ADVANCE PRAISE FOR *MY GOOD SON*

"A tailor . . . asks an American customer for help sponsoring [his son] Feng, and what results for the tailor and his family shines a light on vast, abiding disparities in opportunity."
—*Electric Literature*

"The novel, about parental expectations, social class, and sexuality, highlights both the similarities and differences between Chinese and American cultures."
—*The Millions*

"*My Good Son* is a mesmerizing portrait of at least two societies in flux, seen in the story of one Chinese family challenged to change their sense of what a 'good son' is and what it would mean to love and support him. Provocative, funny, charming, Huang's novel takes on the challenges of this moment of sexual politics with affection and honesty."
—Alexander Chee, author of *How to Write an Autobiographical Novel*

"In a country where a couple is allowed only one child, overly protective Mr. Cai's ambitions for his son create an inevitable clash. But what could go wrong when they become involved with an American family—from Texas? The story takes surprising twists and turns, both comic and poignant. The gentle humor, deceptive simplicity, and joyfulness of Yang Huang's prose makes this novel a delight to read. With a cast of unforgettable characters, *My Good Son* is an exquisite novel, kind and true."
—Bobbie Ann Mason, author of *In Country* and *Dear Ann*

"Yang Huang weaves her story with great patience and a steady hand. Her compassion for her characters is matched only by her sharp, unrelenting narrative eye, one which draws the reader deeply into the growing complications of Mr. Cai's world. An engrossing and compelling novel."
—Shanthi Sekaran, author of *Lucky Boy*

Also by Yang Huang

*My Old Faithful*
*Living Treasures*

# MY GOOD SON

BY YANG HUANG

UNIVERSITY OF NEW ORLEANS PRESS

The University of New Orleans Press
2000 Lakeshore Drive
New Orleans, Louisiana 70148
unopress.org

Cover photograph: Yang Huang
Cover design: Jirachaya Kiriruangchai
Author photograph: Nancy Rubin

Library of Congress Cataloging-in-Publication Data

Names: Huang, Yang (Linda), author.
Title: My good son : a novel / by Yang Huang.
Description: First edition. | [New Orleans] : University of New Orleans
    Press, 2020.
Identifiers: LCCN 2020035249 (print) | LCCN 2020035250 (ebook) | ISBN
    9781608012015 (paperback ; acid-free paper) | ISBN 9781608012039 (ebook)

Classification: LCC PS3608.U2249 M9 2020  (print) | LCC PS3608.U2249
    (ebook) | DDC 813/.6--dc23
LC record available at https://lccn.loc.gov/2020035249
LC ebook record available at https://lccn.loc.gov/2020035250

First edition
Printed in the United States of America on acid-free paper.

*To Qin, Victor, and Oliver*

# MY GOOD SON

# CHAPTER 1

If he could have exchanged a limb for a wish, Mr. Cai would have traded his gladly in order to unleash Feng, his only son, into a life where he could live and prosper on his own.

Afternoon sunshine slanted into the northwest-facing kitchen, hot and stuffy with the carp soup simmering in a slow cooker. Mr. Cai unfolded a letter on the dining table and saw a hint of blush come into Feng's pallid face. He was lean and willowy, like a beanpole, towering above his mother beside him. Despite their height difference, the mother and son had faces looking strikingly similar, so in a way, the chiseled nose and high cheekbones were too pretty on Feng for his own good.

Now that Mr. Cai had their full attention, he read aloud a "love letter" written and signed by Feng, to a young cook working at the canteen of his continuation school: "I can't wait for the class to end and the day to go dark, so I can slide my hand under your apron to touch your dudou, the lushest satin I've ever stroked."

"What the hell is this?" Mr. Cai pounded the dining table so hard that his cup jumped up from its saucer.

Feng shuddered and stepped back. "Nothing, Dad."

Mrs. Cai reached out a hand to stroke Feng's hair, but he pulled away before she could touch him. This should teach her not to pet him like a baby, Mr. Cai could only hope.

"She complained about unwanted attention, and I, your old dad, was called to your school to be given this!" Mr. Cai swept the letter off the table. "You tell me if this can be called a love letter."

"I only—"

"Speak up!"

Feng's finger shook as he pointed it to the floor. "When I wrote the letter, I only wanted to feel her dudou. It was made from a rare silk brocade embroidered with—"

On another day Mr. Cai might have indulged Feng, for his son had a fascination for silks and other fine fabrics. But not today. "What do you take me for, some old dimwit?" Mr. Cai ripped the reading glasses from his nose. "I was a tailor before you were born. Have you ever seen me touching a woman's underwear when she tries on new clothes?"

Feng wiped his eyes with the back of his hand. Mr. Cai rarely saw tears from his son. Feng had an inner strength that belied his fragile appearance. As a young boy he had taught himself by making rag dolls with scrap cloth. By the time Feng was in middle school, Mr. Cai had made him quit his hobby until his grades were ranked among the top 30%. As a result, Feng had not made another rag doll, nor had he shed a tear about giving it up.

Now Mrs. Cai set the small table, where Feng usually took his meal after he failed an exam. "He is really sorry," she said. "Go study now, and dinner will be ready in a few minutes."

Mr. Cai was too angry to look at Feng, and turned his face toward the windows. A magpie landed on the windowsill to comb its tail with its beak. Even the birds chose a season to mate, lay eggs, and raise their young. Why couldn't Feng remain abstinent for a few more months?

July was Feng's last shot at the college entrance exams, because he was twenty-two years old and would soon be disqualified for the university admission. Meanwhile, Ouyang Jiao, the neighbor girl who grew up with Feng, had gone to Beijing Normal University four years ago and would return home in May with a B.A. in Chinese. At the end of April, Mr. Cai had erected a new fence bordering on Jiao's yard and planted a row of roses along it. That way, Feng didn't need to say hello to anyone on the other side of the fence unless that person called out to him. Once Jiao was back, Mr. Cai would hint that she should not disturb Feng before his exams. Feng would not be a free man until the late afternoon of July 9th, 1990.

"You may not care about your future." Mr. Cai heard the tremor in his own voice and cleared his throat. "But you're indebted to your parents, who work until their backs break in order to provide for you."

Feng stomped on the letter and kneaded the paper under his sole with vengeance, until the letter was torn in the middle. Mr. Cai had never seen his son so distraught before. If Feng poured a half of his passion into his studies, what might he have not achieved?

Seeing Feng's cheek damp with tears, Mr. Cai managed to choke down his scolding. "Son, you have to be smarter. As the old saying goes: the worth of other pursuits is small." He waited for Feng to finish the sentence.

"The study of books exceeds them all," Feng whispered.

"Now act on your promise like a good son." He rubbed Feng's back and drummed his hard spine. "Let's put this trivia behind us."

Feng returned to his room and shut the door. Mr. Cai told his wife to move Feng's place setting from the small table to their dining table. It would be easier for him to lecture Feng if they were seated at the same table.

*          *          *

Mr. Cai Liang always had to correct other people: his family name was Cai 材 as in aptitude, not the Cai 才 as in talent. He had grown up without a father, and his mother hadn't given him her surname, Bai 白 as in white, a synonym for chastity. Instead, she chose him a name composed of the two best words in the dictionary: timber 木 combined with talent 才 that promises aptitude, and Liang 良 which means fine quality.

Cai 材 wasn't a traditional surname. Mr. Cai had never met anyone with his family name. Therefore, he was overjoyed to beget a son, who would carry on his lineage. Mr. Cai named him Cai Feng 材丰, abundant aptitude. To this day, Feng's name remained one of the two things about his son with which Mr. Cai was satisfied. The other was Feng's good looks. His eyelashes, long and dense, shaded his eyes like little fans.

"All we ask of you," Mr. Cai told Feng at dinner later that evening, "is to enter a college this year." He turned aside to let his wife put the fish soup on the table. "It's about time. You know, China's War of Resistance against Japan lasted eight years, and you've been in the continuation school for half that long."

"Eat it while it's warm," Mrs. Cai said, putting a soup spoon by Feng's hand.

"We're not unreasonable parents," Mr. Cai said. "After making your way to a university campus, you can find and date a nice girl. But, you've got to wait a few months. If you get distracted, you may regret it for the rest of your life."

Feng sipped the carp soup. "It's fishy," he said and put down his spoon.

"You don't eat it for the taste, but for the nutrition." Mr. Cai scooped up a spoonful to put it in front of Feng's mouth. "Come on, have some more."

"Now you're feeding him," Mrs. Cai said. "No wonder the newspaper said the one-child policy has produced a generation of little emperors—"

"Feng is not like the other only children." Mr. Cai pinched his wife's thigh under the table. She slapped his hand away. "We have relatives in Taiwan. Feng may write to his cousins, whom he's never met."

Feng swallowed the soup and pouted his lips. "Why would I want to do that?"

"Not everyone can boast of an extended family nowadays." Mr. Cai pushed the soup bowl toward his son. "Remember, blood is thicker than water."

Feng sipped a half spoonful of the creamy, white soup. He had been a strict vegetarian ever since he had come down with food poisoning from eating lamb hotpot when he was six. Throughout his teenage years Feng had not touched eggs, meat, or seafood, and prevented Mr. Cai from killing any fish or fowl in his presence. Feng had grown tall and bony, with a pale complexion and large, expressive eyes. After he failed the college entrance exams four times in a row, Mr. Cai suspected that Feng was undernourished and pressed him to eat eggs. The lack of animal protein might have hampered his brain function and stultified his killer instinct. But Feng refused vehemently and resorted to drinking fish soup as a compromise.

For the past year, carp stew had been a regular course at their dinner table. At least three times a week Mr. Cai killed a carp, sliced it up, and salted it before Feng came home from school. His wife fried the carp chunks, then simmered them in a crock pot with oyster mushrooms, black fungus, and lily flowers, until the soup became fragrant and milky white. When Feng initially protested, Mr. Cai told him that the carp was previously frozen and so was already long dead. Luckily Feng had no culinary experience, or he would've known that frozen seafood does not make good soup.

"After the exams, I won't eat this anymore." Feng pushed the soup toward his mother.

Mr. Cai didn't oppose Feng being a vegetarian so long as he did relatively well among his peers. Otherwise, what would become of him when his parents were old and gone? The age-old saying holds true: he who does not plan for the future will find trouble at his doorstep.

\*     \*     \*

As usual Mr. Cai checked on Feng before he went about his own business. Through the keyhole to Feng's bedroom, Mr. Cai saw his son hunch over the desk with his right hand moving a pen across his notebook page. This picture of diligence was a result of fifteen years of schooling.

Feng had been left-handed when he was in kindergarten. Mr. Cai learned that many left-handed children stuttered when they started school. To help Feng ease into the transition, Mr. Cai spent a summer training him to write with his right hand. Not until his left hand suffered enough whacks from a ruler, did Feng gradually succumb to the discipline. By the time he started school, Feng only used his right hand to wipe the blackboard clean for his teacher. In spite of Mr. Cai's success Feng began to stutter, which lasted for eight months until his classmates grew tired of mocking him.

Having seen that Feng was studying, Mr. Cai returned to his workroom, nestled in the back of his shop. With the ceiling fluorescent light turned off, the shop front was dark, and back lights illuminated the workshop where four tables formed a rectangular space. The worktable faced the shop in the front. On the long wooden table, he laid out assorted fabrics and paper patterns alongside chalks, scissors, ruler and tape. Against the back wall was the ironing table, one end of which touched upon the archway that led to the kitchen and bathroom in the back of the house. In the west corner was the fabric table, stacked with silks, brocades, and various blends sorted by content and colors. Against the east wall was an end table with rotary cutter, seam ripper, tracing wheel, and other tools. Everything was within his reach. It felt cozy in this space where Mr. Cai and his wife spent most of their time together. The clutter was stashed away inside the sewing room at the west side of the house, so the large hall of the shop and workroom was spacious and welcoming to both tailors and customers.

Feng had grown up playing with the fabrics and watching his parents cut and sew and serve their customers. As soon as the customer left their shop, the tailor's work was done and forgotten. In a way, a tailor's accomplishment was superficial—it only made people look good on the outside. Besides, there were myriad styles to try, none better than the other. Mr. Cai had been cooped up inside his shop making clothes for other people, but he had harbored a grander ambition for his son. Feng should venture into the world and become a scientist, an engineer, or a physician, to whom ordinary people would turn in their time of need. So in spite of Feng's interest in cloth and perhaps because of it, Mr. Cai had made it a point to keep Feng from tailoring, so that his son could focus on his academic studies.

"What'll we do if he fails the exams again?" he asked his wife. "I haven't taught him one skill."

Mrs. Cai moved a rack full of new clothes to the ironing table and collected the ham, seam roll and clapper for him to use. She was deft at managing the shop and household without breaking a sweat. Having spent almost every minute with his wife, Mr. Cai still found it thrilling to look into the gentle eyes set in her round face.

"Feng is only twenty-two," she said. "Many young people live with their parents until they're allotted apartments to get married. It's nothing to be ashamed of."

"That doesn't make it right." He hit a cotton coat with the clapper to flatten its surface. "What is a son good for if he's cooped up with his parents? We ought to get rid of him." He misted the coat with water, then pressed his iron over its breast pocket.

"If he moves out, you will miss him more than anyone."

"A son ought to brave the world." He slid the coat onto the ham to iron its sleeve. "I'd rather support him to study in the States than have him stay home to save money for me."

Mr. Cai had pressured Feng to pass the Test of English as a Foreign Language last year in order to expand his options. After applying for several universities in the U.S., Feng found that an American citizen was required to be his financial sponsor in order for him to obtain a student visa.

Mr. Cai had no idea where to look for an American citizen. Living in Yangzhou, a medium-sized city in Jiangsu province, they hardly saw any foreigners except for a few times in the Slender West Lake Park. In late summer, a tourist group was occasionally led by a young woman who carried a loudspeaker and waved a red flag. Mr. Cai never mustered his courage to approach those big-nosed strangers, who wore white berets and toffee sunglasses printed with their travel agency's logo.

"It's not his fault that he cannot study in the States." Having sewn the frog closures, Mrs. Cai hung up the coat to sweep its back with a felt brush. "Isn't it enough that he's doing his best, and that he's goodhearted and handsome?"

"Looks don't buy him three meals a day." He swiped some starch onto a pair of pants and ironed its leg immediately. "Face it: he isn't a girl who can marry up with her looks."

His wife waxed a needle in her hair before she sewed a button. Having been married to him for more than twenty years, she remained slim and with few gray hairs. Only two weeks ago, one of Feng's classmates had asked if she was his sister. Mr. Cai was proud that Feng had inherited her fine skin and gentle eyes, yet she had almost no eyelashes.

"Although I've never been to a university, I do not consider myself a failure, because I have you." He wished she would look up at him, for he meant what he said. "But Feng is flirting with a cook. Do you really want a country girl for a daughter-in-law?"

"You've never met her. How do you know she's a country girl?"

"A city girl can tell Feng off in person and not resort to going to the school authorities. Besides, who wears a dudou nowadays? Any city girl can afford to buy a bra, which is more figure flattering." He pointed at a red skirt hanging on the rack. "The city girl bares her legs when it's below zero outside. Why? To show off."

Mrs. Cai kneaded the woolen skirt with two fingers. "This is warm enough for April," she said and returned to her sewing.

*     *     *

Around midnight, Mr. Cai left his wife to clean up the workroom. He felt restless after having chastised Feng earlier. Since his son was asleep, Mr. Cai took a bowl of longan and egg soup to eat in Feng's room. With the ceiling light from the hallway, Mr. Cai could see Feng's mosquito net was down, the room stuffy with the warm scent of his son. It was still a month away from the mosquito season. Outside the windows, a lonely streetlight attracted throngs of moths and locusts. It was Mr. Cai's favorite time of the day, when he could relax after a hard day's work.

Eating at the rosewood desk was an indulgence Mr. Cai rarely allowed himself. Last year he had bought the desk from a neighbor who taught at a university overseas and later moved his entire family abroad. Mr. Cai imagined that the desk was blessed with scholarly fortune. Plump grapes and songbirds piled and strung together to form the crossbar that could be used as a brush-holder. Most of the carvings were smooth to the touch, except that the swallowtails were sharp as scissors. Mr. Cai spat a longan pit into the wastebasket. It hit a paper ball before springing out of the overfull basket. Mr. Cai reached down to pick up the stray pit and took the paper from the basket to use for collecting the pits. He opened the paper ball on the desk. With the light from the hallway, he made out several pencil sketches on pieces of scrap paper. A busty woman wore a dudou, the halter top that draped over her breasts and tummy.

"Why are you here?" his wife whispered as she added a ladle of soup to his bowl.

"Look what our son did with his precious time." Mr. Cai nudged her outside and quietly closed the door behind them. "While we sweat to earn every cent for his keep, he fools around like he owes us nothing."

She studied the drawings one by one.

"If I feed a pork bun to a dog, it will at least wag its tail to please me." He choked on his own words.

"It couldn't have taken him a whole night to draw these." She led him to the kitchen. "In case you didn't notice, he added a different pattern to each dudou, as if designing a wardrobe for her."

"That's not the point." He plunked into a chair. "I must have another talk with him in the morning."

"And what will you say?" She fed him a longan to keep his mouth busy. "That you went through his trash?"

"I'm his father." He spat the longan pit into his palm. "I can't let him waste these two months courting a country girl. Can you?"

Mrs. Cai said nothing as she ate the rest of her husband's longan soup. Then she rinsed the bowl in the sink.

"Why don't you go wash?" She turned off the light in the kitchen without looking back to see if he followed her.

*          *          *

Mr. Cai woke to the burnt smell of potstickers in the kitchen. The bright sunlight on the curtain showed it was past seven.

"Damn!"

He leapt out of the bed to pull on a shirt and pants, then dashed into the kitchen, still fastening his belt. "Feng, I have to talk to you."

Feng glanced at his watch. His eyelids were swollen, as if he hadn't gotten a wink of sleep last night. Wrinkles appeared on his once-smooth high forehead. He seemed to have withered overnight. His mother handed Feng his backpack before Mr. Cai could open his mouth.

"You'd better go now," she said. The parents followed Feng to the courtyard and watched him mount his bicycle. "Ride safely," she added.

"Why didn't you wake me?" Mr. Cai asked his wife after they returned to the kitchen.

"Leave his doodles alone," she said. "Do you want to ruin a fine morning for all of us?"

Mr. Cai reached for a potsticker, before she snatched the enamel bowl to slide it onto the top shelf of the cupboard. Mr. Cai eyed the potstickers, and his mouth began to water.

"Those were my bribes for you to keep quiet." She shut the door of the cupboard. "Our son is going through something difficult. Can't you step back and let him breathe?"

"Why am I always wrong? Did he tell you his trouble?"

"No, but I can tell he's struggling." Her somber eyes looked back at him without derision.

No wonder people say that a mother's heart is as soft as tofu. This left Mr. Cai no choice but being tougher on Feng because his wife refused to discipline their son. When Mr. Cai went around her to retrieve the potstickers, she didn't stop him. He put a potsticker in his mouth and offered the enamel bowl to his wife.

She shook her head. "I bought them for you." She added a new coal cake into the stove and closed its air shutter to dim the fire.

*     *     *

After breakfast, Mr. Cai followed his wife to the sunny shop that faced the courtyard. She opened the pinewood plank windows to put her potted orchids on the windowsill.

Mr. Cai believed that sunshine and flowers bring good feng shui for business. He had allotted the entire south hall, half of their townhouse, for their home tailoring shop. During the Cultural Revolution, Mr. Cai had asked a famous calligrapher, then a known "counter-revolutionary intellectual," to inscribe "Cai's Formalwear and Wedding Wardrobe" beneath the eaves of the house. Mr. Cai paid the calligrapher with a bowl of pork and shepherd's purse wontons, a treat back then for a starving artist beaten by Red Guards. More than a decade later, the calligrapher passed away as a "rehabilitated patriotic artist," according to his eulogy. His works became so popular that they were auctioned overseas for astronomical prices. Mr. Cai vowed never to move his shop away from the house, partly because the calligrapher's ink was etched above their front door.

Every day after dinner, his wife dusted the doorframe and swept the doorsteps. She couldn't do it in the morning for fear of losing their luck. Like most townspeople, the Cais entertained few superstitions, but being shop owners, they held a few beliefs out of abundant caution. The god of wealth didn't care if it was money or dust; the act of sweeping would tell the god the shop wasn't intent on accumulating money or anything else.

The shop itself was about the size of their workroom but seemed spacious and airy. A rack of finished clothes were displayed in the front, flanked by a cashier's front desk in the southeast corner, and a full length mirror mounted on the western wall. In the northwest corner was a fitting room behind a screen. Two carved mahogany chairs and a sofa were stationed in the northeast corner as the waiting area. Behind it across the hallway, the bedroom doors remained closed during the business hours.

From behind his worktable, Mr. Cai could see Mr. Ouyang's tinted shop windows across the street. "Show off," he muttered and spat in his hand.

Ouyang Rong, who specialized in youth wardrobe, had separated his shop from home and moved it across the street to double its size. Mr. Cai speculated that the cute outfits spilling onto the sidewalk were returned goods, clothes made a size too small for pubescent customers. Mr. Cai rather took pride in not having such "samples" for show.

Mr. Cai dipped his fingers into a bowl of talcum powder, then rubbed the powder over his palm and between his fingers. He disliked leaving sweat stains on anything he touched, from paper patterns to silk brocade. He opened a sleeve pattern that he had cut out yesterday. After trimming the edges of the paper pattern, he pinned it against two layers of blue velvet and placed them inside his scissor blades. *Snip snip*, his day officially began.

An hour later, his wife greeted their first customer of the day. "Good morning, Sir. We specialize in formalwear, wedding wardrobe—"

"I must see Mr. Tailor himself."

Mr. Cai didn't look up but frowned at the awkward title. Who would say this as if he were the only tailor in the neighborhood?

"I want to make a vest from this Matka silk," the customer said.

The first customer should never be slighted because he might bring good luck. Mr. Cai put down his scissors.

"My husband will take care of you."

She walked over to hand Mr. Cai the Matka silk. It was stone yellow, solid and heavy like burlap, with bold cloud prints.

"Would you make a vest for my shirt?" the man asked in lightly accented Mandarin. His jaw moved gingerly as he pronounced every word in a clear and even voice.

The young man was about Feng's height. He had such translucent skin that it seemed to be washed-out from drinking too much milk. His blond hair parted in the middle and hung above his nearly white eyebrows. What really caught Mr. Cai's eye was a pair of sapphire earrings. The azure stones twinkled and reflected the color of the man's eyes.

A little short of breath, Mr. Cai stepped back. He had never seen a man wear earrings.

"A vest?" the customer repeated.

Mr. Cai pinned the silk to the man's chest, and he straightened to his full height. Mr. Cai caught a whiff of powdery scent, not an unpleasant odor but distinct enough from a foreigner and stronger than Feng's scent. He felt the bump of chest hair under the man's shirt and removed his hand. "This will do." He backed away to his worktable.

"Will it look okay?" the man asked.

In spite of his unease Mr. Cai chuckled. The man could've worn rags and looked smart with those chiseled features and blue eyes. "I am sure," he said simply.

The man grabbed Mr. Cai's hand so suddenly that he almost stumbled forward. "I went to Mr. Ouyang's shop, and he told me to make a coat instead, but I didn't listen." The man shook Mr. Cai's hand vigorously. "Thank you for doing me the service."

Mr. Cai smiled and pulled the tape off his neck. The man raised his arms to let him wrap the tape around his chest. Ninety-nine centimeters for his chest, seventy-three for the waist, ninety-six for the hips, and thirty-eight for his neck. His admirable proportion and chest hair made him look more grown-up than Feng, though his face appeared quite young.

Mr. Cai cleared his throat. "May I have your name, Sir?"

"Jude."

"Mr. Jude." Mr. Cai jotted down his measurements. "Where're you from?"

"I'm American."

Mr. Cai wrote "American" and drew a star beside it. "Do you happen to be a model?"

The man frowned as if he didn't understand the word.

Mr. Cai stuffed the tape in his pocket and closed his notebook. "You have an ideal figure, if you don't mind my saying so."

"I'm not tall." The man clicked his heels. "I have short legs."

"Your legs are *proportional*," Mr. Cai corrected him. "Do you want a Chinese or western vest?"

"I want the hip-length vest, with the mandarin collar and frog closures, the traditional Chinese style."

"Anything else, Mr. Jude?"

"You can call me Jude." He pulled out a Parker fountain pen from his shirt pocket. "I'll write down my Chinese name for you." He wrote legibly and fluently with his left hand.

Mr. Cai read his running script. "You write very well, Mr. Red Moral. Do you know it's also the name of a famous Chinese general?"

"My teacher picked it out as a transliteration for Jude." He smiled and showed his straight teeth. "I like it."

Mr. Cai couldn't help but smile back at him. Jude was the only American with whom Mr. Cai had ever talked. Was he a distinguished person as both his looks and name suggested? Amazingly, Jude had good manners and spoke near-perfect Chinese. If Mr. Cai did not seize this opportunity for Feng's sake, he would consider himself a negligent father.

"You may come and try on your vest in a couple of days," Mr. Cai said. "It's my pleasure to serve you."

\*　　\*　　\*

Mr. Cai waited for Jude to turn onto the main road, then capered into the sewing room. "Guess what order I just took?" he said to his wife, who was basting a border onto a dress front.

"Is that why you're hopping like a gorilla?" She finished sewing and bit off the end of a thread.

"I told you not to ruin your teeth." He handed her a pair of scissors.

She put the scissors in a drawer. "Was it a good deal?"

He opened the Matka silk to drape it from his arm. "Isn't this grand? Feel it."

She stroked the silk and grinned. "He has the yellow hair to match it, you know."

He showed her Jude's handwriting. "This Red Moral may be of some help to Feng. He speaks Chinese. Why don't I ask him to be Feng's financial sponsor in the States?"

"Don't make a fool of yourself." She covered her mouth with her hand.

"He can say no. What do I have to lose: my face or Feng's future?" Mr. Cai dropped the silk in a basin that they used to shrink new fabrics. "You mustn't tell Feng about this. He has to give a hundred percent to the exams."

"Of course."

They looked at each other, feeling the excitement and gravity of this commitment. Mr. Cai took the basin to the bathroom and filled it with water. His wife followed.

"He was turned away by Mr. Ouyang before he walked into our shop. What a stroke of luck for us." Mr. Cai watched the stone yellow silk turn into a light taupe.

Mrs. Cai handed him a towel. "Go see Mr. Ouyang and find out who this American is."

Mr. Cai, reluctant to visit Mr. Ouyang's store, dried his hands as slowly as he could. During the last two years his neighbor's business had doubled while Mr. Cai's had more or less remained the same. The demand for Tang suit could not rival the clothing market for youths, who were cheaper to dress and had more diverse tastes. Still, Mr. Cai was uneasy to think that he was not as successful as Mr. Ouyang, who was not a better tailor than he, but a fashion stylist who had more original ideas than his scissors could handle.

His wife took out his coffee tunic and Oxford shoes. "Be tactful when you talk to Mr. Ouyang. Don't forget to ask him when Jiao will come home. He'll be happy to know that you're interested."

"I'm not going to fawn over him."

"No one is asking you to." She stroked his hair a few times. "You're just a kindly neighbor who is asking him for some information. I will go if you don't want to."

Her soft touch calmed him down. Mr. Cai gave in and said he would go. After all, he had never befriended a foreigner before; being stubborn could hurt his chance with Jude. He needed advice, and since he would conceal the plan from Feng, who knew English, he had to consult elsewhere.

"Take care of the shop while I'm gone." He put on his favorite peaked cap and pulled it over his eyebrows. Passing a mirror, he smiled at his own reflection, thinking he looked like a Kuomintang spy from an old movie.

*     *     *

Mr. Ouyang's shop was crowded with women who were planning their children's college wardrobes, though the exam results wouldn't be announced until the end of July.

Mr. Cai envied those mothers who were certain enough about their children's successes to invest in their wardrobes. If only he had such faith in Feng, who'd been wearing the same old clothes since entering the continuation school. Maneuvering around the chattering women, Mr. Cai sighed. Feng was not a dumb kid, but he needed a bit more leeway than the top students in order to make it to a university. Once he was enrolled, Mr. Cai was sure Feng would survive the university curriculum as well as the smartest in his class.

"What wind has blown you here, Busy Man?" Mr. Ouyang's baritone voice startled him. "My shop isn't worth your inspection at this hour." Mr. Ouyang seemed to have grown a double chin since Mr. Cai had last seen him while putting up the new fence between their backyards.

Mr. Cai held up both hands and bowed a little. "Your business is booming, Neighbor. When is Jiao coming home?"

"In a month or so." Mr. Ouyang kneaded his mustache, which hid his beak-like mouth. "You are not one for idle chatter, Mr. Cai. How can I help you?"

"Not help really, more like curiosity." Mr. Cai stood aside to allow the customers to pass through the entryway. "I wonder if a foreigner recently visited your store."

"A blond kid?"

"Did he ask you to make a vest?"

Mr. Ouyang led the way into the store. "He had a piece of silk but nothing else. I told him my specialty is youth wardrobe, not formalwear." He showed Mr. Cai to a seat on a sectional Italian leather sofa. "My favorite customers are those mothers who are in charge of their family banks."

"I hear you." Mr. Cai adjusted himself to face Mr. Ouyang. "Did you see his Matka silk?"

"Of course. He called me Mr. Tailor and said a friend had sent him. I knew immediately he was looking for your shop."

Mr. Cai thanked him. "The material is quite good for a vest, but the stone yellow is a little dull." He licked his dry lips. "Perhaps a bright-colored border will liven up the muted yellow."

"I leave it to your able hands." Mr. Ouyang got to his feet. "Excuse me, but I have a business to tend."

Mr. Cai tried not to mind being shown to the door so abruptly. Mr. Ouyang wasn't an expert in silk or Tang suit, after all, and had broken off the conversation perhaps to avoid showing his ignorance.

Mr. Cai was curious which friend had first sent Jude to his store, but Mr. Ouyang might not know this. Mr. Cai bowed slightly and put on the warmest smile he could manage. "We'll chat again soon. Let me know when Jiao is home, and we'll congratulate her with some post-graduation gifts."

"Please don't bother with any gifts." Mr. Ouyang grinned so wide that his mustache stretched out to a straight line over his mouth. "I'm just glad that she has made it through four years and is coming home in one piece. We were worried sick last year when she protested in the streets with her schoolmates. Before the night the shooting broke out, I was ready to go to Tiananmen Square to drag her home." He patted Mr. Cai on the shoulder. "At a time like that, I envied you that you could keep your grown son at home."

The confidence he'd felt in his superior skills evaporated. Mr. Cai racked his brains but couldn't find a dignified reply.

"So long, Neighbor." He waved and backed out of the store, and was almost run over by a tractor loaded with red bricks.

"Watch it," Mr. Ouyang said.

Mr. Cai cupped his burning cheek with a hand and hurried home. Too ashamed to look up, he kept his eyes glued to the asphalt road and veered around a fresh pile of cow dung by the sidewalk.

*          *          *

At home Mr. Cai was greeted by a scent of yulan magnolia. The young woman waiting for him on the sofa chased the thought of Mr. Ouyang from his mind.

As their eyes met, she stood up to gaze at his face, as if Mr. Cai were a friend she hadn't seen for a long time. The white magnolia was tucked into her waist-length braids. Her face might've been pretty, but for the cherry-sized purple frostbite scars on her cheeks. A country girl shouldn't forget to wear her scarf while working in the fields, Mr. Cai thought as he took off his tunic suit and peaked cap.

"May I help you, Miss?" he asked.

"The lady explained to me that you were busy with my friend's order."

Mr. Cai glanced at his wife with a raised eyebrow. Why had he been sent on a fool's errand while he could have waited at home for a moment longer?

"She knows Jude." Mrs. Cai pressed her lips together to suppress a smile.

"We met at the Slender West Lake," the girl said. "He's an art student from Texas. He likes to take pictures of local women."

If Jude were trying out his charm on this girl, she might have been a lost cause. Mr. Cai gestured for her to sit down. "Did you refer him to my shop?" He lifted a candy jar toward her.

"Yes, I heard you do good work." She pushed away the sweets. "I just had two cavity fillings. No, thank you."

Mr. Cai asked his wife to refill the girl's teacup. "What's your name?" he asked.

"Ye Jinhua," she said. "My coworkers call me Little Ye. I work at the Yangzhou Hotel." A pair of dimples indented her cheeks as she smiled.

"People say that the hotel hires the best looking young people," Mrs. Cai said. "Now I believe them."

"I didn't go through the regular recruitment." Little Ye bit her lower lip. "I recently left another job to fill a vacancy in the diner after the last girl working there married a Japanese businessman." She crossed her legs and blushed a little. "I came here to have my uniform altered."

Mr. Cai picked up his tape.

"My skirt is a bit of hip-hugger. I hope you can loosen it up for me." Little Ye remained sitting with her hands clasped over her lap. "I'm carrying. I don't want my belly to show before it has to."

"Formalwear is our specialty, Ma'am," Mr. Cai said. "I'll alter your uniform to give it the most slimming effect. Satisfaction guaranteed."

"Is this your first baby?" Mrs. Cai asked.

Little Ye's lips parted, but she said nothing.

"Silly me. You can only have one child nowadays." Mrs. Cai lowered her voice. "My husband can keep you covered until you're about five months. After that, it's up to your belly."

"I came to the right place, then." Little Ye grinned, showing her buckteeth.

Her yulan magnolia fell to the floor. Mr. Cai picked it up.

"Is your husband in town?" he asked and handed her the flower.

"Yes, but he's very busy with his work." She slid the magnolia into her pocket and peered at the closed bedroom doors behind the waiting area. "I haven't told him, because this is only my sixth week. He will be surprised. I hope he won't take it hard." She opened a parcel and showed him a white uniform with gold trimmings. "The cap doesn't need any alteration," she said and put it on. With her hair covered, she looked like a teenage boy rather than a mother-to-be.

*     *     *

Around noon, Mr. Cai drew the pattern for the front piece of Jude's vest on old newspaper. Then he heard the dings of a bicycle bell in the courtyard. The screen door opened.

"Dad, I'm home." Feng dropped his backpack on the sofa and asked his father, "Is that real Matka?"

Mr. Cai said with a smile, "You know more about silk than Mr. Ouyang."

"Feng?" Mrs. Cai hurried out with a ladle in her hand. "Are you unwell, Son?"

"No." Feng hung his jacket on the back of a chair. "I'm sick and tired of the smell at the canteen, always cabbage and meatballs. I want to eat my lunch at home, if you don't mind."

"Mind? No!" Mrs. Cai ran back to the kitchen. "We're only too glad, aren't we, Husband?"

"You should've let us know earlier." Mr. Cai pointed at the kitchen with his chalk. "We could have added a vegetarian dish."

"What's that smell?" Feng sniffed the air.

"You must be hungry." Mr. Cai dropped his work and went to the kitchen. "Hurry up, Wife. Feng has to return to school in an hour." He reheated the vegetable chop suey from the night before, as she chopped a piece of green onion to garnish the mushroom soup.

"I smell perfume." Feng strode to and fro in the hallway, as if looking for the source of fragrance.

"Oh yeah," Mr. Cai said. "We had a girl customer in here not too long ago."

Feng looked disturbed, but before he could say more, his mother asked, "Will you eat lunch at home from now on?"

"I hope so," Feng said.

Mr. Cai made a few trips to fetch the dishes. Feng moved a coaster to let him put down a bowl of mushroom soup.

"This was made especially for you, Son." Mr. Cai took out a bottle of whiskey to pour himself a shot. "A toast to your academic success." Mr. Cai clinked his shot cup with Feng's soup bowl and drank up.

His face grew warm as the alcohol seeped down his throat. Mr. Cai could never stay angry at Feng for long, his own flesh and blood. Having Feng home for lunch already cheered him up. Moreover, Mr. Cai rejoiced at the prospect of sending Feng abroad. All his striving seemed worthwhile, for a son so gentle and pliant.

"Everything we do is for you." Mr. Cai blinked as the bitter whiskey stung out a few tears.

Feng kept scooping the mushroom soup into his mouth as if his thirst couldn't be quenched.

CHAPTER 2

The next day Mr. Cai scotch-taped a handful of patterns cut out of newspaper, which formed a muslin for Jude's vest. He put on the paper vest and shrugged it into place. What he saw in the mirror didn't catch his fancy: a middle-aged man with thinning hair, neck too long for his still handsome face, marred by crowfeet of worry that looked like a map of stunted hope. His head stuck out of the hole that was to become the collar, so he looked like a turtle emerging from its shell.

"How can we impress the American with this?" he said to his wife. "He can step into any Friendship Store and find something fancier."

The colorful Tang suits displayed in Friendship Stores dazzled on mannequins, but the blend fabric, combined with sloppy fit, didn't hang well on real bodies. Mr. Cai couldn't compete with the cheap price of mass production, especially when customers did not know the quality of traditional Tang suit.

"But he didn't go to a Friendship Store." She tied a knot and bit off the thread with her teeth. "He came to you instead."

Yet her confidence didn't assure Mr. Cai. He lifted the vest over his head, careful not to tear its taped edges. "I'm afraid of disappointing him," he said. Perhaps Feng was tall enough to carry it off and gave him a better picture of the vest.

He flung open Feng's door. "You have a minute, Son?"

As usual Feng pretended not to hear him, but Mr. Cai knew how to entice him.

"I want you to try on a test vest for a customer."

Feng sprang to his feet. "Does he have my build?" It was his favorite kind of distraction.

Feng followed his father to the workroom, slipped into the vest, and shifted it into place. The vest reached to his hips and fit him loosely. Mr. Cai pinned the silk to Feng's chest and pulled his head as far back as he could to take in the full view of his son. Mr. Cai tried to imagine Jude standing in Feng's place, his skin milkier, his hair blond instead of black.

"It almost fits me." Feng glanced at himself in the mirror. "What's the problem?"

"Your dad worries that it may look boring on a young man."

"You could add a red border to break up this stone yellow a bit." Feng drew on the vest front with his fingers. "A stripe of red border with piping will add a look of prosperity to it."

"Did you just think of that?" Mr. Cai was amazed.

"Jiao wore a red and yellow cashmere sweater the last time she was home." Feng smiled for the first time since the love note fiasco.

Mr. Cai cast him a sympathetic glance. Feng was a few months older than Jiao. They had played together as children, with Feng always acting the part of a big brother. One day Jiao had sprained her ankle jumping off a tree, and Feng carried her home on his back, making quite an impression on Jiao's parents. Mr. Cai wondered if Feng had missed Jiao during these four years. Jiao might have had her share of boyfriends at Beijing Normal University, while Feng was cooped up at home with his high school textbooks.

Mr. Cai didn't want to say anything that might embarrass Feng, so he turned to search the fabric shelf and threw a few bolts of red satin on the table. "Which one will do?" he asked Feng.

Feng rummaged through the red silks printed with such words as Prosperity 福, Longevity 寿, and Happiness 喜, before his fingers clutched a piece of satin with golden Love 爱 prints. "Did you say it's for a young man?" he asked.

Mr. Cai nodded.

"Take Love. I'm sure of it."

Feng folded a strip of Love-printed satin alongside the Matka silk. The golden motif lit up the stone yellow silk, while the red and yellow silks contrasted and complemented each other like yin and yang. Mr. Cai couldn't wish for a better match.

Mrs. Cai let out a low gasp. "Aren't you becoming a tailor!" She pinched Feng's cheek.

"You can go back to study now." Mr. Cai lifted the paper vest off Feng. "Thank you, Son," he murmured, "for lending me a designer's eyes."

Feng, with his natural gift, could become a creative craftsman and help Mr. Cai expand his business way beyond his neighbor Mr. Ouyang's limited success. But, Mr. Cai preferred for his son to brave the world of science and technology rather than be cooped up in a family workshop like himself.

"It looks great, but must it say Love?" His wife shelved the rest of the satin bolts. "Jude isn't a girl."

"Of course we want Love." Mr. Cai measured the width of the satin. The Love motifs needed a forty-five degree bias-cut across the fabric's grain in order to form a continuous strip. "Jude is too young to be burdened with fortune and prosperity and longevity, etc. All he needs is love for his parents, who will take care of the worldly fortunes for him." Mr. Cai chalked along the golden Love 爱 prints with a ruler. "A student like Jude may not have enough assets on paper to prove his ability to sponsor Feng. I will then ask his parents in the States to help us."

"Aren't you going a bit too far?" She helped him fold the Love satin. "We don't know his parents."

"It won't hurt us to try," he said. "It may hurt Feng if we give up."

She held down the strip for him to cut through the satin. The Love motifs came off like a string of golden coins. She filled a basin with cold water to shrink the satin strip.

*       *       *

Mr. Cai asked his wife to have a chat with Little Ye when she picked up her altered uniform. Little Ye might give them valuable information about Jude, and more importantly, about Jude's parents in the States. Mrs. Cai agreed to her task, though she insisted on doing it her way.

Little Ye arrived shortly after Feng went back to school after having lunch at home. She tried on her uniform and found the waistband of her skirt four centimeters too wide, just as Mr. Cai expected. He dropped his work at hand to add a few contour darts for her. If later she needed more room in the waist, she could simply take out those darts. Little Ye thanked him for the clever fix.

As he went to the back of the shop to finish up the skirt, Mr. Cai heard his wife offer Little Ye spiced sunflower seeds and tea while she waited. Listening to the women talk, he began to add the contour darts.

"How come you're so skinny?" she asked Little Ye. "Are you really expecting?"

"I lost some weight, but my stomach feels bloated." Little Ye cracked a sunflower seed with her teeth. "I crave dried shredded squid."

"Do you have morning sickness?" Mrs. Cai lowered her voice. "I vomited a lot when I was carrying my son. A friend of mine who had a girl didn't feel any bother throughout her pregnancy."

"I don't feel sick, but tired every day." Little Ye was silent for a while. "I hope to have a baby girl, because my husband doesn't like boys."

Many families in the countryside preferred boys to girls, because they needed men to work in the fields. Perhaps her husband was a progressive townsman. Mr. Cai wished his wife had asked about Jude instead.

"A son is a little easier to raise, though. You don't worry about him as much as you do a daughter…until he grows up." Mrs. Cai sighed. "Then you want him to have a good career, and a mess of things that go with it. He can't be married off like a pretty daughter."

Mr. Cai finished sewing the darts and took the skirt to Little Ye. "Ma'am, you can try it on."

She thanked him and went behind the canvas screen to change.

"Quit talking about the baby and get some useful information out of her, would you?" Mr. Cai whispered to his wife.

Mrs. Cai cupped a hand around her mouth. "I don't think anyone is taking care of her."

"Don't be so gossipy." He squeezed her shoulder.

Little Ye's heels clicked as she stepped out from behind the screen. "I don't know how you did it so quickly, Tailor Cai, but you made me look thin."

Mr. Cai smiled at his work. "I'm glad it fits you."

"If you cut your hair short and perm it firework style, you'll turn many heads when you walk down the street," Mrs. Cai added.

"The firework perm requires a lot of hairspray for daily upkeep." Little Ye waved her hand with a blush. "I have to avoid chemicals."

Mr. Cai wished his wife hadn't changed the topic so needlessly. "How's your job at the hotel?" he asked Little Ye.

"I have no complaints." Little Ye disappeared behind the screen to take off her skirt. "It's much cleaner than the school canteen where I used to work, and the menu is mighty fancy."

"Which school canteen did you work at?" Mrs. Cai asked.

Mr. Cai was irritated at his wife's irrelevant questions.

"Last time, you mentioned Jude was your friend," he cut in before Little Ye could answer. He stood in front of the screen to wait on her. "Do you know him well?"

She appeared in her old clothes. "I teach him papercutting, you know, cutting out pictures from colored paper with a pair of scissors."

Mr. Cai folded the skirt for her. "Do you know what his parents do?"

"His dad runs some kind of a fabric store. His mom died, and his father remarried. Jude hasn't gone back in three years. He likes to study art and feels at home here."

"You must be a very good friend of his, to know all these details." Mrs. Cai refilled Little Ye's teacup.

"I've known him for a while." Little Ye accepted her skirt from Mr. Cai. "He's real friendly, and doesn't put on airs like some city folks, you know what I mean?"

Mr. Cai didn't know what she meant, and suspected that she felt contempt for his prying into Jude's life. Offended by her scorn, he excused himself and returned to the worktable where Jude's silk lay spread out.

He watched as his wife gave Little Ye a receipt for her payment.

"Come back to our shop any time." Mrs. Cai walked Little Ye to the door. "If you want to have some baby clothes made, we'll give you a discount."

Mr. Cai said to his wife after she returned, "I didn't know we make infant clothes." "Relax." She latched the screen door. "That girl may not come back at all. If she does, you may ask her more questions about Jude."

Mr. Cai didn't laugh at her joke but continued to work on Jude's vest.

*       *       *

Feng's small innovation proved no easy task. After Mr. Cai basted the red satin onto the front of the vest, the bias strip stretched out like hand-pulled noodles. He took them apart, pressed the satin again to make it shrink to its proper width, then stitched it with the piping. To his dismay, he found that the seam of the border became rippled.

"Look at the mess!" He showed his wife the crumpled vest front. "I shouldn't have listened to Feng. What did he know?"

She spread the vest on the table and ran the steam iron over the wrinkled border, which pressed out like a dream. Mr. Cai's eyes widened. The vest was a success after all.

"How could I be so dim?" Mr. Cai knuckled his forehead. "Like the old saying: after traveling the five seas, my ship was capsized in the sewer."

"You would say anything to save face." She hung up the vest. "Doesn't Feng take after you!"

Mr. Cai rubbed his balding head. If he argued that he wasn't like Feng, it would only prove that he was indeed like what she said, one who would say anything to save face. If he didn't defend himself, she could not accuse him further of vanity. Besides, he didn't mind terribly being like Feng, who was young and handsome with a full head of ebony hair.

\*       \*       \*

That evening Feng dashed inside and threw his backpack on the floor. Before Mr. Cai could tell him to close the door, he ran to the kitchen waving a piece of paper.

"Mom, look!"

Mrs. Cai came into the workroom and wiped her hands on her apron. "What is it? Did you pass this time?" She turned the paper over. "Old Man, Feng got ninety-eight points on his physics exam!"

Mr. Cai hesitated to close the door. Good news like this was hard to come by. It wouldn't hurt to let his next door neighbor overhear it. "Is it an exam or a test?" he asked with his hand resting on the door handle.

"It was a test on the law of universal gravitation." Feng leaned against the worktable. The crinkles at the corners of his eyes showed that he was suppressing a smile. "Not that it was a big deal."

"Don't you belittle a success!" Mr. Cai closed the door halfway. "Of course it's a big deal. Haven't I told you time and again that a good beginning is half of the battle?"

Mrs. Cai returned to the kitchen, followed by her husband and son. Then without a warning, Feng rolled up his paper and tossed it in the garbage can. Mr. Cai dove to fetch it.

"What did you do that for?" he scolded Feng, scraping off green onion skin and a yellow bok choy leaf from the paper.

"I don't need to keep it. I know the whole test by heart, Dad. I only lost two points, remember?"

Mr. Cai used a damp napkin to wipe off the stain from the paper. "It's the first time you scored high in physics. I would've framed it and hung it in our living room."

Mrs. Cai poured cornstarch water into the stir-fry to create a thick broth. "You do that when he brings home the perfect score next time. Right, Son?"

"It may be just around the corner, Dad."

Mr. Cai studied Feng's face for the hint of a joke, but Feng seemed to mean it. "Good!" Mr. Cai exclaimed. "It's dogged that does it. You give me hope, Son."

Feng carried the steaming hot cauliflower and shiitake mushroom stir-fry to the dining table. "I'm not really dogged. Just an underdog, that's all."

"The dogged or an underdog, it doesn't matter which one you are. So long as you're the dog who can sniff out a way to a prosperous life, we will unleash you happily." He tugged his wife's apron. "Right, Old Woman?"

"Right." She took off her apron. "But I'm not as old as you." They burst into laughter.

"I could've done this years ago." Feng shrugged. "Well, better late than never." He joined them in laughing.

As if blown by a knowing wind, the kitchen door to the back porch squeaked wide open. As the scent of roses permeated the room, Mr. Cai realized that he had been right to plant the flowers after all. Even if Feng didn't need to be shielded from Jiao's triumphant return, he could still inhale the sweet fragrance of roses.

*       *       *

After dinner Mr. Cai felt like taking a stroll. The setting sun painted the sky with its rosette footprints. Mr. Cai couldn't tell whether it was Feng's good news or the warm south wind that touched him with optimism. When he had mended the fence a week ago, he vowed never to take a walk in daylight until Feng was admitted to a university. Today he would make an exception and visit the campus of Yangzhou Normal University with his family.

Feng came out carrying his father's peaked cap. At the doorstep, Feng dropped the cap onto his own head and straightened his collar. "It fits me, too, Dad."

"It's yours." Mr. Cai waited for his wife to lock the door and then take his arm. "I would give you the clothes off my back, too, if you want them."

"Nah, I don't want to look like Vladimir Lenin in 1918." Feng pulled the cap over his eyes. His shapely red lips reminded Mr. Cai of an opium poppy in full bloom.

"You're a good-looking kid, Feng," Mr. Cai said. They walked a few steps in silence. "You could've had your pick of a girlfriend, had you gone to college right away."

Mr. Cai remembered those drawings that he had discovered in Feng's bedroom a few days ago: who was the half-nude girl? Or had Feng imagined a model wearing his dudou designs, as his mother had supposed? Mr. Cai wanted to find out more without sounding too critical.

A pedicab that carried a young couple approached them on the narrow lane. Feng stepped aside to let it pass. Mr. Cai nodded at the old man, who pedaled hard and wiped his sweat with a towel hung from his neck. From behind, the old man's bare torso reminded Mr. Cai of a dry roasted duck displayed in a deli window.

Mr. Cai strode to catch up with his son and pulled his wife along. "If you don't go to a university, you may end up working a pedicab, like him."

Every now and then, a poster of a family of three—a father, mother, and baby daughter—wearing the identical smile on their raised faces showcased the slogan, "It is good to have one child." Rarely was there a baby boy in the propaganda posters, because many families still preferred to have boys, and there were more males than females in the society. Feng peered into the peddlers' shops as he passed by the storefronts. A woman finished washing spinach and poured out a basin of dirty water, which swept over the covered drain and flowed onto the street. Feng stepped over the rivulet and trod on.

His son was used to his nagging. Mr. Cai had to be candid with Feng in order to get his attention. "The other night I found a drawing. Don't ask me where or how I found it." His wife squeezed his hand, but Mr. Cai ignored her. "I was surprised to see the sketch of a half-naked girl in a dudou."

Feng pushed the peak of his cap backwards.

"You don't wear it like this." Mr. Cai tugged the visor from behind so hard that Feng lifted his chin.

"It's my cap now." Feng skipped ahead.

"Stop it, both of you." Mrs. Cai plucked the cap from Feng's head. "I have a husband and son, not two sons who fight each other over every little thing."

"I'd listen to Mom if I were you."

"The patterned dudous were pretty," Mrs. Cai said, "as well as comfortable, end of discussion."

Mr. Cai only patted her hand.

Ahead of them, Feng stopped at the gate of Yangzhou Normal University. Beside him, a column glistened as the dying sunlight was reflected in the thousands of glass shards mounted into the cement.

"Who're you going to see?" an old man hollered from the gatehouse.

Mr. Cai noticed that only people wearing school badges were entering the university.

"Mr. Cheng Xiefang teaches at my continuation school." Feng introduced his family to the guard. "My parents would like to meet my tutor and thank him for his guidance."

"Go." The old man turned up his radio and took another bite of his supper.

Mr. Cai kept quiet until the gateman was out of earshot. "Is he going to call your tutor?" he asked.

"Not likely. My tutor lives in the dorm and doesn't have a direct number."

Mr. Cai decided that telling a white lie once in a while didn't amount to a sin. "It's only natural that you are drawn to a pretty girl." As he began, Mr. Cai worried that he sounded goofy. "All we're asking is that you focus on the entrance exams."

Feng stretched out his arms to balance himself as he tiptoed on the edge of the sidewalk.

Mrs. Cai poked his side. "Someday we will walk this campus as the parents of a university student."

Feng swayed and fell to the grass field. "Not you, too, Mom."

As they passed by a white mulberry tree, Feng reached up to pick a few fruits to chew. "Sour mulberries." He spat them out and wiped his lips. "They were good three weeks ago."

"You've been eating the mulberries?" Mrs. Cai pinched Feng's cheek. "I bet they spray pesticides. You could get poisoned."

"No wonder the tree has grown so lush." Feng lifted a heart-shaped mulberry leaf from the ground. "I once left a silkworm on the tree hoping it would feed on the new leaves. The next day when I passed by, it had fallen to the ground and was feasted on by ants."

"Where did you get the silkworm?" Mr. Cai asked.

"It was a girl's pet. She raised a couple of them to keep her company. She said you could tell season change from watching how the silkworms feed."

It surprised Mr. Cai that Feng had revealed a secret without being pressed—for once he wanted to be heard. Feng looked up as they passed the female dorm. The wind chimes rang softly outside the windows. On the clothesline nearby, white bras on plastic hangers danced in the breeze along with grass green, orange and apricot skirts. Gray partridges strolled on the roof cooing melodiously. Feng peered back at the girls' dorm, full of vibrant colors and soft sounds.

Feng asked his mother, "Why do you suppose a girl would save a love note for years before telling its sender off?"

"Is she the girl who raised silkworms as her pets?" Mrs. Cai let go of her husband's elbow and walked alongside her son, as Mr. Cai followed them behind.

Feng nodded and stood still. He put his hands on his upper arms, as if bracing himself for a good shake. Mr. Cai had not seen his son so pensive before. This glimpse of fragility made Feng look arresting and grown up.

"Her silkworms might've told her that the season has changed," Mrs. Cai said. "There's a time to fall in love and a time to leave your lover."

All three stood beside one another and reveled in the simple truth of her words. Feng forced a smile and reached overhead to pluck a mulberry leaf. He resumed walking, followed by his parents. Feng tore the leaf and sprinkled its pieces on the path they walked.

"In the twinkling of an eye, a silkworm changes into a cocoon," he said to himself.

Mrs. Cai slid her arm across her husband's waist and squeezed him. She told him to keep quiet and not scold their son when he was melancholy over a breakup. It was generous of Feng to have shared this much with his parents. They wouldn't antagonize him by probing the details of his failed relationship. In his heart, Mr. Cai couldn't blame Feng for dating, be her a country girl or not. After all, Mr. Cai had had his younger days, too, when love seemed to be the only thing that mattered. Not until he had Feng did he realize how shallow and naïve he had been to have lusted after a woman ill-suited for him.

*       *       *

For many years Mr. Cai had been in love with his cousin Xiu who lived in Jiangdu countryside. His mother, Ms. Bai, had brought him to see Xiu and her grandaunt every August, when muskmelon, sugar cane, and water chestnut were plump and ripe. Three years older than himself, Xiu used to be a head taller than Little Liang (the name Mr. Cai was called back then). Unlike the girls in his class who wore bobbed hair or ponytails, Xiu had long braids that reached to her waist, and they swayed from side to side with her every step.

Each summer when they visited Xiu, Ms. Bai would bring her a skirt, a sunhat, and a pair of galoshes or sandals from the city. She always bought the clothes a size larger because she didn't want Xiu to outgrow them too quickly. The next year when they returned, Xiu would greet them wearing the dress she had gotten the year before, almost new and fitting her like tailor-made.

One summer, Little Liang was surprised to see Xiu greeting them wearing a skirt that had faded from red into pink. The skirt appeared short, hiking up on her behind and showing more of her shapely thighs.

When Ms. Bai gave Xiu a new yellow dress, Xiu didn't exclaim how pretty it was. Instead, she went into the bedroom and locked the door.

"She's grown into a looker, hasn't she?" Ms. Bai told her mother, Xiu's grandaunt.

"Tell me about it." Liang's grandma was weaving a wicker basket, which she would sell at the farmers' market. "At the rate she's growing, I can't keep her in this house for long."

Xiu whirled into the room like a yellow butterfly. Before Little Liang could have a good look at her, Ms. Bai sprang up to lead Xiu to the bedroom while whispering into her ear.

When Xiu appeared again, the yellow dress looked tight on her. "If you wear a bra instead of the shirt inside, the dress will fit you." Ms. Bai held Xiu's shoulders. "I'll go to town tomorrow and buy you a bra."

"Thank your auntie now," Grandma told Xiu. "She knows how to dress you up like a city girl. Your grandaunt can't do that for you."

Xiu said her thanks and fiddled with the ends of her braids.

"Don't be so modest," Ms. Bai said. "It's you who makes the dress look good."

Liang didn't know until much later that Xiu often received gifts of fresh produce such as peanuts, sugar cane, water chestnuts, and muskmelon from the neighbor boys. It was Xiu herself who told him about the local tradition of acquiring a wife.

"You can't marry a girl until her family accepts your betrothal gifts," she told him one night and showed him a glass jar filled with fireflies. "Zhang's eldest gave me this. The second boy from Yuan's family bought me apples. Which one would you prefer?"

"I prefer you." He touched the lit spot where a firefly bumped into the glass jar. "Is it hurt?" he asked, worried.

She let out a laugh that tickled his ears. "We'll free them in the morning." She set down the jar inside a lotus paper lantern. "Have you seen a prettier lantern?"

Liang hadn't. He blew on the lantern. *Puuuuu*! The lantern seemed brighter than ever. Not to be outdone by her, he opened a tin box to show her General, the cricket with which he had won many fights in the neighborhood.

The next summer Liang contracted chicken pox that forced him to stay home for weeks. By August, he was so far behind in schoolwork that he had to spend the remaining weeks catching up. When he went to visit Xiu again a year later, Liang had grown almost ten centimeters and became scrawny. Meanwhile, Xiu had become the belle of the village.

Ms. Bai said Xiu had the bearing of a seventeen-year-old, two years ahead of her real age. Wearing her stockings and heeled sandals, Xiu reminded Liang of an actress in a Shaoxing opera.

One afternoon, Xiu and Liang were eating sugar canes in the field before a long wail pierced the screeching of cicadas. He parted the sugar canes and looked out onto the ridge. What a scene he saw! A donkey put its forelegs onto another donkey's haunches to push it downward.

"They're going at it again." Xiu spat out the sugar cane fiber.

"What're they doing?" Liang asked.

"Copulating."

The boredom in her voice reminded Liang of another word he'd learned in botany: pollinating. Both sounded technical and mundane. Xiu tossed a stalk of sugar cane at the pair. It hit the donkey underneath, but it seemed to have no effect. The donkeys were pushing and shoving as if they were in a tugging war.

"You couldn't pull them apart with two wagons." Xiu lay on the pile of sugar canes with her hands locked behind her head. Her lashes cast two half circles of shadow over her lower lids.

"Do you pluck your eyebrows?" Liang asked.

"No. Why?"

"Because my mom plucks hers." Liang touched the end of her braid so lightly that she didn't seem to notice. "Your brows are perfect."

"You're nice, Liang." She rolled to lie on her stomach. "What can you do for me?"

"Do?"

"Remember what I told you? You can't marry a girl until her family has accepted your gifts. The eldest from Zhang's family just gave me a silk purse. The third boy from Yuan's family bought me a bottle of floral water. What will you get me?"

He thought hard amidst the loud braying. Sweat trickling down the back of his neck, he blurted out, "My mom gave you pretty clothes. Don't they count?"

She pulled her braids away from his fingers. "I'm talking about *you*, City Boy."

"What do you like?" he asked.

She chewed the end of her braids for a while. "I do have a soft spot for nice city clothes," she finally admitted.

"I'll become a tailor and make city clothes for you!" he exclaimed without thinking.

"I'd like to see you try, Cousin." She chopped off a stalk of sugar cane and put it to his mouth. "Eat more, and grow up quickly. You may outshine all my beaus here."

Liang bit into the bark of sugar cane to peel it with his front teeth. He did it clumsily, and the sharp bark cut into his lips. Xiu looked at him with pity.

"It doesn't hurt," he said.

Then Xiu did something unexpected: she closed her eyes and kissed his lips, so gently he wasn't sure if he had imagined it. When he licked his lips, he tasted sweet blood. Just like that, an invisible knot was tied inside him, which couldn't be undone.

Liang didn't tell his mother that he wanted to become a tailor. He never excelled in his academic studies, perhaps because he hadn't worked hard enough. After high school, he didn't get into a college. Rather than waste money on continuation school, he entered a trade school to study tailoring.

Looking back, Mr. Cai wished he had not given up college at a tender age in order to please his pretty cousin.

*     *     *

Back from the walk, Mr. Cai took Jude's vest off the wooden hanger to give it a last check. The red border parted the yellow cloud patterns in the middle, pretty with a string of Love prints. The vest was cheerful, prosperous, and youthful all at once. He couldn't wait to show it to Jude.

His wife began to sweep the floor. "Will you explain to him why you added the Love print border? He didn't ask for it."

"It's a new style, especially designed for him." Mr. Cai stroked the vest front. For the whole week, he had been mulling over a style worthy of Jude's good looks. Now his work was done, and he could find nothing to say about the vest. Perhaps Feng was able to explain it better.

He knocked on Feng's door. "Do you have a minute, Son? I want you to try on the vest."

Feng came out promptly.

"It's finished now." He held up the vest for Feng to slide it on.

Mrs. Cai put down the broom and led him to the full length mirror.

"Who is it for, anyway?" Feng asked, buttoning up the frog closures.

"A special customer." Mr. Cai straightened the vest shoulder. The vest was slightly loose on him, and its muted colors made Feng's face look fair.

"See, how nice it looks." Feng smiled at himself in the mirror.

"Yes, with your mother's help." He patted Feng's shoulder. "Do you mind going to school a little late tomorrow?"

"Why?"

"This is a showcase piece." Mr. Cai unbuttoned his frog closures. "You may be able to explain to our customer how we came up with this design."

"What's there to explain?" Feng asked.

"He's an American," Mrs. Cai said. "Although he speaks Mandarin, your dad wants you to say a few English words to make him feel welcome."

"Exactly." Mr. Cai was grateful to his wife for the explanation. They weren't ready to distract Feng with the prospect, which was a long shot. And yet, Feng's explanation could elevate the vest to be a showcase piece. This was a chance worth taking. "We may ask for a good price, if he likes our design."

"I can take the day off if you need me." Feng's face was wrinkled with a smug grin.

"That won't be necessary. He will be our first customer, so you can leave by 8:30."

Mr. Cai let Feng return to his studies. Tailoring was a menial job, not a lustrous career that a man could be proud. Hopefully one day, Feng would understand that Mr. Cai had kept him from the workroom for his own good.

Still, Mr. Cai was proud of this dazzling vest, the first fruit of labor made by all the members in his family. Their shop was little but inventive, thanks to both Feng and Mrs. Cai. From across the room, Mr. Cai watched his wife dump the scrap cloth from her dustpan into the garbage can, all the while with her eyes down-cast, so she didn't see the smile on Mr. Cai's face. In the midst of his ecstasy, Mr. Cai felt a bit lonely and doubtful about tomorrow. He had done his best, and when it came time to collect the fruit of his labor, he could only hope he wouldn't be let down—by Feng or Jude.

# CHAPTER 3

Mr. Cai was awakened at the crack of dawn by a peculiar noise. It sounded like an infant's cry, subdued but insistent. He lay in bed wondering if it was an ill omen. Conversely, the first customer could bring good luck to the store. Therefore, Mr. Cai decided to start his day with a treat for Jude.

Jude probably drank coffee, which gave Mr. Cai an excuse to open his New Year's gift from his in-laws: Nestlé coffee and Coffee-mate. They had bought these expensive imports with Feng in mind, not realizing what a frail child he was: last year, the coffee ice cream Mr. Cai had given his son prior to his exams had caused Feng a severe stomachache.

However, one man's poison might be another man's meat. The only thing missing was cube sugar. Fortunately, Mr. Cai had recently seen some displayed at the Number One Department Store, alongside bags of Hershey's and M&Ms.

There was already light on the curtains. A cat meowed outside, followed by a tomcat's howl. So the strange noise wasn't a child's cry at all.

Mr. Cai decided to break up the copulating cats before they woke up his entire family. He got up from the bed and tucked the blanket around his wife. The cats whimpered and screamed while he made his way toward the porch. As soon as he stepped outside, they were chasing each other away and slithered underneath the fence, heedless of the honeybees buzzing among the rosebushes. He stood to listen for a minute. All was quiet again, so he went into the bathroom.

On a chilly morning like this, Mr. Cai wished he had installed a water heater. His neighbor Mr. Ouyang had bought a porcelain bathtub with a shower nozzle in anticipation of Jiao's return. Mr. Cai told himself he wasn't envious. He would never spoil Feng the way that Mr. Ouyang pampered his daughter; small hardships could toughen up a young man and increase his endurance. Hence, Mr. Cai hadn't wasted a cent on installing hardwood floors, wall paneling, or a gas stove either. Well-kept cement floors and limewashed walls were luxury enough for his family. His wife got up early every day to light the coal-cake stove and cook breakfast. Mr. Cai's plan was to spend all their savings on Feng's tuition. Certainly it would be easier on their family's finances if Feng studied at a college in China, but Mr. Cai would do whatever necessary to make Feng successful.

He laid the wooden bathtub on the floor, his teeth chattering noisily in his mouth. He was concerned that a bath might not cleanse his body as well as a shower. So he used an enamel washbasin for clean water, and let the large wooden basin collect the soapy water. He poured cold water into the washbasin, then added hot water from a thermos bottle until it was lukewarm. He undressed quickly and got into the tub. The chill raised gooseflesh on his arms when he rubbed a cake of sandalwood soap over his body.

After a long bath, a strong scent of sandalwood rose from his skin. He dabbed on some of his wife's lotion to neutralize the smell. All perfume stinks, he thought. He couldn't understand why any man would let his woman waste money on perfume instead of relishing her natural scent. Mr. Cai had a sensitive nose and always preferred the natural scent of a clean body to the expensive perfume that showed a person's status.

Hearing his wife get up, he poured out the dirty bathwater and propped the bathtub against the wall.

Mrs. Cai entered with her eyes narrowed.

"Be careful." He guided her hand as she stepped onto the wet cement near the drain. "It's slippery."

"You're already up." She bent down to the squat toilet. "How come?"

"I took a good bath. You and Feng should do the same. We want to look neat for Jude."

He ran his comb in her matted hair. She tossed her head and pushed his hand away.

"I'm going to boil your bathwater, fix some breakfast, and wake Feng up," he told her. "He needs to go to the department store and buy some cube sugar."

She muttered how expensive the cube sugar might be. He didn't bother to argue with her. Experience told him that the gesture of hospitality would be paid off doubly, if he carried it out with tact.

*     *     *

An hour later, Mr. Cai wore a tank top and was busy pressing his white shirt. His wife approached him holding a cup of hot tea.

"Can't you wear something cheerful? White looks like a funeral worker's uniform." She sipped her tea and then squeezed his bicep playfully. "You're only forty-four. There're dozens of colors that look flattering on you."

Mr. Cai glanced at his wife, who had on a blue rayon shirt with purple flowers, one of her favorites. "You look nice." He hung up the white shirt, then laid Jude's vest on the ironing board. "But you know I never upstage my customers. Jude is no exception."

In truth, he had worked with fabrics for so long that few patterns appealed to him—they all looked interchangeable. He had dressed countless bodies to camouflage their flaws, either with fabric, color, pattern, or tailoring craft. Clothes doesn't create beauty but only enhances it. In the case of natural beauty, less is more. Being a hard worker, he didn't want to be enslaved by the standard of beauty in his own life. During twenty years of making clothes for other people, he had only worn black pants and white shirts at work.

She held out her cup to his lips, but he shook his head and backed away.

"Go make some coffee," he said. "Jude will be here any minute."

"But Feng isn't back with sugar!"

"Just do what I said."

She made a face and then left. It was his habit to be alone with his prized garments before he parted with them. He knew she didn't mind.

After he changed into his work shirt, warm on his back, he began to press the vest one last time.

Mr. Cai was glad that he had let Feng lend a hand. Although he hadn't taught Feng any tailoring skill, he had shown his son the mundane life of a tailor. If this hadn't scared Feng off but rather attracted him, was this not a credit to himself as a father? Feng hadn't listened to his advice but learned by his example.

Why did a tailor craft pretty clothes? In addition to their practical uses, clothes had the potential to attract a mate, real or imagined. When a tailor took sexual attraction into consideration, he might have more creative ideas at his disposal. Creativity might be an extension of one's sexual imagination.

Unfortunately Mr. Cai had had a traumatic experience before; afterwards, he had given up his fashion design apprenticeship to study traditional tailoring instead. For decades he had made clothing in sophisticated traditional methods with limited variations. Repetitions never bored him; if anything, they confirmed the lasting value of Tang suit styles.

Pressing was his favorite job, polishing the garment before putting it onto the body for which it was fit. All his planning, cutting, and sewing took final shape. In the end the garment itself made sense. Take the vest, for example. Matka silk needs minimum handling in order to keep its shape. Its natural good looks reminded him of Jude, whose friendly face seemed to suggest an open nature and kind understanding.

As Mr. Cai ran the iron over the red piping for the last time, he prayed that Jude would fall in love with the vest as he had.

\*   \*   \*

Mr. Cai put down his scissors when footsteps approached. He was disappointed to hear a woman's voice speaking. "Is Tailor Cai in today?" she asked.

Mr. Cai turned and found Little Ye accompanied by Jude. With her braids coiled on the back of her head, she looked ruddier and prettier than the last time he had seen her. The uniform fit her nicely.

"Good morning." She waved a hand at him. "Jude asked me to come see his vest. I told him to get a Tang suit robe to go with it. Then he wanted my help choosing one."

"She has good taste." Jude winked at her.

Mr. Cai clasped his hands and blushed in spite of himself. He had not expected that Jude had a wardrobe adviser. Perhaps he had to win over Little Ye in order to please Jude. Mr. Cai lifted the vest from the hanger, careful to keep his hands steady.

Jude slid the vest onto his beige short-sleeved shirt. He stared at his reflection in the mirror as if he didn't recognize himself. Mr. Cai held his breath for a verdict.

"You look fine," Little Ye said. "In fact, you look like a million yuan."

Jude pinched the red border. "I didn't expected it to look like this."

Before Mr. Cai could explain, Little Ye replied, "This is the best part. It says Love, as you can see. The red color gives the whole vest a prosperous look, doesn't it, Tailor Cai?"

Mr. Cai nodded eagerly, pleased that Little Ye seemed to want Jude to like the vest as much as he did.

Jude tilted his head this way and that to examine himself from several angles. The red border gave more coloring to his milky complexion and made him look semi-Chinese despite his yellow hair. Mr. Cai studied his face for signs of disapproval. The tip of Jude's tongue darted out between his lips before withdrawing behind his teeth as quickly as it had appeared. Mr. Cai never saw a Chinese man wet his lips this fast.

Little Ye said, "A blue Tang suit robe will top it off."

"You think so?" Jude fastened the bottom three frogs so slowly that Mr. Cai wondered if they weren't sewn well. "I prefer green. What does Mr. Tailor think?"

"A dark shade of green looks better." Mr. Cai was amused by the way Jude had addressed him. By now he took it as a term of respect since he was the only tailor working with Jude.

Little Ye helped Jude hook the top clasp over his throat. With an easy gesture, she smoothed down his blond hair over the collar. They appeared to be so comfortable with each other as if they'd grown up together on the same street, like Feng and Jiao. Neither the white man nor the country girl seemed to be concerned about their mutual attraction. Their closeness had gone beyond normal friendship or even the initial stage of intimacy, as they seemed dependent upon each other. Mr. Cai was so absorbed that he didn't notice when Feng returned.

"What're you doing here, Jinhua?" Feng's voice startled everyone in the room.

Little Ye took her hands from Jude's collar and hid them behind her back. Her eyes widened, fixed on Feng's face for a moment, and then peered at the door.

"She's my friend," Jude said with a smile.

"Don't talk, Jude." Little Ye grabbed her purse and strode outside. "Good day, you all," she called over her shoulder.

Feng glared at Jude, as if the white man's smile were a cruel affront. Yet he couldn't look away. Feng bore his gaze into Jude's face as if in search of an answer, which never came. Feng banged the bag of cube sugar against the cashier's desk.

Mrs. Cai carried out two cups of coffee. "Feng," she said. "Come here and give our guests some sugar."

"I'll help myself." Jude took a cup with both hands. "Thank you."

"How did you know Jinhua?" Feng asked impatiently.

"We help each other." Jude sipped his coffee. "She teaches me papercutting and helps me with Chinese."

"And I wonder what you do for her. Excuse me." Feng dropped the sugar bag on the sofa and picked up his backpack. "I have to go to school now."

"But Feng," Mrs. Cai called out.

Feng unlocked his bicycle and rode away.

"Did he offend your friend?" she asked Jude. "She left so suddenly."

"I don't think so." Jude chuckled and then shook his head.

Mr. Cai was puzzled why Feng had taken Jude for an enemy— on Little Ye's account? But she was married, and her husband was in town. He apologized to Jude, "Feng is not usually this rude. Lately he has been under a lot of stress "

"I know," Jude interrupted. "Feng didn't want to be late for school."

Mr. Cai was grateful for his understanding, and so disappointed in Feng that he almost wanted to thank Jude for not minding him. On second thought, though, he decided that it was better to stop apologizing for his son.

He opened the bag of sugar to offer Jude. "Would you like a few?"

Jude reached a hand into the bag and picked out two broken sugar cubes.

"Take a good one." Mr. Cai opened the bag wider. "Take a few more. Your friend is gone. These are all for you."

"Thanks, but I've had enough." Jude covered his coffee cup with a hand. "I want to thank Feng for buying the sugar."

Mr. Cai smiled and showed Jude to a seat on the sofa. "I haven't asked you, what do you think about the vest?"

"It's fine." Jude touched his vest. "But it's different from what I had in mind."

Mr. Cai burst into a smile. "To tell you the truth, I can't claim the credit for such a youthful style. It was Feng who designed the vest."

This seemed to surprise Jude, as he leaned forward and put down his coffee cup. "Is Feng a tailor, too?"

"Not really. Feng has always wanted to do things his own way, but I've kept him from learning my trade. So he may have better prospects, instead of holding a job early in life like me." Mr. Cai was comfortable talking to Jude, a young man like his son. Jude's striking blue eyes no longer intimidated him. Rather, they encouraged Mr. Cai to confide in Jude, an American who had little conception of life in China and found his experiences interesting rather than boring. "I spent my prime years in the Cultural Revolution, so I couldn't have done better than making an honest living with my hands. Feng is luckier than me. He grew up studying mathematics, physics, chemistry, and English. He is well-prepared to study abroad and become a respected engineer."

"Does Feng want to become an engineer?" Jude sat back in his chair.

"He's too young to know what is best for him," Mr. Cai said.

"Would you like your coffee refreshed?" Mrs. Cai asked Jude. "This must be cold."

"No, thanks."

"Have another cup," she insisted. "We have Nestlé, good coffee."

"Yes I know." With a grin Jude lifted his cup. "No cream, please."

She nodded and took the cup to the kitchen.

Mr. Cai returned to the pressing subject. "Feng passed the TOEFL exam two years ago. He would've been able to study at a college in the States, if he had an American citizen to sponsor him."

"You mean a financial sponsor?" Jude asked.

"Exactly." Mr. Cai was so excited that he jumped a little in his seat. "We'll never ask for a cent from his sponsor. All Feng needs is someone who gives him a legal sponsorship so that he can obtain a student visa to the States."

"A lot of people have asked me to be their sponsor." Jude tugged at his bracelet, round and barrel jade beads strung together by a rubber band. "I'd like to help you, but I can't. I haven't lived in

the States for three years or paid any taxes. I can't sponsor anyone. Sorry."

"What about your father?" Blood rushed into his face as Mr.
Cai brazened out the question. "He has lived in the States all
these years, I presume?"

By the time Mr. Cai finished his second question, Jude had
leapt to his feet and bumped the cup in Mrs. Cai's hands. The
coffee seeped into his vest like brown paint. Jude's cheeks turned
into a deep shade of pink that Mr. Cai had not seen before.

"I'm so sorry." Mrs. Cai wiped Jude's vest with her hand. "Would
you give it to me to wash?"

It took Jude a little while to take off his vest. "It was my fault."
He flicked the ugly brown stain on his shirt.

"Let me wash your shirt, too," she said.

Mr. Cai asked, "Would you wear a shirt of Feng's while you
wait?"

"I'm much obliged." Jude's smile looked forced.

*       *       *

Jude looked comfortable wearing Feng's blue plaid shirt. He
wasn't very thin, though. Mr. Cai was surprised to see the bulges
of his biceps inside the short sleeves. His chest and shoulders
filled out the shirt nicely, while the shirttail draped over his pants
just below the hips. If not for his blond hair and blue eyes, he
could pass for a very handsome brother of Feng's.

"You don't look too shabby." Mr. Cai clucked approval.

"It fits me." Jude smoothed down the shirt. "Sorry about the
coffee. I just didn't expect you to ask about my father."

Mr. Cai was glad that he had gotten the hardest part over with,
and Jude was still with him. Now he needed to proceed with more
finesse. "I have never met your father," he began. "But I know
one thing for sure. If I had a son like you, I wouldn't refuse anything you asked of me, so long as it was not hurtful."

"Anything?" Jude raised his eyebrows.

"Look at you." Mr. Cai pointed at Jude, but was too shy to praise his beauty, so he tried to compliment Jude in a roundabout way. "You may assume that your future wife will appreciate your body the most. I tell you it's not true. Any person will find fault with his or her mate after they have lived together for a time. Do you know who will never find fault with your physical appearance? Your parents. Yes, your father and mother. No matter what you look like, these two people always think you're perfect."

Jude chuckled and rubbed his neck. "I'm not so sure."

"Trust me." Mr. Cai patted Jude on the shoulder, before realizing that he had touched a foreigner. Jude's shoulder was more muscular than Feng's. "Parents are the same all over the world. They'll do everything in their power to make their children happy. You know why? Because you're their flesh and blood. Making you happy makes them happy." Mr. Cai paused and wondered if he had digressed from his point.

"Your theory is intriguing." Jude opened his hand with palm up. "But in reality, parents say and do all sorts of things that ruin their children's lives."

"How?" Mr. Cai regretted it as soon as he heard himself. He regarded Jude as a youngster and used the same tone as he did with Feng, forgetting that Jude was a special guest as well as the first customer of the day. Mr. Cai ought to have respected Jude's opinions and not argue with him over some trivia.

"Sometimes a scolding look can wound a young person for life." Jude shot Mr. Cai a glance that sent a chill down his spine.

Mr. Cai said after an awkward silence, "I hope I'm not one of those parents."

Jude grinned and touched his earlobe. "I didn't mean you, Mr. Tailor."

"Of course." Mr. Cai titled his head back and chuckled to show Jude that he didn't take offense.

Jude laid his arm on the back of Mr. Cai's sofa. "Suppose I give my dad a call." He squinted sideways as if contemplating the possibility in his mind's eye. "I haven't talked to him much in three years. I don't know if it's going to do any good."

"Of course it will." Mr. Cai tried not to raise his voice. "It won't hurt you to try."

"You have no idea." Jude withdrew his arm from the sofa and kneaded his bracelet with his left index finger, one bead at a time. Mr. Cai watched Jude go through all the beads at least once. He wondered if Little Ye had chosen the bracelet for Jude. If not for his pale skin, the bracelet would've made Jude look like a bumpkin.

"Heavens," Jude said. "My dad is going to be shocked."

Mr. Cai could hardly believe his good luck. He was afraid that Jude might change his mind, and attempted to occupy him with friendly chitchat. "Do you have any brothers and sisters?" he asked.

"I'm an only child, like Feng." Jude swept his bracelet onto his forearm. "An opportunity like this doesn't come along every day, does it?" He seemed to speak mostly to himself. Before Mr. Cai could nod, Jude leapt to his feet. "I'd better go home and make that phone call. My dad will be in bed soon."

Excited by his initiative, Mr. Cai called out for his wife. "Are Jude's clothes ready? He must go now."

"So soon?" Her voice echoed in the bathroom. "I need to soak the shirt a little longer. Won't he stay for lunch?"

"He can't." Mr. Cai turned to Jude. "Where do you live? I'll bring them over to your place tonight."

"Don't bother. I'll stop in again." Jude shrugged his shoulders. "Can I keep this for a couple of days?"

"The shirt is yours," Mr. Cai burst out. "Feng is lucky to have you help him. How can we repay your kindness? We won't charge you for the vest. If you want a Tang suit robe made, we'll do that for free, too."

Jude stared at his face as if he didn't understand the bargain. Then he grabbed Mr. Cai and pecked him on the cheek. "See you later."

Jude left the shop before Mr. Cai realized what had happened.

Mrs. Cai came out, her hands wet with soapsuds. "You didn't ask him to stay?"

"He kissed me." Mr. Cai wiped his face. "What a foreign devil." He didn't say anything more about it, though he wasn't unhappy. Jude was the first grown man who had ever kissed him, while Feng hadn't pecked his father's cheek ever since puberty.

*       *       *

Mr. Cai and his wife agreed not to disclose the deal with Jude until success was in sight. In the next two months, Feng would create a future for himself. Meanwhile, Mr. Cai was waiting to hear from Jude and his American father.

"Why did Jude agree to call his father?" Mrs. Cai pulled out a chair for him to sit at the dining table. "Feng wasn't a charmer this morning."

"Now that you mention it, Jude said that he hadn't talked to his father much for three years." Mr. Cai touched his cheek where Jude had pecked him. "Maybe he wants to break the ice."

"What did you get yourself into?" She tossed her head. "Jude is having trouble with his dad. You have your hands full with Feng. Now you want to get involved with Jude's problem, too. Good luck."

Mr. Cai pressed her hand on the table. "You're such a cynic."

"Then you're a shameless opportunist." She stood up and patted his shoulder. "It isn't for the fainthearted. I wish you luck."

Mr. Cai decided to reason with his wife, a smart woman. "You've heard of an old saying: when the husband and wife are of one mind, they can turn yellow soil into gold. Neither you nor I amount to much, but together we can bring prosperity to our family."

"I would like that." She added a cup of water to the vegetable hotpot for the third time. "What's keeping Feng at school so late?"

"I hope it has nothing to do with that"—the word "pregnant" was on the tip of his tongue, but Mr. Cai checked himself—"country girl."

"Feng called her Jinhua. Do you think they were friends? Little Ye said she left her job at a school canteen." Mrs. Cai sighed. "Who got her into trouble?"

"What trouble? She told us she was married." Mr. Cai turned off the hotpot. "You'll say nothing of this, unless Feng brings it up." He shook his wife's shoulder. "Are we of one mind?"

"Now you're the cynic." She slapped away his hand. "I'm on your side. Don't you know that?"

Another half hour passed, before a familiar bicycle bell rang in the front yard. Mrs. Cai switched on the hotpot and put a finger to his lips. "Let *me* ask him why he is so late."

Mr. Cai nodded and folded his arms on his chest.

Feng opened the door and dropped his backpack on the floor. "Dad. Mom." He changed into his slippers and entered the kitchen.

"Did you get to school very late?" she asked cheerfully. "Come, let's eat the hotpot. All veggie and tofu, your favorites."

"What're we celebrating?" Feng said.

"No celebration for our family until July." She pushed a plate of bean threads into the boiling water and stirred them with her chopsticks. "We just thought you would be tired and hungry after a long day."

Feng didn't need to know that they were celebrating their first successful dealing with Jude. "Help yourself, Son." Mr. Cai echoed his wife.

Feng wiped his face with a dirty hankie. His cheeks were grayish with sweat and dust.

"You left in a hurry this morning," his mother said. "Is everything all right?"

Feng nodded and looked up at the ceiling. He drew a deep breath.

Mr. Cai gave him a spoon. "Next time, please be polite to our customer."

Feng tilted his chair back on its two hind legs. "What were they doing in our shop?" Before Mr. Cai could answer, Feng lurched forward to let the chair land with a thud. "I went after Little Ye this morning, in case you wondered. I lost her in the hotel lobby when a guard stopped me." Feng rubbed his bloodshot eyes. "We had dated for four years before she turned in my note to the school and broke up with me. There, say whatever you want about it."

In his shock Mr. Cai swallowed a spoonful of hot soup. There was no reason why Feng had to disclose so much so fast and ruin a fine dinner for all of them. Mr. Cai licked his scalded lips and inhaled slowly.

"Was it the note we saw?" Mr. Cai asked.

His wife said softly, "Let's eat first, and talk about it later."

"Did you think I wrote her that note recently? No, it was four years ago. If I hadn't met her, I wouldn't have been able to stand staying home all these years." Feng stomped out of the kitchen. "I'm not hungry."

The hotpot lid clanked softly with the boiling water.

Mrs. Cai gave the sieve to her husband. "Let's save some for him." She found a thermos mug from the cupboard and banged the door closed. "He'll be hungry later."

Mr. Cai filled the mug with tofu, spinach, and bean threads. "Carve us some mutton, Woman. We have the hotpot all to ourselves tonight."

Mr. Cai sipped some whiskey and watched his wife rock a knife up and down to slice the mutton. Red meat streaked with white fat fell to form a small pile. Mr. Cai wondered how Feng had managed to keep the secret from them all these years. Since Feng had spent a great deal of time and energy courting Little Ye and covering up their romance, his failing the exams couldn't have been entirely due to ineptitude.

A young man capable of such deception might be good material for a spy. But Mr. Cai didn't want a spy for a son.

*       *       *

Mr. Cai and his wife ate their dinner in silence. He dipped a slice of bright red mutton into the boiling water for a few seconds until it lost its blood and became pink. Then he dabbed it with spicy satay paste. The tender meat melted in his mouth. His wife ate little, her face grim with the determination not to speak. She'd rather hurt herself than shout at Feng. While he was making his instant-boiled mutton, she stood up to put her dishes in the sink.

"You leave the dishes to me," he said. "I will talk with Feng."

She turned on the faucet.

"Don't be so upset." He picked out the food from the soup base and turned off the hotpot. "We don't know if Feng made Little Ye pregnant. They broke up already. Little Ye is now Jude's friend."

"She and Feng dated for four years! What do you take your son for, a monk?"

"*Our* son." Mr. Cai stood up from the table. "Feng doesn't eat meat, does he?"

"Being a vegetarian doesn't make Feng a saint," his wife replied. "Look at him, he has the fair face of a heartbreaker."

"Don't think the worst of him." He turned off the faucet to speak to her. "We're his parents and have watched him grow up. We have been in love ourselves. Love isn't a monster for a twenty-two-year-old man."

She wiped her hands on her apron.

"Why don't you rest?" He undid her apron and led her toward the bedroom. "I'll have a man-to-man talk with Feng. It's not the end of the world."

He took off her shoes and moved her legs onto the bed, then pulled the quilt over her. "You just relax and watch TV." He put the remote control in her hand.

He left the room and closed the door quietly. Then he stood to press his ear to the door. A minute later, the TV was on. The canned laughter of American sitcom *Growing Pains* poured out. Mr. Cai walked down the hallway to knock on Feng's door.

*        *        *

Mr. Cai spent ten minutes coaxing Feng to open the door. Leading the way to the kitchen, Mr. Cai told himself to remain calm. If Feng had dated a country girl to spite his parents, who knew what he might do in a fit of anger? Mr. Cai sat at the table and watched Feng wolf down his dinner from the thermos mug and drain the soup. The good food should nourish Feng and calm his nerves. Afterwards Mr. Cai let Feng do the dishes while he cleaned the table. The teamwork would encourage Feng to be cooperative, he hoped.

Mr. Cai wiped the dining table twice, first with a wet dishrag, then a dry one. "Did you meet Little Ye at the canteen?" He unplugged the hotpot and carried it to the sink.

Feng nodded. "She gave me dried radish and lotus seedpods, sometimes salted bamboo shoots with fried peanuts. She made them herself."

"She was good to you, wasn't she?"

Feng scrubbed a plate with his sponge.

"Is she married?"

Feng shook his head. "I wanted to marry her." He pulled out another dirty plate, making the rest of the dishes clatter. "She was willing to wait for me to pass the exams and then get married. She said so herself."

Mr. Cai shook his head. "How can you marry while you're in college, huh? It's against school regulations. You wouldn't get your marriage license."

"Maybe I won't go to college," Feng muttered under his breath.

Mr. Cai felt the ground under his feet soften as if he stood in marsh. He gripped the kitchen counter in order to keep himself from slapping Feng.

Neither of them spoke for a while. There was only the noise of a sponge scrubbing against porcelain.

Feng started to wash the hotpot. "I mean, I can go to a trade school and be married."

Mr. Cai wondered if Feng would use the pot for self-defense if he struck him.

Mr. Cai retreated to the dining table, at a safe distance from the sink. "What're you going to study at a trade school?" he asked.

"Apparel design." Feng waved the sponge in his hand and splattered a little detergent on the floor. "Then I'll be able to help you with the family business."

"What family business?" Mr. Cai shouted. "There is no family business, only a job for your mom and me."

Instead of answering, Feng turned on the faucet to rinse the dishes. The running water drowned out his words as Mr. Cai complained how they worked day and night to provide Feng with the best education he could attain. These were the words Feng had been told hundreds of times but never seemed to take to heart. Perhaps it was impossible for a selfish son like Feng to appreciate the loving sacrifice his parents made for him. Until finally, maybe, he would be learning all about that for himself.

With this realization, Mr. Cai shut his mouth and listened to the water splashing on Feng's hands like pouring rain.

*        *        *

By the time Feng finished with the dishes, Mr. Cai had calmed down. There was no use in blaming Feng for his lack of ambition. If Feng planned to enter a trade school in order to marry Little Ye, Mr. Cai had better bring him to reason.

Mr. Cai made a cup of tea for Feng. "Why did she break up with you?"

"I suppose she had a change of heart." Feng scratched the mouth of his teacup with his fingernail. "Her blond boyfriend may take her abroad. I'm nobody in comparison."

The scratching noise made Mr. Cai's hair stand on end. "It's just a flaw in the china." He snatched Feng's teacup away and gave him a new one.

Feng poured his tea into the new cup. "She won't marry me, because I have nothing to my name."

What sort of woman would turn away her unborn child's father? Mr. Cai wondered. Perhaps Little Ye had been made pregnant by Jude, or someone else.

"She won't see me until I pass my exams," Feng continued. "She leaves me no choice. I have to do well this time, or I'll lose her for good."

"Did she mention some . . . trouble?" Mr. Cai stopped short of saying "pregnancy."

"She is working at the Yangzhou Hotel, a big step up with bonuses, even tips from foreigners, and who knows what else. Her friend married a Japanese businessman. Maybe she will get lucky, too." Feng lifted his hung head to drink up the tea.

If Little Ye hadn't told him about the baby, Mr. Cai saw no need to burden Feng with the anxiety. Since Feng and she had broken up, her baby probably didn't concern Feng. Mr. Cai was grateful that Little Ye kept the news of her baby, which could shatter their tranquil life, to herself. Even if Feng would become a father, he could deal with that after his exams. On the other hand, Little Ye must've known what was best for her baby. Therefore, Mr. Cai would presume nothing until she told Feng about the pregnancy.

Mr. Cai stretched out his legs to put his feet on the opposite chair. His hurt was alleviated somewhat now that he knew a secret Feng didn't.

"Was she your first girlfriend?" Mr. Cai asked.

Feng nodded. "I was hoping she would be the last, too."

"Were you her first boyfriend?"

"She had only a dozen silkworms to keep her company before she met me." Feng smiled with tears in his eyes. "She was the flower of the canteen. Most of the cooks there were old and cranky. I saw one married man try to grab her several times. He thought that a country girl like her must be an easy catch."

Mr. Cai cleared his throat. "It was wrong of you to keep us in the dark about your girlfriend. But after all these years, what's done cannot be undone. We forgive you, only if you'll spend every minute of the next two months studying for the exams." Mr. Cai patted his hand. "Will you promise us that?"

"I have to, or she'll never see me again."

Mr. Cai grinned. "For her, for us, and for yourself, you have to pass those exams."

Feng pushed up from the table. "I'm going back to study."

Alone in the kitchen, Mr. Cai poured himself a shot of whiskey. He lifted the cup toward Feng's door and drank up. He was glad that now Feng had a better reason to study hard and strive for success. It was noble of Little Ye to give Feng the ultimatum. He wondered why she hadn't done it years ago. Perhaps the baby was the cause of her resoluteness. If she was carrying Jude's baby, her urging Feng to go to a university enabled her to dump him without breaking his heart. And if the baby wasn't Jude's . . .

Alcohol dulled his mind and made his head throb. The anger he felt toward Feng mellowed into pity while he recollected from his own experience that one's first love could be a bitter mistake.

Mr. Cai's first love had long been dead and buried, yet the look of Xiu's tomb remained fresh in his memory. A blue stone and green bristle grasses were her only companions. He had wept remembering how she used to love pretty clothes. Xiu was the reason he became a tailor, though he never made a dress for her.

\*      \*      \*

Little Liang had noticed Ms. Bai bought Xiu new clothes in the same size, yet with more lace and embroidery each year. No dress had been too pretty for Xiu. She wore a skirt better than the model on the clothes label. Her shins were slim and white, her cheeks a delicate coral. She didn't look like other peasant women, most of whom were swarthy and stout.

Ms. Bai once said that Xiu had the looks of a mistress but the fate of a servant girl. Xiu could've had her pick of a man if she were a city girl. Back in the village, a boy named Zhuzi was regarded as a learned man because he graduated from middle school and could use an abacus.

When Liang visited Xiu in the summer of '60, she told him that Zhuzi had asked her to marry him.

Liang followed her to the vegetable plot. "Will you marry him?"

"What're you talking about?" She pouted and pushed his chest.

"Will you?" he insisted.

"Why would I settle for him?" She stamped her foot, her face flushed.

He couldn't tell if she was angry or shy. "Has he given you any betrothal gifts?"

"What I want he doesn't have."

Before he could ask her what she meant, Grandma called for Xiu to fetch a bucket of well water to chill a watermelon for dinner. Liang took a pail and went with Xiu to the well.

"Has Zhuzi given you any betrothal gifts?" he repeated.

She dropped her bucket into the well and flicked her wrist to sink the bucket into water, then pulled it up with all her strength. "Don't you spill it." She stopped him from helping her. "Here, it's your turn." She lifted her bucket away from the well's stone ledge.

He threw down his pail and tried to sink it into the water, but it kept floating as if it had a will of its own. "How did you do it?" he asked.

"City Boy, don't sprain your wrist." She was already on her way home.

Liang swung the bucket over and again. If he used too much force, it skipped on the water and hit the well. With too little force, it wouldn't flip over. It took him fifteen minutes to tilt it enough and submerge it in water. Finally he waddled home carrying a full pail of water, feeling triumphant.

"I did it!" he called out to Xiu as he entered the courtyard.

She smiled and took the pail from his hand.

"So, was Zhuzi disappointed?" he asked her.

"Am I not pretty enough to marry a townsman?" She lifted the pail to pour the water into the vat, then put the heavy wooden lid on the vat. "Can't I pass for a city girl when I have a nice dress on? You tell me, Cousin."

Liang almost slipped on the wet dirt floor. When he looked up, he saw Xiu's eyes, dark and hurt as if he had insulted her with his slow reply. "You're prettier than all the girls in my class," he said. One day he would make Xiu a magnificent silk gown that everyone envied. None of her suitors could compete with such a perfect gift.

Not until years later did he understand that her beauty would be her only means to marry up. It was harder for a country girl to marry a townsman than for Feng to enter a college. This hadn't changed after three decades. Little Ye reminded Mr. Cai of Xiu in both her looks and situation. Knowing how Xiu's life had ended, he wished for a better future for Little Ye, even if she wasn't carrying his grandchild.

*       *       *

Mr. Cai returned to the bedroom and closed the door. An episode of *The Dream of the Red Chamber* was playing. Two cousins in beautiful Hanfu were having a catfight. His wife pointed the remote control at the TV to turn it off.

She clutched a pillow. "Are we having a grandchild?"

"I doubt it." He took off his shoes to get into the bed. "Feng doesn't know anything about the baby. It could be Jude's. You saw how sweet she was to him."

"Are we going to tell Feng about the baby?"

"This is Little Ye's call, not ours." He pulled the pillow from her arms and propped it behind his head. "First of all, the father of her baby may not be Feng. Our son thinks she dumped him for Jude. You can guess her reasons. Even if she is carrying Feng's baby, she does not want to marry him. Little Ye is the mother, so she has the sole right to her baby."

"Feng has nothing but his good looks. Jude is even better looking to some." Mrs. Cai chewed her thumbnail. "Stupid youngsters! Why did they jump into bed before they were married?"

Mr. Cai took his wife's hand and held it between his palms. He wanted to joke that he would've done the same with her if she had let him decades ago, but he didn't dare. Instead, he leaned forward and gave her a gentle embrace.

"Feng is not the only one to blame," he whispered. "He couldn't have done it without Little Ye's consent."

"I know." She nodded with downcast eyes. "They made a handsome couple."

Feng might be too whimsical for his own good, and for once Mr. Cai was grateful: his indolent son was not so thick-skinned as to impose himself on any woman.

## CHAPTER 4

Mr. Cai didn't know about Jiao's return until Sunday morning when he saw Feng standing at the fence talking to her. Feng looked put together wearing his gray striped pants and a new powder blue shirt. His hand rested against the small of his back and held a pink hairpin. Jiao finished brushing her hair and slid her boxwood comb into a hole in the fence. The lime green sleeveless dress was just tight and short enough to show off her modest curves. Feng handed her the hairpin, which she used to clip a strand of hair on the top of her crown. Her ebony hair was shiny and damp in a lifting fog. Jiao looked up with a smile.

"Good morning, Mr. Cai." Her cheeks were dimpled. She seemed to have plumped up a little since the last time he had seen her. "Feng was telling me about his studies."

Mr. Cai strolled to the fence with his hands clasped behind his back. "Was he asking you for advice? He's not a Chinese major, you know."

"Chemical engineering is my life," Feng quipped. "Jiao will teach Chinese at Yangzhou High School in the fall." The comb fell to the ground. Feng extricated it from the rosebush and wiped it on his shirt before handing it to Jiao. "She's already preparing her lectures."

Jiao accepted the comb and thanked Feng. "I'm the only new teacher assigned to a graduating class. I feel pressured, like a duck driven onto a perch."

Was she trying to put Feng to shame by belittling her own accomplishments? "Please don't be so modest," Mr. Cai said. "Surely, you're the swan in our neighborhood of ducks."

Feng blushed deeply. He let go of the fence and walked back inside, the screen door slamming behind him. Mr. Cai regretted having hurt Feng's pride.

"Mr. Cai, I have to disagree." Jiao's droopy eyebrows made her face look mournful. "On my way home, I wondered if I wasted these four years. My hometown is tranquil and beautiful. Why did I go to Beijing Normal University to study Chinese? I was raised speaking Chinese, for goodness sake." She stepped back from the fence and waved a hand at him. Mr. Cai thought it was an abrupt way of saying goodbye. Perhaps his comment about Feng had offended her as well.

Mr. Cai gazed at her back while she leapt onto the porch, like a young doe. Her skirt flipped upward and showed her white calves. Her college education had given her dignity and poise, Mr. Cai thought with some envy. Jiao had not been born a looker, like Feng. But after living in Beijing for four years, she had become a lady inside and out. Her cheeks were ruddy, and her hair grew long and lustrous.

Along the fence, a couple of rose stems stretched out into Ouyang's side of the yard. Mr. Cai reached out a hand to pull those roses back, careful not to touch the thorns.

\*     \*     \*

At the breakfast table, Feng seemed to have lost his appetite. He stirred the red bean porridge with his nose wrinkled, as if it were bitter cough medicine. Finally Mr. Cai couldn't listen to the clinking of Feng's spoon any longer, and pushed the honey bottle toward him.

"What?" Feng's eyes widened.

"Take some honey if you want." After a pause, Mr. Cai added, "Unless you were thinking about some other kind of honey."

Feng sat back in his chair. "I'm not hungry."

Mrs. Cai nudged a plate of pickles toward Feng. "You can't go study until you finish the porridge."

As if taking an order, Feng lowered his mouth to wolf down the porridge in a few savage gulps. Mr. Cai was afraid that Feng might choke.

"I'm going to visit Jiao and borrow some lecture notes," Feng said and pushed up from the table.

"Her notes are four years old," Mr. Cai said. "Can they be useful to you? Your textbooks have been revised several times already."

Feng looked at the windows. "I want to borrow her *lecture* notes, you know, the ones she'll use to teach her graduating class." He pressed a fist on the table. "She'll help me with my studies, while I can tell her if her notes are pertinent to the exams. You see, this is a fair trade."

Mr. Cai was at once grateful for and embarrassed by Feng's honesty. This time Feng didn't, and indeed could not keep his visits to Jiao a secret. Those days when Feng had courted Little Ye during lunch at the school canteen were over. Suddenly Feng was eyeing a girl who seemed too good for him.

"There's an old saying that those who are able to help themselves can help others as well. I may add that the reverse of this is also true." Mr. Cai cleared his throat. "Son, you are like a clay idol fording a river, hardly able to save yourself. Do you really think you can help Jiao?"

Feng ignored the question and stood with his back to the table. Mr. Cai couldn't see his face.

"Can I go now?"

"Go then," his mother said, "and come home for lunch."

"See you." Feng closed the screen door behind him.

"What do you mean by contradicting me, Woman?" Mr. Cai coughed up some phlegm and spat it in the kitchen sink. "I counted on your help to keep our son at his desk."

"It's Sunday." She collected dirty dishes to pile them on the kitchen counter. "He had a trying week. Let him take a break."

Mr. Cai stepped aside to let her wash the dishes. She rubbed three pairs of chopsticks against one another to rinse them under the running water.

"Did you live like this when you were his age, nose constantly to the grindstone?"

Mr. Cai felt blood rush into his face. "I wish I had a father who had pushed me to study hard, then I wouldn't have wound up being a tailor." He pointed at the workroom. "Who in his right mind wants to be cooped up in here day and night?" Mr. Cai stopped, lest he might say things he didn't mean.

He didn't hate being a tailor—it was the only job he knew how to do. Nor did he love it. He regretted not having considered other choices, such as becoming an engineer or a scientist, before he had decided to become a tailor for Xiu's sake.

Mrs. Cai piled clean dishes on the kitchen counter. "Feng may like being a tailor," she said. "He prefers to hang around our worktable rather than sit at his desk. Isn't it a credit to you, Old Man?"

"Don't flatter me, when Feng tries to outsmart me." Mr. Cai hesitated for a moment. "He told me that he had wanted to marry Little Ye—he could go to a trade school and study tailoring."

"It could have been a good life: she cooks while he designs clothes. But they broke up." Mrs. Cai sighed. "Go out if you want to. You have the yearly pass to the park."

Mr. Cai then remembered the pass, which he had gotten for Feng eight months ago. Feng had started to appear hunchbacked after he failed last year's exams. Concerned about Feng's defeat, Mr. Cai urged his son to practice martial arts. He bought Feng a summer training session that came with a yearly pass to the Slender West Lake Park. Feng had dropped out of the class after three days. He claimed he was too old for the painful leg pressing. Fortunately, Feng stopped hunching his back after Mr. Cai bought him the rosewood desk.

"Are you coming with me?" Mr. Cai asked his wife. "We can go fishing for a couple of hours. It's a beautiful day."

Yawning, she dried her hands on the apron. "With all of you gone, I'd rather take a nap."

"You're getting old, Woman." Mr. Cai patted her cheek, her skin cool and a bit rubbery. In spite of her youthful appearance, his wife wasn't as energetic as he. Middle age took a greater toll on a woman than a man, Mr. Cai thought. Perhaps that was the reason that she was more lenient with Feng. He didn't press her any more and went to the closet to dig out his fishing gear.

*     *     *

Mr. Cai was tightening up the meshes of his fishing net when he heard his wife lead Jude to the closet.

"Excuse my husband. He'll be with you in a minute. Would you take a seat?" She offered Jude the sofa chair opposite the closet.

Mr. Cai scrambled to his feet. "You caught me at a funny time." He peered at Jude, who was in a white tank top and blue shorts. The pale skin on his naked shoulders had light brown moles like a sika deer's dapples. "Would you like a soft drink? Plum juice is good for one's skin."

Mrs. Cai left to prepare the drinks.

"I'm going to swim in the Slender West Lake later." As Jude looked at his own shoulder, Mr. Cai averted his gaze.

"We're going to the same park!" Mr. Cai said. "But swimming in the lake is prohibited. A park ranger will fine you for it."

"The ranger on duty today is a friend of mine." Jude winked and then handed him Feng's shirt, neatly folded with its buttons fastened.

"Good for you." Mr. Cai accepted the shirt with both hands. No doubt Jude could charm anyone, even a park ranger, at will.

"I talked to my father." Jude lost his smile. "He was surprised that I have such a good friend here. He asked what sort of a friend Feng is to me." He ran a hand in his hair.

Mr. Cai took a deep breath. Jude's father had asked a reasonable question before he would help a stranger. It was foolish of Feng to make a rival of Jude because of a girlfriend whom he wasn't able to keep. Mr. Cai was obliged to exaggerate Feng's goodwill toward Jude.

"Although you met Feng only a couple of days ago, he's your age and could be a brother to you, considering you are an only child."

Jude tapped a finger on his lips. "My father may think it strange of me to take a Chinese brother." He stood to accept a tall glass of plum juice from Mrs. Cai.

Mr. Cai talked to his wife in the dialect that Jude might not understand. "Get Feng home, would you? We are planning for his future. It would be courteous of him to be present."

"Do I tell him about the sponsorship?"

"Not yet, just ask Feng to be friendly to a man who can help him."

She nodded and left.

Mr. Cai then asked Jude why he had not seen his father in three years.

Jude turned his face away. "We disagree about certain things."

"Like every other family, I suppose." Mr. Cai made chitchat as he waited for Feng. "My mother once told me that not until I became a parent, would I appreciate what she had done for me. It was true. Not until I had Feng did I realize what a burden I had been to her, as well as a joy. You see, a man's maturation doesn't occur at his marriage, but at the birth of his first child."

Jude glared at him. "What if I don't become a parent?" His eyes were so blue it was as if they were filled up with sky.

Mr. Cai blurted, "What a waste that would be! Can you imagine? You could teach your beautiful children to be bilingual while they are still toddlers."

"So?" Jude pressed his fist into the arm of the sofa.

"So?!" Mr. Cai was shocked. Jude had looked and talked like a bright young man until now. "There's an old Chinese saying: there are three unfilial acts, and to have no posterity is the greatest of them." Jude folded his arms on his chest.

Mr. Cai wondered if he had offended Jude. He tried to soften his speech. "I think some mores of parenting are universal. For example, parents all over the world want the very best for their children. Even though I don't know English, I dare to bet on this: as the father of a son, I can talk to your father better than you about family matters."

"Really?"

Mr. Cai nodded without any hesitation. For a moment, he felt powerful and wise, as if he were an old sage enlightening his disciple on the secrets of parenting.

Jude clutched the arm of the sofa with both hands. "Well, if I invite him here for a visit, would you talk to him?"

"What do you mean?" Mr. Cai stammered and put his hands between his knees.

"My father owns a fabric store. He takes a trip overseas every year to buy cheap fabric, mostly from Mexico. When I first came here, he said he wanted to visit China, but I didn't invite him. I know he'll make a trip out here, if we help him buy some quality silk. Once he meets Feng and hears him talk, my father may believe in our friendship and agree to sponsor Feng. What do you say?"

This was too much information for Mr. Cai to absorb. He had hoped that Jude would appeal to his father on Feng's behalf. Upon seeing his son after three years, his father might be in a sanguine mood to indulge Jude's whims. Why did Jude assign a critical mission to Feng, who was deft at jeopardizing his responsibility? Besides, neither Feng nor Mr. Cai knew how to impress an American businessman. Perhaps it was Jude's way to go through the motions without actually helping them. Mr. Cai was afraid to imply that Jude was insincere, so he thought of an innocuous excuse.

"Where will we receive your father?" He scanned the crowded room, much too shabby to welcome a rich guest from afar. "Why can't you go to the States and visit your father, since you haven't seen him for so long?"

"What good does that do," Jude asked, "unless you arrange for Feng to come with me and meet my father?"

Mr. Cai fell silent. An airfare across the globe would cost him a fortune. Besides, Feng didn't have time to travel.

"I rest my case." Jude shrugged. "I suggested this for Feng's sake. If you want to quit, let's do that and not waste any more time."

Mr. Cai felt hurt that Jude gave him an ultimatum. People rarely talked to him in a tone that allowed no negotiation. Afraid that Jude might retract his support, Mr. Cai hastily promised, "I will do my best to receive your father. In fact, I'm going to call a friend tomorrow and arrange for a tour of the Yangzhou Silk Factory." Mr. Cai caught a whiff of his sour perspiration and wiped the back of his neck with a hankie. The room seemed to be much hotter than the morning.

To Mr. Cai's relief, Jude burst into smile. "I'll make a reservation for him at the Yangzhou Hotel. You, me, and Feng can talk to him there."

"Excellent," Mr. Cai said, rather worried about what he had committed to.

The door opened. Mrs. Cai had returned with Feng.

"Good, Jude is still here." She held Feng's hand to drag him inside. "Feng, meet Jude. He's a kindly young man."

Jude stood up to shake Feng's hand. "We've already met. Your dad and I were just talking about you."

Mr. Cai coughed dryly. He didn't want Jude to disclose their deal before his father agreed to visit China, but he couldn't signal Jude to keep quiet.

Feng bowed stiffly and looked at Jude's bare shoulders and arms. Then he stepped back and fanned himself with a handful of lecture notes.

Jude lifted the shirt from the tea table. "Thank you for lending me your shirt. I've washed it."

Feng didn't know that his father had given Jude the shirt. Now Feng accepted his shirt with a frown. He studied Jude's chest and arms, as if picturing the American inside his own shirt. Then he raised the shirt to his nose and sniffed it. "Did you spray perfume on it?" he asked Jude.

"No." Jude's face flushed like a red pepper.

Feng dashed out of the room before Mr. Cai could stop him. As Feng passed the bathroom, he tossed the shirt in the washing machine. Mr. Cai moved to the doorframe to block Jude's view of the hallway.

"He's a shy kid," Mr. Cai said with an apologetic smile.

\*        \*        \*

Mr. Cai saw Jude out, all the way to the main road. Then he came home and went straight for Feng's room. The door was wide open, as if Feng were expecting him.

"Why did you insult our guest?" Mr. Cai let his displeasure show in his voice.

Feng didn't raise his eyes from the exercise book. Mr. Cai would've been pleased by his absorption any other time.

Feng finished writing a geometric equation, then put down his pencil. "I didn't," he said.

"You tossed the shirt in the washer right after he said he had washed it!"

Feng sneered. "It had a smell."

"What do you mean?"

Feng retrieved the shirt from the bathroom to thrust it under Mr. Cai's nose.

Mr. Cai sniffed it. There was a doughy smell on the fabric, like baby powder. Could it be a scent—from Little Ye? Mr. Cai was afraid to make Feng jealous. "It's healthy body odor." Mr. Cai returned the shirt to the washer. "It was dumb of you to offend our guest over such a trivial matter."

"Was he offended?" Feng plopped into his chair. "So what? What's he to me anyway?"

Mr. Cai became tongue-tied. He wasn't going to disclose the deal, so he decided to give Feng a lecture on courtesy instead. "I hope you won't be so rude next time when he, or another guest, visits us. A Chinese or an American, it doesn't matter. It can't hurt you if you make our guests feel welcome."

"Dad, you'll be better off if I just hide my face." Feng pouted.

"Nonsense!" Mr. Cai's voice softened. When Feng acted like a young boy before his difficult father, Mr. Cai couldn't help feeling forgiving and protective toward him. In the back of his mind he knew Feng wouldn't live at home for much longer.

He sat on Feng's bed and drew up his legs. "Now would you be a good son and tell me what you did at Jiao's house?"

Feng tapped the lecture notes with the tip of his pencil. "While I was asking to borrow these, Mom dashed over to drag me home. What could I have done?"

"Are you fond of her?" Mr. Cai asked. "She's prettier than last year."

"Give me a break!" Feng closed his exercise book. "I was just dumped by one girl. Now you make fun of me with another."

"I'm not making fun of you. I just want to know what's going on." Mr. Cai tried to sound reasonable. "I had no idea that you had been seeing Little Ye, or I would've been able to advise you then."

"This won't happen again. I won't date anyone until I finish my exams." Feng stuck his pencil into a sharpener and rolled it quickly.

"I want to believe you." Mr. Cai watched his son blow the shavings from the tip of the pencil. "But you of all people know how easily I can be played for a fool."

"Dad!" Feng pounded his desk so hard that the pencil sharpener jumped. "If I fail again this year, I'll be nobody. I'll disappear from this neighborhood for good. I might as well be lost to you and Mom."

Mr. Cai was terrified to hear Feng's vow. "Who put this in your head?" He wanted to stroke Feng's head but was afraid to distress his son even more, so he kept his hands tightly about himself.

"Who else?" Feng knuckled his temple. "You, of course. 'Career first, and love second.' Dad, you made me see my errors."

"All right." Mr. Cai was at once relieved and hurt to hear his answer. Feng had a right to resent his discipline. That didn't matter so long as Feng would have a good future. He patted Feng on the arm and chuckled with tears in his eyes. "We're of one mind, then."

Feng returned to his geometry problems.

Mr. Cai rose from the bed and left the room. After he closed the door, he pressed his ear to the door and heard the soft scraping of Feng's pencil on the paper. Gone were those days when Feng had drawn erotic doodles—now he was solving a geometric problem. Mr. Cai tiptoed away in order not to disturb Feng any more.

\*        \*        \*

Mr. Cai was happy to skip his afternoon nap and go fishing. Since Jude would swim in the Slender West Lake, Mr. Cai dared to go there, too, where fishing was prohibited. Not only would it be more fun to catch fish there, he would also be in a scenic and perhaps eventful place. Indeed, Mr. Cai hoped to bump into Jude and his ranger friend, who might advise him on how to cast in the Lake.

Mr. Cai didn't take a fishing pole, which would cause him to be caught by the first ranger he met, but brought a small net instead. He could drop the net in the lake and let its floats signal him when fish struck. With such a neat gear he would be able to kill a few pleasant hours.

Mr. Cai strolled the long pier toward the Fishing Platform, looking splendid with its persimmon-colored walls and a double-tiered roof. Walking through the large rectangular entrance, he took in the views of the lake from the Platform's circular openings on three sides. Out of one circular opening he enjoyed the sight of White Pagoda, and another the Five Pavilion Bridge. Decorated rowboats and an occasional motor boat ruffled the water while tourists meandered alongside the shores with their cameras.

Mr. Cai settled at the lee side of the Fishing Platform. The Platform was not a public fishing site. In the Qing Dynasty, Emperor Qianlong and his ministers were entertained there. The two people who had fished there in recent years were Richard Nixon from the States and Norodom Sihanouk from Cambodia. The latter had caught a monstrous catfish. The rumor had it that Sihanouk had such a fondness for catfish barbels that his chef made them into a gourmet dish for him, with barbels taken from hundreds of catfish. However, ordinary people were only allowed to have a stroll and take pictures at the Fishing Platform.

It wasn't crowded in the early afternoon. Mr. Cai cast his net and opened a large book on his knees, *The Latest Styles of Cheongsam*. He fixed his eyes on the white floats in the green water.

Several rowboats drifted downstream from the Five Pavilion Bridge. One boat came within a hundred meters, where a red umbrella was rolling like a pinwheel. The bittersweet red would scare away any fish within a kilometer. Mr. Cai wished he knew the woman holding it, so that he could ask her for the favor of closing her umbrella. Instead, he stared at the boat helplessly.

Then, white waves approached the boat, before two arms reached up to the side of it, followed by a man pulling himself out of the water.

Mr. Cai's eyes popped with amazement. It was Jude! What a stroke of luck. Mr. Cai put down his book and stood up.

Jude wiped himself with a moss green towel, then slid his white tank top over his head. The woman behind the umbrella handed him a bottled water. Jude drank, then took an oar and started to row. The boat headed for the Fishing Platform.

Mr. Cai thrust his hands in the air and waved. "Jude!" he called. "How have you been?"

Jude shielded his eyes to peer at him. "Mr. Tailor, are you enjoying the breeze here?"

"I sure am." Mr. Cai glanced around to make sure no ranger was at the Platform. "I've cast a little fishing net here for some game."

Jude leaned over to say something to his companion. The red umbrella stopped spinning.

Jude nodded and shouted at Mr. Cai, "We're going back!"

"So soon?"

Jude rowed with both his oars. "We'd like to explore a bit upstream. So long, Mr. Tailor."

"Have a nice row." Mr. Cai was puzzled why Jude was in such a hurry to leave. Did he resent Feng's rudeness this morning? Even if so, it was surly of Jude not to introduce his friend.

The red umbrella diminished on the lake like a faded flower. Mr. Cai decided whoever was behind that umbrella was not worth meeting. Then he was able to return to his fishing.

A couple of hours later, Mr. Cai fastened his double plastic bags filled with lake water and a dozen carp, the size of goldfish. Mr. Cai would raise them as pets. From now on, when he felt bored and trapped working at home, he could take solace in the little carp he had caught at the Fishing Platform, a feat none but VIPs and royalties could have done.

*       *       *

Mr. Cai bought a fish tank on his way home. It felt heavier in his hands than it looked in the display window. The splurge without his wife's permission made him feel audacious. He poured the bag of carp into their new home. The carp glided swiftly from side to side as he carried the tank home. In two months, once Feng passed his exams, they would grow big. Then, Mr. Cai could make a delicious soup for his victory dinner.

Glad of the double use of his pets, he nudged the door closed with his elbow.

His wife came up to him. "No wonder it took you so long. What is this?"

"Is Feng home?" He laid the tank on the tea table. "I want to show him."

"He went to return the lecture notes." She tapped the tank with her fingers, causing the carp to dart about in panic.

He moved the tank to the far end of the table, out of her reach. "Back to Jiao's house? He has wasted a whole day over there."

"He said he would be back shortly." She glanced at the windows. "It's going to rain. Would you take in the laundry? I have to set the table for dinner."

Mr. Cai went to the porch at the back of the house. He moved the bamboo pole that hung wet laundry inside the hallway over the doorframes. Then it started to rain, cleansing the gravel on the back road until it glistened with a violet hue, the water echoing loudly in the sewer. His wife stood beside him on the porch as the rain pelted down in hard sheets.

Mr. Cai said, "I saw Jude rowing in the Slender West Lake with a woman."

"Who?"

"He didn't introduce her. She hid behind a red umbrella." Mr. Cai sighed. "If Jude has a girlfriend, she may want to monopolize him. She can talk him out of helping Feng."

"But you told me Jude wanted to invite his father to visit us!"

"Why not? We can help him buy cheap silk." As rain splattered onto the porch, he entered the kitchen with his wife and closed the door. They returned to the front room together. Seeing the fish tank on the table, Mr. Cai had a sudden revelation. "It might be Little Ye!"

"Who?"

"The woman in the rowboat with Jude. Jude said hello to me, but she talked him into turning away. Maybe Feng was right: Jude stole Little Ye from our son, and she didn't want me to see it. Then why does Jude want to help Feng?" Mr. Cai grunted. "I'm getting a headache trying to figure them out. What are these young people up to?"

"I'll ask Little Ye next time," Mrs. Cai said, "if I see her."

At the sound of Feng's voice out in the courtyard, along with a girl's giggling, Mr. Cai exchanged a glance with his wife. Then the screen door opened. Feng entered with his palms upturned to shield Jiao from rain.

"Mom! Dad! Guess what? Jiao saw me off and locked herself out. She just got home and isn't used to bringing her keys yet. It's pouring outside. Can she stay with us for a little bit?"

"Of course." Mrs. Cai gave Jiao a dry towel to wipe her face. "Would you have dinner with us?"

"I can't." Jiao brushed her wet bangs aside with her fingers. "Dad will be home soon. I'll have to help him with dinner."

Mrs. Cai said, "You're a good daughter, unspoiled after those years at college."

Mrs. Cai moved an extra chair to the dining table. Jiao helped her move the place settings.

"What's this, Dad?" Feng knocked on the fish tank, making a dull sound.

Mr. Cai smiled. "As you can see, I am raising young carp. They're our mascot, Son. After you pass the exams, I'll make a delicious soup for you."

"You will *not* fry them." Feng embraced the fish tank as if to protect it. "Let's make a deal: we'll release them after I pass the exams."

"Deal!" Mr. Cai was excited by Feng's optimism. "Now you have more at stake than your own future. Do your best!"

"Where did you catch them?" Feng sat down at the dining table.

"At the Fishing Platform."

"But fishing is not allowed there!" Jiao said.

"Only if you don't know how." Mr. Cai winked at her.

Jiao smiled and showed her dimples.

Mrs. Cai gave her a bottle of orange juice. Jiao took a seat between Feng and Mr. Cai, like a daughter in the family.

"Jiao has told me a lot about Beijing Normal University." Feng piled stir-fried vegetables in his bowl and sat sideways to face Jiao. "Her friends were among the bravest protesters at Tiananmen Square last year. Jiao, tell my parents about the protest."

Jiao sipped her juice. "Thinking back, we were just dumb brave. Ten of my classmates joined the hunger strike. Two dropped out after the third day, and the rest stuck it to the end." She averted her eyes from Feng's face. "Every night we sat on the Square and sang 'The Internationale' and patriotic songs. A good friend of mine wrote his last words, in case he wouldn't make it."

It made Mr. Cai wince that someone Feng's age was willing
to die for a cause. Remembering his baby carp, Mr. Cai took
a spoon of cooked rice to sprinkle in the fish tank. The carp
swarmed to gobble up the food. They must've been starving.

"What happened to your friends?" Mrs. Cai asked after a long
silence.

Mr. Cai returned to the dining table.

"Nobody died." Jiao forced a smile. "None of my friends, I mean.
A number of students were missing after the 4th, as you could
imagine. For most of us, the consequences didn't come until graduation. One of the smartest men in our department was denied
his application for graduate school." She looked down at the table
and chewed her lower lip. "Instead, he was assigned to teach at a
high school in the countryside of Gansu province, thousands of
kilometers from his hometown. So basically, he was sent into exile."

Feng added, "He can't return to the east coast for five or ten
years."

Mr. Cai was surprised to see the grin on Feng's face. If this student had been Jiao's ex, now his absence created an opportunity
for Feng. But what about Little Ye?

Nobody else commented on the sad story about the young man.

Feng glanced at Jiao every so often as he ate his dinner, as if he
were afraid that she might disappear. Jiao sipped her juice with
the straw gripped between her fingers.

There came a knock on the door, and she jumped up to open it.

Mr. Ouyang entered carrying a plastic bag. "Sorry that Jiao
troubled you." With his wet hair stuck to his skull, he looked bald-
er than usual. "I bought pig's tongue and duck feet, your favorites," he told Jiao.

"Jiao is a doll." Mrs. Cai brought a chair for him. "Why don't
you sit with us for a while? Our children must've talked more
today than we did in a year."

Mr. Ouyang thanked her and took his seat.

"I want to ask you for a favor." Mr. Cai poured a shot of whiskey
for Mr. Ouyang. "A friend of mine is interested in visiting the

Yangzhou Silk Factory. Do you think a tour can be arranged?"
He pushed a plate of fried peanuts toward his neighbor.

Mr. Ouyang picked up several peanuts. "I can write a note for
you to give to the director of the printing shop." He rubbed the
brown skins off the peanuts before putting the white kernels in his
mouth to chew, one at a time. "Make sure that you bring a carton
of 555 cigarettes for Director Xu. Then he'll give you an agree-
able tour." He sipped the whiskey and frowned as he swallowed it.
"Who's your friend, someone I know?"

"Sort of." Mr. Cai chuckled. "I do appreciate your help." If
not for Feng, Mr. Cai wouldn't stoop to ask his neighbor for
favors.

Mr. Ouyang ate the rest of peanuts along with his whiskey. "Let
me know when you need my note." He dusted his hands. "Jiao
and I had better go home. The rain has stopped."

Mr. Cai went to see them off. At the door, Mr. Ouyang thanked
him again for taking care of Jiao.

"Not a problem. She's a doll." Mr. Cai was surprised to hear
himself say it.

When Mr. Cai returned inside, Feng was explaining to his
mother, "Jiao was talking about her ex-boyfriend who is in exile.
She misses him like crazy."

"How unfortunate," Mrs. Cai said.

"A female student from Jiao's university was sent to a prison
farm after the 4th. That girl was raped three times in a month.
After hearing that, Jiao decided not to go with her boyfriend to
Gansu."

Feng still didn't know that Little Ye was pregnant. What would
he do when he found out? "Are you as sensible as Jiao?" Mr. Cai
asked.

"How can you compare people like that?" Feng blushed to the
root of his hair. "I'm a man, and she is a woman. Male intelligence is not the same as female intuition."

"It's funny you should say that." Mr. Cai wasn't in the mood to
let Feng off. "You and Jiao are the same age. She just graduated

from college, while you're still trying to enter it. You tell me how the society may compare your statuses."

Feng bit his lower lip, the corners of his mouth drooping unhappily.

"Did you think of Little Ye before you started going after Jiao?" Mr. Cai regretted it as soon as he heard himself say this.

"I'm not *after* Jiao!" Feng kicked a table leg and made the dishes clatter on the dining table. "Both she and I were dumped. We're in the same miserable lot."

"You two, calm down." Mrs. Cai sat between them to push their chests away. "Feng, when you live at a university dorm, you won't have to answer to your dad for everything."

"I can't wait." Feng stomped out of the kitchen.

Mr. Cai bit his tongue to keep his silence. He and Feng could never be of one mind, even though they wanted the same thing. They must arrive at Feng's success via the routes of their own choices. Along the way, Mr. Cai had to be careful not to trample on Feng's fragile self-esteem.

# CHAPTER 5

After a night of tossing and turning, Mr. Cai decided to visit the Silk Factory early rather than late.

If Jude was dating Little Ye, he might not be keen on helping Feng. In order to give Jude incentive, Mr. Cai planned to take him to the Silk Factory and choose some fine brocade for his Tang suit robe. Being socially graceful, Jude was unlikely to take his favors for granted.

After breakfast, Mr. Cai took a spoonful of rice to his fish tank. When he rapped the tank to warn his baby carp of the feeding to come, he was amazed to find rose petals and duckweed floating in the muddy water. Mr. Cai sprinkled the rice over the surface of the water, and the carp darted about, crisscrossing each other's paths, only to ignore the rice and start chewing the same piece of duckweed at opposite ends. To Mr. Cai, it looked as if they were in a tug-of-war.

"Did you muddy up my fish tank?" he asked his wife, who was opening the shop.

"I didn't touch it." She slid the rack stuffed with finished clothes to the front windows.

"Our son sticks his fingers in everything except for his own studies . . . and worse, wasting my roses."

His wife peered at the fish tank and smiled. "Now it looks like a living place, not just dead water."

Mr. Cai used a ladle to scoop out the fish into a clean bowl.

"Didn't you see the carp eating the duckweed?" she asked. "Why are you cleaning out their food?"

"I'm not a carp farmer at a fishery. They're my pets." He washed the tank with dish detergent. "You heard Feng. He wants to release them after they grow big. They're too good to be our food."

"Stop it."

Mr. Cai returned a few carp to the clean tank. "If Feng wants to raise them, he can have his own." He found an enamel basin to put the rest of fish into. Then he compared the carp with those in the tank and evened out the fat and thin ones. "I'll compete with Feng to see who raises the biggest carp." He filled the basin with water. The lotus flower print lifted from the bottom of the basin and became alive, as carp swam to and fro rippling its reflection.

Mrs. Cai prodded him with her finger. "How childish you are over a few minnows!"

"The drinker's heart is not in the cup." He put a fist to his lips while saying the proverb. "Likewise, I have another purpose. If Feng has pets, he is more likely to stay home rather than chase after Jiao."

"Feng is twenty-two years old, not a young boy."

Her wistful tone made him think of Little Ye. "He is our boy," Mr. Cai said to his wife. "Trust me, Feng won't grow up until he learns to take care of his own things."

Mr. Cai then went to the bedroom to find his pickle-colored cotton shirt. He would visit Mr. Ouyang rather than waste time arguing with his wife, who didn't speak for Feng any more than he did.

*     *     *

After knocking on Mr. Ouyang's door, Mr. Cai straightened his collar and raised his chin. It surprised him when Jiao opened the door.

"Is your father home?" he asked. "I'd like to pick up that note."

"He went on an errand and will be at the shop in a little bit." She pointed at the front road. "You can leave a message with me."

Mr. Cai was ready to turn and leave until he glimpsed red roses on the tea table. Mr. Ouyang grew only orchids in his yard. The price of roses was steep this time of the year. Could they have picked the roses from his side of the fence?

Jiao saw his glance and smiled. "Thank you for asking Feng to bring us the lovely roses. They really break up the monotony of our orchid display." She opened the door wide. "Would you like to see my flower arrangement?"

Mr. Cai nodded involuntarily.

Jiao led Mr. Cai to her bedroom. "I keep the best ones here." There were at least a dozen pink and red roses in a crystal vase, mixed with red, blue, purple, and yellow orchids, all creating a stunning bouquet. Her room smelt like a delicious nursery garden. "I dote on pink roses." She stroked a bud with her fingertips.

Her words stung him. Mr. Cai had planted the roses and mended his fence to shield his son from the potential humiliation of Jiao's success. Now the roses were in bloom and used to decorate her vase. A dozen roses in red and pink, no less!

Silenced by his exasperation, Mr. Cai leaned against the wall with his head hung low.

"When Feng came over last time, I practiced my lessons with him. He told me when I got boring." She pulled out a chair for him. "Have a seat, please."

Mr. Cai sat down without hesitation. Normally he would never loiter in a young woman's bedroom. But he felt misused just now and wanted some form of payback. Mr. Cai was also curious about a college graduate's living environment, which might prepare him for the future if Feng would pass the exams. Jiao plugged in an electric mosquito repellent, then sat on the bed opposite him.

Her room seemed much larger than Feng's, since she didn't use a mosquito net. The cream-colored wallpaper must've cost her father a fortune. The hardwood floor was waxed to shine like a splendid tabletop. On the wall above the bed hung a poster of the Statue of Liberty.

Mr. Cai pointed at the picture. "Is this the idol of college women?"

Jiao glanced up. "I can't speak for others. I adore her."

"Why not a young man's picture?" Mr. Cai knew he shouldn't pry, but knowing he might never have a private chance to find out what Jiao thought of Feng, he allowed himself. "You must have had many admirers at the university."

"What's the use?"

Jiao pinched a rose bud to make its petals open like a pouting mouth. Mr. Cai looked away to avoid snatching the poor bud from her.

"Love affairs in college rarely have any future," she continued. "Once people graduate, they just go their separate ways. It can't be helped."

Mr. Cai recalled Jiao's ex-boyfriend who had been a student leader. "You told us about a young man in exile. I can't imagine how sad his parents must be—"

"He paid his price for speaking a few honest words," she interrupted him. "The disciplinary committee sent him as far away as they could, so that he wouldn't implicate our school authorities, some of whom had once demonstrated with the students." The coir rope-strung bed frame jolted as Jiao slid back. "Everybody was brave in late May last year. After the crackdown, people ran for cover like scared rabbits. You can't help feeling that the spilt blood has gone to waste."

Mr. Cai stared at her mouth as it spoke those passionate words. She was, after all, an intellectual, Mr. Cai thought with envy. Her political zeal seemed otherworldly to the locals. Perhaps that was what drew Feng to her. But did Feng stand a chance with someone like her?

"Supposing Feng passes his exams this time. Will he find a nice girlfriend in college?" he asked Jiao jokingly. "I wonder because he's four years older than most people."

The sparkle in her eyes faded. "Older guys tend to get dates in college, because they're less shy with girls."

"What do *you* think of Feng?" Mr. Cai asked.

"He has good looks." Jiao lifted her pinky, then her ring finger, middle finger, and index finger. "He is also gentle, smart, and romantic. He will attract girls, especially those who aren't too ambitious."

Mr. Cai was at once gratified and hurt by her honesty. She was entitled to her opinion, being a college graduate while also being three months younger than Feng. Yet, Mr. Cai was not satisfied with her answer.

"May I ask if you're interested in him at all?" The question flew out of his mouth as if it had wings.

Jiao hugged her knees and rocked herself gently from side to side. For a long time she didn't speak, as if debating whether she wanted to be forthcoming.

Mr. Cai swallowed hard. "I don't know what came over me," he muttered.

"Feng is a good guy." Her eyes became wistful as she spoke. "Both of us have had a first love. The second love, however good it may be, tends to be less devoted and more pragmatic." She bit her lip and blushed briefly. "You give your whole self to your first lover. When the second person comes along, you only have the rest of you to offer him."

Why must she talk in circles! Mr. Cai racked his brains about her meaning. Then, blood rushed to his face, making him so hot that he opened the top button of his shirt.

"Are you okay?" Jiao asked.

Suddenly he noticed how narrow the space between his chair and her bed was. He ought to have stayed in the living room instead.

"I must be leaving." He stood up to press his back against the wall. "Your dad may be at the store. Sorry to bother you."

"Not a problem." Her face was flushed, too. Perhaps she was embarrassed that he knew her secret.

Mr. Cai left Jiao's bedroom in quick steps, feeling as though the fragrance of rose and orchid hung at his sleeves.

They said goodbye. Mr. Cai glanced at Jiao when she closed the door behind him. He should've guessed: a virgin couldn't have her swaying hips and talking eyes. Perhaps it wasn't college but sex that had ripened her. Mr. Cai was both uneasy and excited about his discovery. He might reveal the secret to Feng if such a need should arise.

*     *     *

Mr. Cai caught Mr. Ouyang surrounded by customers at his store. After a few words of exchange, Mr. Ouyang tore off a calendar sheet and wrote a note on its back, which Mr. Cai accepted with a gush of thanks. For the first time in years, Mr. Cai was proud of his resourceful neighbor.

Mr. Cai went home with his head held high. Just before crossing the street, he helped a man pull his wheelbarrow loaded with winter melons, so that the cart gently rolled down the steep slope. The young man stammered his thanks. Mr. Cai shook his head and walked gaily away. It had been a triumphant morning. He had not talked to Jiao in vain. The poor girl had lost her virginity to a man in exile. No matter how open-minded Feng was, this would surely affect his opinion of her.

Mr. Cai was in the kitchen chopping a turnip leaf to feed the carp when he heard the shop door open.

At the front desk his wife called out, "How have you been, Jude?" Her plastic soles tapped the cement floor as she led Jude inside.

Mr. Cai hurried to the shop front and held out both hands for a warm handshake. "Jude, just the man I want to see."

Jude's hand was sweaty and limp. After shaking it, Mr. Cai wiped his hand against his sleeve.

"My father booked a flight. He'll be here next month." Jude wiped his forehead. "Are we still up to it?"

"Why would I go back on my word?"

Jude bit his lip and nodded. "This won't be a relaxing trip for my father."

"Don't worry." Mr. Cai showed him Mr. Ouyang's note. "I've gotten us the passport to the Silk Factory."

Jude read the note aloud: "Please give Mr. Cai and his friends a tour. Yours, Old Ouyang." He turned the piece of paper over but didn't find more words. "Is this going to work?"

"I see you have doubts." Mr. Cai pinched his chin with his finger and thumb, like a wise Zhuge Liang kneading his goatee and advising the generals in a battle. "Here is an example of how Chinese people make good use of their relationships. If Mr. Ouyang had written me a formal letter, Director Xu at the textile printing shop would know that I had been sent through normal channels, which would make me a nobody to him. Since Mr. Ouyang wrote a personal note, Director Xu will understand I'm a friend of Mr. Ouyang's. Therefore, Director Xu will treat me like his own friend. In China, friendship snowballs." Mr. Cai clasped his hands in front of his chest. "So, my friend, can I interest you in visiting the Silk Factory sometime this week?"

Jude looked worried. "My parents haven't arrived yet."

"This is a preview, especially for you." He patted Jude's shoulder for emphasis. "Silk is a local specialty, and you will see why."

"Sure. I'll cut a few classes tomorrow."

Mr. Cai would've scolded him if he were Feng. "Can't you choose a day when you're free?" he asked in a gentle voice.

"Let's make it the day after tomorrow," Jude said, "if you don't mind."

"Not at all." Mr. Cai jotted down the address of the Silk Factory and handed the paper to Jude.

Instead of taking the note, Jude reached up to knead his earlobe, and Mr. Cai realized that Jude's left ear was bare.

"You should take off jewelry while swimming." Mr. Cai chuckled. "So fish in the Slender West Lake won't claim one earring!"

Jude's pale face reddened, his blue eyes defiant. "I *prefer* to wear one earring."

Mr. Cai wouldn't quarrel with Jude about a fashion choice; after all, he had never worn any jewelry in his life. "I appreciate your coming here, but you didn't have to. You could've called to tell me that you had arranged the visit for your father." He waved the note in front of Jude's face.

"Some things are better discussed in person." Jude watched Mr. Cai's face as if he were searching for some tacit understanding. The fervent light faded in his eyes, and his cheeks recovered its pallor. "I'll talk to you at the factory. It won't be too late."

Mr. Cai assured him, "We can go as early as you like!"

Mr. Cai extended his hand, but Jude's mind seemed to be elsewhere. "Wednesday!" Mr. Cai said. "Bright and early."

They shook on it. This time, Jude squeezed Mr. Cai's hand back. When their eyes met, they broke apart. Mr. Cai walked Jude to the courtyard. Jude unlocked his bicycle and rode away. His spandex pants made his legs look long and delicate.

Mr. Cai returned to his worktable with a tight feeling in his stomach. He had both dreaded and longed for this day when he had to inform Feng about their deal with Jude. Mr. Cai didn't speak English, yet he wanted to arrange for Feng to study abroad. Feng might laugh at him for meddling, even try to thwart his plans. Mr. Cai would endure Feng's belittlement as long as his son would go along and make the best of his situation.

*       *       *

As soon as Feng stepped inside that evening, Mr. Cai stopped him from changing into his slippers. "We're going out to dinner!" Mr. Cai snapped his fingers, trying to sound lighthearted.

"What for?" Feng asked. A strand of hair fell into his eyes.

Mrs. Cai reached out a hand to brush it away from his face. "You've studied hard and we have worked hard," she said with a broad grin. "Don't you think we deserve a night out?"

Feng straightened her velvet coat. "Mom, you're all dressed up!"

"I'm not." She slapped away Feng's hand. "This is a perfectly normal coat. Can't I wear it without being laughed at?"

Her coat, made in Hong Kong, had been Mr. Cai's gift for her fortieth birthday. The royal purple velvet had a soft hand and subtle shine that blotted out the blemishes in her face and took five years out of her appearance. The tailoring was impeccable. Once Feng had tried it on and marveled how elegant it looked. Feng had even challenged his father, "Can you make something like this?" In response Mr. Cai had shooed him back to his desk.

Now they took seats inside Fuchun Teahouse, while people were filing in during the early dinner hour. Soon customers would crowd the entrance and even wait at the tables for other diners to leave. The ceiling fans were twirling above the noisy crowd. Mr. Cai looked at the tall windowpanes with wood etching, antique imitation of an affluent home. Colored paper with food items written in brushstrokes were pasted at the ordering windows and throughout the dining hall, like a street fair.

Feng ordered spicy tofu and white rice, and the fried turnip cakes for appetizer. His mother asked why he didn't try the specialty, vegetarian three-treasure buns.

"They use lard in the filling." Feng drummed his fingers on the table.

Mr. Cai squinted his eyes to read the orange menu posted on a nearby column. "I'm going to have the three-treasure buns. It's what Fuchun is known for." He gave his wallet to his wife to buy the coupons for the dishes. Then he poured Feng a cup of tea. "This is jasmine. It should be okay, even for you." The tea was a pale yellow.

"You didn't have to do this, Dad."

"I should've steeped the tea for a while longer," Mr. Cai said.

"Actually, you could've just told me whatever you want to talk about. You didn't have to take me out for dinner." Feng pointed at Mrs. Cai, who was jostling her way to the ticket window. "Look at Mom." He smiled. "They're going to rumple her favorite coat."

Mrs. Cai lost her place in the queue when a large man shoved her aside. Just before the man could take a good look at the menu, she slithered back into the queue in front of him and stood at the ordering window. Mr. Cai could trust his wife to beat out anyone who dared to stand in her way.

Mr. Cai glanced at other tables, most of which were occupied by dating couples. He felt assured of their privacy. "I have news for you, Feng. How good it is depends on what you do with it."

Feng dipped a finger into his teacup, then drew smiley faces on the table.

"You passed the TOEFL last year," Mr. Cai continued, willing himself to ignore Feng's fidgeting. "Would you like to go study at an American university?"

"How? My transcript is sitting at the ETS with nowhere to go."

"Because we didn't have a financial sponsor then. Suppose I found you a sponsor. How would you feel about that?"

"Super."

Mr. Cai was relieved to hear Feng's answer. Before he could go on, Feng wiped away his drawings with his sleeve.

"My food is here." Feng rubbed his hands together.

Mrs. Cai put down a plate of fried turnip cakes. Green onion speckled their light, crispy skins. Its savory smell attracted glances from the neighboring tables.

Mr. Cai lowered his voice. "I've asked Jude to sponsor you."

Feng doused a cake in vinegar, then bit into it. Its crust fell from the corners of his mouth. Mr. Cai felt hungry watching him.

"Jude was kind enough to ask his father to be your sponsor." Mr. Cai poured tea for his wife. "Now, his father is coming to see us in a few weeks."

Feng finished the first cake and reached for a second.

His mother slapped his wrist. "Have you got nothing to say about that?"

"Why all this fuss? What do I have to do with it?"

Mr. Cai said, "Feng, if you convince Jude's father that you're a good friend of Jude's, he may sponsor you to study at a university in the States."

"I'm not Jude's friend." Feng started on his second cake. "For all I know he stole my girlfriend."

"We don't know that. Can't you be friendly with him for a half-hour or so?" Mrs. Cai wiped Feng's greasy palm with a napkin. "How hard can that be? Would you rather waste the opportunity of a lifetime? When will you ever grow up?"

"I'd like to grow up, very much." Feng pressed the whole cake into his mouth and mumbled with a thick tongue. "But do you let me? You don't even allow me to date."

Mr. Cai held his wife's hand to keep her from chiming in. "You understand, 'Career first, and love second.' This is a necessity."

When the cashier called for their table, Mrs. Cai went to pick up the rest of their dishes.

"Who would be so stupid?" Feng asked. "Do you really think if I pretend to be Jude's friend for a couple of minutes, his old man will support me through college?"

"*We* will support you." Mr. Cai drew a circle with tea to connect himself with Feng and his wife, who set the spicy tofu and three-treasure buns on their table. "Jude's father will be your sponsor only in name. I won't ask him to spend a cent on you. Why wouldn't he take kindly to a good family like ours?"

Feng didn't answer but studied his food with a pout. "Didn't I ask for tofu only? What's wrong with the cook?"

"We'll help you with it." Mrs. Cai scooped out dried shrimps from the tofu. "If I go ask them to throw away the shrimp, they'll think me slow in the head."

"Take them all, please." Feng sat back with his arms folded on his chest. "I can't believe you want me to cheat Jude's dad. I thought you were above telling lies."

"We didn't ask you to lie," Mrs. Cai said, "but to be friendly with Jude. What's wrong with that?"

Mr. Cai wanted to ask Feng, if he was so against lying, how he had kept Little Ye a secret from them all these years without batting an eye.

Instead, he picked up a dried shrimp and put it in his mouth to chew. It tasted like sand.

*          *          *

"I don't see what's so great about this restaurant." Feng rinsed his mouth with tea and swallowed it. "You cook much better, Mom."

Mrs. Cai collected the two leftover buns in a doggie bag. "You didn't order the right food. Your father told you the three-treasure buns are their specialty."

Feng stood up to leave. "The air in here is so greasy that I took a breath and felt full." He bumped into a stool someone had pushed into the middle of the aisle.

If it was in Feng's nature to disobey and disappoint his parents, Mr. Cai had to try a roundabout approach to wear him down. "This will not do." Mr. Cai returned the stool under a nearby table. "Imagine you're in the States: all around you people are eating hamburgers, cheesesteaks, and fries. Will you survive breathing the air in that restaurant?"

Feng swung outside and held the door for his parents. "I'd much rather stay home."

Feng's attitude made Mr. Cai's blood boil. How could he deliver a wakeup call to his unruly son?

"Don't be a loser." Mr. Cai slapped his back so hard Feng stumbled forward down the sidewalk. "All my labors are wasted if you end up like me."

Mrs. Cai cast her husband a sympathetic glance over her shoulder. "What your dad meant was, if you end up being a poor tailor like he is, then you let him down." She rubbed Feng's back to whisper into his ear, loud enough for Mr. Cai to hear, "However, he is a good father and husband. I won't be disappointed if you turn out like him."

When they passed the Hanjiang Cinema, people swarmed into the streets and broke them apart. Feng grasped his mother's hand, who held Mr. Cai's hand to form a line and pushed through the crowd. Mr. Cai was dragged toward the littered sidewalk, as his soles stepped on popsicle wrappers, sunflower seed shells, banana peels, watermelon rinds, and broken eggshells.

"How long has it been since you took me to a movie, Dad?"

"A couple of months? Not that long." Mr. Cai wrinkled his nose at the earthy odors emanating from the bodies around him. Despite his best effort he bumped into people with every step: soft breasts, hard shoulders, bony elbows, groping hands, and worst of all, the stem of a palm fan that stabbed his waist. He groaned with pain.

They huddled together after the crowd left. The streetlights went on and illuminated Feng's face, which made him look sallow. Mosquitoes and moths gathered under the source of light into a ball, humming like a fleet of mini-helicopters. Feng slapped Mr. Cai's wrist so hard that he moaned.

"A mosquito." Feng showed his palm. "I missed it, darn!"

Mr. Cai rubbed his wrist with a forced smile.

They resumed walking. The evening sky was smoky gray with shimmering stars. Ahead of Mr. Cai, Feng dragged his heels as if he were intent on ruining his shoes. What would Jiao think of Feng if she could see him now?

"It's going to be sunny tomorrow," Mr. Cai said. "Good for the roses, you know."

Feng kicked a rock and sent it gliding down the path.

"I went to Jiao's house to see her father today," Mr. Cai said. "Guess what I found there? A dozen roses. Our roses, she told me."

"I gave them to her." Feng glanced over his shoulder at his father.

The Cais veered around the bridge under construction. Inside the bridge opening, a slum family sat around an upturned wooden bathtub, which they were using as their dining table. A man cracked a hardboiled egg and peeled it for his daughter.

Mr. Cai cast a sidelong glance at the family before walking on. Their poverty looked cozy at this distance.

"A family should stick together," Mr. Cai said as they ascended the ramp to the main road, Feng leading the way. "We should look out for each other instead of plotting against one another. Don't you agree?"

"Stop beating around the bush. I gave the roses to Jiao." Feng thrust his hands into his pockets. "They're just flowers. What's the big deal?"

Mr. Cai slowed his pace, his chest tightening with anger. What if Feng wanted to stay home in order to court Jiao? Feng would be throwing away a career opportunity that would never come his way again, while Jiao used him as a neighbor boy to practice her lectures.

"If I don't give the roses away, they'll just wither in our yard," Feng added.

"Perhaps." Mr. Cai strode to catch up with Feng, for he didn't want to shout the rest of his words. "When I spoke with her today, we discussed many things. I have reason to believe that she and her ex-boyfriend were—" he sighed—"*lovers.*"

Feng whirled around to face his father. "What?"

"Feng, you understand she's not untouched."

Feng grabbed hold of his arm and shook him hard. "Why are you telling me this, Dad?"

"I thought you would want to know, since you are so sweet on Jiao." Mr. Cai said every word slowly and clearly.

"Suppose I am fond of Jiao." Feng stamped his feet. "You're trying to ruin my image of her. What's the matter with you? You're a bully who plays with people's feelings."

"Son." Mrs. Cai pried Feng's hand from her husband's arm and waved him down the path to get the group walking again. "Your father is only the messenger. It's up to you to think well or ill of her."

"I can't believe you: this is 1990. If Jiao could go to a political protest, she is entitled to have a boyfriend." Feng turned to his mother. "How can you stand him, Mom? Your husband is a sick man."

Mrs. Cai said, "Keep your voice down, Feng."

"I didn't even know I was falling for Jiao until now. How's that for what I think of your message?" Passing a holly shrub, Feng ripped a handful of leaves. "You know what? I changed my mind about Jude, too. I'll pretend to be his friend. I'll go study abroad. What the heck? I want to get as far away from you as possible." He ran ahead, his long hair flying behind him like a pony's mane.

Mr. Cai was too angry at Feng to be happy about his consent. He wanted to shout after his son: *You think I'm asking a favor from you? It is I who has arranged everything for you. We'll have to spend every cent we have saved just to get you through the first year abroad. That is, if you can make it to the States after you've fouled up everything else* . . .

But none of these words escaped his lips, as he realized, in spite of Feng's emotionality, the goal of this expensive dinner was achieved: he would be able to carry out his plan.

"You didn't have to do that." His wife tugged his arm with surprising force.

"I didn't . . . do it on purpose. It just came out."

"I know." She sighed. "Like father, like son."

\* \* \*

The ticket seller rapped the bus window with his metal hole-puncher and announced the stop, Silk Factory. Mr. Cai clutched the plastic gift bag in his hands to peer out of the windows. The Yangzhou Silk Factory emerged with a row of bright red, yellow, green, and blue banners lining up its main avenue. Morning breezes teased the silky soft flags and made them flutter like gigantic butterflies. Mr. Cai marveled at the extravagant display.

He stepped off the bus behind a stream of workers. As he headed for the factory gate, a familiar voice called to him, "Morning, Mr. Tailor."

He was surprised to find Jude standing by the reception office and waving at him. Jude wore a jade green shirt that brought out his fair features. To Mr. Cai's delight, Jude wore both his earrings, so he hadn't lost one after all.

"Morning, Jude! I thought you'd be a few minutes late. Don't young people need more sleep than old folks?" Mr. Cai let out a hearty chuckle.

Jude didn't smile but glanced at Mr. Cai's plastic bag. "Do you need a hand with that?" he asked.

"No." Mr. Cai was touched by how attentive Jude seemed. Feng wouldn't offer help so readily to an elder.

The guard pointed them to the textile printing shop. "You're in luck today," he said. "Director Xu just returned from a business trip in the States."

Jude nodded at the guard. "Thank you, Sir, much obliged."

Mr. Cai was proud to be seen in Jude's company, cordial and handsome as Jude was. As they entered the factory, Mr. Cai talked about specialty silks while Jude remained silent. Other people peered at them curiously as Mr. Cai spoke to a foreigner in Chinese. When they reached the printing shop, Jude jogged ahead to hold the door for Mr. Cai.

"There's something I need to tell you," Jude said and looked around as if in search of privacy.

A young receptionist interrupted him from behind the counter. "Good morning. Are you here to see Director Xu?"

Mr. Cai nodded and handed her Mr. Ouyang's note. "I'd appreciate it, Miss, if you gave this note to him."

"Please seat yourselves. I'll be back shortly."

Mr. Cai then turned to Jude. "What did you want to tell me?"

Jude gazed at the side door which the receptionist had left half-open. "Maybe later." He stepped aside to study the silk patterns in the exhibit case.

The receptionist returned with a stout middle-aged man. Director Xu wore a white polo shirt and gray pants that seemed to be tailored for his potbelly.

Mr. Cai shook Director Xu's hand and nudged him aside to whisper, "I have a small token of appreciation for your kindness." He sniffed Director Xu's cologne, an exotic and pleasant scent. For a man with average looks, using cologne made him appear well-groomed and cultured.

Director Xu peered into the bag with a carton of 555 cigarettes. "Thank you, Mr. Cai." He wrapped the handles of the plastic bag over his wrist. "Would you and your friend care for a tour of our shop?"

\* \* \*

Inside the large printing room, six printers spilled out fabrics cascading from the metal rolling guide suspended at three meters high. Several workers wearing hats and aprons inspected the silk and replaced the full bolts with empty ones on the flat bed, where the silk was collected and rolled. A rack against the wall displayed the silk in dazzling patterns sorted by color groups: red, orange, yellow, green, blue, indigo, and violet. The humming of the machines filled the workshop with a constant buzz. None of the workers looked in Mr. Cai's way. Perhaps they were trained to ignore visitors.

"Gauze silk is our new specialty, introduced from Hangzhou, Zhejiang province. Hang Gauze is reputed to be the finest gauze on the market. Made of pure mulberry silk, Hang Gauze is noted for its simplicity and tight fiber formation. The satin weave on the fabric facilitates ventilation, which makes it a popular fabric for summer clothing." After a pause, Director Xu told Mr. Cai, "Advise your friend to buy a pajama set, because he won't find better fabric on the market."

Mr. Cai saw Jude's eyes twinkle and knew that he had understood Director Xu.

"You would look fine in any color," Mr. Cai said to Jude in Chinese. "But if you want a Mandarin robe, get the red." He pointed at the bright red silk with dragon prints cascading from the printing machine.

"You didn't tell me he knows Chinese." Director Xu slapped his thigh. "Come here." He led them to another machine that spilled out black silk with gold snake prints. "This is a hot item on the overseas market."

Jude shook his head with a shudder. "I'm not into dragons, snakes, or anything that crawls. I'm interested in this pattern here." They followed him to the printing machine by the windows. "Can Mr. Tailor make a Tang suit robe out of such a pretty thing?"

The light ginger-colored silk he pointed to was printed with turquoise butterflies teasing peonies. Mr. Cai was amazed. He realized that Jude's chiseled facial features seemed fragile for his strong body, looking rather feminine.

Director Xu broke into loud chuckles. "You don't want to buy that, unless you're a teenage girl with a peachy complexion."

"Is it the flowers?" Jude asked.

"Peonies are fine for a man's Tang suit robe," Mr. Cai advised Jude. "They embody nobility, prosperity, happiness as well as beauty. However, butterflies are never used in men's clothing. A Tang suit robe should inspire respect for your masculinity. It can't represent both men and women." Mr. Cai knew this pattern was too pretty. Even Little Ye couldn't pull it off, but Jiao might. Once upon a time, Xiu could have but never had a chance.

"It's the only pattern I like." Jude stood by the cascading silk. "Do you think it'll look ugly on me?" His blue eyes darkened with something like hurt.

"Ugly is the wrong word." Director Xu pulled some silk to place beside Jude's face. "Our designer will be flattered to see you wear this. With your complexion, you'll make our silk look gorgeous."

"I'll buy it." Jude burst into a mischievous smile. "I want my first Tang suit robe to be made from this."

Mr. Cai was insulted because Jude ignored his advice. On the other hand, he was relieved that he could make a Tang suit robe with the Hang Gauze that Jude adored.

"Do you have a girlfriend?" Director Xu asked Jude. "She'd envy you if she sees you wearing this."

"I don't have such a girlfriend, fortunately." Jude's face was flushed like a ripe peach.

"Why? Don't you like Chinese girls?" Director Xu winked at Jude. "I've been abroad, you know. A number of white men have told me Chinese girls are rather pretty."

"They *are*," Jude said. "They're intelligent and kind as well. I'm sure to be interested in them if I was looking for a girlfriend." He swallowed. "Though I'm not, at present."

Mr. Cai understood that Jude wanted to evade the personal question. With his exotic looks and perfect Chinese, Jude must have been stared at everywhere he went and harassed often by curious local people.

Mr. Cai came to Jude's rescue. "You're young. No need to hurry and find a wife. If you like this silk, very well, I'll make you a Tang suit robe. You may wear it when your father comes to visit."

Director Xu nodded like a pecking chick. "If our silk looks good on you, we want to photograph you."

"I expect to be paid." Jude stuck out his chest with arms akimbo. "How else will I attract a wife?"

*       *       *

Later at home, Mr. Cai rinsed Jude's Hang Gauze and hung it on the bamboo pole to dry. The moonlight tinted the silk a faint teal. The butterfly wings became transparent, as if they would lift from the cloth. Jude seemed to have the aesthetic eye of a Chinese painter. Now he found a silk almost as beautiful as himself. What did it matter that Jude was a man? His face and body would become the perfect canvas for this image of exalted natural beauty.

Mr. Cai was removing his hand from the gauze silk when the screen door squeaked open behind him.

Feng walked onto the porch. "Mom said you gave me some carp to raise." He walked to the silk and stroked it with the back of his hand. "My goodness, who gave you this?"

"I took Jude to the Silk Factory."

"Why didn't you take me?" Before Mr. Cai could reply, Feng switched on the light, the silk on the pole turning ginger-colored again. "I've always wanted to go."

"You had class. We live here and can go later, but Jude is a rare guest." Since Mr. Cai couldn't appease Feng's jealousy, he decided to distract his son. Mr. Cai picked up an enamel basin from the floor. "These are your carp. Stop filling my fish tank with mud. You do whatever you please with yours."

"Fine." Feng accepted the enamel basin with both hands. "They're going to sleep in my room."

"After your exams, we either release all of them." Mr. Cai lowered his voice. "Or just yours."

"You're cruel, Dad."

"Let me revise the rules. You may enter a Chinese or an American university. In either case, we release all our fish."

Feng laid his basin on the floor. He wiped his hand on his tee shirt before he shook his father's hand. "Deal."

Mr. Cai squeezed Feng's cold hand. "What did you give my carp, anyway?"

"Mud from the riverbank. Carp love that junk. I don't want to spoil them. They're just fish, you know."

"Aren't yours pets?"

"Sure." Feng flashed a smile that disappeared as quickly as it had appeared. "I'll take good care of them. They won't starve."

"Let's see who can raise the strongest carp," Mr. Cai proposed in a half-hearted effort to make amends with Feng from last night.

"Is this a contest?" Feng tossed his head. "What's the prize?"

"The winner gets to be Dad for a day." Mr. Cai chuckled. "Would you like that?"

"Fair game." Feng lifted the basin from the floor. "I can't wait to beat you."

"Will you run the tailor shop for me?"

"A piece of cake." Feng scoffed. "I won't even complain."

Mr. Cai held the screen door open for Feng. He was pleased with his own cleverness. He wasn't at all afraid of losing to Feng. To be a dad was more difficult than Feng could ever imagine, even if Feng's children were only carp.

# CHAPTER 6

Mr. Cai was drawing the paper patterns for Jude's Tang suit robe when his wife answered the ringing phone.

"Jude is asking for you," she called from the hallway.

Mr. Cai had to drop his work in the middle of calculating the sleeve length. At a time like this, he wished he had a cordless phone like the one that people used in the sitcom *Growing Pains*.

"Why, Jude, I just laid out the patterns for your robe," he said.

The voice on the other end was hesitant. "Is this Mr. Tailor?" it whispered.

"Of course." Mr. Cai raised his face as if to show Jude. "You don't sound good, Jude. Did you catch a cold? You should take care of yourself. Your parents are coming to see you soon."

Jude muttered something that Mr. Cai didn't hear.

"You have to speak up!" he said.

"I couldn't tell you the other day at the factory," Jude said so loudly that Mr. Cai had to move his phone away from his ear. "The fact is, Mr. Cai . . . I'm *gay*." He said the last word in another language Mr. Cai didn't understand.

Mr. Cai waited a few seconds for Jude to continue, because he didn't understand. "What is *gay*, Jude?" Mr. Cai wiped his handset with his over-sleeve as if that would help him hear more clearly. "This phone is so old. I need to buy a new one. Anyway, don't let me cut you off. What do you mean you're *gay*?"

"I'm homosexual."

Mr. Cai's hand opened and dropped the handset. He leaned against the wall to collect himself for a moment, before he pulled up the phone with its cord. "Sorry about that," he said faintly. "I almost lost you."

"I thought it would be better if I told you over the phone. If you don't want to see me again, there won't be hard feelings between us."

Jude's voice was fading at the other end of the phone line. Or did Mr. Cai's ears start ringing? He was afraid that Jude might evaporate even as they were speaking. "Why shouldn't I see you again? I'm making your Tang suit robe and want you to come in for a fitting in a couple of days." He wrapped the phone cord around his wrist as if to keep Jude on the line. "You're my friend, Jude. Why would I have hard feelings against you for no reason?" he asked in a scolding tone. After the initial shock, he felt hurt that Jude wanted to end their relationship over a simple statement.

There was a long silence at the other end. When Jude spoke again, he sounded like he was sobbing. "Thank you, Mr. Tailor. Thank you. You don't know how much this means to me."

Mr. Cai was puzzled by his gratitude. "Why do you say that?"

"You took a heavy load off my mind." Jude muffled a dry cough. "I haven't told my father. He may disown me if I do. I went as far away as China to keep my secret from him."

"Why would he disown you, Jude, when you're his only son?" Mr. Cai sat down at the corner table to brace himself for a long talk.

"You don't know my dad."

Another long silence followed. Mr. Cai propped his arm on the table and waited patiently.

"He thinks gay people are wrong in their heads," Jude said with a sigh. "I've always been afraid of him."

"Your head is fine," Mr. Cai said. "You speak Chinese almost as well as Feng."

"You know I didn't mean it like that, Mr. Tailor."

Mr. Cai was glad that he wasn't talking to Jude face to face, or he might have stuttered while he told some half-truths. "You're a university student and an artist. If I had a son like you, I would've flaunted your achievements in front of all my relatives."

"You think everything is so simple."

"How complicated should it be?" Mr. Cai waited for his answer, but Jude gave none. "You're your father's son, his flesh and blood. How can he sever a blood relation with some petty excuse?"

"Thank you, Mr. Tailor." A kissing sound through the receiver made Mr. Cai's ear tingle. "The more I think about it, the more I'm convinced I did the right thing to invite my father for this visit. For three years I have not gone home for Christmas, and used up all my excuses to keep my father from visiting me. But I can't cut myself off from him forever. You helped me see that, Mr. Tailor. I cannot thank you enough."

Mr. Cai felt the pinch of his handset against his cheek and realized he was smiling. He enjoyed the praise, for he knew Jude would be more willing to help Feng from now on.

"When you asked if my father would sponsor Feng," Jude continued, "I realized you also gave me an opportunity to come out to my family."

A sobering revelation dawned on Mr. Cai that he had been blinded by Jude's fluent Chinese; there was a side of Jude that was utterly foreign. The Chinese had a motto: don't discuss private problems with outsiders. But Jude was doing the opposite, a risky move that could bring dire consequences.

"Do you have to 'come out' during this visit?" Mr. Cai swallowed the rest of his words: *you could jeopardize Feng's case.*

"This is the perfect time." Jude sounded like he was smiling. "I'll explain to my father that I haven't been avoiding him all these years. Rather, I've been trying to come to terms with who I am. Then I'll tell him what a great friend Feng has been to me, who not only taught me Chinese but also helped me come out to them. If my father asks why I want to help Feng, can I tell him that Feng is my best friend?"

"Or you can say that Feng is like a brother to you," Mr. Cai suggested. The word "best" gave Mr. Cai a queasy feeling. Did

Jude imply physical intimacy in such a friendship? Mr. Cai didn't ask Jude to clarify, lest he sound presumptuous.

"A best friend is more natural," Jude replied, "because I have one of those. I just need to act friendly with Feng instead."

Mr. Cai's heart was pounding so hard he was afraid Jude could hear it on the other end of the phone line. "You have to give me time to talk to Feng." He licked his dry lips.

"Of course. That's why I'm telling you this now."

Mr. Cai said goodbye. The handset slipped a few times before it clicked into the phone cradle on the wall. Who was this young American, who feared his own father? What desperation had driven Jude to turn toward a stranger for help? Most importantly, how could Mr. Cai navigate this brand new territory?

*        *        *

Mr. Cai didn't hear his wife's steps. When her hand touched his shoulder, he turned around to hold her tightly to his chest.

"What's wrong?" she asked.

"You were right about the American." Mr. Cai could not continue.

She trembled. "What?"

Mr. Cai squeezed her hard.

"Tell me." She pushed him away to look at his face.

"He is . . ." Mr. Cai took a deep breath. "Gay."

"Go on."

He grew impatient. "Do you know what a gay man is?"

"I told you about it first. Now you're asking me? Old Wang, the barber, had been married for ten years with a nine-year-old son. He divorced his wife last year and went to Guangzhou. People said he was gay." She sighed. "What are you getting at?"

"Jude wants Feng's help to come out to his family."

Mrs. Cai reached behind him to turn on the light in the hallway.

He shielded his eyes with a hand. "What're we going to tell Feng? He could barely stand the sight of Jude. Now he wants

Feng to pretend to be his 'best friend.'" Mr. Cai pushed her into
their bedroom and shut the door, lest anyone might eavesdrop.
"Jude said this might persuade his father to sponsor Feng, or his
father could disown him. Our chance is slim. Who knows what
Jude's really after? What if he's attracted to our son? We can't
push Feng into his trap!"

She sat on the bed and hugged a pillow in her arms. "Is a best
friend the same as a boyfriend?"

Mr. Cai shrugged, feeling defeated. "Who could say?"

"You'd better tell Feng and let him decide what to do."

"Are you out of your mind? The exams are a month and a half
away. You don't mess with his mind, unless you want him to fail."

"How do you know he'll fail?" She threw the pillow at Mr. Cai's
chest. "He has never made a real decision in his life. All he does
is obey your orders. It's about time he takes some responsibility. I
bet it'll help him get over Little Ye as well."

Mr. Cai fell silent at her mention of Little Ye. If Feng had made
her pregnant, he might not be corrupted by Jude. But then, the
gay barber had survived a ten-year marriage in this very neighborhood, and no one suspected a thing. Apparently, Jude could
just as likely have made Little Ye pregnant as Feng.

Mr. Cai walked to his fish tank, which rested on a trunk. Like
Feng, he kept his carp in the bedroom. He dipped a finger into
the water. A large silver carp swam to the surface while the small
ones dove to the bottom. Mr. Cai was disappointed that the stout
carp was eager to feed despite any danger, like himself.

Mr. Cai only wanted his son to go to the college, whether in
China or the States. Why did Jude have to make his goal perilous?
For a moment, Mr. Cai wished he had not laid eyes on the gay
American who had sauntered into his shop.

But neither was he willing to pass on the hard-earned opportunity without giving it a try. He had to listen to his wife—perhaps
the time had finally come to test Feng.

He wiped his wet finger on his over-sleeve. "I wish there were
some other way."

\*     \*     \*

Mr. Cai didn't want Feng to waste a night of studying, so he waited until Feng was ready for bed to approach him for a chat, a basin of warm water in tow. He hoped Feng would go to bed with a general idea, wake up the next morning, and return to his studies, the usual routine uninterrupted.

Instead, as Mr. Cai told Feng about Jude's plan, Feng became animated while washing his feet.

"I had no idea he was gay!" Feng tapped his feet, splattering some water. "This is too cool!"

Puzzled, Mr. Cai asked, "What's so cool about that?"

"He likes men! He can't be with Jinhua. Boy, was I dumb to take him for my enemy. I owe him an apology."

Mr. Cai exchanged a glance with his wife.

"What do you think about acting as his best friend?" she asked.

"No objection whatsoever. I'll have to practice my act with Jude before meeting his father." Feng dried his feet with a towel. "When will he come?"

"Next month," she said.

"I don't have much time." Feng peered at himself in the mirror. "Should I put on some weight? I've heard that one of the gay partners is 'butch,' and Jude is pretty feminine."

Mr. Cai was shocked. "What do you mean?"

"That I'll be more convincing if I look gay. Better yet, there should be chemistry between Jude and me. Then his father will believe we are close. Do you need any help finishing up his robe, Dad? I'm happy to try it on."

This was too much for Mr. Cai. "Jude did not ask you to play his gay friend!" He was almost shouting.

Feng seemed not to hear him. "I knew Jude had something up his sleeve," he said. "But I didn't expect it to be so simple. I once heard that a girl got her sponsorship to the States by promising to bear her sponsor a child. No marriage, just a baby for her sponsor's family. Of course, she started to take pills as soon as she landed in Miami.

"Jude only asked me to act as his friend. This is nothing. I could do much more for him!"

Mr. Cai didn't know whether he should laugh or cry.

His wife handed Mr. Cai the foot basin and said, "You go pour it out. I have a few words to tell Feng." She shoved him so hard out the door that he nearly spilled the dirty water.

Mr. Cai hurried to the bathroom. When he rushed back, his wife was closing Feng's door.

"Sleep tight, Son."

Mr. Cai dropped the red plastic basin, which rolled a half circle before plopping flat on the floor. "What did you say to him?"

She took the basin to the bathroom, and he followed her. She rinsed and refilled it with warm water. "Here, wash your feet."

Mr. Cai raised his voice. "Are you going to tell me, or conspire against me together?"

"Hush, Feng is trying to sleep." She laid the foot basin on the floor. "I didn't want you two to quarrel, so I told Feng to take it easy and sleep on it."

"Was that all?"

She nodded.

"Then why did you make me leave?"

"Take a look at yourself." She nudged him toward the mirror.

Mr. Cai saw a haggard man with a pasty face, three days' stubble, and bloodshot eyes. "I'm aging rapidly." He stroked his sunken cheeks. "I worry about Feng so much that my hair is graying."

"You can't blame it all on Feng. When you were ready to jump on him, he saw the opportunity to tease you."

"What do you mean?"

"You don't understand why Feng wants to help Jude." She handed him a stool. "Living with us, Feng has few ways to assert his independence. Acting as Jude's friend gives him a chance to stand up to Jude's father." She bit her lip to conceal a smile. "Feng told

me that he and Jude could be sworn brothers. Both keep secrets
from their fathers."

Mr. Cai sat on the stool and rolled up his pant legs. "Secrets."
He put his feet in the basin and flexed his toes. "What am I going
to do if Feng turns gay just to spite me?"

"You underestimate him." His wife walked away shaking her
head.

Mr. Cai rubbed his feet against each other. The water was a
little too hot and scalded his skin. He lifted his feet from the basin
and called his wife to bring him some cold water.

"You're the one already in the bathroom!" she called from the
bedroom.

Padding to the faucet with wet feet, hand against the wall,
Mr. Cai wondered if he had invited unforeseen trouble into his
home.

                    *        *        *

All night long Mr. Cai had dreamt about being chased by mon-
sters and jumping in front of trains, before he woke to the noise
of a passing bus. His wife snored softly beside him. It was half
past six, when the sky was gray like a gloomy winter afternoon.
He lay in bed and listened. The house was quiet as a grave. Mr.
Cai wondered if Feng was sleeping soundly, or dreaming about
flirting with Jude in front of their dumbfounded fathers.

His wife stirred beside him. "What time is it?" she asked.

"A quarter to seven. Go back to sleep. I'll rustle up some breakfast for Feng." Mr. Cai got up and tucked the blanket under her.

"Don't forget to buy fried breadsticks." She buried her face in
the pillow.

Mr. Cai entered the kitchen to slide open the air shutter of the
coal cake stove. Then he put a saucepan of porridge on the stove.
It would take at least ten minutes for the top coal cake to blaze up.
So he headed for the snack shop to buy soybean milk and fried
breadsticks.

At the fried breadstick stand, Mr. Cai caught sight of Jiao in a red-dotted rayon dress, waiting in line. As he stood behind her, the crackling of dough in hot oil and odor of grease didn't bother him anymore.

"Good morning," she greeted him with a smile.

"Good morning to you, Jiao." For some reason, Mr. Cai was glad to see her dimples. With her hair pulled back into a tight bun, Jiao's face looked plump and feminine. Perhaps his son had not been frivolous to court Jiao. After all, if Feng entered a university, Jiao would be more or less a social equal for Feng. Mr. Cai would prefer to have Feng be friendly with Jiao rather than Jude, exams be damned.

"You're a diligent girl," Mr. Cai said.

"Why do you say that?" Jiao reached out her enamel bowl to the cook, who gave her four fried breadsticks, dripping with hot oil.

"You could've slept in. It's your summer vacation."

"No, I can't. I'm a morning person."

Mr. Cai bought his breadsticks and then started walking home with Jiao. "I was awfully chatty at your house the other day," he said. "I hope I didn't waste too much of your time."

"You were my guest. I was happy to talk with you." Jiao's bamboo slippers gently tapped the asphalt road as she walked.

"I really admired your flower arrangements." Mr. Cai eyed her long neck and delicate collarbone. Perhaps Feng wouldn't insist on acting as Jude's gay friend if his friendship with Jiao was encouraged. "I'll ask Feng to cut some fresh roses for you, if you like."

"Thank you, Mr. Cai. You're too kind." As Jiao raised a hand to wave goodbye, a jade bangle slid down her round forearm.

"You're welcome." He added, "It's Feng's privilege."

At home, Mr. Cai found Feng eating porridge with fermented tofu. "Dad, I didn't know you were up." Feng pulled out a fried breadstick from the enamel bowl. "Did you buy soybean milk?"

"Darn! I was talking to Jiao and forgot. Won't you drink milk instead?"

"Dad," Feng drawled. "You don't want me to be sick for my exams."

"What exams?"

"We have three-day mocks every week until July." Feng ripped the twined breadsticks apart and started to eat one.

"Did you sleep okay last night?" Mr. Cai studied Feng's face for signs of fatigue.

"Like a log. I haven't slept so well in months."

"I just talked to Jiao, you know." Mr. Cai took a seat beside Feng. "She's a fine girl. I promised her that you will cut fresh roses for her to make new bouquets."

Feng stopped chewing. "What came over you?"

"What do you mean?" Mr. Cai began to eat the other half of Feng's breadstick. "I don't dislike her. You two grew up together. She's practically like a daughter to us."

"I'll let you have the last word." Feng washed down the bread-stick with his porridge. "My exam starts at eight o'clock sharp." He leapt up to grab his backpack. "By the way, do you know where Jude lives? I may stop by his place later to practice English. Won't I be more convincing if I talk to his father in English?"

"Son, you shouldn't go overboard just now." Mr. Cai swallowed hard. "The entrance exams are still your top priority."

"Just kidding." Feng laughed a little too loudly. "Good day, Dad."

Mr. Cai scooped a bowl of porridge for himself and took it to the porch. He blew on his porridge to cool it, then ate it slowly with dried pork floss. Perhaps he had outsmarted himself trying to send Feng abroad. No education in the world would be worth it if Feng turned gay. Mr. Cai had no idea what made a person gay, but it must be more difficult to correct than left-handed-ness. He suddenly recalled Jude was also left-handed. Was there any connection between left-handedness and gayness? Mr. Cai sighed with relief that Feng had at least been right-handed for some fifteen years.

Yet, Feng's fixation on Jude worried him. Last time Feng had thrown the shirt lent to Jude into the washer out of spite. On the other hand, Feng had kept looking at Jude's bare arms and chest under the tank top with thinly disguised jealousy. Now that Jude was no longer a threat, could Feng's jealousy turn into admiration, even infatuation? A little stomach sick, Mr. Cai put down his porridge. With his exotic charms, Jude seemed to be a great attraction not only to Feng, but also to Little Ye: she had left Feng and become a friend of Jude's. What was the nature of her close friendship with Jude? Who was the father of her baby?

Mr. Cai bent down his head in silent exasperation. The pork floss had now soaked in his porridge for so long it looked like vomit. Returning his bowl to the kitchen, Mr. Cai decided to finish up the robe for Jude.

*     *     *

Mr. Cai watched Jude button his Tang suit robe up to his chest. Bright sunlight tinted the silk fabric a high gloss finish and made it look almost sheer. It lent the foreigner a Chinese and youthful air, so that Jude's good looks appeared ageless, raceless, and genderless. There was one problem. With the top clasps open, the collar enveloped Jude's neck like a cabbage leaf.

"You can't leave the top button open," Mr. Cai said.

"Why not?" Jude pressed a hand to his muscular chest. Perhaps his beauty lay in the androgynous features that Mr. Cai only now saw for what they were.

"A Tang suit robe is not worn this way." Mr. Cai stepped forward to hook Jude's top clasps. "That's much better."

Jude gazed at himself in the mirror and turned from side to side. The robe swung around him like a weeping willow. "It's too loose for me." Jude peered back over his shoulder.

"That's the way it's supposed to be." Mr. Cai retreated to the sofa. "Tang suits are loose-fitting. We aren't stingy with fabric. If we want a new Tang suit robe, we use the best material available and plenty of it."

Jude unhooked his top clasps. "But the robe doesn't fit me. My body is lost in all this gauze silk. Look." He pinched the sides of his robe. "I could be this big and wear it well—I'm fifty pounds short for your robe."

Jude's complaint upset Mr. Cai more than he had expected. "If you know anything about a man's Tang suit robe, you won't ask for it to fit you as tightly as a woman's stockings."

Jude looked taken back, even a little hurt. Mr. Cai was sorry that he had sounded unkind. A foreigner didn't know how Tang suits should fit, so he had to be patient and not mocking.

"Tang suit isn't designed to show off a person's body, especially of a man. A tailor's job is to enhance a woman's beauty, but for a man, less is more. A Tang suit robe fits a man when he diminishes in it and becomes one with his robe. Look." Mr. Cai pointed to the patterns on Jude's robe. "There're peonies and butterflies, creatures of nature, and you inside it, also a creature of nature. Only when you're immersed in the peonies and butterflies, will you become one with them." Mr. Cai took a handful of Hang Gauze. "The silk is in ginger and turquoise, the colors of soil and sky. The peonies and butterflies are scenes of summer. As you wear them on your robe, you become a part of the summer scene, Jude."

"That sounds nice." Jude pulled up his robe to his knees. "But do I have to be covered from neck to toe? I'm a swimmer, you know. In the summer, I'm in shape and tan well."

"Maybe a Tang suit robe isn't for you." Mr. Cai helped Jude to undress.

"Little Ye talked me into having one made. Of all people, she knows how I like to dress."

Mr. Cai's hands shook as he peeled the robe from Jude's back. "How is Little Ye doing these days?" He tried to sound casual.

Jude lowered his voice. "She forbids me to tell anyone."

"Then you mustn't betray her confidence." Mr. Cai heard disappointment in his own voice.

Jude was silent for a while, frowning. "I know she really loves Feng," he whispered.

"You shouldn't be telling me this." Mr. Cai wanted to ask whose child Little Ye was carrying, but he was afraid of hearing the answer.

Jude's blue eyes were earnest. "She's my best friend. I'm worried about her making a mistake."

The familiar phrase "best friend" made Mr. Cai's heart leap in fright. He shook his head as he hung up the robe. "I don't presume to know how Little Ye goes about showing her love. You know, she broke up with Feng."

"She did, for his own good." Jude stood with his back to Mr. Cai. "This is all you're going to hear from me."

Mr. Cai wondered what else he might get out of Jude in spite of his protest. He was marking the spots where the robe needed slight modifications, when a bicycle bell rang in the courtyard. Feng had returned from school.

"Why are you home so early?" Mr. Cai asked Feng in a scolding tone when he stepped inside.

"It's the last day of the mocks."

Seeing Jude, Feng burst into a smile and said something in English.

"It's okay. No offense taken." Jude offered his hand and added something in English.

Feng shook his hand and repeated some words with exaggerated surprise. Mr. Cai stared at Feng's gleeful face but couldn't understand a word he had said except for a brief mention of "Cai Feng."

"All my Chinese friends have teased me about it," Jude said in Chinese and chuckled. "I just inherited the name from my father."

Mr. Cai coughed dryly in order to interrupt their exclusive conversation. "What did you say to him?" he asked Feng in Chinese.

"I asked him about his family name," Feng replied in Chinese. "His full name means Jude is a darling."

Jude blushed and winked at Feng.

Mr. Cai didn't smile. He had planned to have Jude come in when Feng wasn't home. Instead, the young men were being

friendlier with each other than he would've liked. Mr. Cai wanted to order Feng to his room, but he was afraid of offending
Jude.

Feng said something in English and hugged his own shoulders.

"My father is the opposite," Jude said in Chinese and glanced
at Mr. Cai.

Mr. Cai became more and more annoyed with Feng, who insisted on speaking in English. He stepped between the young
men and waved his hand decisively as if to sever their commu-
nication. "You come to pick up the robe in a couple of days, Mr.
Jude. We're very busy right now. If there is nothing else, I'd like
to see you out."

Feng put his hand on Mr. Cai's shoulder. "Dad, Jude said the
Tang suit robe is too big."

Mr. Cai stepped aside to let Feng's hand drop off. "It's supposed to fit loose."

"Can I have a look?" Feng turned to Jude and spoke to him in
English.

To Mr. Cai's disbelief, Jude lifted the robe from the hanger and
slid it over Feng's back. The young men stood side by side in front
of the mirror to appraise its fit. Mr. Cai was a little dazed by what
he saw: like Jude, Feng appeared ageless, raceless, and genderless.
If Little Ye could see Feng now, she would have been envious of
his glowing complexion against the luminous silk.

"The light coloring also makes it look wide. Dad, you can take
it in a bit more. It's not a crime to give it a little shape." As Feng
turned aside to look at his own profile, Jude swept his eyes at Feng
from head to toe.

Mr. Cai had heard enough. "Do you want to finish this robe?"
he asked his son.

Feng exchanged a few words with Jude in English. "He said he
can use it for casualwear, like a caftan for a slumber party, something like that."

Mr. Cai had never heard of a caftan or slumber party. Why
did Jude suddenly stop speaking Chinese to him? Were the young

men talking about something they didn't want him to know—
some secret knowledge of being gay?

"Thank you, Mr. Tailor." When Jude spoke to him in Chinese,
Mr. Ca was startled out of his reverie. "I'd better go." Now there
was glee in Jude's eyes.

Quickly Feng slid out of the robe and returned it to the hanger.
"Dad, I can show Jude a shortcut to his university."

Intentionally or not, they seemed to have coordinated efforts to
annoy Mr. Cai.

"You shouldn't treat Jude like a stranger." Mr. Cai forced a
chuckle. "He comes here all the time and knows his way around.
He is our friend."

"But I don't know the shortcut back." As Jude stepped toward
Feng, Mr. Cai backed away involuntarily. "Feng just finished his
exams. Perhaps he can use a walk to relax himself."

They both switched back and forth in Chinese and English at
Mr. Cai's expense. Suddenly Feng found an ally in Jude. What
was going on in front of Mr. Cai's nose?

"Be back in a half hour, Dad." Feng left with Jude before Mr.
Cai could think of another excuse to detain him. As they waited
to cross the road, Feng wrapped his arm around Jude's shoulders
as if they had been best friends since elementary school.

*    *    *

When his wife returned from fabric shopping, Mr. Cai didn't tell
her what Jude had revealed about Little Ye. Actually Mr. Cai was
too preoccupied with his son to worry about Little Ye's situation.
At the dinner table, Feng talked of nothing but his interaction
with Jude. He compared Jude's apartment to a luxurious hotel
suite. Feng said that he didn't have to gain weight in order to look
butch after all; Jude had told Feng that he could pierce his right
ear, for it was a recognized symbol among gay men. Finally Mr.
Cai slapped down his chopsticks and ordered Feng to shut up,
which his son answered with roaring laughter.

In the three days since Jude's visit, Feng hadn't mentioned Jiao once but kept saying he wanted to practice English with Jude. While Mr. Cai's tolerance was tested, he considered telling Feng about Little Ye's pregnancy but decided against it. Even if Jude had told him the truth, her covert love for Feng was problematic; her baby didn't belong to his family until she married Feng.

None of these speculations eased Mr. Cai's worry that his only son might fall prey to Jude's charms. Feng didn't have a conventional backbone. Jude could have added fuel to his rebel flames and brought out the wildness in Feng that he himself didn't know. Sometimes it was hard for Mr. Cai to imagine that Feng would settle down and get married in the foreseeable future. To top it all, Mrs. Cai laughed at him for letting Feng get to him. Mr. Cai suspected that a woman might have a soft spot for a gay man, and decided to take the matter into his own hands. If he told Feng a cautionary tale about his own disgrace in youth, would Feng heed his lesson or brush him off like a fool?

On Monday afternoon, Mr. Cai told his wife that he was going to play badminton with Feng.

She threaded a needle and fastened a knot with her nimble fingers. "Badminton?" She whetted the needle in her hair. "But you haven't played with him for years."

"Feng hasn't gone out since he had his mocks. Fresh air will do him good." Mr. Cai groped for more excuses. "Playing badminton will not only help him relax but also train him to be alert and competitive."

"Go. Don't talk so much." She slid on a thimble and started to sew. "Come home at seven. I'm making chive wontons for dinner."

In the sewing room, Mr. Cai took the racquets from the wall and chose two yellow-feathered shuttlecocks from a shoebox. "We won't be late."

\*          \*          \*

At the university playground, Mr. Cai veered onto the quiet gravel road behind the stands where some stone benches were scattered. Feng walked with his one hand inside the pant pocket. Mr. Cai chose the bench with the least moss and wiped it with his over-sleeves.

"Have a seat," he said.

Feng plopped down and crossed his long legs at the ankles.

"What I'm about to tell you, I haven't told anyone, not even your mother." Mr. Cai thought of his wife at home, chopping the chives for their wontons, and felt a pang in his chest. "In fact, I wish you never gave me a reason to tell this story."

Feng didn't blink, and appeared to be listening to him for the first time in months.

Mr. Cai mustered his courage to continue. "Before I tell you my secret, I want your complete confidence. Swear that you'll never tell anyone, not even your mother, about what I am going to tell you."

Feng rubbed his soles against the gravel. "I'm wearing loafers. Won't Mom suspect us when she sees me in these? She's not stupid."

"You leave that to me. Now, do you give me your promise?"

"Yes." Feng pinched his temples.

Mr. Cai hesitated, then asked Feng the question that had been on his mind for the last few days. "Why do you want to act as Jude's gay friend? Be honest with me."

Feng watched a group of men playing soccer in the grass field. "Why not?" he said. "If I can help him."

Mr. Cai couldn't believe his ears. "Jude is afraid his father might disown him. What chance will you have with his father if you present yourself as a gay man?"

"What difference does it make?" Feng picked up a shuttlecock to toss it in his hands. "If Jude's father is going to disown him, will he bother to sponsor me just because I'm straight?"

"But you don't have to lie about it."

"I like Jude. He's different, not a boring person. He's brave to leave America, come to China, and be gay."

"We like him, too." After a pause, Mr. Cai brazened it out. "Are you curious about . . . *that?*" He swallowed the words "being gay."

"A little."

Speechless, Mr. Cai raised his eyes toward heaven.

Feng let the shuttlecock drop to the ground. "Like, what did Jude sacrifice for being gay? Is it worth it? I want to get to know him."

Before he could press Feng further, his son stooped to pick up the shuttlecock. "Get on with your story, Dad."

Mr. Cai lit a cigarette and offered it to Feng. "Do you want a puff? It's 555, one of the most expensive cigarettes."

Feng shook his head. "We both hate cigarettes. Why don't you savor it for me?"

Mr. Cai coughed as he inhaled. "Before I met your mother, I had an affair with a girl named Xiu. I was sixteen when she seduced me. She grew up in the countryside, you know, and was three years older than I. She was the village belle, a golden phoenix in the chicken coop. I was a city boy who had never dated girls. During the Cultural Revolution, premarital sex was considered criminal, even counter-revolutionary. There was one man in our neighborhood who had sex with his girlfriend and was caught in the act by the disciplinary committee. The Red Guards forced the girl to accuse him of rape. After he was executed, the girl lost her mind and jumped from a building." Mr. Cai saw Feng yawning and realized he had been long-winded. "Anyway, that was the political atmosphere at the time."

"Which dynasty was that, Dad?"

"Less than three decades ago. We were too innocent to question such policies."

"You mean gullible." Feng peered at him out of the corner of his eye. "Naïveté is not a thing to be proud of, Dad."

Mr. Cai was not in the mood to argue with Feng, so he went on with his story. "One day Xiu took me as her lover, out of the blue. Boy, did I feel lucky, until she told me she was pregnant."

"What?" Feng flicked the shuttlecock to the ground. "Do I have a half-sibling I've never met?"

"It didn't quite come to that." Mr. Cai picked up the shuttlecock to put it on the bench. "Xiu told my mother about what happened between us. My mother beat me for the first time ever, with a big fire poker." Mr. Cai drew on his cigarette until smoke filled his lungs. "I've never seen an earthquake, you know. Whenever people talk about the horror of quakes, I think of the longest night of my life."

Mr. Cai proceeded to tell his son about that night, straight from his memory, indelible after almost three decades. Feng didn't interrupt him once.

*     *     *

"It seemed to be the hottest day of the summer. Although it was breezy outside, my mother shut all the windows while Xiu repeated over and again that I should marry her. I would be a cad to leave her and make her a laughingstock in the village. I couldn't argue with that."

"'But how can he marry you?' My mother was calm and firm, though not unkind. 'He's in high school and underage.'"

"'I don't care,' Xiu muttered through her hankies, which had covered her face for more than half an hour. 'Why didn't he think of that earlier?'"

"But she hadn't given me any time to think. She had shown me what to do with her body, which was not easy. I was shaken and confused afterwards. The pleasures were forgettable compared to the upheaval days later."

Mr. Cai flicked off ash from his cigarette and took a long drag. He began to enjoy the warm smoke filling his lungs. He hadn't expected that losing his virginity could be such an ordeal, as if he had been pushed off the cliff: at first he had thought he could grow wings and fly, but after a painful landing, he had been forced to crawl on his mangled hands and knees. He exhaled the smoke and continued with his story.

"My mother said to Xiu, 'He's just a boy who lost his head for a minute.' She slapped my face so hard that I stumbled. Still I returned to stand by her side, at a safe distance from Xiu. 'Do you really see a husband in him? Tell me the truth.'"

"'He ruined me.' Xiu's shoulders shook as she sobbed into her hankies. 'How can I live in the village now?'"

"'Don't say that, silly girl.' My mother walked to Xiu and held her shoulders. 'You're not yet twenty and can have your pick of any man.' She opened Xiu's hand to put a red envelope in her palm. 'Take this money and find yourself a good doctor. You'll be back on your feet in no time—'

"Before my mother finished her sentence, Xiu sprang up and threw the red envelope in my face. 'You're a black-hearted cad! I'll go to your school and accuse you of rape if you don't marry me. You can't get away with this!'

"I still remember the red envelope, embossed with a golden double-happiness, the kind of envelope that my mother used to send Xiu gift money for her birthdays."

*          *          *

"Xiu was out of line." Feng shook his head. "A woman can get so emotional sometimes."

"If she'd done what she said, I would have been jailed or executed. Yes, back then it was okay to eradicate a counter-revolutionary, the dregs of society, even if he was a minor."

Feng gripped Mr. Cai's hand. "She was talked out of it, right?"

Touched that Feng cared, Mr. Cai squeezed his hand back. "Do you think a girl in that state could be persuaded?" Since his cigarette had gone out, Mr. Cai put down the butt on the bench. "My mother was a clever woman. She talked Xiu into going to sleep. Then in the middle of night, she woke me up and we walked ten kilometers to the intertown bus station. We left the town on the first bus. That was the end of my affair with Xiu."

"Couldn't Xiu go to the city and find you? The bus station was not far away."

"You don't understand." Mr. Cai fiddled with a shuttlecock and avoided Feng's eyes. "Nor did I realize at the time how leaving could make things better, until my mother told me a secret."

"Xiu's father had been a wealthy landowner in Anhui province. He had a son and daughter, and the girl was Xiu. My mother married the landlord's younger brother when she was sixteen. That year, her hometown was flooded just before the harvest. As the eldest daughter from a peasant family, she married for money and saved her parents and brothers from starvation."

"Grandma was a child bride?" Feng said in disbelief.

"Your grandma did what she could to survive." Mr. Cai took such a deep breath that it hurt. "When the Land Reform Movement gained momentum in Anhui, several landlords in the eastern region were tried and executed by the Red Army. My mother was pregnant with me at the time. She was scared and missed her family. At last she persuaded her husband to let her visit her parents in South Anhui. He asked her to take Xiu, then three years old, as a measure of precaution. Being so young, my mother wasn't allowed to take the teenage son, who was later executed alongside his parents and uncle and grandparents as the 'Oppressors of People' by the Red Army."

Feng stared at a locust that leapt from one blade of grass to the next.

"Soon after Xiu became an orphan, my mother's family fled to Jiangsu province to live with their relatives. After the liberation, my mother was recruited into a textile mill in Yangzhou. My grandparents adopted Xiu to raise her in Jiangdu countryside." Mr. Cai massaged a chip in the stone bench. "Xiu was my first cousin. My mother said Xiu was indebted to her for life. Instead of being grateful, Xiu had to seduce me, of all people. I never saw my mother so furious."

"Poor Grandma," Feng said. "I wonder if she made up the story to punish you."

"How dare you accuse your grandmother of being spiteful!" Mr. Cai pushed Feng's shoulder. "She was not the sort of woman who would tell lies to upset people. She used to tell me that my father had been a Red Army soldier killed in the war against Japan. Imagine that! She must've hated the Red Army in her bones, but she never showed it. Why? She was a pacifist. She didn't want any trouble. It wasn't until after our affair that Xiu and I learned the truth about our fathers."

Feng gazed at the soccer players in the field. One team had just scored. Several young men clapped one another's hands.

Mr. Cai resumed his story. "I got car sick and threw up on the bus. My mother told me Xiu would be all right. I asked how. She said that being a young woman, Xiu would learn to look after herself. In retrospect I realize she spoke from her own experience. She raised me as a single mother, which was rare in those years."

"Why didn't she remarry? Grandma was pretty."

Mr. Cai thought for a long while. "Maybe her first marriage was enough of an ordeal for her."

A flaxen locust dropped to the ground. Feng stepped on it gingerly. The insect lost one hind leg and crawled into the tall grass. "Did you ever see Xiu again?"

"No, but a few months later I received a letter from her. Listen, this is the part that killed me." Mr. Cai slapped the stone bench hard. "She confessed that she had tried to coax me into marrying her. She had been pregnant before she seduced me. She didn't want to marry a peasant and live in the village for the rest of her life. So she decided to make me marry her, then she could become a city resident. As an only child, I could remain in the city while millions of young people were sent to the countryside to be reeducated by peasants."

"Why did she tell you all this?" Feng shook his head. "Stupid woman."

"She must have felt remorse after she learned that she had been indebted to my mother. If she accused me of raping her, she would throw me in jail and probably get me killed. So she came clean and relieved me of a terrible burden. Looking back, I must give her credit for loving her child more than herself."

"Xiu married the father of her child and raised a family. Her ambition was to become a townswoman. With her beauty and brains, she could've made it if she had been more discreet. My mother said Xiu had sinned when she used me. Then she asked me to forgive Xiu, who had been deprived of her parents' protection and guidance in her upbringing. Xiu had to fend for herself."

"Xiu bore her husband a daughter, but he wanted a son. When Xiu got pregnant the second time, she went into hiding in the woods from the one-child policy workers, who would've forced her to have an abortion even at the full term. She had a miscarriage just before the Spring Festival, and died in the woods by herself."

*　　*　　*

"Did you love her?" Feng plucked off a bright yellow feather, which rendered the shuttlecock useless.

"Of course I did." Mr. Cai's eyes grew moist in spite of himself. "I had known her since we were children. I wanted to become a fashion designer to make beautiful dresses for her. But it hadn't worked out, so I became a tailor."

"She betrayed you."

"Perhaps, but I couldn't hold a grudge against her after her death."

Feng frowned at his father. "Did you love Xiu more than you do Mom?"

"No." Mr. Cai held Feng's hand to examine it. Feng's fingers were thin and strong, each capped with a pink nail. "Before you were born, I had recurring nightmares about your mother giving birth to a monster. Every time I woke up in cold sweat. I told myself it's better to marry a woman suitable for me. Love, like other good things in life, ought to be healthy and rewarding. After we had you, a perfect baby, I've loved you two more than my own life."

"Why haven't you told Mom?"

"This has nothing to do with your mother. My past was my burden, not to mention, Xiu was buried long ago."

"Dad, I never thought you had a past." Feng patted Mr. Cai's chest.

"I was a knockout, too. Where do you think you got your looks from?"

Feng smiled and shook his head.

"You should learn from my lesson that you ought not to lose your head in the matters of heart. 'Falling in love' has its own evil. Too often people pay for easy pleasures for the rest of their lives. Just imagine, if I had married Xiu, would that be real love?"

"But you didn't." Feng bounced the broken shuttlecock with his racquet. "You weren't a saint at my age. I take after you, Dad."

Mr. Cai blushed in spite of himself. "You may think of me silly, but I told my story for your benefit. I want you to be immune from Jude's charm. You may not think you need to be worried. Then again, you may."

"Don't be ridiculous. You learned about gayness a couple of days ago. Now you think everyone is in danger." Feng spread his legs wide and placed one foot upon his opposite knee.

Mr. Cai thought of the son and wife of the gay barber. What had they felt during the ten years of living with a gay man?

He patted Feng's shoulder and said simply, "Better safe than sorry."

"If you want me to be safe, you should keep me home. Let me help you expand the family business."

Mr. Cai shook his head. He was not such a selfish father who would keep his son close to home, so that Feng could care for him in his old age. "You are bound for greater things."

"If you send me to the States, who knows what I'll do?" Feng fluttered his eyebrows. "I may marry a white woman. You won't be able to talk to your future daughter-in-law."

Mr. Cai was stunned. It was the first time Feng spoke about marrying someone other than Little Ye. Perhaps Feng was beginning to accept the breakup after their monthlong separation.

"Or I may marry a black woman twice my age. Or I may fall in love with a homeless man." Feng caught the shuttlecock with his racquet. "I'm hungry." He jogged away.

Mr. Cai collected the other racquet and shuttlecock and got to his feet. He hadn't dragged Feng here to lecture him, but instead to give Feng his old heart. Mr. Cai had few secrets in his life. Feng had heard the only one worth remembering and laughed it off. Perhaps he was a fool to let this old love haunt him after all these years.

Feng headed a soccer ball and sent it back to the teams at play. A young man gestured a thank-you to Feng, who grinned proudly at his father. Mr. Cai smiled back, wondering if he was twenty years too old to be his son's friend. If he had made a fool of himself, so be it. One day Feng might need to confess something difficult. He would remember how his father had bared himself despite the teasing. Hopefully, Feng would feel comfortable to come to Mr. Cai rather than turn to a stranger for help, like Jude did.

CHAPTER 7

When Feng and Mr. Cai returned home, the aroma of chive, fried gluten and shitake mushroom permeated the air. Rows of wontons were lined up on the dining table like a fleet of boat-shaped ingots.

"This is beautiful, Mom. I'll help you!" Feng peeled a sheet from a stack of wonton wraps, which Mrs. Cai had covered with a wet towel to keep them from drying out. "What're we celebrating?"

"You owe us a proper celebration, Mister. It's long overdue." She slapped Feng's hand. "Do you want us to eat the dirt off your hands?"

"My hands are clean."

"You heard your mother." Mr. Cai pushed Feng toward the kitchen sink. "Wash up after playing badminton." He passed Feng a bar of soap.

"Who had the upper hand," his wife asked, "you or our son?"

"Feng was no match for me," Mr. Cai said. "I taught him a lesson."

"You should've seen how well Dad played. The old man is still a man." Feng dried his hands on a towel.

Mr. Cai averted his gaze to discourage Feng from prattling on. He scrubbed his fingers and nails with soap, then rubbed in a blob of lemon-scented dish detergent to neutralize the cigarette smell.

"I wouldn't poke fun at your dad if I were you." Mrs. Cai added more pepper to the stuffing and gave it a good stir. "You take after him more than you know."

Feng picked up a glob of stuffing to set it down in the middle
of a square wrap. Then he folded the wrap twice and dipped his
finger in a bowl of water. He wet two corners of the wonton wrap
and pressed them tightly together.

"Mom, how come my wonton doesn't seal well?"

"You overstuffed it." She opened his wonton to scrape away a
quarter of the stuffing with her chopsticks.

Mr. Cai strode to the dining table. "Stop making trouble here,"
he said sharply. "Go study, and I'll help your mom."

"I don't need much help," she said. "Just boil water, and we'll
eat in a few minutes."

Mr. Cai pushed Feng out of the kitchen. "Don't you have math
problems to solve?" He pulled down the kitchen curtain in front
of Feng's reluctant face.

*       *       *

At dinner, Mr. Cai watched Feng smack his lips over the wontons
and wished he had his son's appetite. The vegetarian wontons
were a little too bland for his taste. Why had his wife treated
them to a lavish meal on a school night? He gave his last three
wontons to his son. Feng devoured them and ate every piece of
green onion in his soup.

"Do the dishes, Son," his wife said. "I need to talk with your dad."

"Sure, Mom." Feng smiled as if he knew some secret that Mr.
Cai didn't. "Have fun."

Mr. Cai followed his wife to the sewing room, his heart thump-
ing inside his rib cage. "Is there something the matter?" he asked
in a low voice.

She closed the door to shut out Feng's curious glance. "I've kept
a secret for over a week," she said.

"A week?" He heard the tremor in his own voice and cleared
his throat.

She removed a bridal gown from the chair to let him sit down.
"When you went to the Silk Factory with Jude the other day, Little

Ye stopped by and asked me to alter her uniform again." She cupped her hands in front of her stomach. "Little Ye said it's Feng's."

Mr. Cai heard a loud clamor in his head: it's not true, it's not true. For fear of losing his composure in front of his wife, Mr. Cai gingerly lowered himself into the chair. This ought not to be a shock, he knew. But it was. The time had come for him to stop believing that Jude could be the father, or even that Feng's friendliness with Jude could become something more than silly rebelliousness. Now it was time for Mr. Cai to cast aside his illusions.

Yet, his old misgivings lingered, partly because he had just told Feng a story he wouldn't have shared otherwise. It had been foolish of him to warn Feng against Jude, when he should have been worried about Little Ye instead.

"Why did she break up with our son?" he asked.

"She wouldn't tell me." His wife sighed. "Poor girl, she must've put up with a lot from Feng."

"Don't cry for her yet." Sitting down had done him good, because his head began to clear up. "Jude is her friend. He must've told her that Feng may study abroad. This makes Feng a good catch. She may want to keep Feng, and therefore she befriends us as her future in-laws."

"What're you talking about?" She backed away to the sewing table.

"Believe me, Wife, not every woman is as pure as you are."

"You're wrong. Little Ye promised me that she won't see Feng until after his exams." She measured several yards of piping for the bridal gown.

Mr. Cai recalled that Jude had revealed about Little Ye's continued affection for Feng. "Does that mean she'll get back with Feng after his exams?"

"I don't know." She slid on her thimble and picked up a threaded needle. "She's keeping her baby. Old Man, we're going to be grandparents."

"We're *not* grandparents until they are married." Mr. Cai leapt
up from his chair. "Don't forget: a couple can only have one child,
and we can only have one legitimate grandchild. I won't bother
with any bastard grandchild, even if he is Feng's!"

"Why are you shouting?" she asked.

He lowered his voice. "Why did Little Ye get pregnant?"

His wife cast him a scolding look.

"They're both so young," he argued.

"We had Feng when we were his age."

"We were married. Anyway, we had nothing better to do during
the Cultural Revolution." Mr. Cai sank down in his chair and
crossed his legs. "Now, my big plans for Feng will go down the
drain because of that baby."

"That baby has a mother, Little Ye." His wife tied a knot and
bit off the end of her thread. "She's been a breadwinner all these
years while Feng was spoon-fed his fish soup. Did you know she
quit school at age thirteen to support her family, so that her two
brothers could finish high school? If she had been raised in a
home like ours, Little Ye would not have ended up as a cook."

"So what?" Mr. Cai said. "Our son is at least good enough for
a country girl."

"Her name is Little Ye." Mrs. Cai rotated the gown to do the
other side. "She will support Feng to finish school. She's good
to our son." Her needle paused for an instant before it resumed
flying in and out of the fabric. "Little Ye said she will wait four
years for him if Feng enters a university."

Mr. Cai watched her baste the piping onto the bridal gown, the
image blurring as his eyes filled with tears. University regulations
disallowed students to marry. Four years was a long time for a
single mother to raise a baby, and still Little Ye had urged Feng
to succeed in the entrance exams. What had Feng given her that
could induce such a loving sacrifice?

"Unless Feng enters an American university . . ." Mr. Cai wiped
his forehead but couldn't continue his supposition. This chance
was so remote that it seemed a waste of time for him to speculate.

Mr. Cai didn't doubt that Little Ye loved Feng. She would be doing her child and herself a favor by making Feng a successful man. Mr. Cai was glad that Little Ye understood this, too.

"I've been thinking about this for a whole week—and I've made up my mind." His wife hung up the gown to inspect its front. "We will become grandparents, whether they marry or not."

Mr. Cai looked into his wife's eyes and knew that she meant it.

"I suppose they ought to marry," he said, "sooner or later."

"Look at this." She fingered the crimson piping that outlined a stunning contour. "Its bride is not half as pretty as Little Ye."

"You sewed this dress stitch by stitch. You know better than anyone that the gown makes the bride."

"This is more than a dress." She smoothed out the hips of the gown. "Little Ye said her baby is due in January."

*     *     *

Mr. Cai wondered why Feng left the door of his room open that night. Perhaps Feng hoped to hear some gossip from his parents. Mr. Cai was ironing while his wife sewed frog closures onto a bridal gown. Looking up from his worktable, Mr. Cai saw his son sitting erectly at the desk reciting some lecture notes. Mr. Cai ran his iron over Jude's Tang suit robe in quick short strokes. The little creases diminished as the gauze silk became soft and warm.

Mr. Cai hadn't admitted to his wife earlier that he did not want to become a grandfather until Feng was properly established. He slid the ham inside the robe to press its shoulder. Little Ye had a strong constitution and was unlikely to have a miscarriage. Most women in her situation would have demanded a marriage right away, regardless of whether she would keep the baby. How could Little Ye have such faith in Feng, who had never worked a day in his life? Love made a woman reckless, which might lead to a battle of wills between the couple. Would Feng submit to her wishes and become the husband and father she needed?

Feng fidgeted in his seat and flirted his fan, then turned and met Mr. Cai's gaze. "What, Dad?"

For a while Mr. Cai couldn't speak. Anger, sadness, pity and disappointment swelled in his chest. He propped the iron on the board and unplugged its electrical cord, understanding now why his wife had been reluctant to share her burden a week ago.

"You're an adult now," he said to Feng, using the mildest words he could find. "I had you when I was your age."

"You guys married young." Feng winked at his mother.

"When we got married, your dad and I wore the same thing: blue uniforms with wide brown plastic belts. Cultural revolution chic!" She sewed a crimson frog onto the burgundy bridal gown. "You're lucky, Son. We can make your bride a prettier gown than the ones sold in the department store."

"What're you talking about?" Feng peered at Jude's Tang suit robe hanging on the rack.

Mr. Cai wanted to wipe the smirk off Feng's face, but instead he let out a dry chuckle. "Your mother has made wedding wardrobes for more than two decades. Will you give her the pleasure of doing it for you someday?"

"Sure, if you'll find me a nice girl." Feng came over to touch Jude's robe. "How much did you take in?"

Mr. Cai said, "About four centimeters."

Feng took the robe off the rack to slide it on. "It fits better now. Don't you think?"

Buttoning up the robe, Feng looked willowy and dainty, resembling Jude in a way that irritated Mr. Cai.

"Give it back here!" Mr. Cai peeled the robe off his son.

"Do you ever shout at Jude?" Feng walked with a rolling gait. "You don't dare." Feng returned to his study and shut the door.

Mr. Cai was indignant. "Will our son ever grow up?" he asked his wife.

"He is a boy in a man's body." She picked up a new frog to sew. "Children and fools speak the truth. What he just said is quite true."

"You know as well as I do that Jude is a customer, and Feng is my son. Why should I treat my son with such courtesy that I show my customers?"

"Why not? You want him to become an adult whom you respect." She pressed the frog with her thumb, then continued to sew it.

*       *       *

Jude was supposed to pick up the Tang suit robe the following morning. Yet as the hours went by, there was no sign of him.

Mr. Cai turned up the radio when his favorite lute solo "Ambush from All Sides" came on. The sound of string plucking kept his mind busy as he tried not to glance at the courtyard every thirty seconds while he worked. It was almost noon. A suspicion gnawed at Mr. Cai's mind that perhaps Jude hated the robe so much he didn't want to see it anymore.

As the solo ended, Mr. Cai heard women's high voices at the front of the shop. He increased the volume of the music in order to drown them out.

"Little Ye is here," his wife called out from the front desk. "She's come to pick up Jude's Tang suit robe."

Mr. Cai spun around on his heels. Little Ye wore a pair of lemon-dotted culottes and asymmetrical short hair that hung beside her cheeks. In a short month, she had evolved from the unadorned country girl into a chic young lady.

Mr. Cai let out a nervous chuckle. "To what do I owe the pleasure of seeing you today?"

"Jude is sick," Little Ye said quickly. "I have the day off, so I decided to stop by. Anyway I have to pick up my altered uniform."

Mrs. Cai took out her jacket and skirt. "Would you try them on?"

Little Ye went behind the khaki screen. Mr. Cai listened to the rustle of her clothing. He had been so preoccupied with Jude's deal lately that he hadn't even noticed his wife working on the uniform.

Little Ye gasped.

He asked, "Is something wrong?"

"A button fell off," she said.

He gave his wife a safety pin and signaled for her to help Little Ye.

"I would prefer that Jude try on his Tang suit robe," Mr. Cai thought aloud. "Is he very sick?"

"He has an upset stomach, as he hardly gets any sleep these days." Behind the screen, Little Ye told his wife something in a low whisper, then continued, more loudly, "He asked me to pick up the robe, and said it isn't supposed to fit him very well anyway."

Mr. Cai felt blood rush into his face, as if someone had slapped him. "I made some alterations for him," he said.

"I will tell him that," Little Ye said.

His wife led Little Ye out from behind the screen. "Who could tell she's three months pregnant?" Mrs. Cai said. "She looks all peaches and cream."

Mr. Cai glanced at Little Ye's protruding breasts and slightly bulgy belly. He wished Feng were here. Mr. Cai had no right to appraise her fertile belly. "Lovely," he agreed.

Little Ye stared into the mirror and sucked in her cheeks.

Mr. Cai could find nothing suitable to say to Little Ye that didn't pertain to Jude. "It's bad timing for Jude to get sick," he said, "when his parents are coming."

"He's not ill, but worried sick." Little Ye looked at Mr. Cai through the mirror. "He's afraid that his father may disown him."

Mr. Cai looked uneasily at his wife, who was busy threading a needle to reattach the button.

"An old-fashioned father is not likely to disown his son," Mr. Cai said. "A daughter can get married and join her husband's family. Thus she belongs to two families. A son has nowhere to go but his own home."

Little Ye blinked with her brow furrowed. "So you think it's better to disown a daughter than a son."

"Don't put words in my mouth, Miss. I did not say that." Mr. Cai dusted his hands.

Little Ye was in the precarious position of being an unwed expectant mother. Would her own family, that she had helped to support, accept her decision if she should have the baby out of wedlock? Mr. Cai had inadvertently reminded her of the potential fallout.

"Excuse me." Little Ye took off her coat and gave it to Mrs. Cai to resew the button.

Mr. Cai wished his wife would say something to smooth over his blunder. Instead, Mrs. Cai sewed the button in silence. Perhaps she had a tacit understanding with their future daughter-in-law. Their alliance was stronger than Mr. Cai had realized.

"Jude told me he was closer to his mother." Little Ye's voice made him turn his head. She got over his blunt remark quickly, he thought. "When Jude was little, he used to hide behind his cereal box and pretend that his father was not in the room." Mr. Cai was struck by how dark her irises appeared. There was a gentle humility in them that he had not seen in the eyes of city girls. "Jude left the States after his mother's funeral. He needed a change."

Mr. Cai was grateful that his wife returned from the worktable with the fixed jacket.

"Perfect." Little Ye took out her wallet. "How much does Jude owe you?"

"His Tang suit robe is free," Mr. Cai said. "Didn't Jude tell you? He bought the gauze silk, and I made the robe for him without charge."

"He gave me a hundred yuan to pay for the robe."

Mr. Cai pushed her hand away. "Jude is our friend. This is but a token of our appreciation."

Little Ye's buckteeth sank into her lower lip, as if Mr. Cai had told her a good joke. "Jude likes to pay people for their help. I'm his best friend, and he pays me to do stuff." She pulled out a few bills.

"Really?" Mr. Cai voiced his surprise rather than doubt.

"Jude says it's important that friends don't owe each other goodwill." Little Ye followed his wife to the front desk.

Mr. Cai returned to his worktable. He envied Little Ye her intimacy with both Jude and Feng. All his painstaking labor for Feng was eclipsed by her supple body, as she held the key to Feng's heart.

When the front door banged closed, Mr. Cai peered out of the windows. His wife and Little Ye walked into the courtyard arm in arm. Their hips swayed slightly from side to side. From behind, they looked like a mother and daughter.

*　　*　　*

Mr. Cai closed the windows halfway when his wife returned inside. "Did you take the money?" he asked her.

"It's Jude's payment." She patted her pocket.

"I meant to do Jude a favor. I told you and Little Ye that."

"You heard Little Ye." She pushed the windows open and hooked the latch. "Jude didn't want to owe anyone goodwill."

Now his wife echoed Little Ye and opposed him. Well, it helped Little Ye to have Mrs. Cai on her side. Soon Feng would have to contend with both his mother and ex-girlfriend about his future happiness. Mr. Cai had to be a bit more neutral. It seemed to be easier to work with Jude.

"He doesn't owe me goodwill. I'm his friend." Not knowing what else to do, he cut a scrap cloth into little pieces with his scissors. Then an idea came to him. "I'll visit Jude and bring him some get-well fruits!"

"If you think that's necessary."

It wasn't her words but her tone that irritated Mr. Cai. "How can you be so uncaring?" he asked. "Jude is sick with worry. I should at least go see what I can do to help him."

"I'm not stopping you," she said.

"Little Ye must know that Jude is helping our son." Mr. Cai's voice softened. "I didn't have the heart to ask her: what if Feng isn't ready to settle down and raise a child?"

His wife glanced out of the windows. "Little Ye believes he will marry her. He's asked her before—many times."

"Maybe he was infatuated, or just trying to win her favors." Mr. Cai paused to look for the right words. "I'll only say this between us. She hasn't endeared herself to Feng with the breakup or her pregnancy. Feng never says anything about her anymore. Who knows what he's thinking? You see how friendly he is with Jiao." *And Jude*, he added to himself.

His wife raised her voice. "It's too late for that."

"He's only twenty-two—nothing is too late for him. But let's not quarrel." Mr. Cai rubbed his wife's back with a consoling hand. "I have my misgivings. Neither you nor Feng may agree with me, and I seemed to offend Little Ye pretty well. Will you take this burden off my shoulders?"

"What do you mean?" She prodded his chest with a finger to push him away.

"I don't know how to talk to Little Ye. I can't just go up to her and ask, 'How's your pregnancy?' I might sound like an old lecher. Obviously Little Ye prefers you to me. Why don't you take care of her while I concentrate my efforts on Jude?"

His wife snickered. "You can't avoid Little Ye if she becomes our daughter-in-law."

Mr. Cai threw the scrap cloth on the floor and dusted his worktable. "Little Ye is not my problem, but Feng is."

"She's not a problem." His wife bent down to sweep the scrap cloth into a dustpan. "She's the mother of Feng's child."

"Good. Then remind her: Feng is not a puppet or little brother to be ordered about. He has wandering eyes, like a lot of men."

His wife's face grew solemn as she considered his words. "After the exams she will ask him to marry her, regardless of the results. Where will they live after they're married?"

Mr. Cai looked at the cramped workroom and Feng's bedroom behind the closed door. "Where else?" he said.

When the baby began to walk, they would have to hide away the needles, scissors, knives, and other sharp objects, as they once had done with Feng.

*          *          *

The next day Mr. Cai searched several farmers' markets for the most expensive fruit. At the high end downtown market, fresh fruits were displayed inside the gleaming aluminum stalls. While not a single fly could be seen, the peaches were firm and unripe, and grapes were sour. Next he passed a seafood market, then elbowed his way into a crowded banana stand. The banana skins were spotted, tainted with a fishy smell. Finally he walked all the way to the end of city limit, beyond which rapeseed and tomato fields stretched out under the bright sunshine. Here, farmers brought their fresh produces to sell every morning. He stopped beside a wicker basket piled high with lychees like a hill of maroon ping-pong balls.

"Where are these from?" Mr. Cai asked the peddler. "Give me three bunches. Pick your best ones."

"From my southern relative's orchard." The peddler dug the scale pan into his basket to scoop up the lychees. "Uncle, I reckon you have guests from out of town."

"I sure do." Mr. Cai pinched a fruit with his two fingers. "I want the plumpest lychees, none of the rotten ones."

"There isn't a rotten one in my basket." The man plucked a lychee to give Mr. Cai. "You taste it and tell me if this is any good."

Mr. Cai broke the shell to squeeze its white fruit into his mouth. He rolled his tongue over the pulp to tear it from its pit. "Not bad." He added a cluster onto the scale.

The string bag weighed him down as Mr. Cai carried the lychees to approach the Foreign Students' Dorm #6, a cream-colored townhouse. What would he do if Jude had a guest? Perhaps he should've let the receptionist at the housing office call Jude after she looked up his address. However, Mr. Cai was afraid that Jude would refuse his gift, as he had with the robe. Mr. Cai came in part to make amends with Jude: after all, he had wrongly and willfully blamed him for both Feng and Little Ye's problems, when his son had been the culprit all along.

Mr. Cai stood to collect himself for a minute, then knocked on the door twice.

When the door finally opened, Jude was there with a fleece blanket wrapped around his bare shoulders. "Why it's you, Mr. Tailor."

Mr. Cai lifted his string bag. "I heard you're not well, so I came to see you."

"Please come in." Jude waved him in. "My place is a mess."

Colored paper littered the whole room, with books, magazines, sketches, and newspaper strewn all over the desk, bed, chairs, and floor. Mr. Cai could barely find a spot to stand.

"Where do you sleep?" he asked Jude. The bed was covered with red, black, and brown paper scraps.

"I haven't slept much. Here, have a seat." Jude patted a recliner and sat down by its foot.

Mr. Cai eyed the books on the floor. "You must be studying hard."

"I haven't set foot outside for three days." Jude stretched out his legs and pushed apart several books and a backpack. "I told the cleaning lady to leave me alone."

Feng was right: apart from the mess, a luxurious hotel suite might look like this, Mr. Cai thought, noting the maroon carpet and matching ruffled curtains. A powdery smell permeated the air, which reminded him of the shirt Jude had returned to Feng. This familiarity comforted Mr. Cai, for the room smelt of Jude, not some strange incense.

On the floor, Mr. Cai saw the sketch of a woman and a water-color painting of Five Pavilion Bridge. He recognized the plastic bag lying at the foot of the bed. "I hope you found the Tang suit robe satisfactory. Feng asked me to make some alterations, and it looked good on him." Jude should've at least hung up the robe after Little Ye had delivered it. Even Feng wouldn't be so sloppy with his new clothes. "We didn't see you yesterday. I was worried to hear that you were sick."

"Bad news travels fast." Jude ripped open the string bag to pour out lychees on the floor.

Mr. Cai noticed the dark circles under his eyes. Without his shirt on, Jude looked rather emaciated since the last time Mr. Cai had seen him.

"It is a joyful event that your parents are coming to see you," Mr. Cai said. "You ought to look your best for them."

Without a word, Jude put a whole lychee to his mouth.

"Not like that!" Mr. Cai shouted so loudly that Jude dropped the lychee with a shudder.

Mr. Cai picked up the lychee and husked it just enough to show Jude the white meat inside. "Squeeze this into your mouth," he said in a soft voice, "so you don't spill any juice."

Jude pushed the lychee nut into his mouth and chewed it. He closed his eyes for a moment, then spat out the pit. "Good." He wiped his chin. "It's very sweet."

Mr. Cai leaned back in his chair and smiled.

"I'm getting the hang of it." Jude husked a second one and ate it. "I can do this all day."

"Help yourself." Mr. Cai looked away in order to curb his appetite for the lychees.

"Mr. Tailor, I wish I could tell you that eating lychees will cure me." Jude dumped the shells on an old *China Daily* and dusted his hands. "Sorry. This is all the help you can give me today."

Mr. Cai watched as Jude husked the lychees with both hands. His shapely fingers reminded Mr. Cai of his son's.

"Hear me out," Mr. Cai said patiently. "I'm not in this just to make you help my son. As I told you before, people are connected by a network of kin. Only when you're on good terms with your family will I feel comfortable sending Feng abroad. Your well-being affects us all."

"I appreciate your concern." Jude folded his legs under himself. "Look, Mr. Tailor. Am I the first gay man you've ever met?"

Mr. Cai nodded, then shook his head. "Actually we had a neighbor. He was married with a son. I didn't know he was gay until he moved away."

"I'll never marry like some fools." Jude popped another lychee into his mouth and said with a slurp, "You still don't understand why I'm afraid of seeing my father."

Mr. Cai rubbed his chin. This claim was not entirely true. "I don't think your father will disown you," he said instead.

Jude peered up, his eyes so blue and piercing they seemed to diminish all other features on his face. "Suppose that Feng told you, I'm not saying it's true, but suppose he told you that he's gay. How would you feel?"

Mr. Cai leapt to his feet. "Feng is not gay."

Jude frowned. "I know, but suppose he told you he's gay. Would you disown him?"

Mr. Cai strode to the windows, shaking his head. "You're not listening to me, Jude. I just told you, Feng is not gay."

"I heard you." Jude got to his feet. "You have less of a problem with my being gay, because I'm only an acquaintance. But Feng is your son, so you react strongly about it."

Jude picked up a tee shirt from the floor. Mr. Cai peered out of the windows when Jude threw down his blanket.

"Likewise," Jude continued, "my father will try to tell me that I'm not gay. So I have to prove to him that I am."

Mr. Cai didn't dare to look back until he saw Jude dressed by his reflection in the windows.

"I couldn't choose to be gay even if I tried," Jude said. "But I am."

Mr. Cai almost stopped breathing. "Is gayness inborn?" he asked.

Jude nodded. "Like my pale skin."

Mr. Cai considered this carefully. How could he explain Feng's sudden fascination with Jude—or had Feng always been curious? "You said you tan well in the summer."

Jude gave a half-smile, as if he were pleased with Mr. Cai's insight. "It only becomes a shade of ivory." He raised his forearm, covered with blond hairs. "I'll live and die as a gay man."

Mr. Cai stared at Jude's thin, brooding face. There he stood in the middle of a messy room, half a world away from his native home. It was inauspicious for a young man to speak of death, yet Jude didn't look sad. Somewhere on the other side of the globe, an old man and his deceased wife had given Jude all the gifts that he had: his good looks, his talent for language and arts, his tact and sense of humor. What they did not know was that their son was gay. Upon discovering this gift that they had given Jude, his father—the one man on earth who was related to Jude by blood—might turn his back on his son and in doing so, shatter his young life.

In the silence, Mr. Cai brooded over Jude's question. Could he accept his own son if Feng were ever to come out to him?

"I tried to kill myself once before." Jude sank into the recliner. "Even then, I wasn't so depressed as now."

"You're not serious!" Mr. Cai gasped, putting a hand on Jude's shoulder. "You must never give up on yourself." He almost said, "for your parents' sake." Instead he said, "If only you knew, that you are the apple of their eyes."

"We'll find out about that in a couple of weeks." Jude hugged his knees. "Last time I saw my father was at my mother's funeral. I couldn't bring my partner, out of grief and . . . my father. Then I quarreled with my partner, and we drifted apart. After our relationship ended, I wanted to disappear, and came as far as China. Where do I go now? If my father rejects me, how would I even pay for school? And then there's you and Feng."

"Don't despair." Mr. Cai squatted beside the recliner. "Let me talk to your father."

Jude threw the green blanket over his head. In his mind's eye, Mr. Cai saw that young boy who had once hidden behind a cereal box from his father, as Little Ye had described. He wished to reach out to that frightened boy across time and space.

"I have a plan," Mr. Cai said to the green blanket. "I'll tell him that Feng is my gay son, and that doesn't make me love him any less."

The green blanket sighed. "Lies. You couldn't even answer my hypothetical."

Mr. Cai pulled the blanket from his head. "The end will justify my means. So what if I tell a white lie? I'll use it to tell your father the truth. You taught me what it's like to have a gay son, and I'll share what I learned with your father."

Jude covered his mouth to stifle a laugh. "Will Feng go along with this?"

"He wants to help you more than anyone. After you walked with him last time, Feng started talking about wanting to pierce his right ear." Mr. Cai blushed as he admitted, "It got me worried, actually."

Jude smirked. "How do you know if he's pretending?"

Mr. Cai blushed more deeply. "I can't tell the difference between a real gay man and fake one."

"Well, neither can my father." Jude gripped Mr. Cai's wrist, then let him go gently. "Mr. Tailor, thank you for helping me." He grabbed one of the lychees from the floor and offered it to Mr. Cai. "Feng, too, if he thinks he can handle it."

"No need for thanks." It gave Mr. Cai satisfaction to accept the fruit. "We're your friends."

Rising back to his feet, Mr. Cai peeled the lychee and devoured it. It tasted even sweeter than the first one he had had at the market.

\*     \*     \*

Half an hour later, they had finished three clusters of lychees and started on the last bunch.

Mr. Cai wanted Jude to have the rest, so he looked around the room for some chores to do. "Do you mind if I clean up the scrap paper for you?"

Jude rolled the old newspaper into a giant cone to seal the shells and pits inside. "But you're my guest."

"And you're a patient. Let me help you." Mr. Cai picked up colored paper scraps and balled them into a wad. "What are these for anyway?"

"Papercutting. This is more intricate than the paper snowflakes I once made as a kid." Jude showed him a framed papercut that featured the profile of a pregnant woman. Her belly didn't swell yet, but the way she craned her neck with a hand resting on her stomach showed her elation to be a first-time mother.

"I've never seen a pregnant woman as a subject of papercut." Mr. Cai was fascinated. "How long have you been doing this?"

"A couple of months. I'm still learning." Jude opened an envelope to take out the papercut of a woman fanning a coal-cake stove with her palm-leaf fan. "This is my best one so far."

The papercut was torn at the woman's elbow and knee. Jude had mounted the whole papercut onto glossy brown paper, and fixed the broken spots with clear glue.

Jude opened a sketchbook to show the drawing of a nude woman. Her face was an empty oval, waiting to be filled in. Her body, full and voluptuous, lay inside a rowboat that barely contained her. "I think a pregnant woman looks divine. Why aren't they everywhere?"

"Did you draw it with a model?" Mr. Cai pointed at the missing face. "It's hard for any woman, let alone an expectant mother, to sacrifice her privacy for the sake of art."

"I'm working with her. A pregnant body, to me, is a fruitful and empowered human form. I wish my art could do her justice." Jude closed his sketchbook. "We'll have a student work exhibition next month. Just another reason I'm nervous about my dad's visit. Please come if you're interested."

"Sure." Mr. Cai rubbed his hands. "I've never studied at a university. I would love to see what art students have learned in the classrooms."

Jude opened the desk drawer to take out two tickets. "Bring Feng with you."

The tickets were dated July 11th. "Feng will be done with his exams by then." Mr. Cai smiled. "All right."

"So the two of you, my father, and my stepmother will all be there judging my work." Jude bit his lower lip. "I have some work to do."

"What's it about?" Mr. Cai scanned the room for an unfinished painting.

"It will be a surprise." Jude winked.

"Feng and I look forward to it." Mr. Cai held out his hand. "By then we'll be ready for your father, won't we?"

"I'll never be ready." Jude's forehead was wrinkled with a deep frown. "I'm just dying to get it over with."

"I'll see it through with you." Mr. Cai pressed a hand on Jude's shoulder. "Don't worry, and get well."

Jude stroked Mr. Cai's hand then held it. Jude's fingers were cold and wet, like melting icicles hanging from a roof in the winter sun. Jude squeezed so hard that his old bones began to hurt, but Mr. Cai didn't move his hand.

CHAPTER 8

For the next few weeks, Mr. Cai kept a close eye on Feng but found nothing to reproach him with. Every morning when Mr. Cai got up, Feng was already reciting English lesson on the back porch. The weather had warmed up considerably, turning the air in the house stuffy. Feng, in his boxer shorts and a tank top, sat on a stool with his back to the kitchen, chanting English sentences like a monk reciting his sutra. At night he worked even harder. If Mr. Cai didn't drag him out for a walk after dinner, Feng would have cut out his physical exercise completely. Sometimes Mr. Cai lay in bed and watched the light leak inside from the hallway, wondering what had finally driven his lazy son to such single-minded determination.

One day, Mr. Cai was tending his roses in the yard. The midday sun beat down on the earth without reserve. The pink Tea Roses had opened their last flowers, while Crimson Glory were just coming into bloom. It was less than a week to Feng's exams, and schools were out on summer vacation. Red bean popsicle stands were always crowded with youngsters, and swimming pools opened all day to students. In a week and a half, Feng would be rid of his misery and free like everyone else. But before then, he had to undergo the exams of his lifetime.

Mr. Cai snipped the faded roses and collected them in a basket. How did other people breeze through those exams? He peered at Jiao's house, wondering. She must have had a few tricks that helped her achieve academic success. Feng hadn't visited her or mentioned her name since he walked with Jude a month ago.

Perhaps Jiao was peeking out of her windows in search of Feng just then, hoping it was he who was out cutting her roses.

When Mr. Cai stood up to wipe his sweat, sure enough, he saw Jiao looking at him from her windows. Before their eyes met, Jiao lifted a hand to press it against her forehead, so that he couldn't fully see her face.

Mr. Cai withdrew into the shade on the porch, put on a straw hat, and returned to the yard to cut off three half-open Crimson Glories and six pink Tea Roses that would make a pretty bouquet. Then he went to ask his wife to pipe a strip of periwinkle satin, while he trimmed the rose stems with a sharp cleaver. Mrs. Cai bound the roses with the satin ribbon, and warned her husband not to stress out Feng with undue advice. Then Mr. Cai took the small gift to see Jiao.

He presented the bouquet humbly as if he were but a messenger. "Feng will visit you after his exams," he said. "The roses will be in full bloom by then and not fit to be cut off. So he asked me to pick a few to give you now."

"How sweet of Feng! I wish I had something nice to give him in return." Jiao ushered Mr. Cai into the living room before she went to a cupboard to look for a vase. "I offered him orchids before, but he didn't care for them."

Mr. Cai glanced at the calligraphy hanging on the opposite wall, a gigantic "Diligence" in bold, vigorous strokes. "You may give Feng a few tips on taking exams," he said. "How did you do so well? Although it was four years ago, you probably haven't forgotten."

"I'll remember that July as long as I live, the battle and carnage. 'Millions of troops cross a single-plank bridge.' Less than four percent of graduating seniors in Yangzhou were accepted into universities and trade schools." Flowers in water and placed on the counter, she offered Mr. Cai some plum candies.

He peeled the wrapper and put the candy in his mouth. Its sour sweet taste made his teeth ache, so he pushed it under his tongue, careful not to suck in its juice.

"I like to work under pressure." Jiao's eyes grew intent as she spoke. "I watched the TV show the night before, and was refreshed the next day and ready for my exams. I did better than my mocks, which surprised my teacher."

Mr. Cai was intrigued. "Did your father let you watch TV?"

"He lets me do anything." Jiao's smile froze in her face, and left only her brows arched in a peculiar fashion. "Except for demonstrating in the streets while I studied in Beijing. He didn't believe in dying for a cause. To be honest, neither did I."

"Do you miss being in college?" Mr. Cai tried to imagine the campus inhabited by bright young people: what a nice place for his son to spend four carefree years.

"I do." Jiao shook her head resolutely as if to dismiss her nostalgia. "But it will pass. I must move on."

"To what?"

"Life goes on. I have a job now and am self-sufficient. I want to get married and have a child. It's pointless for me to be burdened with the romantic notion of a democratic China. A lot of my friends who study Chinese literature are prone to such idealism, which I think is bookish and naïve. What is the use of mere passion? Red Guards in the Cultural Revolution were passionate. Look what they did!"

Mr. Cai had never seen the pragmatic side of Jiao before. In his eyes, she was a mere child who had passed from school to school living the sheltered life of a scholar.

"After I become successful and well-established in society, my child will have a better chance to fight for China's future," she said. "Democracy cannot be achieved in a day, a month or a decade. It takes generations of effort, sacrifice and struggle."

Mr. Cai lowered his head in silent exasperation. He hadn't come to hear her grand talk. She wanted to have a child and also continue the revolution. What did she know about raising a child?

"If you were a mother, the only thing worth dying for would be your child's safety." Mr. Cai watched her face redden. Even her ears became pink.

"My parents told me to be more practical." Jiao looked down at her hands. "A month at home feels like a year at the university. I'm aging rapidly."

"Don't worry: you have the high school kids to keep you young." Mr. Cai tried to undo the damage. His wife was a much better conversationalist, though she would not have fawned on Jiao and given her flowers.

"I've got to tell you," Jiao said suddenly, "my dad cooked me victory noodles for breakfast before I took the exams."

Mr. Cai pricked up his ears.

"The noodles are soft boiled, seasoned with soy sauce and sesame oil. The key ingredients are two fried eggs."

"Why eggs?"

Jiao lifted the index finger of her right hand, and made an O with her thumb and finger of her left hand. "The noodles stands for a one, while the eggs are two zeros. Together they spell a hundred points, the perfect score."

"Feng doesn't eat eggs." Mr. Cai coughed into his cupped hand and spat out the sour plum in his fist.

"He may be tempted if you make them delicious."

"I'm afraid the victory noodles are not for Feng." Mr. Cai stood up. "Thanks for your suggestion."

"Anything round will do." Jiao followed him to the door. "Why not give him two cherry tomatoes?"

"You're a sweet girl, Jiao." Mr. Cai patted her arm. "Feng may talk to you after his exams."

"I look forward to that." Jiao brushed loose hairs behind her ears.

Mr. Cai waved goodbye and left. As soon as he was outside, he flung the sour candy into the weeds.

*     *     *

The night before Feng's exams, Mr. Cai woke to a beam of light in his face and saw his son's head poke in from an opening of the mosquito net.

"What's the matter?" Mr. Cai asked.

"I can't sleep." Feng scratched his neck and chin. "I feel as if a thousand ants were crawling on my skin."

His wife stirred awake. "What time is it?" she asked.

"Almost three o'clock," Feng said.

"Are you all right?" she asked. "Why aren't you asleep?"

"He has insomnia." Mr. Cai nudged her. "Would you sleep in his bed tonight? I want to take care of Feng."

She yawned and sat up on the bamboo mat. "Get some sleep. You have a big day tomorrow." The mosquito net quivered as she crawled out.

Mr. Cai patted the mat beside him. "Hop in, Son."

"Will it do me any good?" Feng asked.

"I have a cure for you." Mr. Cai opened the drawer of the night-stand to take out a few yellow tablets.

"Will I be able to perform if I take sleeping pills?" Feng scrambled inside.

"These are quick-acting pills with short-term effects. Trust me, I won't let you go to the exams drugged."

Feng swallowed the pills and lay down with his hands folded on his chest. Mr. Cai tucked the mosquito net under the bamboo mat and turned off the light. The unfamiliar weight of his son beside him made Mr. Cai wide awake.

"Would you like victory noodles for breakfast?" Mr. Cai smacked his lips. "Soft boiled noodles seasoned with soy sauce, sesame oil, and two fried eggs. Very delicious, I heard."

"Victory noodles, no less!" Feng chuckled. "Where did you get the recipe from, a fortuneteller?"

"It worked before." Mr. Cai pointed toward the Ouyangs'. "She passed the exams years ago."

Feng was silent for a while. "Jiao ate two fried eggs before the exams?"

Mr. Cai nodded. "Eggs are good for you."

"Nutrition isn't everything. Confidence is the key." Feng shifted his weight on the mat and caused his father to slide toward him.

"Can I sleep in your room for two more nights? It's a lot cooler at night."

"It was my fault that I didn't think of it. Of course you're welcome here." Mr. Cai stroked Feng's forehead, damp with sweat. "Go to sleep, and don't worry about a thing." He yawned out a good night and turned to the wall.

Feng had never had trouble sleeping before his previous exams. Mr. Cai was both amazed and saddened to see this change. Perhaps, in the face of his last college entrance exams, Feng had finally grown up, feeling the weight of adult responsibility on his shoulders. Mr. Cai was glad that the multi-enzyme tablet—not a sleeping pill at all—had helped put him at ease.

Soon Feng was snoring softly. In the dim light, his head was slanted as if its weight were too much for his neck to bear. His ebony long hair spread on the bamboo mat pillow. Even after all these years, Mr. Cai never ceased to be stunned by the beauty of his son. Too bad a pretty face wouldn't do a son as much good as it would do a daughter. Mr. Cai listened to Feng's even breathing, and pressed his body against the wall to give his son more room.

\*      \*      \*

In the morning, Mr. Cai was pleased that Feng was not only well-rested but also requested victory noodles with two fried eggs, just as Jiao had recommended. After breakfast, Mr. Cai and Feng rode their bicycles to Yangzhou High School, where the exams would last for three days. They came upon a majestic gingko tree in the middle of the avenue. Having been split into two halves by lightning long before Mr. Cai's birth, the four-hundred-year-old gingko stood like a silent giant, with its thousands of fan-shaped leaves quivering in the breeze.

It was the fourth year Mr. Cai had taken this route. This time, his legs were weak as he pedaled. In front of him, Feng stretched out his long leg to brake his bicycle while a tractor passed. Mr. Cai gazed at Feng's erect back, trying to find some solace in his poise. Feng lifted his foot from the ground and resumed pedaling. Mr. Cai followed his son to enter the gate of the school, where he spotted others who would be waiting on the lawn while their loved ones took the exams.

A dozen red banners lined the main avenue with a prominent sign, "Good Luck to Examinees!" Mr. Cai pushed his bike to the parking area and locked it beside Feng's. Feng retrieved his backpack from the rack and swung it onto his shoulders.

Mr. Cai took out a bottle of orange juice from his handbag. "Take it with you." He gave it to Feng.

"No." Feng pushed his hand away. "They're going to search my bag."

"So what? It's only juice, not a reference book!" Mr. Cai was almost shouting.

Feng twisted open the bottle lid to take a few gulps.

The loud speaker announced, "This is the first call for examinees to enter the test halls."

Feng returned the bottle to Mr. Cai. "I have to go, Dad."

"Don't be nervous!" Mr. Cai called with his hands cupping around his mouth, "Just give your best!"

Feng turned and walked a few steps backward. Mr. Cai waved at Feng, his hand shaking. Soon Feng merged with the crowd that swarmed into the test halls. Mr. Cai stared at Feng's black head until it disappeared in the classroom building.

A young teacher pulled a red plastic tape between two poles where a sign read, "Non-examinees are not allowed beyond this point." As Mr. Cai met her eyes, her face bloomed into an innocent smile. "Good luck to your child, Uncle."

Mr. Cai nodded and averted his eyes, suddenly blushing with shame. She looked to be Feng's age.

\*     \*     \*

Mr. Cai approached a group of parents who stood in a circle discussing something in a low voice. A middle-aged woman with bobbed hair listened intently to others. When she saw Mr. Cai, she gave way to let him into the circle.

"Is your child in there, Uncle?" she asked kindly.

"He sure is." To his surprise, Mr. Cai burst out, "He's been there since last night, because he couldn't sleep at all."

"Isn't it wicked hot this year?" the woman said sympathetically. "I had the electric fan on all night for my daughter."

"Weren't you worried that she might catch a cold?" he asked.

"Not if you have the fan blow on her feet. Nobody should sleep with a fan blowing on her head." She covered her mouth and giggled. "I have another trick: soak the bamboo mat in ice-cold water drawn from a well. And be careful not to let your son eat too much iced watermelon because he might get diarrhea."

Mr. Cai said he wouldn't and thanked her for the advice.

"What university did your child apply to?" a man in glasses asked.

"Yangzhou Normal University," Mr. Cai said.

"Is it his 'safety net' school?" the man asked.

Mr. Cai lowered his head. Feng was not so arrogant to put a perfectly good university as the last option, in case he might fail to enter all other schools. Mr. Cai didn't answer the other father, who might have an extremely bright child.

"What university did your child apply to?" Mr. Cai asked with a polite smile.

"Beijing University," the father said.

A gasp of admiration rose from the crowd.

"It's a good school," the lady with bobbed hair said, "if you don't mind sending your child to the military training."

"What military training?" Mr. Cai asked.

"Haven't you heard?" the lady asked. "The students' big waves in the 1989 turmoil have brought disciplinary treatment on freshmen. Now Beijing University freshmen must go through a long military training before they can start their academic year. Fewer seniors applied as a result."

"The size of the freshmen class has also shrunk," the proud father said. "So it's no less competitive to enter Beijing Univer-

sity. My child is among the top five students at Yangzhou High
School. He doesn't want to bother with any second-rate university. What can I do?"

The man's smug grin made Mr. Cai's stomach turn. He couldn't
listen to those parents any longer without feeling ashamed of his
son. There was a pecking order even in the way that a person received political persecution: only the elites were capable of making waves with their political demands while the silent majority
had their noses to the grind, living one day at a time, without a
grand vision. Feng's lack of competitiveness had prompted Mr.
Cai to look for ways to send him abroad, though by now he had
grown used to disappointments in spite of his extraordinary efforts. At a certain point, one had to accept defeat, and there was
grace in forbearance. How else could a parent live with himself?

Mr. Cai strolled to the far side of the gingko tree, where the
shade was sparse. A few parents squatted under the tree without
looking at other people, most of whom were probably in a similar
situation as Mr. Cai. So he spread a handkerchief on the ground
and sat waiting patiently for Feng to undergo the test of his life.

*     *     *

As soon as the bell rang, Mr. Cai unlocked his and Feng's bikes
to push them to the side of the road. He wanted to beat the
crowd who came to retrieve their bicycles. Looking out at the sea
of pensive faces pouring out of the test hall, he glimpsed Feng's
smile. It didn't hurt that Feng was a head taller than most high
school seniors.

"How did you do?" Mr. Cai waved the juice bottle in his hand.

Feng beamed broadly as if the world were at his feet. "Swell."
He took the orange juice, gulped down a half bottle, and wiped
his lips with the back of his hand.

Mr. Cai pushed his bike forward. "Let's get moving. You need
to take a nap after lunch."

Feng followed him. "I nailed it pretty good in my composition."

"What did you write about?" Mr. Cai said.

"I was asked to write an essay about an allegory. Twin girls are playing in a rose garden. One girl tells her mother, 'It's an awful garden!'"

"'Why, my child?'"

"'There're thorns underneath every flower.'

"A moment later, the other twin runs to tell her, 'Mom, it's a nice garden!'

"'Why, my child?'

"'Because there's a flower at the top of every thorny bough!'

"The mother watches the girl who has a bleeding finger, and reflects on what her twins have said. Isn't it an interesting story?"

"It sure is—my roses gave you a head start—but don't you dwell on it." Mr. Cai stretched out a leg to brake his bike. "A good beginning is half of the battle. Keep it up, Son."

The traffic light turned green. They rode side by side and left the crowd behind.

*          *          *

Mr. Cai glimpsed his wife craning her neck and waiting at the side road. As soon as they were within earshot, she cried out, "How did you do, Son?"

Feng jumped off his bike, looking embarrassed. "I did fine, Mom."

"I already prepared the lunch, so I came out to wait for you." She led them inside to the dining table. "I hope the dishes are to your taste."

"These are your favorites." Mr. Cai pointed. "Bamboo shoots stewed with shiitake mushrooms, and hotbed chives stir-fried with spicy tofu."

"Do you know what I want for dinner?" Feng asked. Before anyone could venture a guess, he said, "Three-treasure buns from Fuchun Tea House."

Mr. Cai exchanged a wary glance with his wife. "You said they use lard in vegetable three-treasure buns."

"I want to eat meat, fish, and dairy for these three days." To Mr. Cai's shock, Feng picked up a thin slice of pork to douse it in soy sauce, then ate it off of his fingers. "I need protein. The eggs this morning did me good."

"Sit down and eat with your chopsticks." Mr. Cai pulled out a chair and nudged his dumbfounded wife. "We'll get you the three-treasure buns for dinner. Right, Wife?"

She nodded with her mouth agape.

"Although I lost sleep last night, my mind was crystal clear this morning. I wasn't nervous and had no trouble concentrating. Maybe you were right that I was undernourished." Feng pushed his short sleeves onto his shoulders and pulled the meat dishes closer. "Animal protein seems to agree with me."

"Are you becoming a carnivore?" his mother asked.

"Of course not." Feng dug his chopsticks into the streaked pork stewed with preserved potherb mustard. "I'm only doing this for the exams. I'm pulling out all the stops, you know." He smacked his lips over the fatty pork as if he had been a meat lover all his life.

\*     \*     \*

Mr. Cai didn't know whether the warm milk did the trick or if Feng had been exhausted by the exams that day, but Feng fell asleep as soon as his head touched Mrs. Cai's pillow. Mr. Cai lay there staring at the ceiling wide awake, pondering Feng's change of diet, when the mosquito net shook around him. His wife's face appeared at the opening of the net.

"Can we talk for a minute?" she whispered.

Mr. Cai climbed out of the bed and tucked the net back in. He followed her to Feng's bedroom and closed the door. "You could've woken Feng," he scolded his wife.

"I can't go to sleep without telling you this." She looked startled with wide eyes. "Little Ye came to the shop this afternoon while you were away."

"Again?" He groaned.

"She wants to go to Yangzhou High School tomorrow. She'll stay out of Feng's way. You don't know this, but she went to the exams every year and watched Feng from a distance."

"That's why he failed every time," Mr. Cai said sharply.

"That's not fair, Husband." The rims of her eyes turned pink as she blinked.

"Did you say no to her?"

"I couldn't say that," she murmured.

"Why not?"

"She said Feng won't look for her this time because they have broken up." His wife put a hand on her brows as if shielding her eyes from the bright fluorescent light. "She hopes it's okay with you."

That was all he needed to hear. His wife had agreed to Little Ye's visit. Mr. Cai saw no use in arguing with her anymore.

He stroked her hair and said softly, "Thank you for warning me. Now get some sleep."

Feng was snoring softly when Mr. Cai returned to the bed. He lay down and pulled the coverlet over Feng's stomach. Feng had eaten four Fuchun three-treasure buns for dinner and a glass of milk before going to sleep. Feng hadn't touched this sort of food since he was six years old. Mr. Cai hoped the animal protein would fuel Feng's killer instinct and catapult him into a university.

\*     \*     \*

The next day Feng had an English exam in the morning and chemistry after lunch. In the heat of the afternoon, Mr. Cai sat under the gingko tree and watched the test hall. His heart clenched for an instant, then fluttered in his chest.

The lady with bobbed hair from the day before cast a sidelong glance in his direction. When Mr. Cai turned his head to look where she was looking, blood rushed into his face. Little Ye was staring in his direction! Although it was cool enough under the gingko tree, Mr. Cai was suddenly so hot that he pulled out the handkerchief from under him to wipe his sweat.

He didn't dare to look back at her, but remained sitting and hugged his knees stiffly like a statue. In all his worrying about Feng, he had forgotten about the late-night conversation with his wife. After the exams, Little Ye would ask Feng to marry her. There was bound to be a scene when Feng would forsake his parents for Little Ye and their child. Couldn't Mr. Cai hear it from his son rather than be confronted by a stranger? Mr. Cai had done all he could for Feng. Little Ye should wait her turn to reap the benefit of Feng's success. Granted, she was carrying Feng's child, and Mrs. Cai wanted them to marry. Couldn't Mr. Cai be left out of this marriage business? Just then he felt a sharp pinch on his skin and caught an ant crawling on his neck. He crushed it and flicked its corpse from his fingers.

Ten minutes passed before he sneaked a peek in Little Ye's direction. She had left. He glanced about furtively but found no trace of her. Then he approached the lady with bobbed hair and asked her if she saw where Little Ye had gone.

"I didn't pay attention," the lady said with a half-smile.

"Sorry to bother you." Mr. Cai returned to his spot, a little sad but relieved.

Jude had said that Little Ye had broken up with Feng for his own good. Mr. Cai wondered if Feng knew this himself. Feng had taken the first offer of female affection that came his way, just as Mr. Cai had done as a teenager. Perhaps Mr. Cai was partly to blame for scolding Feng every day, which robbed his son of his self-esteem and caused him to seek solace outside home.

It was too late to change that now. A child was on the way, as the old saying goes: the rice is already cooked. Mr. Cai folded up his dirty handkerchief and wandered to the side of the gingko tree where the shade was dense.

The proud father whom Mr. Cai had seen yesterday was telling a story to bystanders. "My son was reprimanded by the disciplinary committee because he wrote love letters to a girl in his class. I told him that if he can enter Beijing University, where she is headed, then they will be together. Guess what? From that day on, he spent every waking minute studying as if his life depended on it! So you see, incentive works better than punishment."

People chuckled and a few clapped their hands, applauding the beaming father. An idea struck Mr. Cai: he could invite Jiao to meet Feng after his exams. If Little Ye saw Jiao with him, even as a neighbor friend, she might not approach Feng as if he were readily available. This wouldn't solve everything, but it could give Feng a moment to breathe before Little Ye snared him.

Mr. Cai was so immersed in his plan that he didn't hear the bell ring. Soon a crowd swarmed to the bicycle parking area. Mr. Cai was rushing to fetch the bikes when Feng appeared beside him.

"How did you do?" Mr. Cai asked with a smile.

Feng bit his lip. "So-so, like everyone else, I suppose."

So his premonition had been right: Feng didn't perform well when Little Ye was present. Mr. Cai felt his heart sink and said no more about the subject.

He unlocked his bike and grinned at Feng cheerfully. "Let's go, Son. Mom has yellow croaker and tofu soup waiting for us."

*     *     *

After dinner, Mr. Cai asked his wife to take Feng out for a walk, while he went to Jiao's house to pay her a visit.

She had taken a bath. Her wet hair was smooth and shiny, and her cheeks coral. "Mr. Cai, I was thinking about you!"

"Me?" Mr. Cai pointed at his chest and looked behind him. "You must've mistaken me for someone else," he joked.

She adjusted the electric fan for it to blow in his direction. "How is Feng holding up?"

"He did well yesterday after he had the victory noodles. I want to thank you for the recipe."

"Did you give him cherry tomatoes?"

"No, two fried eggs, like you said. He started to eat meat and fish, too! Just for three days, he said, but we shall see." Mr. Cai closed his mouth as cool wind blew in his face.

"Did you cure Feng of vegetarianism?" Mrs. Ouyang chimed in from the kitchen.

"Let's just say, it was put on hold for the sake of the exams. I was worried that he might have indigestion because his body wasn't used to fatty pork, but he showed no sign of it. Last night, I almost died watching him gobble down four Fuchun buns."

"Was it all in his head that he couldn't eat meat?" Jiao asked.

"Possibly." Mr. Cai collected himself. "The reason I came to see you, Jiao, is that I went with him to Yangzhou High School today. This is the fourth time I've done this, and the last. Tomorrow after he steps out of the test hall, he'll either enter a university or become an unemployed youth. Since you're a college grad and an old friend, I wonder if you'd mind dropping by tomorrow and advising him about life after the exams." Mr. Cai stopped talking because Jiao kept nodding.

"I have to go to the library tomorrow. What do you say I meet you at three o'clock?"

"That's perfect. You're most kind, Jiao."

"Don't mention it. Actually I wanted to go today, but was afraid."

"Of what?"

"Feng might feel weird seeing me there." Jiao's long hairs danced around her face as the electric fan blew in her direction. "I ought to go because I'll be teaching seniors. I need to know how students feel about the exams."

"Feng is lucky to have a friend like you." Mr. Cai glanced at his watch. He wanted to be home when Feng returned from his walk. "Tomorrow I'll see you under the big gingko tree at three o'clock." He said goodbye to Jiao and her mother.

"I'll be there." Jiao stood up to see him out. "I'm glad that you asked."

\*       \*       \*

The next day Mr. Cai stared at the school gate but found no sign of Jiao. It was almost three o'clock, and in a half hour Feng would be outside. Someone touched his elbow and he saw it was Jiao, clutching two ice cream bars in her left hand and some books in the other.

"Would you give me a hand?" She giggled and licked melted ice cream from her palm.

"I didn't see you come up." Mr. Cai took the books on modern literature and pedagogy.

"I told you I was going to the library, remember?" She peered at the other side of the gingko tree. "Why don't you stand in the shade over there? No wonder you're getting a good tan."

"I *am* in the shade." Mr. Cai's face grew warm, since he had kept his distance from the bragging father and other competitive parents. "It's less crowded here." He shifted his feet.

"You can say that again!" She pushed down her sunhat with the back of her hand. "Luckily we have ice cream. I'll have the melted one."

"You really shouldn't." Mr. Cai opened the wrapper carefully to let the melting ice cream drip onto the dirt ground. "I asked you for a favor. It's only right and proper that I treat you to ice cream."

"The pleasure is all mine." Jiao licked the wet wrapper. "I got us lychee ice cream, my favorite."

Mr. Cai watched Jiao roll her tongue over the ice cream. It seemed to taste better the way she ate it.

As Mr. Cai and Jiao talked and bantered with each other pleasantly like a father with his daughter, Mr. Cai scanned the surrounding area. To his relief, he didn't find Little Ye.

Soon the bell rang. Mr. Cai asked Jiao to help him fetch the bicycles. They waited for Feng at the roadside, but few people came toward their direction. Instead a crowd swarmed into the gym opposite the test halls.

"I know where he is," Jiao said.

She led Mr. Cai into the gym, where they found pandemonium. Several men smashed juice bottles on the cement floor, and they popped like firecrackers. A few others were stamping their textbooks, while a scrawny girl set her notebook on fire. Oddly enough, a few teachers looked on with folded arms.

"What're they doing?" Mr. Cai asked, somewhat mortified.

"This is how we felt when we were done, too."

Mr. Cai was surprised to see tears in her eyes. Even a winner like Jiao had reckoned with powerful emotions when she emerged as a young adult, ready to start a new life at the university.

Before he could dwell on it further, he spotted Feng behind a column, tearing up a page of his book and throwing the paper scraps in the air.

"It's snowing!" Feng shouted at the top of his lungs.

Mr. Cai hurried toward his son, and Jiao followed behind.

"Are you forgetting yourself?" Mr. Cai grabbed Feng by the arm. "Come home with me!"

"No! I'm going to have some fun. No more entrance exams for me, you hear? I'm *done*." Feng tossed another handful of paper scraps in the air and started to dance like a drunkard.

"Look who's here." Mr. Cai pinched Feng's arm.

Feng reeled around the column until he saw Jiao, who waved at him with a book in her hand. Feng stood up and straightened his shirt, his head hung in shame. It might have been doubly embarrassing, since Jiao had had this moment four years ago and understood him perfectly.

Jiao greeted him with an innocent smile. "I came from the library and ran into your father, so we stopped in to look at the party."

"What party? Hell." Feng kicked the column, and water squished in his foam sandals.

"Why are you all wet?" Mr. Cai asked.

"The test hall is like a sewer." Feng tossed his head. "Do you guys want to have a look?"

"Sure." Jiao slid her books into her backpack.

The red banners and welcome signs had already been taken down. Mr. Cai pushed his bike and followed them to the classroom building. For four years Feng had not had any success in those test halls. Mr. Cai was reluctant to visit the inauspicious place.

"Come on in, Dad." Feng waved at him.

Mr. Cai lifted his bike to push it into the hall. On the walls were posters exhorting graduates to study hard and become the future pillars of society, full of pictures of starry-eyed teenagers with confident smiles and plump cheeks. In reality few people could be sanguine, and their successes were buoyed by the majority's humiliating defeats. The sound of the bike chain echoed creepily in the hallway. It was much cooler than outside. Suddenly his skin was covered with goosebumps. Beside him, Jiao pulled the sunhat from her head.

Feng led them into an empty classroom, where a small ice cube lay in a puddle. "It was a meter cube yesterday." Feng kicked the ice and sent it sliding across the room, where it hit the opposite wall and slid back. The water on the floor made its glide effortless. "There goes our air conditioner." Feng punched the air with his fist.

"We didn't have ice four years ago." Jiao tapped her feet in the puddle. "This is quite an improvement."

"It's a torture chamber." Feng looked at the empty desks. "Your students will come through here—a half of them will have their hopes dashed. For those from other high schools, they don't stand a chance to compete with the brightest and hardest working students. For four years I have been beaten black and blue and convinced that I'm worthless."

Mr. Cai was stunned. Perhaps Feng was only honest with his friends, like Jiao or Little Ye. If Feng had shown his humility rather than acted nonchalant, Mr. Cai would have been gentler and encouraged him more.

"You have us," Mr. Cai said quietly.

Feng didn't seem to hear him. "Let's get out of here," he said and pounded the teacher's podium.

They were outside in the humid air, surrounded by reuniting parents and students. Feng refused Mr. Cai's offer to go get ice cream and said that he would return to his vegetarian diet. He had eaten too much junk food during these past days, and he was dog-tired. He wanted to sleep for days.

Mr. Cai looked in his eyes and knew that Feng wasn't lying. His face looked sallow and glum, and there were dark circles under his eyes. They would have to leave the celebration for another day. Jiao joked with Feng that he should set a date for a post-exam party, to which Feng made no reply. He might be thinking about Little Ye, and what future held for them.

Jiao rode on the back rack of Mr. Cai's bike as the three of them headed home like a family. Jiao wasn't so light as she looked. Mr. Cai pedaled hard with his back arched. He had a tight feeling in his stomach that this perhaps was the beginning of new hardships.

# CHAPTER 9

Mr. Cai hushed his wife when he realized she was washing dishes in the kitchen. "Would you keep it down? Feng is asleep." He put down the curtain to the hallway.

"He didn't have breakfast." She glanced at the clock on the wall. "Now he's skipped lunch."

"It's not a sin to sleep in after the exams." Mr. Cai returned to his worktable. He needed to catch up on his work after taking three days off for Feng.

He was cutting out a trouser leg when his wife grabbed his elbow. "What're you doing?" he asked, trying to keep his hand steady.

"I need to talk to you."

He finished cutting the damask and raised his head.

She folded up the trouser leg. "Little Ye has asked us for help. She's carrying twins."

Mr. Cai gripped the worktable for support as his legs almost gave away under him.

"She doesn't have anyone else." His wife reached out to touch his hand, but he withdrew and put it behind his back. "She told her colleagues that her husband lives in the countryside. It's been hard on her, as you can imagine."

"I cannot imagine!" Mr. Cai pushed away the scissors, lest they should fall on his foot. "When did you find out about this?"

"On the first day of his exams."

"Why didn't you tell me sooner?"

"Little Ye was afraid that you might leak the news. She begged me to wait to tell you and Feng."

"How considerate she was!" Mr. Cai exploded before he could think. "As if being knocked up wasn't enough, she's giving us a double-happiness!" Mr. Cai stopped short when Feng's door opened.

Feng emerged, looking dismayed with his swollen eyelids. His cheeks were sunken, his hair matted like a bird nest. He seemed to have lost weight on his new diet.

Mrs. Cai asked, "Do you want lunch?" She led the way to the kitchen, followed by her son and husband.

Feng poured himself a glass of sour plum juice. "I'm not hungry."

"Have a bowl of egg flower soup," she said. "It's light and refreshing."

Feng gulped down half the juice and wiped his mouth. "I told you I won't touch eggs anymore." He turned the glass round and round in his hands, then burst into tears.

"What now?" Mr. Cai asked, startled by Feng's emotionality.

"I could've done better in the exams if I hadn't wasted four years courting Little Ye." Feng choked on his sobs. "I could've been done with university already. It's too late now."

Mr. Cai walked to the windows. In the yard, the roses stretched out their thorny boughs toward the midday sun. Their bloom might not last, but they were fortunate, he thought, to be spared the useless regrets of human beings.

"If I fail again, I'm going to shave my head and become a monk." Feng sniffled. "At least in a temple there're no exams."

"But there *are*," Mr. Cai said. Feng could not remain celibate until he finished school. What willpower did he have?

Feng sank into a seat at the table. "I think I flunked the composition."

Mr. Cai turned from the window to glare at Feng. "But you told me you nailed it."

"Now I'm not so sure." Feng scratched his glass with a thumbnail. "I wrote that the girl who says it's a nice garden is naïve because her mother will ask her to tend to the roses, while her sister will be spared the chores. I wanted to be creative, but any idiot knows that's asking for trouble."

Mr. Cai pinched the bridge of his nose. "How could you argue that laziness is the higher virtue?"

Mrs. Cai said to Feng, "The grader may favor your originality."

Feng shook his head. "They wanted us to reflect on how we may look at one thing from two different perspectives, and applaud the optimism of the girl who says it's a nice garden. School taught us to always give positive responses in the exam composition."

"Why did you write the wrong answer if you knew the right one?" Mr. Cai asked.

"I thought of Little Ye. She could've had her pick of the men at our continuation school." Feng had a wistful smile on his face. "But she only had eyes for me. She cooked vegetarian dishes especially for me. When I asked her out, she wept tears of joy." Feng drank up the rest of the plum juice and pressed the glass to his cheek. "I wasn't the best guy she could have. Just the squeaky wheel that got oiled."

"It's possible that Little Ye missed you, too." Mrs. Cai went to Feng and squeezed his shoulder. "Now that exams are over . . ."

Mr. Cai snatched the empty glass from Feng's hands before his son could respond. In the sink, he scrubbed it with a loofa sponge until the glass broke into four pieces under his grip.

His wife hurried over to turn off the faucet and held his bleeding hand.

"You hurt yourself," she said. "Let me bandage your hand."

She dragged him into the bedroom to bind his wound. He couldn't stop his hand from shaking.

"Calm down," she said and drew the curtains. Shadows draped the room like a gray eiderdown. "We will find a way to care for the twins."

"It's Feng's responsibility!"

"I know, but you can't talk to him like this. Lie down for a nap. Then we can tell him calmly."

Mr. Cai thrust his hand under a pillow to keep it there. Otherwise, he might leap from the bed to slap Feng's emaciated face.

*       *       *

Mr. Cai woke to feel a cool breeze on his face. His wife slowed down her palm fan. He glanced at the fishbowl with his carp on the trunk—their days were numbered.

"Feeling better?" she asked him with a smile.

"Is it morning yet?" He closed his eyes.

"It's three o'clock in the afternoon and Feng has gone back to bed."

Mr. Cai wondered about their conversation in his absence. "Good, I hope he won't wake up anytime soon. I may have a heart attack listening to his rubbish talk."

She pinched his cheek gently as if he were a cranky child.

He opened his eyes. "Will Little Ye tell Feng about the twins, or do we have to do it?"

"She wants us to. But we should wait after he has a decent rest." She pulled his bandaged hand into her lap. "He may not be able to handle the news right now."

"Neither can I." Mr. Cai meant it.

"There's more." She leaned to whisper into his ear. "Little Ye said when they were together, Feng refused to study for the entrance exams. He wanted to marry her and go to a trade school. When she found out she was pregnant, she broke up with him. She was afraid that Feng would use her pregnancy as an excuse to marry her and not take the exams. She knew that would break our hearts. That's why she decided to wait to tell Feng."

"This no-good son of mine." Mr. Cai clenched his teeth. "What have I done in my past life to deserve him?"

"All of us have done our best: you, I, and Little Ye." She gently pressed his good hand. "Feng is what he is. He may do the right thing yet."

"What's that, marrying Little Ye? She is as sneaky as Feng. I'm glad that she didn't come to me, or I would've scolded her. She distracted him and kept a secret with him. Why didn't she tell us what Feng was doing? She might not have ended up pregnant if she had."

"Now be fair," his wife said. "Little Ye *loves* our son, don't you see? Feng might not have stayed in the continuation school at all if it weren't for her."

"What did he go to school for, sex or education?" Mr. Cai hopped down from the bed. "The sooner I get this couple out of my sight, the better. I have to prod Jude's father into sponsoring Feng. He should study abroad and raise his family in the States. I can't allow twins to raise havoc in my house."

"But we'll go clean broke supporting them all! Husband, maybe trade school—"

"What can I tell you?" Mr. Cai interrupted. "Little Ye needs our help, as you said, and Feng is our blessing." He opened the nightstand drawer to retrieve the two tickets for the student art exhibition. "I'll take him to see Jude's art show tomorrow."

She glanced at the tickets in his hand. "Jude's art show? You never mentioned this."

"You don't care much for Jude. Consider us even for all of Little Ye's secrets you've been keeping."

His wife sighed. "Fine. When you get back, we'll talk to Feng about the twins."

Mr. Cai folded the two tickets into a small square. Then on an impulse, he put the paper into his mouth. His wife stared at him as if he had turned into a giant panda in front of her very eyes. He kept the tickets on his tongue for a while longer before spitting them out.

"If I swallow them, I may really be going out of my mind." He laughed and wiped his mouth with his hurt hand. The gauze bandage soaked up his saliva without a trace.

*       *       *

Mr. Cai was disappointed at the art show. He had pictured a grand gallery, but the so-called exhibit hall was just a classroom the size of the test hall at Yangzhou High School. Around him, students bantered with one another about artistic topics he didn't understand. Many of them dressed sloppily, wearing clothes either a size too large or too small. Mr. Cai mistook a man with shoulder-length hair for a woman and then was surprised by his deep baritone voice. He noticed a pretty woman with a vacant look in her eyes, gliding across the room like a skater on ice. The room was decorated with paintings, drawings, sculptures, even papercuts! There were more people than exhibits, regrettably.

Feng whispered to him, "College is a zoo."

Mr. Cai felt warm and dull in his pickle-colored shirt. Beside him, Feng looked flamboyant in his fern-patterned seersucker shirt, at home with the motley artist crowd. The father and son stood in front of an abstract painting with multi-colored interlocked triangles, circles, and squares.

"Is it a play structure?" Mr. Cai asked. "Or an unfinished building."

"Look deeper." Feng stepped back, then turned left and right from several different angles. "You can see passion."

The pretty woman stopped by and fixed her haughty eyes on Feng's face. "*Illicit* desire," she said, then left to join a group of friends without waiting for a response.

"Fascinating!" Feng studied the woman and then pinched his chin. "There is no wrong way of creating a piece of art."

As the noises in the room died away, Mr. Cai turned his eyes to the entrance. There was Jude, leading a venerable looking white couple into the room. People gave them twice as much room as a Chinese couple would need. The gentleman with a gray moustache had a pink face as if he had too much internal heat, according to Chinese medicine. A head and half taller than average people, he walked briskly swinging his long arms. The lady with him wore a raspberry dress in thick denim. Her stud earrings and pearl necklace gleamed as she moved. Although her face was perfectly made up, Mr. Cai found her chiseled, bird-like features too sharp to appear beautiful. Jude hadn't told Mr. Cai what to say on their first meeting with his parents. Should Mr. Cai shake their hands or quietly observe them?

Feng shouted, "Welcome!" and clapped his hands.

"Feng!" Mr. Cai hushed him. It was risky of Feng to draw attention to himself before Jude was ready to introduce his "gay" friend.

Scattered clapping rose to join Feng's before murmured conversations resumed. Jude looked in Feng's direction and quickly turned his back.

Jude cleared his throat. "Professor Wang," he addressed an emaciated man in wire glasses who stood near the entrance. "This is my father and his wife, Mr. and Mrs. Darling." Then he said something to the couple in English and ushered his parents to the far corner of the room.

Mr. Cai couldn't help staring at the old couple, especially Jude's father. Would Jude look more like him when he grew old? Although Jude was shorter than the old man, he had the same erect posture and agile limbs. This similarity pleased Mr. Cai.

From across the room, Jude cast Mr. Cai a sidelong glance and tilted his head toward the door.

"Get ready to move." Mr. Cai pulled Feng's sleeve.

Jude kissed his stepmother's cheek, then left the room without looking at anyone. Mr. Cai led Feng to meet Jude in the hallway.

Mr. Cai found Jude behind a column and approached him eagerly. Jude backed away a few steps before Mr. Cai got near.

"Forgive me, I can't introduce you today." Jude folded his arms on his chest. "My parents just got off the plane and need some rest."

It wasn't Jude's words but his tone that made Mr. Cai uneasy. His voice had lost its vivacity and sounded diffident. Even his face looked somber, with his hair combed back from his forehead. Wearing a light blue shirt with its long sleeves buttoned,

Jude looked prim and proper, like an executive secretary. Mr. Cai noticed that Jude wasn't wearing his earrings.

"They haven't seen me in three years." Jude thrust his hands in his pant pockets. "I can't spoil their joy by telling them that I'm gay on the first night."

"Why not?" Feng asked. "You're not lying to them." He cupped his cheek in his hand and gazed at Jude intently.

"No." Jude averted his eyes from Feng.

Mr. Cai asked in a soft voice, "Have you changed your mind about the whole thing?" He knew better than to pressure Jude.

Glancing distractedly toward the exhibit hall, Jude gestured a phone with his thumb and pinkie. "Don't worry. I'll call you when the time is right." He jogged back inside.

Mr. Cai had looked forward to meeting Jude's parents as the next step toward the sponsorship. Now that they were here, Jude had retreated into his shell like a nervous boy. His parents would look out for Jude and might make his problem go away. Jude had pretended to be straight until now—why not a bit longer for his parents' sake? Mr. Cai couldn't hold Jude accountable for his promise. A little stomach-sick with disappointment, Mr. Cai squatted on the floor to catch his breath. He bit his bandaged hand to keep himself from swearing.

"Are you okay, Dad?" Feng stooped to watch his face.

"I'm fine." Mr. Cai wiped away an angry tear and stood up. "We may as well go see more exhibits."

*       *       *

Feng exclaimed, "Look! We'll release our carp back there."

Mr. Cai saw a group of paintings of the Five Pavilion Bridge, a few of them done at sunset, the rest showing the midday sun. He was touched by Feng's optimism. "Hopefully, as soon as your exam results are out." He patted his son's shoulder.

In one painting, lotus flowers filled the lake. The real Slender West Lake was sparsely covered with duckweed at its banks. Lotus flowers only grew in the artificial ponds where rowboats were not allowed.

"You can make up the scenery in a painting," he told Feng.

"That's our job," a stranger's voice replied. It was the man with the long hair, probably the artist.

Mr. Cai pointed at the painting. "I liked the lotus seedpods, very realistic."

The man tossed his hair with a casual air. "It took me hours to get the shadows right. So glad you noticed it."

"Nice work." Mr. Cai nodded at him with a smile and then turned to look for his son. Feng stood three meters away, his eyes fixed on the wall before him. Mr. Cai moved to join him.

"How dare he!" Feng pointed at a painting.

Looking up, Mr. Cai saw a naked woman lying in a rowboat and holding a red umbrella. It cast a round shadow upon her protruding belly. Her swollen breasts stuck up from her chest like two unlit lanterns. Her legs were closed demurely yet showed a dark triangle of pubic hair. Although her face was painted with hazy watercolors, it was recognizable as Little Ye, with the shadows of frost bite scars in her cheeks. There was not coyness but elation and pride in her smile, seducing the audience with her voluptuous fertile body.

"I'm going to kill him," Feng muttered under his breath.

Mr. Cai found the signature at the bottom of the painting: Red Moral, written in Chinese, and in English, Jude Darling. Its caption read, The Woman Afloat.

Feng dashed off to the back of the room before Mr. Cai could grab him. "What the hell have you done, Jude?" Feng shouted.

Jude spun around on his heels. "I'm glad you came." He held out a hand to Feng, as if greeting a friend.

"Cut the crap." Feng shook a fist at Jude. "Did you seduce her into taking off her clothes?"

"Calm down, Feng." Mr. Cai grabbed for his son's arm, but Feng pulled away.

Jude's parents looked to Jude for translation. Their disconcerted gaze swept behind Feng and over Mr. Cai, before returning to their son. Mr. Cai felt at once mortified and useless. Surely the spectacle would destroy the fragile alliance between his family and Jude.

Jude pulled Feng to the side. "Please don't misunderstand us," Jude stuttered in Chinese. "I hired Little Ye using a grant that I earned. I didn't take advantage of her."

Feng slapped Jude's hand away and pushed his chest. "You mean you paid her to strip in public?"

"No! The two scenes were done separately." Jude took a step back and glanced pleadingly at Mr. Cai. "I painted her indoors. Then I did the landscape on a rowboat. It's art, Feng. You're looking at a representation of her, not the real person."

"Jude is right," Mr. Cai said. "It's only a painting. No one here even knows her."

But Feng wasn't consoled. How could he be? Jude's painting divulged Little Ye's beauty that Feng had only seen while she succumbed to his lust. Feng had loved her submission and yielding to his sex. Now he was confronted with her sex appeal out in the open, to the extent that he as a man was entirely superfluous.

"You did more than a fucking painting." Feng pointed at the wall, his finger trembling. Clearly Feng envied Jude for having seen Little Ye in a new light that he, as a lover, had been deprived.

A group of papercuts were displayed in an elegant rosewood picture frame. Each of the papercuts featured a young woman with braids and a protruding stomach. With regrets, Mr. Cai remembered the drafts he had seen at Jude's apartment. Why had he not immediately recognized Little Ye? Why didn't he believe that the country girl could be a magnificent art subject?

"What did you do with her belly?" Feng demanded, stepping so close that he was at the risk of kissing the white man.

Mr. Cai held his breath, but Jude stood his ground and shook his head.

"Trust me, it's nothing I did." He gave Mr. Cai a nod. "Help me out here, my good Mr. Tailor."

With that, Jude nudged his parents toward the exit. Feng shouted something in English. Mrs. Darling peered at Feng curiously, before she was dragged away by her husband.

Mr. Cai clutched Feng's arm to stop him from going after the Darlings. "What did you say to them?"

"I told his parents Jude is a liar." Tears welled up in Feng's eyes. "How could he paint her like that?"

Mr. Cai released Feng and scratched his head. "There's one thing I haven't told you. I was waiting for the right time." He cleared his throat several times, but the words were stuck in his throat like a tough fishbone.

With all the secrecy around Little Ye's pregnancy, Mr. Cai had failed to tell the news to Feng, who should have been the first to know. The well-meaning deceptions had hurt Feng deeply, perhaps more so than the painting. Mr. Cai realized it was unforgivable. Once upon a time he had been shattered by Xiu's pregnancy. He wouldn't have wished this ordeal upon anyone, least of all his son.

Feng stared at his father with tears rolling down his cheeks, in front of a roomful of people. Around the room dozens of eyes were fixed on him, but Feng didn't wipe his tears.

"What, Dad?"

Mr. Cai laid a hand on Feng's back to guide him through the exit. "Jude didn't lie," he told Feng when no one else was within earshot. "I am sorry that you found out this way, but Little Ye is carrying your twins."

Feng gripped his bandaged hand so hard that Mr. Cai choked on his comforting words. He didn't moan or pull away, lest Feng should desert him, run off in a fury and never return. It was better that Feng could vent his anger on him instead.

*     *     *

Mr. Cai arranged a pair of ivory chopsticks on the guest side of the dining table. His family only used bamboo chopsticks,

188

YANG HUANG

which were inexpensive but easier to pick up food with than the slippery ivory ones that Mrs. Cai had stipulated for tonight's dinner.

It was almost eight o'clock. Feng and Little Ye would soon be due. After the incident at the exhibition yesterday, Mr. Cai and his wife had decided it was time for Little Ye and Feng to have a heart-to-heart talk about their future. They were afraid that the young couple might quarrel, so they had asked Feng to invite Little Ye over for a family dinner.

Mrs. Cai laid a crock pot on the table and propped up its lid. Streaked pork stewed with peanuts and lily flowers was Little Ye's favorite, Feng had told them. She scooped out a little soup to taste it, then held the spoon to her husband's mouth.

"Tell me if it's not salty enough," she said.

"You already tasted it."

"I'm not sure if it's all right for our future daughter-in-law." She reached the spoon a little closer to his lips. "They may become engaged tonight. Old Man, we will be grandparents!"

Mr. Cai didn't have the heart to tell her all that had gone down yesterday. Hopefully Feng would calm down and act in good conscience toward Little Ye.

Mr. Cai sipped the soup, a little bland but rather refreshing. "It's fine," he said. "She shouldn't eat too much salt on a summer night. It may not be good for the baby."

"Babies," she corrected him. They exchanged a glance. "I can't believe Feng is becoming a father. Do you remember the day he was born?"

"He peed on the doctor's white coat." Mr. Cai pushed away her spoon. "Our son has been a troublemaker since day one."

"Everybody said he looked like a little angel, with his almond-shaped eyes and tiny mouth."

"Now he sells himself short to a country girl with an elementary school education."

His wife adjusted the dishes on the table and put a pink paper napkin with each setting. "Look on the bright side," she said.

"Feng isn't the easiest man to live with. At least Little Ye can cook for him."

When a bicycle bell rang in the courtyard, Mr. Cai dashed to open the door. Feng had brought Little Ye home on his bicycle. She stepped down from the bike rack and stamped her feet. She wore a pansy-purple maternity dress and black cloth shoes. If not for her stomach, now past the point of concealment, she could pass for a pretty university student.

She handed Mrs. Cai a paper bag. "I brought a little something for you," Little Ye said with a half-smile.

Her eyes were reddish, as if she had cried shortly before. Behind her, Feng was stoic as he locked up his bike.

"You shouldn't have." From the bag Mrs. Cai took out a bottle of ginseng and pilose antler wine, and a piece of silk crepe.

"For Mom." Little Ye pointed at the fuchsia crepe. "This is an auspicious color, worn by some rich ladies who stayed at the hotel."

"You're so sweet to think of us. We should take care of you." Mrs. Cai folded the silk crepe and put it back into the paper bag. "Let's have dinner." She led the way to the dining table and asked Little Ye, "Do you like pork stewed with peanuts and lily flowers?"

"It's my favorite." Little Ye took her seat.

Feng sat opposite her and slid his chair back from the square table.

"I'll move it close to you, then." Mrs. Cai pushed the crock pot toward Little Ye and spilled a little soup on the table.

"There's a lot of meat." Little Ye glanced around the table. "Help me out here."

"Don't worry about it," Mr. Cai said. "We'll throw away the leftovers. It's not that we don't like fatty pork, but we shouldn't indulge in it at our age."

"I understand." Little Ye flashed him a toothy smile. "Many foreign guests at the hotel don't eat fatty pork, either." With her lips twitching at the corners, she looked as if she wanted to cry.

\*     \*     \*

Mr. Cai watched Feng while Little Ye talked about her life on the farm: laboring in the rice paddies, harvesting cotton and yam beans, and feeding pigs, goats and chickens. Feng's face remained inscrutable, showing neither joy, shame, nor lust. He stabbed a piece of tofu with his chopsticks, until it was crushed into a puddle. Instead of eating it, Feng pushed the bowl away.

"My eldest brother graduated from high school," Little Ye said. "Now he can help out with his younger brother's tuition, so I don't have to—"

Feng interrupted Little Ye. "Tell my parents why you took off your clothes for Jude."

"You know," she murmured with her eyes downcast.

"Now tell them."

Mrs. Cai cast a stern look at Feng, but he ignored her warning. Mrs. Cai asked the whole table, "Are we ready for red bean dessert soup?"

"You tell them, or I will." Feng glared at Little Ye.

"Jude paid me." Little Ye wrung her fingers. "I wanted to save some money for my maternity leave. My job at the high school canteen didn't pay much."

"So you sold your looks!" Feng said.

"Jude is a friend of mine. He had a grant that he could use on models, so he hired me." She cupped her cheeks in her hands. "I didn't know his work would be exhibited. He asked me to sign an agreement, which I didn't read."

"The whole world has seen you butt-naked." Feng's voice broke. "How can I marry you now? I'm not so shameless."

Several months ago, Mr. Cai had read an article in *People's Daily* about an oil-painting exhibit in Beijing. The husbands of several nude models filed for divorces afterwards. Mr. Cai had not believed the story until now.

He pressed Feng's hand to calm him. "Don't rush the talk of marriage. Let's finish dinner."

"Are we not talking about marriage?" Little Ye let out a sob. "Will you let my twins be born without a father?"

"Little Ye, let's discuss this rationally." Mr. Cai offered her some tonic wine.

She shook her head. "I'm four months pregnant."

"Sorry." Mr. Cai put down the bottle. "You have to forgive me. It's the first time I've met you as Feng's fiancée."

"Ex-girlfriend," Feng said.

"Hush," Mrs. Cai said. "Let your dad finish."

He nodded to his wife in appreciation. "Marriage, as we know it, should be based on mutual respect and affections. We can't make Feng marry you if he's not willing. As his parents, we shall take certain responsibility for his actions. Namely, if you won't get married, we will pay for your abortion."

As he spoke, his wife frowned at him. Under the table, she pinched his thigh. Mr. Cai moved his knees away. He knew she would not oppose him in front of Little Ye.

"You think I've come this far just for the fees for an abortion?" Little Ye burst into tears. "For four years, I've waited on him as if he were my husband already. I cooked for him, cared for him, and kept a secret for his sake. I've made sacrifices. Is this my reward for loving him?"

"Little Ye." Mr. Cai handed her a kerchief. "Have both of you discussed family planning beforehand? A woman can have babies, but childrearing requires lifelong commitment from both parents. I am awfully sorry, but grandparents don't have a direct say in this matter. Why did you get pregnant before you're married? Why did you let him take advantage of you?"

Little Ye opened her mouth, but Feng was the first to speak.

"Who took advantage of whom?" he demanded, pushing up from the table. "Where were you when I needed you the most? You turned in my letter to the school and broke up with me, remember? You said I was no good if I didn't go to a university. Guess what? I didn't study until you left me. Why didn't you do that sooner? I might've graduated by now."

"That's enough, Feng!" Mrs. Cai held the weeping girl in her arms. "You put her in a miserable position. At least you should be kind to her."

"Why does she need anything from me? Hasn't she made a lot of money posing for Jude?" Feng plunked down on the sofa. "She can go ahead and marry him if he'll take her."

For an instant, Mr. Cai was stunned by Feng's cruelty. He shuddered to think that Feng might have inherited that streak from him.

Yet, Mr. Cai couldn't bring himself to scold Feng in front of Little Ye. Although deeply shamed by Feng, he wouldn't take Little Ye's side in this row simply because Feng was his son and Little Ye wasn't his daughter.

"Slap him for me." Mrs. Cai waved her free hand.

Mr. Cai told Little Ye in a pained voice, "Feng didn't mean it."

\*  \*  \*

Mr. Cai watched Little Ye board the bus for the hotel. She didn't turn her head to say goodbye while the bus pulled away. The way she had averted her eyes made Mr. Cai wonder if she was keeping a secret even now. Feng was not ready to become a father, so he might have asked her to have an abortion. Perhaps Little Ye had appealed to the grandparents for support behind his back, because she wanted to keep her babies. Many years ago, Xiu had blackmailed Liang in order to make a better life for her child. Perhaps Xiu had not meant to harm Liang as much as to protect her baby. A mother was compelled to act in the best interest of her baby, forsaking all others.

When he returned home, Mr. Cai stomped into Feng's room.

"Why were you so cruel to Little Ye?" he asked.

"She made me sick. When I looked at her, all I could see was her floating on the Slender West Lake butt-naked." Feng slammed down *The Popular Cinema* magazine. "And she had the nerve to hold up a red umbrella. Why couldn't she cover her privates with that?"

Mr. Cai sat by the desk. "Little Ye was your lover. You have seen her nude before."

"She was my fiancée." Feng pounded his bed. "No one has a right to see her naked but me."

"You aren't so liberal as I thought." Mr. Cai glimpsed the magazine cover that featured an actress in a red bikini. "Little Ye is also her own person. I don't think you appreciate her struggle as a young woman alone. Besides, she is Jude's friend."

"Jude is a foreigner. He lives in a nice townhouse by himself, and does whatever he pleases, unbound by our traditions and customs." Feng shut the magazine and glanced at its cover before throwing it into the trashcan. "Damn him! Exploiting a poor country girl."

"It was only a painting." Mr. Cai eyed the magazine crumpled in the trashcan. "Didn't you draw Little Ye in a dudou once? I found the sketches in this very room."

"But I didn't hang them at an exhibit hall. I never disclosed our intimacy to anyone, not even you." Feng pressed his finger and thumb on his eyelids. "Dad, you know the saying: face is as important to a man as bark to a tree. When people stared at her privates, I felt as if my skin were ripped off from my body."

"I don't understand why you feel so insecure. She's anonymous in the painting. I bet Jude never had lewd thoughts while working with her. In fact, he made her beautiful. Look, a woman's fertile body is the most precious gift that nature has to offer. It is beautiful because such a body is not made to last."

"Her beauty, as you call it, is for my eyes only." Feng pounded his thigh with a fist. "Why didn't she tell me she was pregnant? I would've married her then."

"Would you have married her *and have the babies?*" Mr. Cai said every word slowly and clearly.

"Maybe." A strand of hair fell in front of Feng's face and obscured Mr. Cai's view of his eyes. "But not so soon."

"So you would have asked her to have an abortion."

"Why are we even discussing the hypotheticals?" Feng brushed his long hair back from his face

Mr. Cai massaged his thigh. "Perhaps she kept the news from you for a good reason: you aren't ready to become a father."

"Would you want me to settle down with a family and not go to the university?"

"Feng, you had refused to study hard for many years. Please do me a favor: don't use me as an excuse now." When Mr. Cai looked into his son's eyes, Feng slid down the bed and stared at the ceiling. "You know, I took responsibility for my own action, and you are the living proof."

Feng made no reply. His lips trembled, his eyes welling up, before he clapped a pillow over his face as if to smother his own breath.

Mr. Cai sat in silence, moved by Feng's shame and defiance. He recalled his wife's words: it was Feng's immaturity that had led Little Ye to take the matter into her own hands. How frightening it was to be confronted with a fragile man-child like Feng! Yet, part of him realized his son wasn't the only one to blame.

Mr. Cai regretted that he had invited Little Ye to dinner so soon and caused everyone great distress.

*          *          *

The weather was so hot that the leftover rice from dinner turned sour overnight, since Mrs. Cai had forgotten to store it in the fridge. The two of them had talked early into the morning, and at last she had agreed not to force Feng to marry Little Ye. Feng had to think long and hard if he could commit himself to a life with Little Ye, beyond a mere sense of obligation.

Yawning, Mr. Cai moved his fish tank into the kitchen. He sprinkled a pinch of sour rice and smacked his lips to lure the carp to feed. At last night's dinner, Little Ye's stories of her life in the countryside reminded him of how Xiu had once fed her chickens this way. He wondered if the carp could hear him as well.

Feng entered the kitchen wearing only his boxers, followed by his mother.

"So how're you feeling, my little emperor?" Mrs. Cai asked.

Feng stood facing the windows. "I won't talk to you, Mom, if you make fun of me." A large stripy-legged mosquito clung to his bare back.

"Don't move!" Mr. Cai said.

Feng froze.

Mr. Cai lunged forward and slapped Feng's back hard.

"Oww!"

Mr. Cai showed him the bloody mess of a crushed mosquito in his palm.

"You didn't have to slap so hard." Feng rubbed at the pink handprint on his back.

Mr. Cai grinned. "Can't you take a well-meaning smack?"

"You were too late. The mosquito had a full stomach." Feng glanced around him. "Do we have fried breadsticks?"

"You haven't had breakfast for two days. Your dad and I don't eat that greasy stuff. Go, scoop your own porridge." Mrs. Cai handed Feng an empty bowl. "You were a real rascal last night. What was wrong with you?"

"Nothing." Feng filled his bowl, then pulled out several pickles from a jar to bury them in the warm porridge. "What do you want me to do, Mom?"

"Why are you even asking me this?" She sat at the dining table opposite Feng. "Little Ye is carrying your twins. You ought to marry her."

"Are you sure?" Feng stirred the hot porridge to blow off the steam. "If I marry her now, I won't be going to a university."

Mr. Cai squeezed his wife's shoulder to calm her. "You can still go to an American university," he said, "if things go well, and do right by Little Ye."

"How?" Feng munched a pickle. "Jude didn't even want to talk to you at the show."

"Thanks to someone who threw a conniption fit," Mr. Cai said. "I hope you will have a chance to make it up."

"Little Ye promised to support you going to any university of your choice," his wife said. "Feng, do you want to marry her or not?"

Mr. Cai knew his wife would only antagonize Feng and get into another row. "Why don't you go cut the culottes? I left the paper patterns on the worktable." He pulled her up from the seat. "Let me talk with Feng."

Mr. Cai yawned again as he pulled down the kitchen curtain. When he returned to the dining table, Feng's rice bowl was empty. "Do you want me to refill it?" he asked Feng.

"No. I'm counting on Jiao to offer me a snack."

"Are you visiting her?" Mr. Cai asked, surprised.

"There's nothing to do at home." Feng got up to put his bowl in the sink. "I'll go crazy waiting for the exam results to be announced. Jiao asked me to visit her several days ago."

"But I have to talk to you." Mr. Cai went to the sink to wash the dead mosquito off his hand. Drying his hands on a towel, he decided to try a subtler approach. "Have you fed your carp lately?" he asked his son.

"I fed them grass and mud." Feng looked inside his father's fish tank. "They've grown stout."

"I hope we can release them soon." Mr. Cai patted his fish tank. The carp darted about like little torpedoes. "I wanted to raise my fish for food, you know. Thanks to you, I changed my mind. Look at that big one! She may grow to be a breeder. How can I eat a mother carp?"

Feng said nothing. Mr. Cai stared at him until he raised his head, a stony look on his face.

"Why don't you lay off Little Ye?" Feng said. "She's not your daughter-in-law and never will be."

"I was only talking about my fish." Mr. Cai felt the warmth of a blush in his cheeks. "You are faced with a major life decision. I want you to act in good conscience. You had a real bond, and she made sacrifices for your sake. Think about how you would wish to be treated if you were her."

"I sure wouldn't take off my clothes for money and lie to my fiancé about it."

"Sometimes in life difficult decisions must be made. Betrayals, even." Mr. Cai's voice quivered, and he cleared his throat. "You've never had to fend for yourself."

Feng peered over his back at the pinkish handprint. "Exactly. How can I be a father, Dad? As you said, I'm like a clay idol fording a river, hardly able to save myself."

Mr. Cai was stunned to hear his own words get thrown back at him. "So her posing nude isn't the real issue here. You know, we can help you raise the twins."

Feng waved his hand and left the kitchen. Through the screen windows, a breeze brought in the scent of withered roses, ripe and tainted like body odor.

*         *         *

At noon, Mr. Cai dropped the culottes on the worktable to answer the phone in the hallway.

"Is it Mr. Tailor?" a familiar voice asked.

The hairs on the back of his neck stood up on their roots. "Jude, what's up?" Mr. Cai shouted.

Mrs. Cai put down her work and came into the hallway to listen with him.

"Are we still going to visit the Silk Factory?" Jude asked. "My dad wants to see Hang Gauze."

"No problem." Mr. Cai lowered his voice. "What have you told them about Feng?"

"Listen, it's a little complicated. Please don't blame it on me." Jude had lowered his also, even though his parents couldn't understand Chinese.

"I'm not blaming you, but asking you where we stand in this deal." Mr. Cai hugged his wife's waist so that she could listen in more comfortably.

"Does Feng still want to . . . after the show?"

"I hope so. I told him to get over the painting." Reading his wife's lips, Mr. Cai relayed, "We invited Little Ye over for dinner last night."

"Good. She's a sweet girl. I care about her." Jude sounded relieved.

"Feng quarreled with her and made her cry. He said it was over between them."

"Why?"

"Feng doesn't like her being seen naked in public. Don't you get it?" Mr. Cai was almost shouting.

"How is it my fault? I'm just an artist." Jude gave a nervous chuckle. "She has a beautiful body. It's nothing to be ashamed of. Feng should appreciate the painting more than anyone!"

"Her beauty is for Feng's eyes only." Mr. Cai was surprised how much he sounded like his son.

"Does Little Ye agree with that? Why did she let me paint her, then?"

Mr. Cai wanted to say: *you made her feel complacent about her beauty, at a crucial time when she ought to have discussed with Feng about family planning or having an abortion.* But Jude was not responsible for Little Ye's decision. And in a way, no one was at fault. Little Ye did what she had thought best.

Jude muffled a cough. "Listen, we would like to visit the Silk Factory very much."

"What's in it for us?" Mr. Cai clenched his teeth.

"We'll see if the factory visit puts my dad in a good mood. Then we can go from there."

"How much longer do I have to wait for your dad to be in a good mood?"

"You want to succeed, don't you? Do you think it's so easy to get a financial sponsor? He doesn't even know Feng, for goodness sake."

Mr. Cai saw his wife nodding. "Okay, we'll go with your plan."

Jude said something in English in the background. "We'd like to visit the Silk Factory the day after tomorrow," he told Mr. Cai. "By the way, don't bring Feng, please. My stepmother keeps asking me who he is. It's not time yet."

"Okay."

"I owe you one, Mr. Tailor. I won't forget it."

Before Mr. Cai could tell Jude that he owed Little Ye one, too, Jude had hung up. Mr. Cai stared at the receiver. Neither Jude nor Little Ye was to blame, but Feng wasn't able to accept her anymore. By overstepping the bounds of masculine pride, the artist had inadvertently caused a crisis.

His wife returned the phone to its cradle. "What does it mean, Old Man? If Feng goes to an American university, he can marry Little Ye."

Mr. Cai leaned against the wall, his knees wobbling. "We'll see."

# CHAPTER 10

For once, Mr. Cai forwent his thrifty habits and took Feng to the best salon in town. The Honorable Guest Salon provided services from haircuts to body massage.

Mr. Cai glimpsed his stubbled face reflected in the coffee-tinted glass door outside the salon. He hoped a good haircut would boost his confidence when he gave the Darlings a tour of the Silk Factory.

As Feng opened the door, a wave of pungent hairspray made Mr. Cai cough. The majority of customers were women close to Mrs. Cai's age, empty nesters who could afford to blow a quarter of their monthly salaries on a good perm. Teresa Teng's love song *Don't Pick the Wildflowers by the Roadside* cooed on the speakers. Her velvety voice, soft as soap, touched and flirted with every heart, young and old alike. Mr. Cai could easily spend beyond his means. Fortunately he and Feng had washed their hair at home, which saved them seven yuan each according to the service menu.

A young woman with stiff bangs fanning up from her forehead ushered Mr. Cai into a chair next to the bathroom. Feng took the seat beside him, which pleased Mr. Cai. As Feng talked to his hairdresser, the young woman pumped Mr. Cai's chair to lift him.

"What do you want?" She snapped a pair of scissors.

"The same as my son's." Mr. Cai pointed to his left.

She exchanged a few words with her coworker. "Good choice," she told Mr. Cai. "The kung fu style is in vogue among townsmen."

"Is it popular with foreigners as well?" Mr. Cai asked.

"Foreigners?" She brushed his hair back and cut along the edge of her comb. "What do you mean?"

"I'm going to see several foreign friends of mine, and I want to give them a good first impression." After the disastrous meeting with Jude's parents at the art show, Mr. Cai wanted to start anew and had dragged Feng along for a haircut, ostentatiously as a post-exam treat.

"If you haven't met them, how do you know they're your friends?" she asked loudly.

Mr. Cai regretted having told his secret to a woman with a big mouth. "You don't have to shout it out for everyone to hear." His neck strained as she pushed his head forward. "Besides, I only asked you about a hairstyle, not your advice on how to make friends."

"I was merely making conversation with you." She snipped the hair around his right ear. "Don't move."

He froze. "I don't want my hair cut too short."

"Short hair makes you look younger."

"I'd rather look trustworthy than young." Mr. Cai held his breath as the scissors prowled behind his right ear. "I want my friends to regard me as a respectable father."

She pressed an electric razor down his neck. "If I were you, I would want them to think I'm in my thirties. You could pass for that if you dyed your hair."

"Go easy on my dad, Miss." Feng leered at them with his head bent to one side. "He's not the flirtatious type."

If Mr. Cai gave a rebuttal, Feng might join forces with the hairdresser, who was his age, to tease him. So Mr. Cai kept his mouth shut for the rest of his haircut. The young woman finally rolled his chair around and handed him a mirror.

"Tell me if you like it," she said.

Mr. Cai studied the back of his head. A triangular strip of hair extended to his nape.

"What's this for?" Mr. Cai pointed at the conspicuous hair.

"It's a part of the kung fu style," she said. "Look, your son wears it well."

Feng stood up from his chair. His head appeared rounder and his face broader than before. His eyebrows stretched toward his temples like two sharp swords. Was this the look of a "butch" that Feng had described as a gay partner? It made Mr. Cai a little uneasy, although he was relieved that Feng would go along with the plan and play Jude's gay friend even after the art show.

Mr. Cai said, "I'm not a looker like my son." His mirror displayed a middle-aged face with a receding hairline and gray stubble.

"You can't see your face until you have a shave," she said. "Do you want me to do you the service?"

"I can shave myself." Mr. Cai rubbed his cheek. "I've got to tell you, Miss, this looks a lot like the monk style, popular in the sixties."

"I wasn't born then." She brushed away fallen hairs and pulled off the towel from his neck.

"This bothers me." Mr. Cai kneaded the strip of hair down his neck. "It makes me look like a hooligan."

She swiped the electric razor across his neck a few times. Then she turned on a blow dryer to point it at his neck, until his skin was scorched by the heat. Then: "Twenty yuan at the front desk."

Mr. Cai stood up to peer at himself in the mirror. The strip had gone and left a straight cut across instead. Perhaps he was dumb to have shaved off the extra bit of hair that distinguished the kung fu cut from the old monk style.

"We got our money's worth. Right, Dad?" Feng put his face beside his father's: a kung fu master and a monk. "It'll take us at least three months to grow our hair back."

Mr. Cai's hairdresser was pumping the chair for a new customer. Overhearing Feng, she smiled at him.

"I spent two jiao for a haircut when I married your mom," Mr. Cai told Feng. "It included a shampoo, shave, pedicure and massage. This haircut alone costs me a hundred times as much. Are you telling me it's money well spent?"

Even now his wife wouldn't pay for an expensive perm to torture and damage her silky fine hair. Sometimes Mr Cai felt guilty that he had never lavished gifts on his lovely wife. Being a seamstress, Mrs. Cai cared more for quality and timeless style rather than trendy fashion. She had never worn any jewelry, either. How could Mr. Cai have deserved a wife so frugal and devoted after his youthful meltdown with Xiu?

Feng took his arm and dragged him to the checkout counter. Mr. Cai paid with the bills in his pouch.

"Hairdressers have to make a living in today's world as well," Feng told him when they were outside, "just like tailors."

As they stepped into the street, a cart stopped in front of them. The donkey pulling it brayed at the top of its lungs, with its hairs standing up on its back. A bald man whipped its behind with a short rope, his other hand holding onto a gas tank on the cart. The donkey didn't budge but hoofed the road hard. A stinging burnt odor oozed from the asphalt road, softened under the hot sun.

"Let's go home and have a shower." Mr. Cai couldn't stand the little hairs that prickled his neck, cheeks, and eyelids.

"A bath," Feng corrected him. Pieces of hair fell like stardust as he tousled his short hair. "You know, we don't have a gas water-heater at home."

Mr. Cai eyed the gas tank with some envy as he waited for the donkey cart to pass. Its driver finally got the cart moving forward, leaving a trail of hoof prints on the melted asphalt.

*       *       *

The next day Mr. Cai arrived at the Silk Factory fifteen minutes early. He buttoned up the long sleeves of his khaki shirt while waiting for the Darlings. When Jude stepped out of a taxi after his parents, Mr. Cai was so excited that he waved his plastic bag over his head. Jude glanced in his direction with dazed eyes. It took him a few seconds to recognize Mr. Cai and wave back, even when Mr. Cai called out his name.

"Did you get a haircut?" Jude asked as they made their way to the gatehouse. Jude's parents followed behind.

"I had it done yesterday." Mr. Cai rubbed his neck and chuckled. "It usually takes a few days for a new haircut to grow into itself."

"You look fine." Jude smiled. "In fact, you look young."

Jude's parents listened attentively to their conversation.

They entered the factory and stood in a circle. Jude turned to his parents and introduced Mr. Cai in English.

"My father's name is Ken and his wife is Carolyn," he said in Chinese.

Mr. Cai made a low bow to show his respect. "How could you call your father by name?" he whispered to Jude.

"Americans call their parents by names," Jude said. "It's just a custom, not a sign of disrespect."

Carolyn offered a slim and soft hand for Mr. Cai to shake, her grip feeble. She wore a delicate scent that Mr. Cai couldn't name. Ken just nodded, and for no apparent reason, pulled up his pants by the belt. They stood smiling at one another for a moment. Then Mr. Cai and Jude led the way to the printing shop.

"I told them that you're an expert in silks," Jude said.

This made Mr. Cai smile. "Have you shown them your Tang suit robe?"

Jude's face turned pink as he stole a glance at his parents. "I showed them the fabric, and Dad wanted to see more Hang Gauze."

"That's good." Mr. Cai lowered his voice. "Have you told them about Feng?"

Jude leapt onto the steps to open the door. "I will, soon."

Though annoyed, Mr. Cai couldn't say more.

Inside, Director Xu was waiting for them in the lobby, sipping his tea. Mr. Cai showed him the gift, two cartons of 555 cigarettes, which Director Xu accepted with an easy grace.

"Welcome," Director Xu said to Jude's parents in English.

Carolyn entered into conversation with him. Both their faces became animated and friendly.

"What're they saying?" Mr. Cai muttered. He wished Feng had taught him more English words at home. The few phrases Mr. Cai understood, such as good morning, thanks, you're welcome, and a beautiful day, were not to be found in Carolyn and Director Xu's talk.

"They're just being polite to each other," Jude told him.

"I asked her where they live in the States," Director Xu explained in Chinese. "She said she lived in Chicago before she moved to Austin, Texas."

Ken's face lit up at the words "Austin, Texas." He struggled to say in Chinese, "Cow . . . boy." He touched his forehead as if to adjust a hat. Then he threw out his chest and pulled up his pants again, although they weren't falling off him.

Mr. Cai beamed at him to show that he had understood Ken's meaning. Perhaps Ken felt a bit like an outsider, too, due to the language barrier.

"Dad had a crash course in Chinese." Jude gave Ken a thumbs-up.

"Now we're introduced. Are we ready to see some silk?" Director Xu led his guests into the workshop without waiting for their answer.

*       *       *

"I assure you that you cannot buy Hang Gauze at our price anywhere else in the province, not of this exceptional quality." Director Xu showed the Darlings a black gauze silk printed with golden snakes and dragons. "Feel the texture. It's almost as thin as a cicada's wings." He pulled out some silk to drape over Ken's shoulder.

Jude translated dutifully; meanwhile Ken and Carolyn spoke to each other in English. Carolyn often smiled at Ken's remarks. Her teeth, though a little yellow, were straight and strong. She had a throaty voice that belied her fragile appearance. Mr. Cai wondered if she had ever asked Jude to call her Mother instead of Carolyn.

Half an hour later Director Xu suggested a cigarette break. The Darlings followed him outside, while Jude remained in the workshop with Mr. Cai. They took their seats in the lobby.

"It seems to be going well," Jude said.

"Good." Mr. Cai had no idea how things were going with Jude's parents. All he had done was smile at the Darlings, though no one seemed to take notice of him.

Mr. Cai flinched. Jude had reached over, taken his hand, and opened it to put an object in it. "Keep this for me." He bent Mr. Cai's fingers closed to make a tight fist.

Mr. Cai was amazed to find a jade beaded bracelet in his palm. "What's this?"

"Don't let Feng pierce his right ear. He may regret it." Jude forced a smile. "When Feng comes to see my parents, I want him to wear this on his right wrist."

"We don't want your stuff." Mr. Cai gave it back. "I told you we won't take a cent from you. We only need your help."

"It's just a prop." Jude slid back on the sofa. "Come on, don't make a scene in front of my parents. They'll think that I annoy you."

Mr. Cai saw beads of sweat on Jude's forehead, his blue eyes bloodshot. He looked haggard with a blond stubble. Then it struck Mr. Cai that since Jude had left the U.S. shortly after his mother's funeral, this was the first time that he met Carolyn. On the surface of a pleasant reunion with his parents, Jude was being tormented in a way that Mr. Cai could hardly imagine. For a moment Mr. Cai didn't care about the sponsorship but was moved to help Jude in any way he could. In spite of Feng's myriad shortcomings, he could at least be honest with his parents about the basic facts of himself, except on one point. Why was he so furious about Little Ye's pregnancy? Was Feng grappling with some fears that he himself didn't know?

Through the dusty windows, Mr. Cai saw Ken glance sideways at them. Carolyn flicked her cigarette and listened to Director Xu with a smile.

Mr. Cai didn't want to embarrass Jude, so he put away the bracelet in his breast pocket. "A loan it is," he said. "When will we come to see you?"

"Soon. My parents will be off to Shanghai in a few days. We should break the news to them right before they leave, so they have some time to think about it before they head back to the States."

As the door opened, Jude stood up.

Everybody returned to the lobby, their faces ruddy from the heat outside.

Mr. Cai pressed his breast pocket with his fingertips. There lay the precious bracelet, a token of Jude's commitment to help Feng. Misgivings aside, Mr. Cai's heart thumped in his chest as if it would burst into song.

"You bought a piece of Hang Gauze last time—a delicate print, if I remember correctly," Director Xu said to Jude. "Did you find it satisfactory?"

"Sure," Jude said and peered at his parents.

"Tell me, how do you look in it?"

"Mr. Tailor made me a Tang suit robe." Jude gestured barrel hips around his body. He told his parents something in English and they smiled.

So after all this time, Jude had not even tried on the altered robe and just assumed that it didn't fit! Oh well, it served Mr. Cai right to fawn upon a young American.

"I mentioned the possibility of hiring you as a model to your parents," Director Xu said. "We have a growing overseas market. A Caucasian model will help us in advertising. We have plenty of menswear in stock." He winked at Jude. "You don't have to wear your fat robe to our photo shoots."

Even Director Xu flattered the white man out of a business need. Yet, Jude looked glum and distracted. If only Ken knew that he was the cause of his son's distress! Mr. Cai felt sympathy toward the father with a pink face, standing with his legs apart and ignorant about his son's true self.

"I will think about it," Jude answered, "after I send my parents to Shanghai."

"Please do." Director Xu shook his hand. Then he told Jude's parents in English, "Your son is beautiful."

The Darlings exchanged a glance before they burst into laughter together. Jude's face was flushed.

"Thank you, Director Xu, but you didn't have to—" Jude was cut short as Ken took hold of his chin and squeezed it.

"Good-looking," Ken said in Chinese.

"Model material," Director Xu added.

In that moment, Jude looked like a diffident boy, meek in front of his elders.

*         *         *

Having acted like a mute servant at the Silk Factory, Mr. Cai headed home with a piece of treasure inside his breast pocket. He couldn't wait to tell his family the good news.

"Look what I've got!"

He pushed the door open and saw his wife and Feng seated on the sofa, looking up at him.

"Jude gave me his bracelet." He flashed it before their eyes, but their faces were somber and joyless. "What's the matter?"

"Feng's exam results were announced." Mrs. Cai turned to Feng. "You tell Dad."

Feng crouched low to hold his head in his hands, refusing to answer, so Mrs. Cai spoke for him.

"His scores are ten points below the cut-off mark for university admission." She covered her mouth with her hand, her eyes glittering with tears.

Mr. Cai plunked himself down on the sofa. His taut nerve snapped like an arrow shooting off a bow. He felt both empty and bewildered. It only took ten points to defeat a twenty-two-year-old man! Surely there was something wrong with this high standard. There were other ways for Feng to make something of

himself, as Mr. Cai held a token of hope in his own hand. In fact
he had begun to resign himself to whatever outcome while sitting
under the gingko tree and waiting for Feng to emerge from the
test hall. In the end, Feng should define success on his own terms,
rather than be beaten once and for all. Some important things
in life had nothing to do with test scores. Mr. Cai wouldn't want
Feng to run away from him, after he had witnessed how Jude was
crumbling in front of Ken's presence.

"Only ten points?" he said. "You were close enough, Son."

Feng seemed taken back by his quiet tone. Feng straightened as
if bracing himself for the other shoe to drop. His mother looked
inconsolable.

"You let us down, Feng," Mrs. Cai said, shaking her head. "Considering all that we've done, how much Little Ye has sacrificed for
you, every day for four years."

"Mom, Dad, I don't want to burden you anymore. Let me go off
to become a monk." Feng wiped his eyes on his sleeve. "I'm no
good for anything else."

This awakened Mr. Cai's anger. While he painstakingly tried
to carve out a future for his grown son, Feng only wanted to
evade his responsibilities, even after he had impregnated Little
Ye. Mr. Cai's worst fear might come true if Feng would live like
a parasite and give nothing back to the society. Before he could
think, Mr. Cai slapped Feng's face hard. "How dare you throw
away your life as if it were nothing?" He backhanded Feng's
other cheek.

His wife grabbed hold of his arm, while Mr. Cai pointed at his
son with a finger. "Take a good look at your face reflected in your
own piss," he scolded. "Do you see a pious face? I would sooner
disown you than have you become a monk."

Feng stood up and left the room. His mother followed him.

To stop his right hand from shaking, Mr. Cai sat on it. His
dream for Feng had finally popped like a balloon that rose too
high in the air. After four years in the continuation school, Feng
had accomplished nothing but fathering Little Ye's twins. Yet, for

the first time, Mr. Cai was able to look past the test scores and see the kind of maturity that he wanted in Feng.

His wife finally returned. "Feng went to bed, and said he didn't want dinner."

"Let him be," Mr. Cai said. "It does him good to reflect."

She sighed. "Why don't you go out with him tomorrow?"

He glared at her.

"To release the carp." She went to the kitchen to wash rice for dinner. "They're lousy to look at now."

Mr. Cai returned to his bedroom. The dying sunlight slanted into the windows and cast a blue gray rim around the fish tank. Feng had also let his fish down. Mr. Cai wished he had the strength to smash the damned tank in the courtyard. He didn't dare, however, make such a scene in the neighborhood.

*     *     *

At breakfast, Mr. Cai told Feng that they would go out to release the carp. Feng covered his eyes with a hand.

"Don't you want to?" Mr. Cai asked.

"Why?" Feng's voice broke. "I failed the exams. It's only right and proper that I should be punished."

"You have been, perhaps for the rest of your life." Mr. Cai filled a pail with water, then put his six carp inside. He said softly, "But your pets don't have to go down with you."

Feng went to his room. A moment later, he returned wearing a pair of sunglasses and carrying his enamel basin. He picked up a carp by its tail to drop it in the pail. Mr. Cai stepped aside as the carp leapt and splattered some water. Without asking for his father's permission, Feng poured all his fish along with muddy water, slimy duckweed, and decomposed rose petals into the pail. Their fish mingled and became undistinguishable. Mr. Cai shook his head but said nothing. After all, the fish would be released into the river.

"We'll be back," Mr. Cai told his wife. He and Feng went outside to clamp the pail on the back of his bicycle.

"Take your time." She saw them off at the door. "Don't hurry back for lunch."

Feng pushed the bike while Mr. Cai held the pail steady on the rear rack. Neither said a word until they reached the gate of the Slender West Lake Park.

Mr. Cai broke the silence. "Do you want me to buy you a popsicle?"

"It's up to you."

Mr. Cai laid the pail on the ground and bought Feng a red bean popsicle, his favorite. As usual, Feng let his father take a bite of his popsicle. Mr. Cai bit off the smallest piece he could chew. Then he purchased an entrance ticket. He showed the ticket and his yearly pass at the gate.

"What's in your pail, Uncle?" the ticket taker asked.

"Some pet fish I raised with my son."

The man peered into the bucket. "They're of good size, just right to eat."

"My son is a vegetarian."

"You would let your dad cook the fish if you're a good son." The man winked at Feng. "Young carp are especially nourishing for middle-aged folks."

Mr. Cai lifted the pail as Feng pushed his bike across the cast iron doorstep. "Don't listen to him," Mr. Cai told Feng. "He's not a vegetarian."

"Neither are you," Feng said. He had spoken little since yesterday, and his voice sounded a bit rusty. He chewed the popsicle and then licked on the stump. "Why did you let me mix your carp with mine? We had a contest."

"They belong to us," Mr. Cai said. "I gave the carp to you."

Mr. Cai remembered his exuberance after capturing the carp. He had met Jude and Little Ye but not known how their lives were intertwined. So much had happened in a month. Mr. Cai was surprised to find a pair of mandarin ducks swimming in the lake. Jude might want to add the famed love birds in his next painting rather than raise havoc with a naked woman.

Feng deposited the popsicle stick in a trashcan. "Sorry, Dad."
"What did you say?" Mr. Cai suspected his ears betrayed him.
"Believe me, this time I really wanted to make it." Feng wiped
his eyes on his sleeve.

It was too late for him to cry over spilled milk. Mr. Cai reached
out a hand to pat Feng's back. "I know, Feng. I know."

"No, you don't. You never ask me how I feel. Would you hear
me out if I were the man of the house?"

The pail slid on the rack as the bike jerked to the right. The
Fishing Platform was still far away. Mr. Cai clutched the pail
tightly in his hands. "We'd better let our fish go before they fall
off the bike."

\*     \*     \*

At the lake, Feng tilted the pail to pour out the fish. The carp
slipped into the lake one after another. "Get away from here,"
Feng said and rinsed the pail.

One fat carp swam backwards and was stranded in the duckweed. It flapped its tail and thrashed a wave of white water.

Mr. Cai prodded the carp with a twig. "Do you want to be
cooked?" he asked the carp, trying to drive it into the deep water.

"You raised it," Feng said.

Mr. Cai studied the black fins of the carp. Indeed, it was his
favorite, the one he'd called a "breeder." Mr. Cai recalled his
earlier talk about the carp alluding to Little Ye. What a tasteless
joke! Looking out to the lake, he could see Little Ye lying in the
rowboat and basking in warm sunshine, like Jude's picture. As
mandarin ducks frolicked in the water, Mr. Cai worried that they
might feed upon the young carp.

"Look at my fish." Feng wiped his soles on the grass. "They
swam away happily as if I had never taken care of them."

"Your fish are at home in the wild." Mr. Cai massaged his aching
wrist. He must've slapped Feng very hard yesterday. "I think you
win our contest." Mr. Cai said this in part to make amends with

his son. His anger from last night was inconsequential. From now on, Feng would have to face the consequences of his own actions. Depending on what would happen with the Darlings, he might need to find a job and settle down to have a family. It seemed a good time to acquaint Feng with his new responsibilities.

"Today," Mr. Cai told his son, "I want you to be the man of the house."

Feng stared at the opposite bank of the river. Mr. Cai wished he could see his son's eyes through those chocolate brown lenses. Quietly, Feng plucked a dandelion and blew a flurry of petals into the breeze.

"What're you doing?" Mr. Cai asked.

"Being my own man for a day." He lay down in the field with his head resting on his folded hands.

"I expected you to take care of the shop for me," Mr. Cai said, half-joking. "See if it was a piece of cake, like you said."

Feng pushed the sunglasses onto his forehead. His eyes were red and swollen, the bags underneath showing that he had slept little the night before. Mr. Cai found his son's haggard look endearing, as if Feng finally began to have the bearing of a grown man.

"You listen carefully, Dad, because I won't repeat myself like you do." Feng closed his eyes. "I don't want to be told what to do. All my life I have wanted to explore and make my own mistakes, but you never let me. You mapped out a straight path for me to enter the university. I hate that. I didn't want to go to a university until Little Ye broke up with me. I would've been happy going to a trade school four years ago."

Mr. Cai watched the last petal of the dandelion sink into a tuft of grass. It was like his disappointment in his son, frail and useless. "You wasted our money then." He'd said the first thing on his mind, and the least important.

"I would've wasted myself just to punish you." Feng pulled down his sunglasses to cover a half of his face. "I thought it was worth it, since I owed my life to you. So long as I live at home, I have nothing to my name. You've given me everything. You told me how to live my life and what to strive for. I wasn't even allowed to write with my left hand." Feng raised that hand in front of his face, splaying its fingers against the sun, casting a shadow on his face. "Dad, you're a tailor, not an educator. Why couldn't you teach me tailoring?"

"I did this for your sake," Mr. Cai interrupted.

"Let me finish. I was pushed to go to a university, for *your* sake. I'm not a person to you. I'm your son, your flesh and blood. You want me to become an engineer because *you* missed out on your own chance. You need me to realize your life's ambition."

Short of breath suddenly, Mr. Cai undid the top button of his shirt. There was some truth to what Feng said, and this complaint put him to shame.

"I couldn't change what you wanted from me," Feng continued, "but I could thwart your dreams by giving myself up. I went ahead and fell in love with Little Ye. I knew you would think I was too good for her."

Little Ye's name roused some pity in Mr. Cai. She seemed to be Feng's biggest victim yet.

"She, of all people, let me down. I was devastated when she left me. For the first time in years, I wanted to pass those exams, not for your sake but mine. But it was too late. I had wasted so much time that a few months of studying couldn't make it all up."

Feng was silent for a long while. Mr. Cai lifted Feng's sunglasses and found that his son was crying.

"I'm sorry, Dad. You don't know how sorry I am."

"You're right for once. I don't." Mr. Cai wiped Feng's wet face with his fingers. Feng's skin was soft and warm to the touch. "You are a young man, Feng. You can make mistakes and correct them. You idled away several years, and still have your whole life ahead of you, unlike your mom and me. We have our best years behind us." He stroked Feng's short hair, remembering his own youth, the shining moment when he had aspired to become a designer, making beautiful dresses for Xiu, and set himself up for the betrayal years later. "You're the generation after the Cultural Revolution. You thrive on acquiring knowledge and technical expertise. A college diploma is necessary for you, just as a good family background was required of us back then. So I'm willing to send you to a university abroad, even if it'll cost us all our savings."

Feng sat up to put his forehead on his knees. "Why do you put up with me, Dad?"

"I'm your father." Mr. Cai heard the tremor in his own voice and cleared his throat. "Your mom and I have spent our lifetime making clothes for other people. What won't we do for you, Son?"

"I am my own reason not to want a son." Feng pulled up some grass by its roots. "I would've said no, if Little Ye had asked me about having children. But it happened. She could've had an abortion, but she didn't."

Mr. Cai remembered another young woman who had refused an abortion, and instead blackmailed him in order to secure a better future for her child. What desperate love had driven a mother to become so reckless?

"Little Ye loves you," he said to Feng. "Do you never want a child, or just not with her?"

"I would be a terrible father." There was remorse, bordering on terror, in Feng's eyes. "Even worse than you."

This barb stung, yet Mr. Cai still wanted to say, "Your mom and I can help." But he knew this would make Feng balk. Meanwhile another difficult subject weighed on his mind.

"Jude gave me this yesterday." He fished out the jade bracelet from his breast pocket. "He wants you to wear it when we visit his parents, soon. You'll act as a gay man, Jude's best friend, according to the plan we've agreed."

"I don't feel up to it anymore." Feng looked away to the lake. "I've done so many bad things. I got Little Ye pregnant. I deceived you and Mom. I'm a terrible son. Worst of all, I used Little Ye to get back at you."

"What's done can't be undone," Mr. Cai told him sharply. "You have one last chance to get ahead in life. You may as well grab it and repent your wrongdoings later, when the chips have fallen."

"Dad, I'd probably be admitted into a trade school with my exam scores." Feng murmured, "I want to go this time."

Mr. Cai was disappointed that Feng only wanted to take the easy path in life.

"Trade school is nothing compared to studying abroad. This is the chance of a lifetime, not only for you." Mr. Cai allowed himself to raise his voice. "Besides, you'd be doing Jude a real favor. He was worried sick about telling his father that he's gay. With your help, he may grit his teeth and go through with it." When Feng didn't respond, Mr. Cai knelt beside Feng with his hands clenched into fists. "Why can't you put your acting skills to good use for once?"

"When the time comes, perhaps. But not today." Feng leapt up and dusted his hands. "Today, I'm my own man."

"Okay." Mr. Cai relaxed his fists and chuckled. "Jude hasn't called me yet. I just want you to be prepared."

"I'm hungry." Feng walked up the slope toward the bicycle. "Let's go home."

Mr. Cai picked up the empty pail. "I miss my fish already," he thought aloud.

Feng took off his sunglasses to gaze at the opposite shore of the lake. "I hope your fish will make it in the wild. You spoiled them rotten, Dad."

"Don't worry!" Mr. Cai swung the pail to hit Feng's behind. "Fishing isn't allowed in the Slender West Lake."

As they set out of the park, Mr. Cai considered telling Feng that he had been wrong earlier—that the life's ambition of father and son, to be a fashion designer, was actually mutual. But he held his tongue. Feng couldn't indulge in his fantasy while he had to forge a career path.

\*       \*       \*

That Friday, Jude called to invite Mr. Cai and Feng to an after-dinner gathering at Yangzhou Hotel. In the end, Jude asked to put Feng on the phone.

"Okay, I won't go overboard," Feng said. His face grew serious as he kept nodding.

Afterwards Feng threw his mother's entire wardrobe on the bed, tried on a dozen pieces, and finally chose her purple velvet coat. It fit him nicely but was five centimeters too short. The sleeves rode above his slim wrists and showed off the jade bracelet. The purple velvet gave his skin a warm glow, accentuated by the berry lip balm that he wore. Mr. Cai averted his eyes and told himself this was for a good cause.

They arrived in the lobby ten minutes early and were directed to the elevator, wherein a uniformed man took them to the sixth floor. Feng wore his mother's floral water and gelled his short hair. The elevator man wrinkled his nose as Feng passed him by on the way out, and flashed Mr. Cai a lopsided grin.

The thick carpet muffled their footsteps as Mr. Cai and Feng walked to the end of the hallway. Feng reapplied lip balm, then nodded at his father. Mr. Cai knocked on the door twice.

Jude opened the door, his eyes glowing and cheeks flushed. He wore the butterflies-teasing-peonies Tang suit robe with its top clasps undone. It fit him surprisingly well in a languid and unkept way.

"I had too much to drink," Jude said in Chinese. "I just told them. Now you have to back me up."

Mr. Cai stepped inside with his son. The Darlings sat on the sofa, sipping white wine and listening to Chinese string music. Neither stood up to shake their hands. Ken looked confused and darted suspicious glances at the visitors. Carolyn gazed at Feng intently and then looked down at her feet. Mr. Cai felt as if they had walked into a trap of their scrutiny. A pungent smell of incense permeated the air.

Jude turned off the stereo and gestured Feng to an overstuffed chair by the bed, on which Jude sat. Mr. Cai took a seat at the desk, away from lamplight.

"Would you like some wine?" Jude asked his guests.

Feng nodded and rested a hand on his cheek.

Jude took out two glasses to fill a half of each, and gave Mr. Cai one and Feng the other. He toasted to them in Chinese, "To our collaboration!" Then he said something in English, and everyone lifted their glass.

Mr. Cai sipped his wine. It was rather sour for his taste.

Jude spoke to his parents in English, while he fixed his eyes on Feng. Feng crossed his legs demurely as if he had something to hide. He listened intently and watched Jude's mouth as if he hung onto Jude's every word. There was frank admiration in Feng's eyes that Mr. Cai had never seen during his conversations with his son. Mr. Cai felt a little short of breath because he wasn't sure that Feng was acting. When Jude finished speaking, Feng murmured a few words with glee and reached out to stroke Jude's hand. This bold gesture seemed to alarm even Jude, who drew back and propped his hands behind him. Mr. Cai blamed the wine, which must've worked quickly into Feng's vegetarian brain.

"I asked my father to sponsor you, my best friend," Jude explained in Chinese. "I told them that you helped me accept myself." He gave Feng a polite smile. "I never said we were involved. Please don't take advantage of me."

Feng bit his lip with a blush. "You look good in the robe."

Jude nodded. "It's comfy, like pajamas."

Although Jude didn't translate this part of their conversation, Mr. Darling sat up with his legs wide apart, kneading the peony print on the carpet with his heels. His face became crimson and was striking against his gray hair. His wife said something to Mr. Cai in English.

"She asked how you felt when you discovered that Feng is gay," Jude translated.

Mr. Cai had a ready answer for the question. "Tell her that his being gay isn't something that I could've helped. I accept and love him, because he's my only son, my flesh and blood."

Mr. Cai glanced at his son. Feng picked at the jade beads and snapped the rubber band against his right wrist. Was Feng punishing himself? After his confession at the park, Mr. Cai wondered how his son had managed to bottle up his resentment all these years. Feng had said that he wanted to make his own mistakes. Mr. Cai suspected that Feng might have more than curiosity and sympathy toward Jude.

"She said you are a loving father." Jude's earrings sparkled as he turned toward Mr. Cai. "Feng is lucky to have your wholehearted support."

Before Jude finished his translation, Mr. Darling sprang up and left the room. His wife remained sitting with a frozen smile on her face. No one spoke for a while. Then she excused herself and went to talk to Ken.

They argued loudly in the bathroom. Ken was stomping, opening and closing the drawers, and shouting English words Mr. Cai didn't understand. No doubt the American father was giving vent to his parenting woes. It might have irritated him to be compared to a Chinese father. Mr. Cai was vaguely comforted by his anger. Ken had begun to process the painful fact. He needed to sort through his feelings and understand that Jude loved him, and this love had given Jude the courage to come out in spite of his father's anger. Eventually Ken would grow to appreciate Jude's honesty, as Mr. Cai was grateful to Feng for having opened up to him at the park. Now was the first step toward eventual reconciliation.

Jude leaned against the bed headboard and listened with his eyes closed. Feng kept his eyes averted with a contrite expression.

Finally Mrs. Darling returned.

"My father needs to think about this," Jude translated for her. "Would you give him some time?"

"Of course." Mr. Cai leapt to his feet. Although he had not expected the meeting would be so brief, he was glad that it was over.

Jude ushered them outside and shook their hands. "Thanks for coming. I'll call you." He closed the door.

\*       \*       \*

The elevator man's eyes popped wide when they returned. "What, you didn't find your friend?"

"We did," Mr. Cai said simply.

"A short visit." The elevator man grinned and pressed the button for the lobby.

Mr. Cai waited for the door to reopen, then exited the elevator after Feng.

"We can never set foot in the hotel without an invitation." Feng veered to the side hallway, out of sight from the front desk and doormen in tasseled uniforms. In the corners of the lobby, vases almost as tall as an adult stood like sentry guards, filled with blooming silk flowers. "We may as well look around a little while we're here."

"What came over you back there?" Mr. Cai asked. "Why did you impose yourself on Jude?"

"I got caught up in the moment." Feng watched his own reflection in a mirror that hung over an ornate credenza. He examined his face critically, like a stranger, and rubbed his cheek against the velvet collar.

"Is there something you need to tell me? I can't take it if you do it like Jude."

Mr. Cai noticed a familiar face reflected in the mirror at the same moment Feng did. He turned and saw Little Ye standing behind them.

"I was hoping to see you, so I took the night shift. I'm on my break." She looked slender and graceful in her navy uniform. It still baffled Mr. Cai, the thought of not one but two babies growing inside her belly. "Did it work out with Jude?"

"What?" Feng asked.

"Don't play dumb with me, Cai Feng. I know about the plan. Too bad I have to talk to you like this, since you won't see me anymore."

Her shrill voice made Mr. Cai cringe. Feng gawked at her face with his mouth open. Despite being a head taller than Little Ye, he looked willowier than she, who wore a skirt and was pregnant.

Little Ye pulled Feng away from the waiting area toward an unoccupied alcove. Mr. Cai followed them.

"Jude helped you for my sake," she said. "He told me that a child born in the States is automatically a U.S. citizen."

Mr. Cai shifted his gaze to and fro, watching their faces flush like a pair of pomegranates.

"What is Jude to you?" Feng asked. "Why did he tell you this?"

"I've known him for a year." The smile on her face disappeared as quickly as it had appeared. "When I met him, you had trouble applying to American universities. I was good to Jude, because I thought he might be helpful to you. As he turned out to be a great guy, we became good friends."

"Why didn't you mention him to me before all this?"

"You know we never had much time together." She bit her lip. "And when we did get together, we were always . . . busy. It didn't seem important."

Mr. Cai looked around for a bathroom. Perhaps he should leave and give the couple their privacy.

"Really?" Feng let out a chuckle almost as strident as her voice. "You talked plenty about that dirty old man who tried to grab you."

"You were the only reason that I stayed at that job," she exclaimed. "You told me to do whatever I wanted on Sundays. Well, I tutored Jude in Chinese, building a future for us all the while.

"Feng. Don't you see? We can get married and live in the States." She stepped toward Feng, her chin raised. "Our twins will be born U.S. citizens. As their parents, we may stay in the States without much difficulty."

"You left out the part where you stripped for him!" Feng glared at her.

Mr. Cai startled when Little Ye slapped the wall with her palm. "With two babies coming, I need money! You're still living with your parents."

Mr. Cai saw a look of hurt cross his son's face, before a sneer replaced it.

"Did Jude promise that I'll marry you, too, Jinhua?"

"No." She averted her eyes from Feng. "*I* told Jude that we were getting married, so he agreed to help us. You didn't know this, but I referred him to your father's shop. When Jude talked about wanting a vest made, I saw the opportunity for us."

Jude had gone to Mr. Ouyang's shop first that day. Why wouldn't a curious artist check out Ouyang's bustling shop? Suddenly Mr. Cai understood why Jude had told Feng not to touch him earlier: even in the deception Jude had held Feng accountable as his friend's lover.

Little Ye looked up at Feng. "I persuaded him to help you, because you are my fiancé."

"I'll be damned!" Feng knocked his forehead against a display window and made it clatter. "You're worse than my father. You want to use your babies to emigrate."

"They're *our* twins." She reached for him. "I want what's best for all of us!"

"No." Feng backed away as if she were a tigress, ready to pounce. "I haven't sunk so low as to marry a double-dealer like you." He dashed for the revolving door.

"We'll see what Jude has to say about that!" she yelled after him.

Mr. Cai stared at her quivering mouth, struck by her determination to make the best of everything, yet would accomplish exactly the opposite with someone like Feng, who resisted the guardian figure despite all he had needed and benefited from them. Feng had used Little Ye to rebel against his father and continuation school. When Little Ye emerged as someone just as domineering, naturally Feng rejected her plan for a perfect future.

"Do you believe me, Tailor Cai?" Little Ye's eyes grew red with tears.

Mr. Cai looked away in order to think. "I . . . appreciate your referring Jude to my shop. Feng is . . . indebted to you." Inadequate as those remarks were, Mr. Cai was embarrassed to contradict Feng's bitter words. So he added, "You could've told us how you were helping Feng."

"You didn't even know me. I thought I should prove myself first." She looked up to the ceiling to keep her tears from falling. "But what difference does it make? Feng doesn't want me now."

Mr. Cai nodded with a sigh. While he racked his brain for comforting words, Little Ye turned and walked away. Mr. Cai watched her enter the arched door of the dining hall. For a moment he wanted to call her back. This young woman embodied the strong work ethic that Mr. Cai had tried but failed to instill in Feng. Alas, Little Ye couldn't be his daughter-in-law, because Feng, with his privileged upbringing and fragile sensibility, was afraid of her strength and resented her meddling. Though he waited, Mr. Cai saw no sign that she might return.

CHAPTER 11

Mr. Cai peered at a young woman who was sunbathing in the grass field opposite the Foreign Students' Dorms. She wore a red bikini and plum-colored sunglasses. Her curly blond hair fell upon the grass like a chrysanthemum in bloom. Her limbs were slender and long. Even more alluring was her taut stomach, white and smooth with a silver stud nestled in her bellybutton. Her cherry bikini bottom—

"Don't stare." Jude shook a finger at Mr. Cai. "It's not polite."

Mr. Cai sat with Feng and Jude at a stone table in the shade. Apparently Feng hadn't noticed the sunbather but fixed his eyes upon Jude. Scantily clad foreign students paced to and fro in front of their dorms. Mr. Cai wished he had not succumbed to Feng's request to have a talk with Jude. He reached a hand to his back and pulled his shirt off his sweating skin.

Beside him, Feng spoke in an anxious voice. "I want to hear it from you, Jude. What is Little Ye's part in our deal?"

Jude pressed a chilled Pepsi can to his cheek.

"She told you that we were getting married," Feng continued. "It's not true. I cannot marry her after what happened."

"What has *happened?*" Jude mocked Feng's serious tone.

"You painted her naked for the whole world to see," Feng said. "I don't blame you because she allowed you. She also lied to me about the breakup. What finally got me was that." Feng coughed into his fist. "She decided to keep her twins without my consent."

Jude took off his sandals and put a foot on his knee.

"We had a deal," Feng said. "I act as your gay friend, while you ask your father to sponsor me. Let's leave Little Ye out of this."

Mr. Cai wished Feng hadn't insulted Jude so bluntly.

"What makes you think it's all about you?" Jude finished his soda and tossed the empty can into a trashcan. "You cling to Daddy's shirttail, but my friend has to fend for herself. Now excuse me." He stood up on bare feet.

Feng deserved the chiding. Mr. Cai was relieved that Jude was cold toward Feng, as he had begun to worry that Feng might have a crush on him.

"How did your father take the news?" Mr. Cai asked in hopes of detaining Jude.

"He hasn't called me since he left for Shanghai." Jude chuckled bitterly. "Maybe he lost my number, for good."

"I wish I could help you in some way," Mr. Cai said.

Jude gazed at Mr. Cai's face. "May I call on you after my father is back in town?"

"Feel free to do so." Mr. Cai got to his feet, so that he could look Jude in the eye. "I'm only a phone call away."

"I'll take you up on that." Jude offered Mr. Cai his hand.

Mr. Cai clasped it and shook it hard. When Jude pulled away, Mr. Cai stepped toward him. He wanted to cheer Jude up, but was afraid of imposing himself.

"Little Ye is my friend," Jude told Feng. "My deal started with her, not you." Jude walked into the grass field to join the white girl who was sunbathing.

"Who is he kidding?" Feng asked. "His parents will know I'm not gay when Little Ye enters the picture."

"Perhaps you don't understand." Mr. Cai wasn't in the mood to lecture Feng about compassion and friendship. "Jude cares about her more than you."

Jude lay in the grass field and took off his shirt. He talked to the girl and she laughed. Both blond and beautiful, they could easily be taken for a couple. This picture of bliss gave Mr. Cai a sharp pang. In spite of Jude's talents and good looks, his fertility would go to waste.

In a way, Jude had disowned his family for these three years by staying in China. Mr. Darling might never have a grandchild by Jude, but what was a grandchild compared to a grown son like Jude? Mr. Cai could never want a grandchild so much that he would risk losing Feng, no matter how disappointing his son was.

"I would go sunbathing, too, if I were born with white skin like theirs." Feng pouted. "But I have to stay in the shade, because a tan makes me look like a country bumpkin."

"Count your blessings." Mr. Cai squeezed Feng's shoulder. "You're luckier than Jude."

*     *     *

Several days later, Feng received a letter from the district agricultural school, the last choice on his college application: *Congratulations! We have accepted you into our class of 1992.*

"Four years of continuation school and this is your reward." Mrs. Cai dropped the letter on the kitchen table. "*Our* reward."

Mr. Cai took a handful of rice to the fish tank, before he remembered that the carp had been released. He washed his hand and put the empty tank in the cupboard.

"Dad, I'm going to the agricultural school." Feng walked to the ironing rack and rummaged through the new clothes as if looking for a favorite.

Mr. Cai nodded. Now that Feng had offended both Jude and Mr. Darling, trade school might be his only alternative. This could be a good time to prod Feng to marry Little Ye.

"When shall we expect your engagement to Little Ye?" Mr. Cai asked.

"Never," Feng said.

"Why?" Mrs. Cai asked. For days now she had deigned to speak to Feng of only two things: food, and Little Ye.

"Why don't you believe me, Mom?" Feng sat down on the sofa. "We broke up."

"She did it for your sake." Mrs. Cai pointed a finger at Feng. "You owe this to Little Ye. Besides, she may teach you more about farming than the lame curriculum."

"I'm not studying to be a farmer." Feng folded his arms on his chest. "My field of study is crop fertilizer. I'll be a chemist."

Mr. Cai cleared his throat. "Whether you'll be a farmer or chemist is not the problem—"

"Little Ye's twins are due in January," his wife interrupted him. "You'd better get your act together."

"How can you be sure they're mine?" Feng asked. "Where do the twins come from? Have there been any twins in our family history?"

Mr. Cai exchanged a glance with his wife, pleading for her to remain calm. Her face was flushed, and a layer of sweat beads appeared on her upper lip. The electric fan blew in her direction and made her hair stand up like a helmet as she lunged at the sofa.

She slapped Feng's back. "You're not going to say that her babies are Jude's, are you?"

"Take it easy, Mom! Hear me out." Feng got up and went to the windows, at a safe distance from his parents. "Little Ye and I didn't spend much time together, even though we dated on and off for four years. All that time, I had no idea that she was a friend of Jude's. One day she dumped me as if tossing out a pair of worn shoes. Now she wants to go to the States to raise some American babies together? She took me for a puppet who would do whatever she pleased. Do my feelings mean anything to her? No, because she has enough life plans for both of us!"

Mr. Cai went to plug in the iron. Although he admired Little Ye, he also dreaded the emotional drama that was associated with her. There was not a moment of peace when an ambitious country girl did everything she could to strive for an American green card. He couldn't see Feng be happy with such a demanding wife. Besides, Feng wasn't ready to become a father.

Perhaps encouraged by his silence, Feng turned to him and said, "Dad, you know what I'm talking about."

Mr. Cai switched the iron heat to medium and started to press a new gown. "Feng has a point."

"Are you taking his side now?" Mrs. Cai leaned on his table and made it tilt sideways.

Nudging her with an apologetic smile, Mr. Cai kept on smoothing out the wrinkles on the gown. "Let me finish my ironing."

As much as he wanted to side with his wife, he wouldn't pressure Feng to marry Little Ye. It seemed like the right thing to do, but it would make Feng unhappy, not because Little Ye was an unworthy match, but because this was his parents' wish rather than his own. Mr. Cai knew his son well enough now to relent on Feng's choice of a mate, because in the end, right or wrong, he would have to—or else risk his son running halfway across the world, and searching for comfort from strangers, like Jude.

Feng raised his voice. "I also told Dad that my falling in love with Little Ye was an act of defiance on my part. Now I have seen my error. I don't love her anymore." Feng walked back to the sofa and sat down. "I just said it," he murmured. "I don't love her anymore."

"You, of all people!" Mrs. Cai pinched the skin on the back of Feng's neck. "You haven't done a day's work in your life. Never cooked, never washed your clothes, not even your own dirty underwear. Now you desert Little Ye after you made her pregnant?! No wonder people say that men are pigs."

"Calm down, Mom!" Feng slid to the far end of the sofa. "You cursed all men, including your father, your husband, me, even Jude and his father!"

"No, just you!" she said. "Son, you cannot get away with this. You will pay."

Mr. Cai felt his wife staring at him for support, so he fixed his eyes on the tip of the iron. When the phone rang in the hallway, he propped his iron on the table, then hurried to answer it before anyone else could.

"My father is back, and he wants to see you." Jude's voice was loud and clear. Perhaps his parents were watching him in the background. "He asks you not to bring Feng. Can you come over tonight?"

"Sure." Mr. Cai gestured for his wife to unplug the iron. "Is your father all right?"

"He's spoken little to me." Jude muffled a dry cough. "Please talk to him. I will be your interpreter."

Out of the corner of his eye, Mr. Cai saw Feng get up and leave the house. The screen door banged.

"I will see you tonight." Mr. Cai hung up and collected himself for a minute, before telling his wife, "Jude is in trouble."

"Feng went to see Jiao." Mrs. Cai came to hold his hand. "You should stay home and talk to him."

"I can't." His voice was sharp with impatience. "I have to see Jude tonight." He softened when he saw tears in her eyes. "Don't take it so hard. The marriage is not your decision, but Feng and Little Ye's. I couldn't even make Feng study for his exams. How can I appoint a woman for him to marry?"

"That settles it." She wiped away her tears. "Don't blame me for the consequence. You have been forewarned."

Mr. Cai was puzzled why she was so intent on making Feng marry Little Ye. Then he remembered their prospective missions: Mrs. Cai was taking care of Little Ye while he worked with Jude. Like his wife, Mr. Cai was embarking on a lost cause. In all likelihood, Feng didn't have a chance to study abroad, but that didn't make Mr. Cai care about Jude any less. He'd begun to take personal responsibility for Jude regardless of the outcome of the sponsorship. In comparison, Mrs. Cai must have been even more committed to Little Ye, who would make them grandparents.

"I trust you, Wife. You're a better person than Feng and I combined." After saying this, Mr. Cai went to his bedroom to look for his new white shirt.

*          *          *

Mr. Cai approached the Darlings' suite with a heavy heart. He would have to face Jude's angry father, who had shouted in the bathroom last week. Would Mr. Darling turn barbaric and hurl insults in his face tonight? Could Jude translate his words with accuracy and goodwill? Would Carolyn intervene if her husband grew hostile? Then he remembered Mr. Darling's large hands and shoes. What would he do if Mr. Darling resorted to using force?

Mr. Cai became so nervous that he barely had the strength to knock on the door, which opened swiftly after one knock, as if Jude had been waiting at the doorknob.

Mr. Cai smiled awkwardly at Ken and Carolyn, who wore the silk jacket and slacks they had bought at the Silk Factory. Jude wore a flaxen short-sleeved linen shirt that looked becoming on his proportional body. He seemed well-rested and calm, without the haggard looks of days ago. Mr. Cai breathed a sigh of relief. He could hardly blame Feng for being attracted to Jude, a talented man exuding decency. Mr. Cai wasn't gay but felt drawn to Jude just the same.

"I hope you haven't eaten," Jude said.

Mr. Cai was astonished to find a table with hot dishes, a bottle of wine and four place settings. He had had dinner but was eager to oblige Jude. "It would be a shame for me to miss such a treat. I saved my stomach for it." He glimpsed a pair of yellow croakers, with deep parallel cuts on their sides that allowed ginger and soy sauce to douse the meat. His mouth began to water.

"My parents have been to numerous banquets for the past week." Jude pulled out a chair for Mr. Cai. "Chinese hospitality agrees with them. My parents are from Austin, you know, right in the heart of Texas."

Mr. Cai sat down and smiled back at Carolyn. It was a good sign that Jude spoke of his family with some pride. Apparently his parents were looking out for Jude in spite of their differences. This dinner was the proof of their effort. How extravagant it was to dim the electric lights and burn the candles!

Mr. Darling nodded stiffly, clasped his hands in front of him and closed his eyes. Jude recited some English words in a solemn voice. The Darlings echoed his last word and opened their eyes.

"I just said grace for the food." Jude lifted the fan-shaped napkin from his plate. "We're a Southern Baptist family."

Mr. Cai wiped his hands with his napkin. The polyester napkin was slippery to the touch. He imitated Jude to spread it over his lap.

Mr. Darling began to speak and fixed his gray eyes on Mr. Cai's face.

"My dad wants to talk to you before he leaves China," Jude translated.

"I understand." Mr. Cai sipped ice water to wet his mouth.

"He wants to ask you a question, which you must answer truthfully." Jude lowered his eyes. "Do you think that living in China made me gay?"

Mr. Cai lurched backward as if someone had pulled out the chair from under him. "No!" he exclaimed. "Your son came to China to *be* gay. China is not a gay nation." Mr. Cai almost gave the example that Feng was not gay; luckily he checked himself. "In China, foreigners don't have as much peer pressure as they do at home. People in Yangzhou rarely talk to foreigners, few of whom speak Chinese. Since we keep a respectful distance, Jude might feel more comfortable living here as a gay man."

"Aren't there a great many gay men in China?" Mr. Darling asked through Jude. "Your son is gay."

Mr. Cai blushed so deeply that he didn't dare to look up. He took a large gulp of water, and in his haste swallowed an ice cube. "I am an unfortunate father, like you."

Mr. Cai tried not to burp as the ice cube squeezed down his throat. Jude translated and glared at him with his cold blue eyes. Mr. Cai felt the ice drop to his stomach.

"My son didn't grow up like a cowboy, but he was never a sissy," Mr. Darling said. "He was a choir boy at the church, and an attentive son at home. I indulged his interest in art. Hell, I'm paying for him to study it." He slapped the table with his palm. "How did he become gay in China?"

Mr. Cai wiped his sweaty upper lip with his napkin.

"I'll stop beating around the bush." Mr. Darling leaned forward. "Did your son seduce mine?"

Jude shook his head slightly after he finished the translation.

Afraid that he might laugh at the accusation, Mr. Cai covered his mouth with his napkin. At the last visit Feng had been bold to stroke Jude's hand. Ken was desperate to vindicate Jude and found a scapegoat.

Ken's eyes narrowed. "Tell me the truth."

But Mr. Cai wasn't intimidated; on the contrary, he sympathized with the American father, for he had also worried that Jude might lead Feng astray. Fathers could be foolish sometimes. Ken needed to learn that he couldn't protect Jude by placing the blame on others. As for the sponsorship, well, perhaps Feng never deserved it in the first place, since he wouldn't marry Little Ye.

"Translate this word for word, Jude." Mr. Cai didn't take the napkin away from his face, lest he might change his mind. "The truth is that I have deceived you. My son is not gay, but Jude is. We didn't tell you this straight out because we wanted to support Jude, our friend."

Jude didn't seem to believe his ears. He muttered, "Do you want to jeopardize Feng's sponsorship?"

"If it comes to that, so be it." Mr. Cai sighed. "It's my own fault. I'm an old fool to think that I could help you by lying to your father. He suspects that Feng seduced you. If I lead him on, he'll lay more blame on Feng for things that aren't his responsibility."

Jude looked stricken. "So you're bailing out on me?"

Mr. Cai gulped down a half glass of ice water, until his mouth was numb with the cold. He could think more clearly now. "I am your friend, Jude. I will do right by you this time."

Jude sat frozen as a statue. His face became whiter than the tablecloth.

Mr. Cai pounded the table and ordered, "Translate!"

"Fine, don't blame me for the fallout." As Jude mumbled English words in a raspy whisper, his face turned deep pink, a blue vein standing out on his neck.

Carolyn let out a low gasp. Mr. Darling pushed up from the table so violently that his chair fell to the floor.

*     *     *

Mr. Cai stared at Jude, who had not said a word in the ten minutes that Ken had been ranting to himself.

"Am I some kind of monster?" Jude finally translated for his father. "Why didn't he tell me the real reason that he invited me here?"

"It was also my fault." Mr. Cai swallowed hard. "I asked Jude to call you. Jude wanted to do our family a favor." Jude cast Mr. Cai a long look but didn't translate his answer.

Ken's gray moustache quivered as he spoke. "Did you teach your son to bear false witness?"

"It was only a means, not the end." Mr. Cai wished there were a hole in the floor that he could crawl in and hide. "Fortunately, I was able to stop that in time."

"How could you lie to us after we came all the way to see our son?" Jude translated and touched his earlobe. His earring glittered in the candlelight.

Before Mr. Cai could answer, Jude had started to argue with Ken. They shouted at each other for at least five minutes. Jude pointed a hand at Mr. Cai without looking at him, perhaps as a way to reduce Mr. Cai's guilt. Carolyn spoke up a few times, but her voice was drowned out by the male voices. Jude kept talking over his father with such courage that Mr. Cai had not witnessed in him before but understood completely now. Likewise, Mr. Cai had stood up for both Jude and Feng rather than himself. While Jude was defending him, Mr. Cai eyed the door for an escape.

Jude shot up to block his way. "I told my father not to blame you, because you only wanted to help me."

"Thank you." Tears blurred Mr. Cai's eyes. The last time he had felt so ashamed of himself, he was but a boy. Almost thirty years later, despite the wrinkles in his face and gray hair on his head, he hadn't found a niche for himself in society as a respectable father. Instead, one lousy lie had brought him to his knees like a guilty schoolboy.

Carolyn stood beside Jude and spoke to Mr. Cai.

"My stepmother says her husband needs some time to cope with this. She believes me that you lied out of goodwill."

Carolyn looked up at them with her gentle green eyes, the trust in them reminding Mr. Cai of his own wife. Mr. Cai had come this far with the Darling family and would not let them down now.

"My goodwill is nothing." Mr. Cai turned toward Mr. Darling. "I care about Jude and am asking you to accept him. He stayed away from home for three years because he was afraid of asking you to understand him. How many three-year spans does a person's life have? We're middle-aged fathers. If I were you, I wouldn't waste any more time and reconcile with Jude."

With inexplicable courage, Mr. Cai marched to stand before Ken, his nose so close to the white man's lapel that he could see the delicate silk threads of Ken's blazer.

Now Jude faltered in English more than he did in Chinese, Mr. Cai could tell.

Ken stepped back and folded his arms on his chest. "This is between Jude and us. Don't meddle with our family affairs anymore."

Instead of backing down, Mr. Cai strode to the windows to grab a handful of the curtain.

"You're a fabric store owner. I know you're an expert in textile weaves." Mr. Cai showed Ken the cloth in his hand, feeling its familiar weight. "See how the warp and weft yarns are woven together. Chinese people think all things in nature are connected. In this light, a piece of cloth is analogous to a person's life. If your family nurtures you like warp yarns, your friends and lover may support you like weft threads. One thread is nothing. Even a steel thread may be bent with my fingertip."

Mr. Cai tried to tear the curtain, but it only hurt his fingers. He went on with a shy smile. "After the warp and weft are woven together, the cloth becomes durable. A shirt on your back can last you a decade before it goes out of style." Mr. Cai wrapped the curtain around his shoulders like a shawl. "Imagine the resilience of human fabric, if it is well woven."

It took Jude five minutes to stumble out his translation. In his struggle, Jude's face flushed crimson like a hen laying an egg. Afterwards, Ken reached out a hand to touch the curtain.

Carolyn walked to Ken and held his hand. "Thank you, Mr. Cai," she said, "for your advice."

Mr. Cai's knees wobbled as if he had just finished a marathon. Though the outburst of passion left him as suddenly as it had come upon him, he knew his words were as much for him to heed as Mr. Darling.

He released the curtain and smiled timidly at Jude. "I'd better go now."

Jude said goodbye for him to his parents, then followed Mr. Cai to the door and pulled him into a hug.

Mr. Cai breathed in Jude's scent mixed with his own perspiration. He kissed Jude's cheek and told him, "Take care of yourself, Kid." Jude's stubble grazed his lips.

"I will." Jude squeezed him before letting him go. "You and Feng, too."

Mr. Cai shook his head and left with a smile. As he walked out of the air-conditioned hotel into the humid air, he suddenly realized that he had not kissed Feng since he became a teenager.

\*     \*     \*

Mr. Cai got home and found Jiao sitting in Feng's room. She was the first girl whom Feng had brought there. Jiao wore a lemon sleeveless dress made of towel cotton, the material best suited for

sleepwear. Soft music and the scent of yulan magnolia permeated the small space. Jiao removed her feet from the rosewood desk
when she met Mr. Cai's gaze.

"You're back." She straightened her dress. "We were just talking
about you."

Mr. Cai backed into the unlit hallway. "Not bad things, I hope."

"Feng said you supported him going to the agricultural school."
Jiao smiled politely, obviously making an effort to have a conversation.

Before Mr. Cai could think of a reply, Feng chimed in from the
bed. "Jiao was telling me what I might expect from the teachers
at the trade school." Feng winked at Jiao.

"And classmates." She giggled.

"You two carry on." Mr. Cai pointed at the bathroom. "I'm
going to wash up."

Mr. Cai washed his face with soap and checked himself in the
mirror. The dim light of a single bulb made his eyes look dull. For
no apparent reason he recalled the white eyeballs of the yellow
croakers lying on the Darlings' dinner table. Mr. Cai shuddered
and switched off the light.

His wife was lock stitching the buttonholes for a dress when he
entered the sewing room.

"Did you see them?" she asked and tilted her head toward
Feng's door.

He plopped in a chair. "I thought they were a couple."

"Feng dumped Little Ye for *her*. Why should it surprise me?"
She stopped her sewing machine.

Pinching his temples, Mr. Cai tried to piece together his
thoughts that had been dashed apart by his outburst at the Darlings'. Somehow Jiao reminded him of his cousin Xiu from long
ago; had Xiu been raised in an affluent family like Ouyang's, she
might have turned out to be just like Jiao.

Mr. Cai and his wife listened to the tittering in Feng's room.
"You can't be too subtle with a girl if you like her." Jiao's voice was
crisp and lively. "Nor should you be brash with your declaration,

or you may scare her away." Her voice lowered to an inaudible whisper. Suddenly they burst into laughter together.

His wife closed the door. "It makes me sick listening to them." She opened the bobbin case to change a roll of thread. "Poor Little Ye, my heart goes out to her."

"Our son knows what he wants," Mr. Cai said matter-of-factly, without praise or disdain. Evidently, Feng didn't consider his acceptance to the agricultural school a letdown, but rather, a means for him to get close to Jiao.

"Feng is courting trouble." His wife threaded the sewing machine and closed the bobbin case. "Little Ye is carrying his twins. She won't let him off easily."

Mr. Cai knew his wife spoke of her own wishes rather than reality.

"Having children out of wedlock gives a woman no special right," he told her. "Feng is under no legal obligation to her or the twins until he marries her. Without a marriage license, Little Ye has only one way to get Feng into real trouble." He whispered into her ear, "She'd have to accuse him of rape."

His wife rose from the sewing machine. "What?! Little Ye would never lie. Where would you get such an idea?"

Mr. Cai didn't want to frighten his wife with his explanation. Anyway, Feng was luckier than he had been.

"A single mother can become desperate," he said instead. "You can hardly blame her."

"I've been on Little Ye's side ever since you asked me to take care of her business." She wrung her hands. "Why did you ask me to fight a losing battle?"

"It's not your battle," he said, rather fatigued by her passion.

His wife sighed. "If Feng won't marry her, I have to persuade Little Ye to let him go." She reached out her hand toward him. "It's the kindest thing for everyone."

He patted her hand with a smile. "Are we of one mind now?"

*     *     *

After breaking the news of his showdown with the Darlings, Mr. Cai asked Feng to help out in the shop as an informal apprentice in order to cheer him up. Feng didn't seem to mind the bad news; in fact, he was enthusiastic to work with fabrics. Within days he had learned to make simple paper patterns and cut fabrics for Mrs. Cai to sew. Now he fetched a young couple the accessories for their wedding wardrobe, and explained to them how each article was used. Watching his son work, Mr. Cai recognized a zeal that he himself had never quite possessed, even when he was first starting out.

"The knee-length cheongsam suits you very well, Miss," Feng told the bride-to-be. "You can wear it to work without looking too dressy. Better yet, this indigo color flatters your complexion."

The young woman came out from behind the khaki screen, clutching the front of her garment. "But I can't snap it on comfortably."

Mr. Cai measured her bust. "I need to give out this much." He showed her two knuckles' width. "You seem to have gained three centimeters since I last measured you."

She lowered her head and blushed.

"The bridesmaid will envy you your curves," Feng comforted her.

Mr. Cai asked the groom-to-be, "How come you lost weight?"

"We've been eating winter melon soup to save money for our honeymoon," he said. "It has finally showed."

The easy tone with which the groom said "we" made Mr. Cai wonder if the bride-to-be had gone on the pill. Mr. Cai had worked with enough of "pre-newlyweds" to know that a new sex life could alter the looks of a young couple as much as any diet.

Mr. Cai marked the young man's Tang suit robe with a yellow chalk. "I'm going to take in some in the waist, and you'll be fine."

Feng poked his waist from behind. "Dad."

"Don't you see I'm busy?" Mr. Cai clamped the sides of the groom's robe with wooden clips, then stood back to study its fit.

The groom fixed his eyes on something behind him, so Mr. Cai turned his head to look. Jude and his stepmother strolled into the shop arm in arm, both nodding at Mr. Cai as if he should be expecting them.

"Mr. Tailor, Carolyn wants to have a dress made," Jude said in Chinese. "We'll wait, if you're in the middle of something."

Something in their postures told Mr. Cai that Ken didn't know his wife and son were at his shop. Having weathered a storm together, Mr. Cai felt a kinship with the Darlings. Now Jude and Carolyn did away with the usual politeness. Mr. Cai had to tread carefully, as if dealing with some volatile relatives.

Mr. Cai told Feng, "Ask your mother to finish this for me."

Mrs. Cai entered the workroom, said hello to the Darlings, and quietly took over her task. The young couple didn't protest that Mr. Cai dropped them to take on a new order; Jude's fluent Chinese might have silenced their complaint, in addition to his pale skin.

Mr. Cai collected his tape and notebook. It was safer to treat Carolyn like any other customer than ask silly questions about Ken.

"May I see your fabric?" he asked.

Carolyn opened a small parcel. Mr. Cai was stunned to see the same Hang Gauze with the butterfly teasing peony print that Jude had bought a month ago.

"She made me buy more of the same fabric," Jude said. "I couldn't refuse."

Mr. Cai nodded, still disbelieving his eyes. "Did Director Xu give you a discount?"

"I agreed to be their model." Jude pressed his lips together to conceal a smile. "Their first Caucasian model."

Carolyn draped the gauze silk over her shoulder and peered at Mr. Cai for approval.

"It looks good on you." Mr. Cai gave her a thumbs-up, then pulled the tape off his neck. "Now let me get your measurements."

*       *       *

The shop remained crowded even after the young couple departed. Although Carolyn and Jude spoke little, their presence seemed to occupy the entire workroom.

"I got what I need," Mr. Cai said. "Is there anything else I can help you with?"

"Carolyn wants to thank you for seeing us last time," Jude translated for his stepmother.

Mr. Cai tugged the measuring tape that hung from his neck.

"She expresses her regrets that Ken will not sponsor Feng."

The news didn't surprise Mr. Cai. Rather, he was relieved to be told the facts and spared the suspense.

"Feng will go to the district agricultural school," he said. "So it's not the end of the world. At least I can sleep at night, without feeling guilty for having lied to you."

"She asks you not to take offence at Ken. He will come around and be grateful for what you did." Jude looked at his stepmother, as if wishing that she would be proven right.

"The gratitude is mutual," Mr. Cai said. "I'm a father, too. For years I've been pushing my son to go to a university. After giving your husband a lecture, I came home and thought to myself, it sure sounds easy when it's not your problem. If Ken had known what I was like at home, he could've challenged me: if you expect me to accept Jude's sexuality, what will you do with your son's talent?"

Jude glanced at Feng curiously as he translated. Mr. Cai, on the other hand, willed himself to speak as if Feng were not in the room.

"My son won't study abroad, which is his loss," he continued. "I'm more concerned that Feng won't like agricultural studies. He has to study it just because he couldn't get into any other program."

Jude translated his message. Carolyn seemed to be puzzled and asked him a few questions, which Jude answered in a subdued tone.

"What does he *want* to do?" Jude asked in Chinese.

Mr. Cai grew shy as he divulged the secret that he'd long ignored in order to push Feng to become an engineer. "He loves to work with cloth. It has been a passion of his since childhood. I don't know if he inherited the gift from me, although I don't enjoy tailoring. I am just good at it." Mr. Cai wrapped the tape around his left hand in order to stop it from shaking. "Feng is so obsessed with cloth that I used to forbid him to set foot in our workroom. Not until he had finished the exams did I allow him in here again. Look, he had so much fun that he forgot to visit his friend next door."

Jude looked sternly at Feng while translating his stepmother's question, "Is Feng a tailor, too?"

"He would be an inspired designer, if only he had the chance to study it. Unfortunately, tailoring is only a trade, and not taught in the university curriculums in China. I served my apprenticeship when I was young, and learned only a few traditional styles that allowed me to make a living." Mr. Cai asked Carolyn, "Did you see Jude's vest?"

Carolyn shook her head.

"You should show it to her sometime," Mr. Cai told Jude. "My son designed the vest. It was classy."

"If Feng goes to the States, would he study fashion design?" Carolyn asked.

Mr. Cai hesitated. Carolyn waited patiently for his answer. Her kind green eyes encouraged him to speak about a fantasy. "If he wants to, I'll support him to study fashion design at an American university. Otherwise, Feng seems likely to drop out of his agricultural studies here."

Feng stood beside Mr. Cai, and for once didn't speak a word, as if stunned by his father's eloquence.

Mr. Cai opened Feng's left hand with its palm down. "There's a saying that left-handed people are artistically inclined. Feng was a left-handed child. It took me four months to train him to write with his right hand. He shed many tears. Afterwards he stuttered for about a year. I did it out of good faith, so that he wouldn't be picked on at school. Left-handedness is treated as abnormal in China. The society doesn't permit you to be different, so you conform at the cost of forsaking your true gifts." Mr. Cai bent Feng's fingers to make a fist. "I don't think it's the same in the States. Jude writes with his left hand."

Carolyn stared at Feng's hand as Jude translated for her. Mrs. Cai left the worktable to come put an arm around Feng's shoulder. Feng pulled his mother closer and leaned against his father as they formed a human wall in front of the foreigners. For better or worse, this must've been what a family business looked like.

"Will you let your son make my dress?" Carolyn asked. "I want it to look different from Jude's robe."

"Of course!" Mr. Cai clicked his heels as if he were a soldier obeying an order. "This will keep him happily occupied for a while."

"Carolyn has to pick up her dress in two days," Jude said.

"Two days it is." Mr. Cai rubbed Feng's back and promised his VIP client, "He'll have it ready for you then."

*     *     *

As soon as Mrs. Cai left the shop to see Carolyn and Jude off, Mr. Cai and Feng began to work on the dress.

"Trust me on this one." Feng flicked his wrists to spread the Hang Gauze on the worktable. "A two-piece dress suits her best."

Mr. Cai stepped back to lean against the wall. "It takes longer to make a two-piece dress. Her fitting will be more problematic as well."

"Either we make a nice dress for her, or you shouldn't have taken this order."

Mr. Cai chuckled, impressed by the streak of perfectionism in Feng.

"Both this material and its color are too light for her." Feng drummed his fingers on the fabric. "She doesn't have the glowing complexion to carry it off."

"She wants to show her support for Jude." Mr. Cai folded his arms on his chest. "I can't see any other reason why she bought this gauze silk."

"Why would a woman sacrifice her beauty—"

"She's his mother," Mr. Cai interrupted him. "Parents will do anything for the welfare of their children."

Feng gawked at him, his eyes dull and mouth agape. How foolish he looked, Mr. Cai thought, and young. Little Ye had staked her love on a fickle man.

"We can add a royal blue border on her dress to bring down the color tone." Feng smoothed down the fabric with his fingers. "It will make her skin look better."

On the other hand, Mr. Cai might've judged his son too harshly. Feng readily accepted Carolyn's taste and determined to make her a flattering dress. When Mr. Cai had once been in training to become a tailor, it had taken him several years to acquire this level of detached professionalism. Clearly his son would surpass him as a dressmaker.

Mr. Cai rummaged the shelf for silk fabrics. "Which pattern is the best: chrysanthemum, orchid, or plum blossom?"

"The bamboo prints will work." Feng folded a strip of bamboo-printed silk to place beside Carolyn's gauze. "The bamboo stripes are unobtrusive alongside the peony prints, yet they fill the gaps and provide an accent for the original prints."

Mr. Cai couldn't help but admire his arrangement. "Where did you learn these ins and outs about tailoring?"

"I have my instincts." Feng patted his forehead. "It's fun to summon them once in a blue moon."

Having collected a stack of old newspapers, Mr. Cai began to sketch the patterns for the dress. If not for Jude and Carolyn, he would never have tailored a two-piece dress designed by Feng. Mr. Cai felt both pride and regret that despite Feng's talent, he would study crop fertilizer at the agricultural school.

Feng stood at his elbow and watched. "Dad, did you mean what you told Carolyn?"

"It was true, wasn't it?" Mr. Cai would never have said those things if it weren't for Jude. The gay American had made him forget that a father should save face by being reticent about the things he couldn't change or make better.

Feng grinned. "I had no idea you knew me so well. Dad, I'm impressed."

"I have my instincts, too." Mr. Cai patted his forehead.

"You should have told me, Dad, how you saw me."

"I didn't, for your sake," he answered, a little sternly. His speech to Ken Darling aside, it unsettled him to reconsider his decisions past, to have them questioned. Mr. Cai drew two sides of a sleeve pattern using a ruler. "I always knew you were born left-handed. It wasn't just a bad habit, like some teachers said. I didn't let you have your way, because it would not do you any good." He added a curve on the top of the sleeve pattern. "If you wrote with your left hand, your teachers wouldn't like it. Your classmates would make fun of you. Later on, girls would take you for a freak, writing and eating with your left hand. It was easier to fix you when you were young and pliant."

"But it wasn't easy for me." Feng leaned against the worktable and made it jolt. "I've hated school ever since."

"What you considered suffering is an unattainable privilege for many others." Mr. Cai thought of Little Ye in spite of himself. Perhaps he was making excuses for Feng's irresponsible attitude toward her, as he was sure his wife would agree. It frightened him to think what the future held for her babies, his grandchildren whether recognized by the law or not. Unlike training a right hand, this couldn't be redone.

For fear that they would quarrel, Mr. Cai did not voice his thoughts, but Feng seemed to know what he was thinking anyway.

"Let me try this part." He nabbed the chalk from Mr. Cai's hand, leaning against his father so he could take his place in front of the spread newspaper. "I know you're talking about Jinhua." He continued the line of the sleeve where Mr. Cai had left off. "Could you put yourself in my shoes? I'm not ready to start a family, not yet, and if I'm pushed beyond my tolerance, I may never want to get married."

"Why did you get her pregnant, Feng?"

"Dad, you made a mistake when you were young, not by your own fault, but you were nearly trapped, had Grandma not rescued you. What if I beg you to rescue me?"

Mr. Cai's legs almost gave away, had Feng not gripped him tightly and pulled him into an embrace. Their cheeks rubbed, and Feng's short stubble grated his father's skin. Feng was trembling, but his voice was eerily calm. He must have turned this over in his head for a while, for he was resolute and succinct. Fortunately Mrs. Cai hadn't returned.

"Don't worry, I'll never tell Mom. But I've been thinking about your cousin, who tried to ruin you. Little Ye was the opposite. We were in love. But months after our breakup, I began to realize that a woman could trap you with her love, to the point that you lose your ambition." Feng pulled back to look his father in the eye. "I have always lived at home. I just learned today what you honestly think of me. Now going to the trade school, I want to explore the world and get to know myself. Who am I, and what am I capable of? What would I have done, if I were allowed to be left-handed? I would never know the possibilities if I don't try out other things."

Feng jerked his chin up. Mr. Cai was afraid to be kissed by an adult son asking for a favor that might not be in his power to grant. But Feng released him and went to sit on the sofa. Looking toward the windows, his eyes began to well up. The desolation in Feng's face reminded Mr. Cai of that stubborn boy who had once insisted on using his left hand even after many whacks on it, until one day, he finally succumbed. Now that boy was begging for a second chance. Feng wiped his eyes and bent down to hold his forehead in his palms. Mr. Cai couldn't find comforting words.

His wife appeared in the courtyard. She returned inside and closed the screen door.

"Where have you been?" Mr. Cai was startled by his own voice, weary but calm.

"Talking to Jude." Mrs. Cai gave Feng a cutting look and then turned to her husband with a smile. "About his friend."

Feng remained sitting like a statue. Mr. Cai returned to the worktable and picked up the chalk. Not knowing where to go next, he traced the lines on the newspaper until the pattern thickened and became blurry in his eyes.

*     *     *

The next day father and son were busy cutting the silk around the paper pattern when someone called from the courtyard.

"Is Feng making clothes?" Jiao's chirpy voice reached them before she entered the house. "I have to see it for myself."

"I'm just helping Dad." Feng's face lit up in her presence. "I can't sew."

"He's my designer while I do the handiwork." Mr. Cai put down his scissors. "My mind is cluttered with details, so I cannot be as creative as he."

"I wish I were dexterous like you guys," Jiao said. "I can't even sew a button."

Mrs. Cai came out of the sewing room to greet Jiao. "You have a mistress's hand." She took Jiao's hand to stroke it. "Your delicate fingers are meant to hold a pen, not a needle."

Mr. Cai was surprised to hear his wife compliment Jiao. He had been too overwhelmed to ask her what Jude had said about Little Ye yesterday. Now he suspected their conversation accounted for her change of attitude toward Jiao. Mr. Cai found he no longer wanted to know everything on everyone's mind, which only made him feel anxious.

"There's no nobility in holding a pen, economically speaking." Jiao pulled away with a smile. "I earn less than a peddler who sells tea eggs. My college education is a waste of money."

"How could you compare yourself with a peddler?" Mrs. Cai offered her White Rabbit toffees. "You have not only job security but also the respect of society. Remember, teachers are the engineers of young souls."

Mr. Cai smiled at his wife.

"Thank you." Jiao sat on the sofa and watched Feng work. "We teachers are merely the leaders of youngsters."

"Students keep you young, don't they?" Feng asked.

Jiao put the toffee in her mouth and folded the candy wrapper into a small square. "Not high school seniors. They worry you so much that your hair grays prematurely."

"My field of study is crop fertilizer. I'm reading about backyard compost." Feng smiled. "I wonder what nickname I will get in two years."

"I'm sure it sounds more prestigious than a head of youngsters."

Jiao's reply gave Mr. Cai pause. Had she made a subtle pass at Feng?

After a quiet moment, Jiao spoke again. "Who is the dress for, an American lady?"

Feng must've told her about the Darlings, perhaps in order to impress her. "Just a customer," Mr. Cai answered before his son could.

Mr. Cai was disappointed that Feng couldn't keep a secret from Jiao. But, had he told her about Little Ye and her twins? If Feng wasn't ready for commitment, why did he start another relationship so soon?

Jiao came to touch the gauze silk on the worktable. "Is she good-looking?"

"A customer's looks are the last thing on my mind when I make her dress," Mr. Cai said. "I only work with her measurements."

"I see." Jiao muffled a dry cough. "My dad wants me to help him with dinner. I have to go now."

"See you," Feng called after her.

Just as Jiao left the shop, Little Ye stepped inside. They looked at each other in the face before they passed. In that moment Mr.

Cai clearly saw the differences in two women. Jiao walked impatiently with bouncy steps, looking like a proud schoolgirl with her quick glances and long slim neck. Little Ye was a woman, her middle beginning to thicken, her feet solidly planted on the ground. She moved slowly and turned around to look at Jiao's back with suspicion.

Mr. Cai finally understood why the nude painting had threatened Feng deeply. During their separation, Little Ye had evolved from a shy caterpillar, so to speak, catering to Feng's every need, to become a dazzling butterfly, answering to a higher power within herself. Feng had not been there to witness her transformation, like Jude had. Perhaps Feng wasn't even the reason for her transformation, while Jude had offered her support that might have led to her decision to keep the babies. When Little Ye looked in his direction, Mr. Cai averted his eyes to focus on the dress in his hand.

Little Ye stood at the door and called Feng by name. "Can I steal you for a minute?"

"I'm busy," Feng said. "Can't we talk here? My parents aren't strangers."

Mr. Cai wished Feng would take her out for a walk instead. Carolyn would come for the dress the next day. Even working steadily as they had, he would have to stay up to finish the piping. But, his wisdom told him not to interfere.

"I have a lot of work to do." Mr. Cai bowed at Little Ye to excuse himself. "Don't mind my being here. You feel free to talk with Feng."

"Would you like some tea?" Mrs. Cai asked.

"No, thank you." Little Ye leaned against the doorframe.

Feng dragged his steps toward her. "How are you?" he asked.

"I feel fat." Her voice broke. "I'll have to take my maternity leave in a few months. They require a marriage license to keep me on the payroll."

Mr. Cai turned the skirt inside out to slip-stitch its waist. Out of the corner of his eye Mr. Cai saw his son lean in toward Little Ye.

"I am so very sorry to have caused you such trouble, Jinhua."
Feng's voice was gentle. "I wish I could take back what I did."

With a meaningful glance at her husband, Mrs. Cai disappeared into the sewing room. Mr. Cai decided that he would join
her when the young people wanted their privacy.

"We did this, Feng." Little Ye glanced down at her belly. "We
did this, together."

Mr. Cai saw Feng's mouth set to a hard line.

"I've thought long and hard about us, but I cannot marry you,"
he said. "Marriage is a lifelong commitment. I cannot treat it like
a game."

"But you promised to marry me," Little Ye whimpered, "or I
would never have—"

"I begged you to marry me, but you dumped me. Have you
forgotten it? I haven't, because I shut myself in the mosquito net
and cried for three nights. How can I trust you after that? What if
you walk out on me during our honeymoon? Do I have to live in
fear for the rest of my life? What sort of marriage would that be?"

Little Ye's cheeks became flushed. "You know I faked the breakup, so that you could finish your exams. Nothing else would get
through to you."

"You sound as if you were doing me a favor!"

"I intended to, because I love you." She pounded the door with
her fist. "If I didn't, I would never have let you touch me."

Mr. Cai dropped the skirt on the worktable and strode toward
the sewing room.

"You don't have to go, Dad," Feng called after him.

"I want to have a word with your mom."

Mr. Cai entered the sewing room to sit beside his wife, who held
out her hand toward him. They said nothing to each other, but
pricked up their ears to listen to the conversation in the front room.

"I need help with our twins," Little Ye said.

"I cannot marry you for their sake," Feng said. "It will never
work, because I don't love you anymore."

"But why?"

"Don't cry like that." Feng sounded frustrated. "We're no good for each other anymore. You are a very capable woman, Jinhua. You broke up with me, posed nude for Jude, and made a deal with him. You didn't consult me about anything. You know I don't want a son. Why are you giving me twins?"

During the long silence that followed, Mrs. Cai pressed a fist against her mouth, and her husband put an arm around her back. Neither could stop their son from acting against his parents' will. Perhaps this was the reason that Feng didn't want to have a son of his own.

Finally Little Ye answered, her voice tiny. "I wish I hadn't loved you so much."

"Say anything you want. I can't stop you."

"Why?" There was a sound of fingernails scratching something hard, perhaps the shop door. The noise made Mr. Cai's hair stand on end. "Why can't you believe that I did everything for us? When did I ever put my needs before yours? Tell me."

"You posed nude without telling me."

"Was it so unforgivable?"

"To me, it is." Feng cleared his throat. "I was the last person to find out that you were pregnant. At an exhibit hall, of all places! I thought to myself, this couldn't be my Little Ye. She wouldn't take off her pants for the whole world to see . . . The idea that she could and had used me to bear a pair of twins!"

Mr. Cai exchanged stunned looks with his wife. She squeezed his hand so hard it hurt.

"Now you want to go to the States to give birth to your American twins," Feng continued. "You never miss out on an opportunity, do you? If Jude were straight, you would've slept with him without thinking twice!"

"You are a pig." A crisp smack in the face startled Mr. Cai. "Listen up, Cai Feng. I pray that you will be impotent for the rest of your life." Her steps receded on the brick road.

Mr. Cai and his wife froze in their chairs, not daring to draw a deep breath. After a long silence, Feng began to hum tunelessly. It sounded like "Moon River," with each note as sharp as a scream.

Mr. Cai strolled into the workroom with his hands in his pockets. "Is everything all right?" he asked in the calmest voice that he could manage.

"Everything is fine." Feng beckoned him closer to show him a chalked line he had drawn on Carolyn's sleeve. "I just thought of making it elbow-sleeved. Not only will it be cooler, it will also wear better on a middle-aged woman."

As Mr. Cai pretended to study the sleeve, Feng's hand shook so hard that the slick gauze slipped from his fingers. Mr. Cai folded the sleeve to put it beside the bamboo-printed cuff, carefully avoiding his son's gaze. The elbow-length sleeve fit with the rest of the garment like a dream.

CHAPTER 12

The handprint left by Little Ye the day before had faded into pale beige on Feng's face. Mr. Cai and his wife waited for Carolyn to change into the new dress behind the screen. Jude studied Feng's face for a while, then walked toward the windows.

"Someone had a bad day." Jude smirked at Feng. "Did he learn a lesson?"

Evidently Little Ye had filled Jude in on her latest visit. Feng couldn't retort, since Jude was a customer. His snide comment made Mr. Cai smile. Then Carolyn emerged from behind the screen.

Carolyn lifted both arms over her head as if she would dance. "This is very comfortable to wear," she said and shrugged her shoulders. Her breasts bounced behind the thin gauze silk.

Mr. Cai looked away from her chest. "Comfort is one of the virtues of Tang suit." He waited for Jude to finish his translation. "What we have here is not purely Chinese, however, as we used the western style of shoulders and front to enable the dress to conform to your contours." Mr. Cai pointed at Feng. "My son contributed the main design."

Carolyn ran her hands over the dress's front. "Can this be called a cheongsam?" she asked.

"Of course," Feng said. "Its borders, frog buttons, and Mandarin collar are taken from the classical cheongsam design."

Mr. Cai could tell that even now Feng was looking for ways of improvement. He was a fast learner but not easily satisfied. He could go far with his meticulous diligence, which had been missing from his academic studies.

"What sort of sleeves are these?" Carolyn pulled her cuff as if to stretch it to cover her exposed forearm.

Mr. Cai explained, "This is elbow-length." Unsure if she favored the sleeves, he hesitated to credit them to Feng.

"They're *fabulous*," she said. "With all these borders and frog buttons, a long-sleeved blouse would've looked tedious on me."

"For a lady like you, less is more." Feng stepped toward her with a smile. "You want to show some skin. Your forearms and neck are more appealing when they're partially covered. In this way, people's imaginations are stirred."

Jude chuckled as he translated the message. "Brownnoser," he added in Chinese.

"What's wrong with making your stepmother happy?" Feng shot back.

Jude just rolled his eyes. Carolyn asked him a few questions, which he answered patiently.

"I told her that you want to make her *happy*," Jude drawled. "Go ahead, knock yourself out."

Feng blushed to the root of his hair.

"Feng didn't fawn over your mother," Mr. Cai told Jude. "What he did was to please a customer. Believe me, it's professionalism in our line of work."

Jude shrugged. "Don't let me stop him."

Carolyn spoke, and Jude translated. "She's really glad Feng designed her dress. Its femininity is pleasing, and markedly different from mine. In fact, this is her favorite souvenir of the trip." Jude leered at Feng. "Are you waiting to hear more praises?"

Feng said nothing but bowed deeply at them. Carolyn shook Feng's hand, and then asked Jude to take a polaroid of her in the dress standing beside Feng, "the designer." The camera spat out a washed-out photo that bled into full colors like sheer magic. She asked Feng to sign the polaroid with his name. Then she shook his hand with more vigor and practiced saying his name multiple times, gaining more accuracy until both Mr. and Mrs. Cai applauded her effort.

Jude scoffed. "Look at you, an ambassador of Chinese culture."
They checked out at the front desk.

"Damn Jude!" Feng exploded as soon as they left the shop. "Why can't he leave me alone?"

Mrs. Cai said with a broad grin, "When his stepmother complimented your work, he envied you in a way that a brother might."

"That's not it." Feng touched his cheek. "He wants to punish me because I won't marry Little Ye."

"Carolyn asked Jude to bring her here to see us." Mr. Cai considered this for a while. "If his mother treats us like her friends, Jude is unlikely to ask her to punish you. This would only hinder his case with his parents."

"His father isn't going to sponsor me." Feng stood on one foot to put on his sandal, tottering a bit as he switched his feet. "As far as I'm concerned, Jude and I owe each other nothing."

"Where're you going?" Mr. Cai asked.

"I need a break." Feng brushed his hair with his fingers. "I've ended my affair with Little Ye. Now I'm a free man."

*     *     *

Feng brought Jiao home near the shop closing time; her skirt had lost a button and she couldn't find a spare. It was a black bowl-shaped button with four holes and a rim in the middle. Mr. Cai gave Jiao a matching button and lent her a thimble, needle and thread.

"You said you couldn't sew a button," he said with a smile. "Now, you can learn." As he and his wife had discussed the night before, there was no reason to be less than friendly to Jiao, despite, as Mrs. Cai had put it, their "misgivings."

Jiao thanked him and sat on the sofa beside Feng. "My best memory in college," she told Feng in a whisper loud enough for Mr. Cai to overhear, "had to be the romantic walks from his dorm to mine." She threaded the needle to sew on her button.

"Have you heard from him?" Feng asked.

"No."

She stretched out her arm high up in the air as the thread extended to its full length. Mr. Cai had never seen anyone waste such a long thread on one button, but he said nothing.

"It's better this way," she added.

"Why?" Feng asked.

Mr. Cai glanced at the sofa now and again as he slip-stitched the polyester lining for a jacket.

"It does me no good to be unrealistic." She tied a knot at the end of her thread. "If he wasn't meant for me, then we parted at graduation for good." She cut off the extra thread, and let out a low gasp.

Feng checked her skirt. Then they burst into laughter.

"Everything you do together is fun, isn't it?" Mr. Cai teased them.

Feng showed him the button that Jiao had sewn. The bowl-shaped button, with its face down, pressed tightly against the waistband of her skirt.

"You have to slide your finger under the button to lift it before you can fasten it," Feng said.

"Why didn't you tell me that I did it upside down?" Jiao snatched the skirt from Feng's hands. "You were watching me all this time."

"I was talking to you. I didn't pay attention to your sewing."

"I'm so embarrassed." Jiao covered her face with a giggle. "Being ham-handed is one thing—being stupid is another."

"Blame it on Feng for distracting you," Mr. Cai told her. "My wife would, if she made a mistake while talking to me."

"I would never," Mrs. Cai shouted from the sewing room.

"Would, too!" Mr. Cai winked at Jiao.

"To err is human." Feng cut off Jiao's button with a pair of scissors. "Let me do it over for you."

"Your hand is meant to hold a pen, not a needle," Mr. Cai comforted Jiao. To his relief, he heard his wife tittering in the sewing room.

*     *     *

The next day Mr. Cai watered his roses in the garden. Within a week he would cut off the withered roses and trim the stems for Feng's backyard compost project. In September Feng would move into the dorm while dating Jiao on the weekends. At least she had a cozy bedroom for them to rendezvous, so Mr. Cai wouldn't have to accommodate the couple and could finally have some peace and quiet at home.

His wife ran to him asking, "Where's Feng? He has a call."

"Where else?" He pointed the watering can at Ouyang's yard.

"Call him back quickly," she said. "Jude is on the phone. His parents are leaving for the airport in fifteen minutes."

Mr. Cai put down the watering can. "Ask Jude to hold."

He dashed into Jiao's house without knocking. As he came to Jiao's bedroom, Feng and Jiao separated hastily to sit up from the recliner.

"What're you doing here, Dad?"

Mr. Cai tried to catch his breath. "You have a call."

"Why didn't you knock?" Feng asked and glanced at Jiao.

"There's no time. Mr. Darling is on the line. They'll leave in fifteen minutes."

Feng got to his feet and left. Mr. Cai stole a glance at Jiao, who lowered her head and brushed a strand of loose hair behind her ear. Mr. Cai nodded at her and then walked away. He knew better than to ask Jiao any more embarrassing questions.

Feng was talking on the phone when Mr. Cai entered the hallway.

"Please thank your father for me." Feng reached out a hand to switch on the ceiling light. "Your stepmother has a beautiful posture that carries off the dress well. The effect doesn't entirely owe to my design. I'm not being modest." Feng glanced at Mr. Cai. "Yes, my dad is here."

Mr. Cai took over the handset.

"My father showered his praises on your son," Jude said. "It makes me sick to translate for them."

Mr. Cai bit his lip to conceal a smile, even though Jude couldn't see him.

"If he's so sweet on my parents," Jude went on, "why doesn't he change his family name to Darling? Feng Darling, adopted from Yangzhou."

"Don't be silly, now," Mr. Cai said. "How can your father love anyone more than you? It's not possible. He accepts your friend, most likely because he wants to please you." Mr. Cai put the handset closer to his mouth. "Listen, your father may be too embarrassed to make amends with you straight away. You should let him save face and agree to his kindly gestures."

"If only they would stop talking about the damned dress! All right, Mr. Tailor." Jude said something in English. "I have to see them off now. Talk to you later."

"Take care, Kid." Mr. Cai waited to hear a click, then hung up his phone.

"Mr. Darling asked me to send him the financial sponsorship forms." Feng turned off the ceiling light. "He wants to look them over. It's a long shot. I may as well give it a try."

"All of a sudden, your star is in the ascendant." Mr. Cai drummed Feng's hard spine. "Would you tell me what you were doing in Jiao's room?"

"Nothing."

"Then why are you blushing?" Mr. Cai followed Feng into the kitchen. "Since when have you become so thin-skinned?"

"I wish you hadn't burst inside as if you didn't know what manners are." Feng poured himself a glass of plum juice and drank it with his back to his father.

*       *       *

For the next three weeks Mr. Cai was absorbed in his work. Making the same Tang suits with different measurements didn't require creativity; his hands dealt with most of the work while his mind remained idle.

He saw little of his son during the day. Feng seemed to have made courting Jiao a full-time job. Mr. Cai believed she and Feng had become lovers. Jiao, who rarely visited them anymore, would blush profusely whenever Mr. Cai ran into her at the fried breadstick stand. Feng spent most of his days at Jiao's house while her parents were at work. The young couple could get comfortable in Jiao's room, a palace compared to Little Ye's shared dormitory with other hotel workers—or, Mr. Cai supposed, Feng's own bedroom.

Mr. Cai could say nothing against their affair, since Feng had officially broken up with Little Ye. Much to his relief, his wife didn't complain about Feng's dating Jiao, even in private. He suspected that she had worked out a solution to Little Ye's problem.

One day Jude called Mr. Cai to meet him after a photo shoot. The matter had to be discussed in person, and Jude had to attend a party that night, so he couldn't make it to the tailor shop. Mr. Cai was amused that Jude had such a busy social life after only three weeks of being a model.

The shoot was taking place on the campus of Yangzhou Normal University, one of Mr. Cai's favorite sights in the city. Now the mulberry trees had dropped their fruits and stained the sidewalks with maroon blotches. Young couples ambled down the campus avenue holding hands. Mr. Cai saw a man drape his arm over another man's shoulder. He used to dismiss men who walked like this as good friends; now he wondered if they might be gays.

Mr. Cai arrived at the scene and found Jude standing in the grass field. As an assistant held up two reflective umbrellas near his face, the photographer pointed his camera at Jude from different angles. Wearing eyeliners and mauve lipstick, Jude lifted his chin with a cheeky smile. Then he turned his face aside to show his striking profile. He squinted his eyes as if he were in some mysterious pain. From a distance, his chiseled features seemed to emanate intelligence and sensitivity.

"Good," the photographer said. "That's a wrap."

Jude shook the photographer's and assistant's hands. "How are you, Mr. Tailor?" he called out to Mr. Cai.

"I'm fine." Mr. Cai pointed at Jude's cream silk suit. "Clothes make the man."

"Don't they?" Jude touched his lapels. "I get to keep this."

"You seem to be enjoying yourself." Mr. Cai noticed that Jude's ears were bare. He looked a bit like a stranger without his earrings.

"Why shouldn't I? I could never be a model in Texas." Jude combed his hair with his fingers. "Chinese ads prefer men with fine features to rugged ones. I'm so lucky. They don't even mind that I'm gay."

"As luck would have it," Mr. Cai reminded him, "your parents gave you a fine set of bones."

Jude's face grew somber at the mention of his parents. "So, I called you here to give you this." Jude took out an envelope from his tote bag. "My father sent it to me."

Mr. Cai couldn't read any English, though the logo on the letterhead was vaguely familiar.

"He has agreed to be Feng's financial sponsor, on the condition that Feng will never ask for money from him." Jude's mauve lips set in a serious line. "I gave him my word."

"Heavens!" Mr. Cai was almost too giddy to stand. "I would kowtow to thank you if we weren't in a public place."

Jude burst into laughter. "Don't be childish, Mr. Tailor."

"Our eight generations of ancestors would prostrate themselves before you if they knew what you have done." Mr. Cai tried to blink away his ecstatic tears. "I'm not joking."

"I am happy, too, because my father mailed the letter to me." Jude's tongue slipped out and brushed his upper lip. "He seems to have done it for me more than Feng."

"I told you so!" Mr. Cai had stamped a kiss on Jude's hand before he knew it. "What a terrific son you are! How can your father not do whatever is in his power to please you?"

"You always exaggerate, Mr. Tailor." Jude led him toward the pine grove. "My father said he had a good time in China. I'm

relieved to hear it. He also helped Feng for a professional reason. He likes Feng's use of borders in his cheongsam design. My
father's store sells fabrics imported from Mexico. Feng may help
him make ethnic costumes by applying colorful borders. If Feng
does well in his studies, my father may hire him to be an in-store
tailor."

"Would Feng study apparel design?" Mr. Cai asked. He had
never allowed himself to indulge in this fantasy, except for the
moment in the shop with Carolyn. How could an American father, in his struggle to accept his son's sexuality, fulfill a foreigner's
dream for a creative career? This act of generosity was more
than Mr. Cai had bargained for.

"Yes. The University of Texas at Austin has a Textiles and Apparel Program."

"But he applied for chemical engineering last year."

"Doesn't he hate it? I have Chinese friends in graduate schools
in the States. I'll be honest: Feng is more likely to get a visa if he
doesn't study engineering."

"Why?"

"Nine out of ten Chinese students major in science and engineering. They hoard too many scholarships. The American Consulate is reluctant to import more of them. Their visa applica-
tions are often declined. But people studying the arts, humanities,
and business are still welcome."

"In that case, Feng seems destined to study abroad." Mr. Cai
rubbed his hands together. "I must raise some serious money."

Jude kicked a pinecone. "I hope you won't be broke after his
first semester."

"I've been saving every cent, jiao and yuan since he was a baby.
I thought this day would never come. A million thanks to you."
Without thinking Mr. Cai picked up Jude and lifted him from
the ground. "You couldn't have been more generous even if you
were Feng's brother!"

Jude let out a nervous cry and kicked his feet to return to the
ground. He was heavier than he looked, and Mr. Cai almost

strained his back. Still, he managed to hold Jude up a moment longer, before putting him down. Then, both laughed so hard they could barely stand.

*　　　*　　　*

At the dinner table, Feng didn't smile after Mr. Cai told him the big news. Instead, he put down his chopsticks and frowned.

"How am I going to make a living in the States?" He made a popping sound with his knuckle. "I have no skills."

"Here is the good news." Mr. Cai held Feng's hand to stop him from popping another knuckle. "Jude's father owns a fabric store. You may earn a little money by helping him out."

Feng shook his head. "He didn't even like me."

"Maybe not, but he has agreed to sponsor you, which means he tolerates you to a degree. And he likes your work. Now you can make him like you more."

"It sounds tough." Feng sank in his chair and glanced about the room. "I was just starting to enjoy being home. We've been working on the backyard compost together. Why do you want to drive me out, Dad?"

Mr. Cai was about to scold Feng—after all this hassle, how could he not be jumping for joy? His wife pressed his wrist for him to remain calm.

"Why don't you talk to Jiao and see what she thinks?" she said to Feng. "You don't have to answer your dad before that."

Mr. Cai grinned at his wife. Judging by the pragmatic bent Jiao had shown in their conversations, he felt confident in her judgment.

Feng nodded slightly with his eyes fixed on the floor.

"Is Jiao going to be our daughter-in-law?" Mr. Cai asked his son.

"Isn't she good enough for you?" Feng replied.

"For *me*?" Mr. Cai smacked his lips. "I don't need a daughter-in-law as badly as someone needs a wife."

"All right. I won't go if she says no." Feng pushed up from the table. "Let me ask her now."

When Mr. Cai was alone with his wife, he took her elbow and dragged her to sit on his lap. "Our son doesn't appreciate what I did for him." He stroked her cheek. "We may get to keep our savings after all. If he doesn't want to go to the States, I'll run out tomorrow and buy you a gas stove and porcelain bathtub."

"Don't splurge on silly things. Husband, we need to save money for a raining day." She kissed him on the neck for a seemingly long time, as if begging for a favor. "What do you say?"

He pretended to be shocked. "With Feng, every day is a raining day."

"You are not so generous as you're cracked up to be." She clung to his neck and giggled. "Like father, like son."

*    *    *

Just as Mr. Cai expected, Jiao became an advocate for Feng to study abroad. What was more, she promised Feng that she would take the TOEFL and GRE exams as soon as possible, and apply to the University of Texas at Austin, so that she could join him in the coming year.

"But we don't have the money to support her," Mr. Cai told Feng.

"You don't have to. She has her father, plus, she'll apply for scholarships." Feng beamed with pride as if seeing himself live in a new world with an intelligent girlfriend and study an exciting university curriculum: everything seemed possible. Who knew? He might even become left-handed again.

Mr. Cai looked to his wife, who drank her tea placidly. "What would she study?" he asked.

"The graduate program in the Foreign Language Education Department," Feng said. "It may lead to a career in teaching English as a second language." He pointed at a page in his Xeroxed copy of *The Most Affordable Universities in the United States*. "This department routinely offers financial assistantships to international students. With her credentials, Jiao has a good chance to be admitted."

Mr. Cai was relieved. For the first time he rejoiced at the boom of Ouyang's business, which would enable Mr. Ouyang to provide for Jiao. As a university student, Feng would be more or less Jiao's social equal in the States. Their love affair seemed to make sense. Feng and Jiao had grown up together and then been separated for four years, during which each of them had experienced a first love. Fate had at last brought them back together when Feng and Jiao were ready to be with each other. But how long would their romance last? Jiao had been chirpy like a silly schoolgirl ever since Feng told her about the sponsorship; Mr. Cai was almost certain that Feng hadn't told her about Little Ye's twins.

A week later Feng went out to apply for his passport. At Mr. Cai's urging, his wife accompanied him, while Mr. Cai stayed in the shop to catch up on his work.

Around noon he heard footsteps in the courtyard and was relieved.

"How did it go?" he asked his wife. "It's time for you to cook lunch."

No one replied. Mr. Cai raised his head and was surprised to find Little Ye standing in the doorway. She wore a peach maternity dress layered with lace. To his dazed eyes she looked like a birthday cake. Her stomach seemed to have expanded five centimeters since Mr. Cai had last seen her.

"Where's Feng?" she asked, her voice tight.

"He went to apply for his passport." Mr. Cai was too stunned to lie.

"So he has decided." The corner of her mouth twitched in a way that suggested she would cry. "He doesn't give a damn about our babies."

Mr. Cai was embarrassed and pleaded for her to stay calm. "Feng doesn't want to go with you. We parents don't have a say in this matter." He peered at the courtyard, wishing that Feng and his wife would return and save him from a scene. "I am sorry."

"When will he be back?"

Mr. Cai glanced at the clock. It was almost one. "I'm not sure. He's pretty busy—"

"I'll wait."

"Make yourself at home." Mr. Cai gestured her to the sofa. "Forgive me, I have a lot of work to do."

*         *         *

After an hour of pretending that Little Ye wasn't sitting mere meters away from him, Mr. Cai was too hungry to carry on. His wife and son still hadn't returned.

"Would you care to join me for lunch?" he asked Little Ye politely.

She shook her head, pulling a long face as if he had owed her a bad debt.

Mr. Cai boiled a bundle of soft noodles and put some leftover meat in the soup base. Then he chopped a piece of green onion and scattered it over the noodles. The sting of green onion would make the soup taste fresher. He sprinkled some cayenne powder and sesame oil to finish, as his wife always did.

Mr. Cai took his noodle bowl to the dining table and started to eat. The soup was so spicy that it burned the roof of his mouth. He got up to fetch a glass of water and realized that he hadn't offered Little Ye a drink.

He walked toward her in the shop. "Forgive me, would you like something to drink?"

She shook her head.

"Not even water?"

"I'm not thirsty."

He returned to the kitchen, poured himself a glass of water, and continued to eat. After he finished half of the noodles, he was not hungry anymore. Only then did he realize that the noodles were overcooked and the soup too salty. He gulped down some water and took the glass to see Little Ye again.

"I don't know when Feng will be back," he said to Little Ye. "It could take him all day. They may go shopping afterwards."

She opened and closed her mouth, but no words came out.

"You want to know if there's a chance for you to get back together," he said.

She nodded and stared at her hands.

"Feng won't live at home for much longer if he gets his visa. School will start in late August." Mr. Cai drank up his water. "This will hurt you, but I have to tell you the truth."

She wiped her lips with the back of her hand, finally meeting his gaze.

"Feng has a new girlfriend now," Mr. Cai said it as quickly as he could, hoping that it would hurt her less. "His mother and I have asked him to marry you. We scolded him for not taking responsibility, but he wouldn't listen to us. What else is there for parents to do? We also want our son to be happy."

Little Ye bit her hand as large tears rolled down her cheeks. Mr. Cai pitied her, as his mother's words from long ago came back to him: without parents, who was looking out for Little Ye? Even Jude, with all his power and friendship, couldn't save her from such misery.

"Who is she?" Little Ye asked.

"A neighbor girl," Mr. Cai said. "You saw her the other day."

"Why didn't your wife tell me?" Little Ye ripped at the yellow lace on her dress. "She promised to help me with the twins. Liar!"

"My wife doesn't lie." Mr. Cai's voice softened. "Feng is the one to blame. Our son is an only child and rather willful. He's less mature than what you might expect of a man his age." As he rambled on, Mr. Cai was aware how different Little Ye was from his cousin Xiu. Little Ye's elongated eyes on her heart-shaped face were full of longing and deep pain, without a shred of aggression. "You are more capable than Feng in a lot of—"

"Are they sleeping together?" Little Ye interrupted him.

Mr. Cai nodded, then retreated to his worktable.

Little Ye let out such a piercing wail that it reminded Mr. Cai of a funeral procession in the countryside. If his wife were here, she would've taken the weeping girl into her arms. His eyes blurred as he listened to her crying. He had not shed a tear when Xiu made a scene decades ago, had simply sat there, stone-like and dazed. For the first time he asked himself: had Xiu ever loved him? What was it, then, about this desperate young woman that led Mr. Cai to still think of her after all these years? That he had not been able to save her? Or was it that she had been unable to save herself?

Xiu had made some mistakes and eventually paid with her life. Now decades later, in spite of all her good intentions, Little Ye had first deceived Feng and then been jilted by him. In contrast, Feng had made countless mistakes and still was able to thrive, after his parents picked up the pieces for him. Was parenting an arms race to amass privilege for your child, so that he could rise while others sank? Was this kind of parenting morally corrupt? Yet, what other choice did you have in order to give your off-spring the best chance to survive—even thrive in a cutthroat society? As long as parental love was unconditional, a parent could not forsake their child's welfare in favor of someone else's.

Now, his old heart could not stand Little Ye's tears. She was carrying his grandchildren and deserved far better.

"If you're devoted to our son, we may help you get back together." He wiped the corners of his eyes. "Feng has not dated his new girlfriend for long. I can arrange for you to meet her. Seeing what Feng did to you, she'd probably break up with Feng."

"Don't you take pity on me. Save it for your son." Little Ye turned her face toward the windows. "After I got pregnant, Feng told me he'll never have children, because he doesn't wish the childhood he had on anyone else. As if he'd be unable to do anything differently! Your son is nothing but a selfish coward. And worse, he resents those who aren't."

Mr. Cai swallowed hard, but found no disagreement to voice.

"He resents me appearing in Jude's paintings?" she went on, growing more passionate. "He resents me putting food in my babies' mouths, when he won't? You're right, Tailor Cai. Feng is not mature. I guess this is the chance I took, getting pregnant by him."

She stood up from the sofa. Mr. Cai stepped back when she got near.

"Tell your son this, because I'll never see him again." She wiped tears with her wrist. "He doesn't deserve my children, nor me." She left the shop, her sobs echoing in the courtyard.

Mr. Cai remained frozen for a long while before dashing outside to call her back, afraid that in her anguish, Little Ye might harm herself. But she was nowhere to be found.

Mr. Cai returned to sit on the sofa where Little Ye had been, still lukewarm. He began to imagine a different reality: if Little Ye were his daughter, she might have grown up to become more beautiful and accomplished than Jiao. Who could tell? His daughter wouldn't even look at a loser like Feng. Finally he was grateful that Little Ye would bring her babies into a world that was grossly unjust. Could Grandpa be of any help? Perhaps there was something Mr. Cai could do.

For a starter, how would Little Ye breastfeed two babies in public? If her maternity dress already looked hideous, Mr. Cai didn't think it would be easy to buy a stylish nursing dress for the twins. He could design one for her to use both as a maternity dress and later for nursing. Since Mr. Cai hadn't made a nursing dress before, he was free to make mistakes. He went through the fabrics on the shelf and pulled out a bolt of jersey cotton in deep mulberry color. The soft slinky jersey was comfortable to wear with a hint of shimmer for glamour. In his notebook he found Little Ye's measurements and increased the bust by five centimeters for a postpartum dress. He sketched a knee-length dress and cut out two holes in the bust as an open nursing panel.

Then he tried several ways to cover up the nursing panel. What if he made the dress double-layered by adding a wrap bodice with extended wings that could be tied behind the mother's back like a sash? This would secure the nursing panel and accentuate the mother's enviable curves. Wearing elbow sleeves and a swishy skirt, she would feel pretty and comfortable in this immensely practical dress.

After reworking his design, Mr. Cai was hungry again. He returned to the dining table. The noodles had swollen up in his bowl like a pile of garbage. Still he ate it with relish, his leaden heart almost bursting into song. This was the magic to have designed something new for the first time. It made him feel young and alive, imagining one day that Little Ye would wear his dress and nurse two ravenous grandbabies.

## CHAPTER 13

Feng's passport arrived promptly after two weeks, during which Mr. Cai breathed not a word of Little Ye's last visit. Instead, Mr. Cai prepared to go with Feng to the American Consulate in Shanghai, where Feng would apply for his student visa. After they reached Shanghai by train, Mr. Cai would remain outside the American Consulate overnight to hold their place in line, while Feng would rest in a hostel to prepare for his interview the next day.

The night before their trip, Jiao came to their house and volunteered to go with Feng. Mr. Cai told her that if Feng obtained his visa, he would have only a few more weeks to live at home. Mr. Cai wanted to accompany Feng, as their trip would become a fond memory. Watching her leave with a smile, Mr. Cai pitied Jiao; there was still no sign that she'd learned about Little Ye's pregnancy.

Mr. Cai and Feng left for Shanghai on a Wednesday. The train was not as crowded as Jiao said it would be. Crossing the aisle, Mr. Cai stepped over burlap bags overstuffed with corn and lima beans. There was a vacant seat beside a man with rolled-up pant legs and mud-caked shins. Mr. Cai insisted on Feng's taking it, while he stood by Feng's booth. Feng fell asleep before the train reached its next stop. When more seats became available, the man beside Feng offered Mr. Cai his seat.

Feng was stirred awake by the commotion of the seating exchange. "Are we in Shanghai?" He yawned.

"We have three more hours to go. You go back to sleep."

Feng closed his eyes, but soon reopened them. He sat up in his seat and peered out of the windows. Was he missing Jiao or thinking about the interview that could change his life?

Mr. Cai decided to tell Feng the old news that he had concealed for weeks. "I forgot to tell you one thing, Son." He cleared his throat. Better late than never, he thought.

Feng glanced at him with wary eyes.

"Little Ye came to see you a few weeks ago. I told her you were seeing someone else."

"How did she take it?"

"She cried." The recollection brought warm tears to Mr. Cai's eyes. "She said she never wanted to see you again."

Feng drew his feet onto the seat and hugged his knees.

"She said you didn't want a child." Mr. Cai asked in a soft voice, "Was that the reason you broke up with her?"

"No." Feng's lips quivered. "I don't want a *son*. A boy is expected to succeed. I don't wish this heavy burden on anyone."

Mr. Cai was silent for a while, torn between guilt and self-defense, remembering Little Ye's final pronouncement of Feng. "A son carries on his family name," he said finally.

"I couldn't care less about my name." Feng wiped his eyes on his sleeve. "What will happen to Little Ye, Dad?"

"She will bring up the twins." Mr. Cai pushed up the window to let a gust of wind pour inside, along with the dust from the field. A few farm houses passed by quickly, looking small and insignificant. Several children at play reminded him of the happier times he'd spent with Xiu once upon a time. The lives on the farm remained the same for generations of people despite the vast changes that took place in the cities. As the train sped by, the crops in the field were flattened.

After Feng sneezed loudly, Mr. Cai pulled down the window.

"Dad, I want to ask you for a favor. If Little Ye ever comes to you for help, any sort of help, please give it to her." Feng blew his nose into the kerchief. "Will you do that for me?"

Mr. Cai nodded. There was no joy in becoming a grandparent like this, but he would have been more worried if Feng hadn't asked for his help.

"Promise me you won't turn her away as I did." Feng's eyes were brimming over with tears. "I'm begging you, because you're a kinder man than I."

Mr. Cai's face was suddenly hot with shame. "Have you told Jiao?"

Feng shifted in his seat. "She knows I had a girlfriend."

"What about the twins?"

"I'm waiting for the right time."

Mr. Cai thought of his wife and Jiao sending them off to the bus station that morning. "Don't wait too long, or it becomes deception."

"Little Ye was my first love." Feng pressed his forehead against his folded arms and sobbed. "I let her down. She gave me her everything, and I let her down."

"Not everything, Son. She will have her twins."

Mr. Cai knew he and his wife would have to pick up the pieces after Feng had caused Little Ye great harm and sorrow. If Mr. Cai had failed his son, how could he have done any better, even in hindsight? Parenting was such a trap. Did Little Ye know about the risks that she was undertaking? Who would ever want to become a parent, if he knew every trouble ahead?

Mr. Cai glimpsed a lamb kneeling on the hay to suckle, before the sheep pen flashed out of sight. Outside the train windows, monotonous rice fields stretched toward the horizon like a hand-knitted green blanket.

*     *     *

After saying goodnight to Feng at the hostel, Mr. Cai headed for the American Consulate. The night was humid with an occasional bracing breeze. The city was bustling at ten o'clock at night. Young women wore short skirts, high heels, and long hair even in this hot weather, walking alongside men who were dressed in well-fitting polos. He heard loud music from the karaoke bar on the street. The smells of grilled lamb kebab, roasted chestnuts, fried chicken, and mini wontons were enticing at the night market.

Mr. Cai had brought a folding stool and palm fan, which he used to drive away mosquitoes. He found the crowd outside the Consulate as soon as he turned onto the street. At a quarter past ten, he was already the twentieth person in line. There wasn't a young person there. Most people looked like middle-aged parents, even older than the crowd at the college entrance exams. Passers-by looked at them with thinly disguised envy.

Mr. Cai unfolded his canvas stool to sit down.

The man in front of him turned and asked with a grin, "Doing it for your child?"

"My son will be here tomorrow," Mr. Cai said proudly.

"Have you heard any news from inside?" The man pushed up the wire glasses on his nose.

"We just stepped off the train this afternoon." Mr. Cai waved his palm fan. "I haven't even warmed up my stool yet."

"You ought to prepare yourself for the worst." The man cupped a hand around his mouth to whisper, "I heard it's pretty tight."

Mr. Cai stopped smiling.

"They require a solid sponsorship for an undergraduate," the man said. "A graduate student must have a full scholarship. Where is your son going?"

"He'll study in the Textiles and Apparel Program at—"

"He must have a killer sponsor. Who dares to study such a fluffy major?"

Mr. Cai didn't know how to answer. Had Jude's advice been inaccurate?

"Yesterday a Ph.D. candidate in computer science at the University of Chicago was denied his visa." The man in front of Mr. Cai lit a Marlboro. "The reason? He only had a half-scholarship."

Mr. Cai waved his fan to disperse the smoke. If only he could move to the upwind side of the smoking man!

A woman behind Mr. Cai chimed in, "It's not good to have too much money, either." Her sandalwood fan gave out a strong scent. "I heard of a young man who had an American relative sponsor him with two hundred thousand dollars. Guess what? His application was denied: immigrant intent!"

"The immigrant intent is a deadly accusation." The man blew a few smoke rings. "You are presumed guilty until proven innocent. But who is innocent? Let me ask you, Uncle: don't you want your son to emigrate to the States?"

Mr. Cai found that he wanted to say yes, but he wasn't sure. It was the first time he heard of the term "immigrant intent." His neighbors were waiting for his answer. Mr. Cai swallowed hard and said, "I'll let my son decide where to settle down. Once he's in Texas, I'll be too far away to advise him. I don't even know English."

"You're an open-minded father," the man said. "Your son is lucky."

Mr. Cai's eyes moistened when he thought of Feng. He wished he could spend this night, perhaps the most important night of Feng's life yet, with him, instead of squatting on a canvas stool and leaning against the brick wall of the American Consulate. Under a dark sky full of shimmering stars, he imagined the tomorrow that would shape Feng's future. He covered his face with the palm fan. It was a long time before he could fall asleep.

\* \* \*

Mr. Cai woke up exhausted. His back ached from pressing against the wall all night, and his neck was sore. His eyelids twitched like crazy. Was it a good or ill omen? He recalled the conversations with his neighbors last night. The woman behind him was gone and a young woman, probably the daughter, had taken her place. She smiled at him for no apparent reason.

Mr. Cai was too preoccupied to talk to her. Meanwhile the man in front of him snored with his mouth agape. Mr. Cai envied the man who could sleep so soundly on the day that might change his child's life. The sun rose to the high branches of sycamore trees, and cicadas began to screech. It was going to be a hot day.

Just then, a bus pulled up some yards from the Consulate. Feng waved at his father as he stepped off. He wore a huge smile. Clean-shaven, his face was spotless. Mr. Cai tried to cast his worries aside and smiled back.

"Did you sleep well?" he asked Feng.

"Okay." Feng tossed his head. "How do I look?"

The kung fu haircut had grown out nicely to frame Feng's face. If only he had the brains to match his pretty face!

"Why didn't you use some gel in your hair?" Mr. Cai licked his fingers and combed Feng's hairs upward. "Now you look fine."

"You go get some breakfast," Feng said. "I'll stand in line."

Mr. Cai glanced at his watch. It was not yet eight o'clock and the Consulate would open at nine. "I'll grab a quick bite."

Before leaving, Mr. Cai introduced Feng to all his neighbors. That way, if Feng needed to step away for a minute, they would allow him back in the queue.

*     *     *

When Mr. Cai hurried back from breakfast, a worker had distributed forms to the people waiting in line. Mr. Cai found Feng filling his form with a ballpoint pen. Feng neatly printed out every alphabet.

"Double-check your answers," Mr. Cai told Feng after he finished.

Feng read aloud: "I am going to the States to study apparel design, which has been a passion of mine since childhood. Mr. Kenneth Darling, who owns a fabric store in Texas, wants to hire me as his assistant during my school breaks."

"Good." Mr. Cai patted Feng on the shoulder. He wanted to encourage Feng some more, but was afraid of making him nervous.

Feng was among the second group of people who were led inside the Consulate.

Mr. Cai cupped his hands around his mouth and shouted, "Go get it, my boy!"

Feng turned his head and nodded. His face was pale. A security guard led the group away, and Mr. Cai's heart left with Feng.

\*       \*       \*

The first group of people came out. A few looked ecstatic, while the rest were somber. A thin middle-aged man burst into tears in front of the crowd.

"I resigned from my hospital post and borrowed a large sum of money," he said. "I gave up everything I worked for and was intent on going to the States, but the Consulate denied me. What am I going to do now?"

Mr. Cai, unable to watch anymore, turned to face the opposite direction. Feng was not in the league of most people who came here for visas. Perhaps his neighbor was right: Feng was too bold to have ventured here. Mr. Cai stood facing the wall, and racked his brains for the comforting words he would have to say to Feng: at least there was trade school; at least there was still Jiao . . .

The crowd began to chatter again. Mr. Cai peered up and held his breath. The second group of people was coming outside. He looked and looked but couldn't find Feng.

"Dad!"

Mr. Cai heard a call and spun around. He almost tripped over Feng's foot before his son grabbed his elbow.

"I got the visa, Dad! I'm going to the States!"

"Really?" Mr. Cai asked.

Feng nodded.

Mr. Cai clutched Feng's arm. "You're not joking?"

"No! You're hurting me." Feng grinned so deeply that crow's feet were etched in his face.

Mr. Cai cried out, "My good son!" and kissed his face.

"What're you doing?" Feng wiped his cheek with his cuff and dragged his father away from the crowd.

"Can't a father kiss his son?" Mr. Cai held Feng's face in his hands and kissed him on the forehead. "Allow me to be proud of you for once, Cai Feng."

"Let's telegraph Mom."

"And ask her to share the news with Jiao?" Mr. Cai winked.

"No," Feng said. "I will tell Jiao myself, in person."

"Let's go." Mr. Cai almost bounded across the street towards the bus stop, but felt Feng pulling his shirttail. As a car whizzed by before Mr. Cai's face, he saw why: Feng had stopped him from running a red light.

Mr. Cai panted and smiled gratefully at his son beside him. Feng stood on the sidewalk, sturdy and erect as a young pine. With spotted sunlight cast on his face, he looked poised, content, and grown up.

*     *     *

Two weeks later, Mr. Cai led his guests to the upstairs suite of the Fuchun Teahouse. At a round table, six place settings lay upon a starched pink tablecloth. A freshly cut bouquet bloomed in the center like a trophy. Their rosewood chairs were embellished with carved grapes and songbirds on their armrests and high backs.

"Here we are," Feng said, holding Jiao's hand.

Jiao nudged him gently. "You should sit beside your parents."

"This is his last supper with us before his departure," Mr. Cai said. "Let him choose where to sit."

Feng moved toward the wall with Jiao. His parents sat down at Feng's right hand, while Mr. Ouyang and his wife took the seats by Jiao's left.

"I'm not gone for good." Feng poured tea for Jiao. "I'll come home and visit you during my school breaks."

"Do us a favor." Mr. Cai sat back as a waiter put down a bottle of green bamboo leaf liquor and several cold dishes on the rolling tabletop. "We can't afford your airplane tickets on top of tuition. You'd better stay put until you have made enough money to travel." Mr. Cai lifted a warm towel from a ceramic dish to wipe his face and hands.

"Don't be so hard on your son." Mr. Ouyang rolled the tabletop to move the appetizers toward Feng and Jiao. "If my daughter studies abroad, I'll let her visit us whenever she cares to. I'll borrow money for her airfare if I have to."

"A father should not pamper a son as he might a daughter." Mr. Cai patted Feng's bicep. "My son ought to brave the hardships. Nobody will hand him a good life on a silver platter. Naturally a parent is more protective toward a daughter."

Mr. Cai meant to advertise Feng to the Ouyang family. His son had had little upon which to recommend himself until a few weeks ago. Knowing that Feng intended to ask Jiao to marry him, Mr. Cai was compelled to exaggerate Feng's masculinity to the Ouyangs, who might not yet view Feng as a worthy match for their daughter.

Mrs. Ouyang put a salt and pepper shrimp on Jiao's plate. "A couple can only have one child nowadays," she said. "We would've raised a son the same way as we did Jiao. We never told our daughter what she couldn't do because she is a girl."

"My parents spoiled me rotten." Jiao frowned after taking a sip of liquor. "I'm helpless with housework."

"Your hand is meant to hold a pen, not a needle." Feng stroked her slim fingers. "I'll do the needle work for you."

"Jiao is a lucky girl," Mrs. Ouyang said. "A fortuneteller once said she'll land a fine husband."

Mr. Cai didn't believe that the fortuneteller had foreseen Feng as Jiao's future husband. Conceivably, Jiao could go to the States, dump Feng, and then marry another man. Since Mrs. Ouyang hadn't clarified it, Mr. Cai was prompted to take her words as a compliment.

"Did the fortuneteller say anything about me?" Feng brushed stray hairs to the back of Jiao's ear. "I am in love with *the one* who has brains to match her looks."

Jiao blushed and lifted her porcelain shot glass. "On this joyous occasion, allow me to toast Feng for his future success!"

Everyone clinked their shot glass. Mr. Cai had seen Feng on cloud nine ever since he beat the odds and got the visa. Having been an underdog until now, Feng was eager to start a new life with a sense of purpose in the States. This could be his moment in the sun. So Mr. Cai forgave him for acting brash in front of his prospective in-laws.

Feng refilled his shot glass and raised it to his brow. "I'll drink to Jiao joining me before the New Year!"

Jiao wet her lips with the liquor. "No need to drink up." She pressed Feng's wrist. "It's not good to board a plane with a hangover."

"Yes, Wife." Feng put down his shot glass obediently.

The whole table fell silent. Mr. Cai stole a glance at Mr. and Mrs. Ouyang, whose faces remained amiable and calm. Jiao's blush deepened, but she did not rebuff Feng.

Mrs. Cai nudged Feng and poured jasmine tea for him. "Who else wants tea?" she asked.

Mr. Cai covered his teacup with a hand. The Ouyangs' apparent acceptance of Feng satisfied him. Perhaps his advertisement for Feng had worked.

"I have a proposal to make." Feng addressed the table in a clear and loud voice. "I would like Jiao to stay with me tonight. That is, if she is willing."

Jiao flushed to the root of her hair. Since Mrs. Cai's subtle warning had failed to deter Feng, Mr. Cai kicked his son's shin under the table. Was Feng drunk? He'd had enough dates with Jiao and should now allow her to save face in front of her parents.

"Are you willing?" Mr. Ouyang asked his daughter in a gentle voice.

Jiao cupped her cheeks in her hands. "Do you have to embarrass me like this?" She pouted at Feng.

"I want to be with you." Feng held her shoulders and pleaded with his eyes. "Would you let me?"

Leaning her head against his shoulder, she nodded. Her parents exchanged a wary glance but offered no contradiction. Mr. Ouyang rolled the tabletop, while his wife doused a slice of pork tongue in soy sauce and put it on Jiao's plate.

The Ouyangs' calm acceptance shocked Mr. Cai. Apparently his neighbors were not at all concerned with preserving their daughter's reputation before marriage. Now he believed that the Ouyangs had indeed raised their daughter like a son.

If Feng had told her about the twins, Jiao seemed to be unfazed. What did she really see in Feng, beyond his plan to study abroad? After they settled in the States, would they start to quarrel? Surely, Jiao would not be as tolerant as Little Ye about Feng's myriad shortcomings. On the contrary, Jiao would be careful and not get pregnant until Feng proved himself to be a good husband. Now Mr. Cai regretted having boasted about Feng's masculinity, for his son might fall short of the expectations of his future in-laws.

Mr. Cai couldn't dwell on his misgivings, as Mr. Ouyang was pouring more green bamboo leaf liquor to refill everyone's shot glass. The whole table toasted the young couple for their future happiness, as if they had just become officially engaged. The liquor left a sharp taste on Mr. Cai's tongue. Beside him, tears gleamed in his wife's eyes.

*     *     *

Outside Feng's room, Mrs. Cai asked Jiao if she needed an extra coverlet. Jiao shook her head so hard that her bangs slid from side to side on her forehead.

Feng put his arm around her waist. "I'll be her coverlet," he said.

They closed the door and left the hallway in complete darkness.

Mr. Cai didn't speak until he returned to the bedroom with his wife. "Feng is practically drooling over her. Do you think she will become our daughter-in-law?"

"Not if Feng treats her like Little Ye."

So his misgivings were not unfounded. Mr. Cai forced a chuckle. "You see how obedient Feng is to her."

"Feng was once sweet to Little Ye. After he got her into trouble, Feng found all sorts of fault with her." She ran her hand in her hair. "You wait and see: he's just enamored by Jiao."

"Do you think she knows about the twins?" Mr. Cai asked.

"I sure hope so. But I doubt it." She sighed and peered at her face in the mirror. "What am I going to wear tomorrow?"

Mr. Cai was glad to talk of something cheerful. "How about your crepe blazer? You look good in forest green."

"I need something that catches the eye." She unlocked an old trunk in the closet. "Will you give me a hand?"

They pulled the trunk to lay it open before the bed. Mrs. Cai fumbled through a pile of old clothes until she found a pink blouse, smoothing out its wrinkles with her fingers.

He smiled. "Aren't you too old for peach blossoms?"

"I wore it inside that blue uniform when I married you." She put on the blouse, which stretched over her torso. "I need to let it out in the chest and waist, then press it well."

"Don't wear it tomorrow." He pulled her sleeve. "You have a dozen nicer blouses."

"Our son is leaving home." Her voice broke. "I want him to see me from the plane, all right?"

He followed her into the sewing room, where she started pulling out the slipstitches from the blouse with a pair of scissors. The peach blossoms became redder and more vivid under the soft lamplight.

"You could've given this to Jiao tonight." He sighed. "It's almost like their wedding night."

"This blouse suits a country girl better. Little Ye would look mighty pretty in it."

He bent down to whisper into her ear, "You sound like you prefer Little Ye to Jiao."

"So what if I do?" She tossed her head. "Feng is my only child. Even though he is a rascal, I want him to marry for love."

Mr. Cai watched his wife craning her neck over the needlework. In spite of her disappointment in Feng, she allowed him to marry for love. In the end no one had a choice in the matters of heart. Mr. Cai had married the best woman, because his happy marriage had nearly obliterated his past disgrace. He hadn't thought of Xiu until he began to worry about Feng's repeating his mistake. Yet, both Feng and Little Ye had surprised him, and so would Jiao.

As Mrs. Cai pedaled the sewing machine, the soft chugging of the wheels broke the silence. Across the hallway, the young couple's room was dark and quiet. Perhaps they slept early, Mr. Cai consoled himself. Both of them had appeared a little tipsy before they retired for the night.

*　　*　　*

The next day Jiao wore a lavender dress that brought out her peaches-and-cream complexion. With her hair neatly braided, she looked more like a schoolgirl than a wife. Mr. Cai invited her to ride the airport bound inter-town bus with his family to Shanghai. After they arrived at Hongqiao Airport, she quickly found a luggage cart for Feng.

Mr. Cai loaded the two heavy suitcases onto the cart. He pushed the cart a few steps, then turned to Feng and said, "You do it. I can't help you after you check into the airport."

Feng released Jiao's hand to push the cart himself. He wore khaki shorts and a jean jacket over a short-sleeved polo. Feng had checked the weather in Austin and said it was hotter than Yangzhou.

"Take good care of yourself," Mrs. Cai said to Feng as they walked along. "Dress warmly when autumn comes. Wear your galoshes when it rains."

"Mom, I'm not a baby."

When they reached the entrance to the airport, Feng set aside his cart and stroked Jiao's elbow with his hand. Facing his parents, he asked, "Look after Jiao for me, would you?" His face convulsed at the mention of her name. Then he let go of Jiao and pushed the cart forward with all his strength.

"Take it easy, Son!" his mother called after him.

Feng strode into the airport without looking back. Through the glass door, Mr. Cai saw him wipe tears with his sleeve. Feng had finally grown up, Mr. Cai thought with some pride: he didn't want to shed tears in front of his parents.

Mr. Cai knocked on the window to get his son's attention for a final goodbye, but a security guard shushed him and ordered him back from the entrance. "My son, my own flesh and blood," Mr. Cai said to himself. His arms ached for a last embrace with Feng, who stood in the check-in line with a hand covering his eyes.

"I have finally unleashed my son." Mr. Cai tried to choke back his tears. "Why do I feel so lousy?"

"Because he's our pride and joy." His wife sobbed into a red handkerchief. "Why do we send him halfway across the globe? I mean, is all this really worth it?"

"I know it is," Jiao said. Her face was so pale that her lips appeared startlingly red in comparison. "Studying abroad is not the only way to get ahead, but it's the best way. He'll avoid the cutthroat competition on the domestic job market. Being a creative person, Feng is more likely to succeed in a relaxed environment like the U.T. Austin."

Mr. Cai couldn't believe what he heard. If not for her pale face and wet eyes, he would've mistaken Jiao for some career counselor rather than a lover.

"Aren't you going to miss him?" Mr. Cai asked her. "I know he'll miss you."

"Of course I'll miss him." Jiao lowered her head. "One night of love marks us for life." She wrapped and unwrapped her kerchief on her wrist.

Apparently Jiao had used her wit and femininity to command Feng's heart—no wonder he was so obedient.

"Poor girl." Mrs. Cai stroked Jiao's hand. "You come and visit us often."

"Maybe when I take breaks from studying for my English exams." Jiao forced a smile and glanced at the taxicabs that lined up by the sidewalk. The shyness and vulnerability had gone from her face. She looked confident and resolute, and seemed a few years older.

Tears filled Mr. Cai's eyes as he imagined the lonely life that Feng would have to face. Feng had never lived at a boarding school or university. Even at the continuation school, he had Little Ye look after him. Would life in the dorm agree with him? Would he get a nice roommate? Could he wash his dirty socks and cook for himself? Who would take care of him if he got sick?

Mr. Cai stood with his back to Jiao and wiped his eyes with his cuff. The Boeing 747 parked on the runway like a giant pigeon. In less than an hour it would take his beloved son to a new life. Mr. Cai held his wife's hand to lead her to the end of the railing, where they could see the passenger windows on one side of the plane.

Spreading a handkerchief on the cement step, he said, "Have a seat, Wife." He smoothed out her hair ruffled by the wind. "Jiao, you don't have to wait with us if you have other things to do."

"Am I not needed here?" Jiao glanced at her watch. "I can wait, you know. I have leave from the teachers meeting."

"We'll handle him all right," Mr. Cai said. "You shouldn't be absent for your first meeting."

Jiao gazed at them for a moment, considering. "Thank you for inviting me here today. I'll see you back home." She swung the imitation alligator skin purse onto her shoulder and made her way toward the bus stop.

"I know she wouldn't insist on staying." Mr. Cai wrapped his arm around his wife's waist. "It's just you and me, like the day he was born."

"Do you think he can see us from the plane?" She blinked her red eyes.

"When the plane takes off, Feng will find his mother covered in peach blossoms, standing on the land that bore and raised him."

They sat with their arms around each other. Hours seemed to slide by before the plane started moving. Mrs. Cai leapt to her feet and waved the red kerchief over her head. Tears streamed down Mr. Cai's cheeks, but he didn't wipe them. He shouted "a safe journey" to the plane that lifted off the ground. His wife cried out "Cai Feng" at the top of her lungs. She kept on waving her kerchief after the plane disappeared into thick clouds.

# CHAPTER 14

Two months after Feng's departure, Jude paid a surprise visit to Mr. Cai. He waltzed into the shop and dropped a fashion catalogue on Mr. Cai's worktable. The magazine featured Jude on the cover wearing a black suit. The picture reminded Mr. Cai of some Hollywood star whose name he couldn't recall.

"Is that really you?" Mr. Cai screwed up his eyes. "Why did you dye your hair black?"

"They decided that black hair would be better for this line of clothing, more enigmatic and masculine looking." Jude pulled out a Parker fountain pen from his shirt pocket. "I can autograph it for you."

"What do you take me for, some bimbo?" Mr. Cai chuckled. "I know you're not such a stud as you look."

"That really hurts my feelings." Jude signed the cover with his Chinese name, Red Moral, in fluent running hand. "I took you for my friend."

"I *am* your friend," Mr. Cai said. "A real friend doesn't need your autograph. I haven't heard from you in ages. How've you been?"

"Just grand." The tip of Jude's tongue slipped out to wet his upper lip. "I met a nice man on the model team. No, I won't tell you more about him." Jude straddled the armrest of the sofa. "You're nosier than my father."

Mr. Cai noticed that Jude wore his earrings, though his right wrist was bare. "Where's your bracelet?" he asked. "Did you give it to your new best friend?" He met Jude's protesting eyes and chuckled. "Your father cannot pry into your life, because he's on the other side of the globe. Both he and I are far away from our sons. We ought to make a deal: I keep an eye on you for him, while he looks after Feng for me."

"Is he bothering you again, Jude?" Mrs. Cai entered with a tall glass of plum juice. "How are your parents?"

Jude thanked her for the drink. "My father sent me some family photos. One of them is my mother in the hospital. She was frail, still beautiful inside and out." Jude broke into a wistful smile. "Dad is coming around, I think. How's Feng getting along?"

Mr. Cai lost his smile. "Feng is pretty lonely out there by himself." Remembering Jude's friendship with Little Ye, Mr. Cai decided not to tell Jude how often Feng pressed Jiao to join him.

"Loneliness is normal when one moves to a new country." Jude made a face that suggested the plum juice was sour. "My first days in China were also hard. I disliked everything from the canteen food to my bedding. There was nothing to watch on TV. When I went shopping, I was stalked like some foreign royalty. The peddlers charged me five times as much as they did the locals. Still, I reminded myself it would've been worse for me to live at home. After a while, my Chinese improved. I began to make friends and learned to bargain. One summer I traveled all over Northeast China on less than eight hundred yuan."

"I hope Feng doesn't feel that his life with us was horrible." Mr. Cai sighed. "It was the only life he had."

"It's because of your persistence that Feng was able to go study in the States," Jude said.

"But I miss him. I miss pressing him to eat fish soup. I miss spying on him to see if he is studying. I miss lecturing him when he wasted his time." Mr. Cai wrung his hands. "I even miss getting upset over him."

"He's just crying happy tears," Mrs. Cai chimed in. "He forgot that he used to call Feng a punishment from his past life."

"Feng is no worse than I at his age," Mr. Cai finally admitted. "He didn't like school. Who does except for a few smart people?

I couldn't leave him to his own devices, so I pushed him hard. Thank goodness, he has aced a statistics exam at U.T." Mr. Cai's eyes grew moist in spite of himself. "I grew up without a father. I tried twice as hard to be a good father to Feng."

"You sure did." His wife winked at him.

Jude looked after Mrs. Cai as she entered the sewing room. "Feng will become a father in a few months, but he's not even here to take part in it."

Mr. Cai frowned, rather thrown off by the change of subject.

"If he made Little Ye pregnant in the States, Feng would have to pay child support. Here, he gets off scot-free!" Jude pulled out the straw from his glass.

"Not scot-free," Mr. Cai said quickly. "We will help care for our grandchildren."

"Is that a promise?" Jude had a look of distaste as if he'd eaten something bad. "What about your son? Isn't Feng afraid of retribution and becoming impotent?"

Mr. Cai couldn't believe that Little Ye had shared with Jude her bitter curse.

"I'm glad to be a foreigner. After living here for three years, I still know nothing about China." Jude bent his straw. "I hurt my best friend not once but twice: first with the painting, then with the sponsorship. How can I ever make it up to her?"

Mr. Cai peered at the sewing room. Its door was wide open. He knew his wife could hear every word. Why didn't she come out and talk with Jude? Had she disappeared on purpose so that Jude could berate him?

"I thought the law would protect Little Ye." Jude shook his head. "I was so wrong."

"Chinese people mostly rely on morals and conscience. To us, laws are inferior to common sense." Mr. Cai licked his dry lips. Normally he didn't drink juice during the work hours. Now he called his wife to bring him a glass of plum juice.

"Well, being a surrogate father—I don't envy you at all, Mr. Tailor."

Mr. Cai cleared his throat. "That's going a bit far. I meant we will send money to Little Ye to help her."

"That's not enough." Jude's face grew stern, almost severe. "Tell Feng that he cannot outrun his problems by relocating. I once ran away to China. It didn't help until I faced my father." Jude drained his juice and got to his feet. "You grow stronger by taking responsibility. There is no shortcut."

Mr. Cai waited for harsher words, but Jude seemed to have finished and was ready to leave. Mr. Cai breathed a sigh of relief. "Come see us again, young man. Now Feng is gone, I have plenty of time to chat with you." Mr. Cai heard himself say these words with little sincerity.

"I will." Jude gave him a hand-salute. "You are my best friend now, because we did each other a real favor." When Mrs. Cai appeared with a tall glass of plum juice, Jude nodded at her and walked away in merry quick steps.

Mr. Cai waited for Jude to have gone far enough away. "Why did Jude chastise me like some petty criminal?"

"Was he chastising?" Mrs. Cai could barely suppress a smile. "Maybe good advice jars on the ear."

"Since when have you liked Jude meddling in our affairs?"

Mrs. Cai reached out a hand to pat her husband's forehead, as if he were a cranky child.

*       *       *

A week later Mr. Cai received a new letter from Feng. He read several passages to his wife: "My roommate lies on the couch drinking beer all the time. Instead of doing homework, he keeps the TV at full blast and falls asleep in front of it. He never takes out the garbage. I have to clean up after his weekend binges with his buddies.

"Worst of all, they love to grill meat whenever the weather is warm. The smell is nauseating. Last week Mr. Darling invited me to a barbecue at his house. I ended up dining on chips, beans, and corn on the cob. Afterwards I took a long shower to scrub off the awful smell from my skin and hair." Mr. Cai turned the paper over. "Please ask Jiao to hurry up and join me. I'm miserable without her."

In the space below, there were several drawings of ponchos with different patterns, colored in with orange, pink, blue and tan lines in varying widths and lengths.

"He didn't mention how his studies are going," Mr. Cai said to his wife.

"Read between the lines." She pointed at the letter. "His room-mate never studies. Can he do as well as our son?"

Mr. Cai admitted that she had a point. He liked the poncho doodles: the vivid colors were eye-catching and pleasing despite the busy line patterns.

After dinner, Mr. Cai visited Jiao to show her Feng's letter. She read it with a bemused smile. "I'm pretty sure I passed the TOE-FL. I'll take the GRE exams in November, just in time for spring admission."

"When do you think you'll join Feng?" he asked.

"January at the earliest." She excused herself and popped open her eyelids to put in a few eyedrops. "It's the best I can do. I'm a full-time teacher. My graduating class demands my utmost atten-tion, you know." She wiped away tears from her cheek.

"I'll leave you, then." Mr. Cai stood up. "Feng and we look for-ward to your good news."

"Wait." Jiao opened a drawer to retrieve a red and blue striped airmail envelope. "Feng wrote me, too. I've been meaning to ask you: what do you know about his ex-girlfriend?"

"Oh." Mr. Cai wanted to sit down but didn't dare, so he squat-ted halfway above his seat. "What did Feng tell you?"

"Not much, but I can tell he's hiding something. You know I will find out sooner or later." Jiao blinked her eyes rapidly as if being irritated by a fallen eyelash.

"Right." Mr. Cai hung his head and thought about Jude's warn-ing. In the States, Feng would have to pay child support by law.

Jiao was too smart to let him off easily. Mr. Cai should have given her a warning. "You met her before."

"When?"

"In passing." Mr. Cai bit the inside of his lower lip. "After your exams, I will tell you everything. You will have time to decide what to do."

Jiao looked stricken, her eyes welling up, but she didn't press him. "Thank you, Mr. Cai. That means a lot to me."

Seeing himself out, Mr. Cai was convinced that Jiao was an overachiever. She would deal with many pressures, even the potential conflict with Little Ye, with a decisive hand.

*     *     *

Jiao kept her promise and made ready for the States in mid-January. She had caused quite a stir at Yangzhou High School: the department chair criticized Jiao for abandoning the students, and she had to pay back the Ministry of Education her four-year college tuition before she could resign from her post.

Mr. Ouyang paid the ten thousand yuan without batting an eyelash. Over a celebratory drink of Maotai with Mr. Cai, he had explained that Jiao would earn back the money in American dollars. For starters, she had won herself a full scholarship for the MA in ESL at the University of Texas. Her stipend as a teaching assistant was fifteen thousand dollars a year, equal to one hundred twenty thousand yuan. As a result, Jiao obtained her student visa from the American Consulate with a "Good luck" and a big smile in addition to a stamp of approval. Similarly, Feng seemed to have earned the Ouyangs' seal of approval, him being the catalyst of Jiao's move abroad. Mr. Ouyang spoke of Jiao and Feng's marriage prospect with stars in his eyes.

On the day of Jiao's departure, Mr. and Mrs. Cai, together with Mr. and Mrs. Ouyang, accompanied her to Shanghai. At the airport entrance, Mrs. Ouyang held Jiao's hand and burst into tears. Jiao promised her mother that she would take good care of herself. Mrs. Ouyang begged Mrs. Cai to tell Feng that he should treat Jiao kindly. Mrs. Cai assured Mrs. Ouyang that she would write to Feng. Jiao cried her way into the airport, as if it were the most miserable day of her life.

Mr. Cai cringed at the sight of their tears. Although Feng had left only five months ago, Mr. Cai found it hard to relate to such strong emotions. A secret worry gnawed at Mr. Cai, as he wondered that Jiao might have told her parents about Feng's twins: had Jiao told her mother, father, none, or both? Among the people who shed tears, Mr. Cai pitied Mr. Ouyang the most, who might've been less distraught if he were sending off a son instead of a daughter.

The four parents waited two hours for the plane to take off. Mrs. Ouyang wept on and off the whole time.

Afterwards Mr. Ouyang treated them to lunch. Mrs. Ouyang ate little but drank plenty of water, perhaps to replenish her tears. After the meal, they went sightseeing at Shanghai Zoo. On that warm winter day, the zoo seemed to be in a state of hibernation. The giant panda exhibit was closed. The chimpanzees were asleep in their cage. Even the monkeys looked bored, scratching each other's back with their eyes half-closed. Much to Mr. Cai's relief, Mr. Ouyang suggested they take a break.

Mr. Cai bought sautéed dried tofu and Coca Cola for everyone. Sitting on the grass field, Mrs. Ouyang dug into her snack as if she hadn't eaten for days. Mr. Cai was glad to see her appetite return, and offered her his carton of dried tofu. She was finally pressed into accepting it. Mr. Cai left the Ouyangs to eat by themselves and went to sit beside his wife.

He clinked her cola with his bottle and toasted, "To Feng's happy days." He took a hearty swig and nearly coughed it back out. The cola, which cost as much as a meal, tasted like cheap cough syrup.

"I never thought I would see this day." She fed him a piece of dried tofu.

He nodded and burped with the taste of cola in his mouth. This time, he could tell the cola apart from the cough syrup: the cola had a hint of tang like smoked meat. Even Feng liked its taste, he had told his parents in a letter. Mr. Cai took another swig and it went down more easily.

"I've been waiting to see what Jiao might do," Mr. Cai told his wife. "One night out of blue, she interrogated me about Feng's ex-girlfriend. I didn't think I could cover it up, so after her exams, I told her about the twins. By then she didn't seem to be surprised, and might have guessed at it." Mr. Cai stole a glance at Mr. and Mrs. Ouyang, who were absorbed in their own conversation. "Do you think she told her parents?"

"Doesn't seem like it." Mrs. Cai fed him another piece of dried tofu and pushed the toothpick a little deeper in his mouth. "Jiao is a sensible woman and will work it out with Feng first, and not frighten her parents needlessly."

"She also really wants to study abroad." Mr. Cai pulled up a handful of withered grass by their roots. "To the extent that she'll put up with Feng."

"How do you know she doesn't love Feng?" His wife pushed his knee. "Feng adores her and is willing to wait on her."

"Maybe she will break Feng's heart as he did Little Ye's." Mr. Cai ripped the grass apart with his fingers, then dusted his hands. "If there's retribution, Feng has it coming." Oddly enough, it gave him comfort that Feng would not get off scot-free, as Jude had accused him of.

"I agree. At least he's in the States and studying what he likes." Mrs. Cai grasped his fingertips. "You know, poor Little Ye needs our help."

"Yes, I already made her a nursing dress. If Jude hadn't chastised me last time, I would have remembered to give it to him. Remind me next time when he comes by."

Mr. Cai smoothed down a few white hairs on his wife's temple. Having known her for nearly a quarter of a century, he had witnessed the surfacing of every piece of white hair, sun spot, blemish and wrinkle on his wife's face, all of which wrote the journal of their lives together. In his eyes, she was even more beautiful now than when they had first met. How could he not have known? Mrs. Cai was his first true love, while his romance with Xiu had been a bittersweet mistake, having faded into oblivion.

Mrs. Cai didn't look at him but was lost in her own thoughts. "Can we afford Feng's second year?" she asked.

He had to consider this carefully. "I have distant relatives in Taiwan. I may write to them if I have trouble raising the money." Mr. Cai put an arm around his wife's shoulder and drew her close. "I've been waiting for this day when my son shows good prospects. Finally I'm able to face my relatives without shame."

After sitting for a while longer, the Ouyangs stood up from the grass field and dusted their pants, then walked over hand in hand. Mrs. Ouyang's eyelids were puffy, though the redness in her eyes had cleared up.

"Do you think Jiao has reached Japan yet?" she asked with a faint smile.

Mr. Cai shielded his eyes with a hand to gaze at the sky. "I reckon she is flying above the Pacific Ocean, free as a bird."

"Seeing the world we've never been able to," Mr. Ouyang echoed.

All four parents stood up to cast their eyes upon the eastern sky. The clouds had parted and left the sky a soft turquoise. As Mr. Cai took a deep, deep breath, it seemed to fill his lungs with the salty air of the Pacific.

\* \* \*

Longan was expensive this year, so Mr. Cai told his wife not to waste money on it. Winter was the busiest season for Mr. Cai. More young couples were getting married in order to go on their honeymoons during the Spring Festival. As the Festival drew near, many customers brought in luxurious brocades for wedding wardrobes and holiday dresses. Mr. Cai often worked late into the night when the rest of his neighborhood was in slumber. His relatives in Taiwan had not replied to his letter; therefore, Mr. Cai would have to depend on his business to support Feng.

Sometimes his wife went to bed early and left him alone in the workroom. On those long nights, Mr. Cai would gaze up at Feng's photo, framed and hung on the wall. In front of a tower that pierced into the blue sky, Feng stood and wrapped his left arm around Jiao's shoulders. He raised his right hand, pointing his pinkie and index finger toward heaven, and his thumb pressing his two remaining fingers down to the palm. "Hook 'Em Horns, Dad!" the caption of the photo read.

This photo had come with Feng's first letter after Jiao's arrival. Since then Mr. Cai hadn't heard from his son. Perhaps the couple were busy getting reacquainted and moving into their new dorm apartment together. Mr. Cai hadn't detected any animosity from his neighbors, so things might have worked out for Feng and Jiao so far. Feng had finished his first semester with straight As, despite his struggle with English, and had been awarded a scholarship that waived two-thirds of his tuition. When Mr. Ouyang asked what Feng was studying, Mr. Cai had answered with some pride, "Feng showed me his course schedule, but damn, it's all in English!"

Now Mr. Cai mimicked Feng's gesture and waved his hand at the photo. "Way to go, Son." All his exhaustion was gone. He could go on for another hour without eating a midnight snack.

Mr. Cai and his wife kept on working until the New Year's Eve. Then, they took a day off to clean the house and prepare several dishes to join the Ouyang family for a New Year's Eve dinner. Mr. Cai went to the farmers' market and bought rice cakes and scallions. Half of the market was empty in the early afternoon after peddlers had gone home to prepare the festive family dinners. He passed by the few stands that sold the Spring Festival couplets, New Year's papercuts, and strings of firecrackers. A young woman sitting on a stool displayed bamboo birdcages, the size of half a cutting board. Each cage contained a straw bird with red and green feathers.

"Uncle, would you like to hear my magpies sing?" When she lifted a birdcage, the straw bird chirped loudly and tottered from side to side by some hidden mechanism, like an opera singer making her grand entrance.

"It sure is loud," Mr. Cai said.

"Would you want one, Uncle?" She flung a red muffler around her neck, her braids reaching to her lap. "Magpies bring good luck to your household and keep everyone well." She reminded Mr. Cai of Little Ye when he had first met her. Now it had been months since he'd seen her face, her finished dress hanging undelivered in the shop.

"Magpies are black and white, not red and green," he said.

"Uncle, I've seen plenty of magpies with green tails and some with red feathers." She was not as pretty as Little Ye, but she was younger. Her cheeks were ruddy and without frostbite scars. "Red and green are auspicious colors. Red stands for festival, and green for spring. Together they celebrate the Spring Festival."

"I'll buy it." Mr. Cai reached into his pant pocket for the wallet.

"These are my last two cages." She gave him his change. "I'll go home and have my New Year's Eve dinner after I sell them." Her voice was a little hoarse. Perhaps she had been waiting on the windy street all day.

Mr. Cai handed the change back to her to buy both birdcages. He would hang one on his shop door to have it greet his customers when they entered. The other would make a nice present for Mr. and Mrs. Ouyang, who might feel lonesome after Jiao's departure. A straw magpie was no consolation to two parents in their empty nest. Yet, it burst into song at a touch of one's fingertip. Unlike a real bird, it never needed to eat or pass its waste.

"Thank you, Uncle." The girl bowed at him so deeply that the muffler slipped off her neck.

"Happy New Year to you, too." Mr. Cai's words were drowned out by the chirping when he lifted his birdcages. He waited for the noise to die down and added, "Wear your muffler, Girl. Don't get frostbite on your cheeks."

With a giggle she wound the muffler tightly around her face. "You're awfully kind, Uncle."

*          *          *

Mr. Cai carried the birdcage to the New Year's Eve dinner covered in a red kerchief. He walked slowly, careful to keep his balance. When Mr. Ouyang patted him on the arm, the straw bird twittered as loudly as twenty real magpies. Mrs. Ouyang was so shocked that she spilled her soup. When Mr. Cai lifted the kerchief to display his gift, all four of them burst into laughter. Mrs. Ouyang put the cage at the center of the dining table, and arranged the dishes around the singing bird.

There was a lot more food than they had appetite for. Mrs. Cai's vegetarian fried rice cakes were barely touched. So were the pork and shepherd's purse dumplings, a favorite of Jiao's. The four parents ate a little of every dish and spent the rest of their evening reminiscing about their children. Whenever their conversation wound down, Mr. Cai prodded the birdcage and made the magpie sing. They all laughed and tried to feel happy, for there was nothing missing in their lives but their children. The night was bittersweet as they found company in each other's loneliness.

It was snowing outside after the Cais said goodnight to the Ouyangs. The ground was covered with a thin layer of snowflakes, gleaming in the moonlight. The northwest wind had died down. An occasional firecracker broke the silence of the night.

"Feng has only written us once since Jiao arrived," Mrs. Cai complained as they passed by the mailbox. "He seems to have forgotten about the Spring Festival." She stamped her feet on the doorstep.

Mr. Cai remembered an old saying: on festive occasions more than ever, one thinks of his dear ones far away. Sometimes he wished Feng hadn't left them. "I'll send him a lunar calendar," he said instead, "and money for him to call us once a month."

The magpie chirped as she unlocked the door. "This is the silliest thing I've ever seen," she said.

"It's been awfully quiet since Feng left." Mr. Cai fumbled for the light switch. "I could use some company now and then."

"A straw bird is no company. It's a waste of money."

The fluorescent light flooded the room and stung his eyes. When the phone rang, his wife answered it in the hallway. "Feng, what time is it for you? You remembered. Happy Spring Festival to you!" She handed the phone to her husband. "He wants to talk to *you*."

"Feng!" Before Mr. Cai could say more, Feng had interrupted him.

"I've been sleeping on the couch, Dad." After a pause he asked, "Did you tell her?"

Mr. Cai began to stutter. "Well, you know, you can't hide a fact like—"

"I thought so. You may be right. I just don't know what to do." Feng spoke quickly as if to save money, which prompted Mr. Cai to hurry up and be as brief as possible.

"Give her some time. If it's not meant to be—"

"But I love her!"

Mrs. Cai leaned forward to listen in on their conversation.

"Then it's even more important to give her time to think it over." After exchanging a look with his wife, Mr. Cai asked, "Did she tell her parents?"

"Not yet, she doesn't want them to worry."

"That's understandable, or they might not have allowed her to join you." After some hesitation, Mr. Cai added, "Jude said in States you would have to pay child support."

Feng sighed. "I'm doing my best, Dad. I worked during the holidays in Mr. Darling's shop and earned a little to pay for this call. I'd better go."

"Okay, don't worry. We will help you any way we can."

There was a pause. When Feng spoke again, his voice sounded muffled. "I know."

Was Feng crying? Before Mr. Cai could think of any comforting words, he heard a click and then the dial tone. He hung up
the phone and looked at his wife's face. "What should we do?"

She forced a smile. "Feng knows what to do. You can help him.
I have my hands full." She headed for the bedroom without turning back to see if he followed her.

*       *       *

Before breakfast the next day, the phone rang again. Jude called
and said that he would like to visit them. In the kitchen, Mrs.
Cai was preparing the red bean and lotus seed dessert soup. She
didn't sweep the snow for fear of losing their luck. The god of
wealth didn't care if it was money or snow; the act of sweeping
would tell the god that the shop wasn't intent on accumulating,
money among other things.

Mrs. Cai laid a rug outside their doorstep so that their visitors
wouldn't slip on the snow. Near ten o'clock, when the dessert
soup was ready, the magpie twittered on the door.

Mr. Cai greeted Jude at the door. "Every time the magpie sings,
our shop has a visitor!" He chuckled at his couplet.

Jude bowed with folded hands. "May you be healthy and prosperous, Mr. Tailor!"

"Happy New Year to you, Jude!" Mr. Cai bowed back. "Why,
you didn't have to bring us a gift."

Jude carried a rattan basket and set it down on the sofa. "Actually, I found this outside your door."

Mr. Cai lifted the plaid blanket that covered the basket.
What a sight he beheld: an infant with a puckered face! Mr.
Cai backed away to lean against his worktable, lest he should
faint.

"What sort of a joke is this?" he asked, trying to catch his breath.

"It was on your doorstep," Jude said.

"It's here!" Mrs. Cai let out a low cry as she entered with
the dessert soup. She laid the tray on the tea table and bent

down to look into the basket. "Is it a boy or girl?" She fumbled under the infant's blanket, uncovered a letter and gave it to Mr. Cai.

Mr. Cai struggled to put on his reading glasses with trembling hands. He read aloud: "Mr. and Mrs. Cai, this is your grandson from Feng and Little Ye. I had the twins, a girl and a boy. I cannot possibly raise two children with my income. I am not giving you my girl, because you don't deserve her. Mr. Cai obviously prefers a grandson to a granddaughter, so I give you Cai Ye. I insist on calling him Ye, as I'm his mother. I don't want him to forget me. It breaks my heart to leave him to you, but I don't have enough milk to feed both twins. I'm going to Shenzhen to look for a well-paid job. People there don't mind hiring an unwed mother, I heard. I entreat you to love and care for your grandson, your flesh and blood. One day he will be reunited with his sister. Happy Spring Festival, Jinhua on her way to Shenzhen."

Mr. Cai ripped the glasses from his nose and asked Jude, "Did you bring the basket here?"

Jude shrugged. His face was inscrutable. For the first time, Mr. Cai hated Jude's blue eyes that seemed to contain unfathomable secrets.

His wife took off the infant's cap to study his features. "He has Feng's nose and forehead." The baby cooed as she gently slid his cap back on. "Our grandson has beautiful hair."

Evidently his wife had been expecting the baby. Mr. Cai studied her face, then Jude's, but neither looked back at him. For months his wife had been acting distracted and secretive. So this was her reason. Indeed he had been forewarned, but why hadn't she told him?

The baby yawned. All his features were squeezed to the middle of his face. The adults burst into laughter together.

"He looks just like Feng when he was a baby," Mrs. Cai said, "except for the freckles under his eyelids, which he got from Little Ye."

Mr. Cai couldn't see the baby's hands inside his swaddle. "Is he left-handed?" he said to himself. "Or vegetarian?"

As if having heard him, the baby opened his eyes and smiled, showing his toothless gums. His grandson liked seeing his face! Mr. Cai's heart was flooded with joy.

"Poor darling, are you hungry?" His wife lifted the baby from the basket for a cuddle.

Now that Mr. Cai was a grandfather, he had to act like one.

"I think we'll manage." Mr. Cai pulled down the cap to cover the baby's ears. "Feng's residence card was canceled. We can try adopting the baby as ours, so he may have the food ration."

"Allow me to visit him from time to time." Jude smacked his lips and cooed over the baby. "I'm your Uncle Jude."

Mrs. Cai said, "I hope this little fellow won't grow up to be a heartbreaker like his dad."

Jude winked at Mr. Cai. "You'll have to raise him differently."

Mr. Cai grinned. By now he didn't doubt that his wife had procured a twin with Jude's help. "You two didn't have to conspire against me like this," he said. "I may be a silly old man, but even a wise man makes mistakes. Next time if I do something stupid, you come and tell me, and please don't smuggle another basket here. Are we of one mind, Grandma and Uncle Jude?"

His wife exchanged a glance with Jude. She turned the baby toward Jude as if showing off a trophy.

Mr. Cai stroked the red satin spread in the basket. It was thick and luxurious to the touch, like velvet. No wonder the baby was snug and quiet lying on it.

"It's as nice as Feng said." Seeing his wife's quizzical eyes, he explained, "It's Little Ye's dudou, the one Feng mentioned in his love letter to her."

She nodded. "I'll dress Ye in Feng's old clothes. I haven't thrown them away."

"Don't be so stingy, Woman. We can make him some new clothes." Mr. Cai prodded her shoulder with his finger.

"Used clothes are good for a baby. Little Ye knew that. That's why she left her dudou."

Mr. Cai was overcome with gratitude for Little Ye: she had named her baby boy after his father. Ye had arrived as the third generation of Cai.

"Look how adorable you are." Mrs. Cai cooed at the baby. "Your mama is so pretty. She also cooked and took care of your no-good father. Auntie Jiao cannot do any housework."

"Why should Jiao do any housework?" Mr. Cai said. "Feng waits on her hand and foot."

"Maybe within a year," Mrs. Cai said, "Feng will be crawling on his hands and knees, begging Little Ye to take him back."

"Forget them," Mr. Cai said. "*I* will crawl on my hands and knees to have a look at my granddaughter."

They both looked to Jude, as if pleading for him to put in a good word with Little Ye.

"I made a nursing dress for Little Ye." Mr. Cai went to the sewing room to retrieve the garment. "If you see her, please give this to her and say that we are grateful."

Jude held up the shimmering dress over his arm. "Very nice, she can wear it in the south." He touched the baby's nose. "Your mama will come and nurse you someday."

Mr. Cai started jotting down a grocery list: milk bottle, milk powder, fresh milk, juice and diapers. And toys, lots of them. Since he would spend a good deal of money on the baby, he couldn't afford for Feng to call home after all; they must wait patiently for Feng's letters. Meanwhile, Ouyang's family would meet the baby. There would be a reckoning, both at home and abroad.

Just then, the baby opened his mouth and started to bawl with all his might as if the world didn't agree with him. Without hesitation Mr. Cai scooped his grandson into his arms and cradled the little head in his palm, as if holding a rare, overripe fruit.

## ACKNOWLEDGEMENTS

My heartfelt gratitude to the wise and passionate people at the UNO Press for believing in this story and bringing it to fruition: Abram Shalom Himelstein, G.K. Darby, Chelsey Shannon, Alex Dimeff, and the students from The Publishing Laboratory. Special thanks to Chelsey Shannon, my editor, for your generous reading and incredible acuity. Thanks to my publicists Leah Paulos and Brianne Kane.

Thank you to my writing group: Clare Willis, Amy Glynn, John Byrne Barry, Joe Gore, Bill Selby, Susan Weiner, and Joe Wyka for reading the early drafts. Thank you to my mentors for inspiring and guiding me over the years: Bobbie Ann Mason, Steve Yarbrough, Yiyun Li, Elizabeth Graver, Vikram Chandra, Elizabeth Evans, and Barbara Kingsolver.

Thank you to the incredible writers and supportive friends: Alexander Chee, Celeste Ng, R.O. Kwon, Vanessa Hua, Shanthi Sekaran, Lucy Jane Bledsoe, Garth Greenwell, Edie Meidav, Micah Perks, Edan Lepucki, Lydia Kiesling, Margo Orlando Littell, Kaitlin Solimine, Marie Mutsuki Mockett, Hasanthika Sirisena, Kirstin Chen, Kate Jessica Raphael, and so many more. I am grateful to walk amongst you.

Thank you to the Sewanee Writers' Conference, the Community of Writers, and the Bread Loaf Writers' Conference for your generous support and camaraderie.

Deepest thanks to my family: Qin for always being there to see every story come alive, and Victor and Oliver for your indomitable spirit that puts me in my place.